A TASTE OF TEMPTATION

"You're safe with me," Chris said, "unless you decide you'd like an introduction to sexual pleasure. There could never be anything more than that between you and me."

"No, thank you," Sophia snapped. "Becoming intimate with you doesn't interest me."

Chris stalked her until he stood before her, his eyes probing deep into her soul. "I could make it interesting."

Their gazes collided. A simmering tension stretched between them. His features wore an expectant look, his expression dark with promise.

"I suggest that you use your powers of seduction on someone who will appreciate your efforts," Sophia sniffed.

Chris chortled. "You do tempt me, my lady, despite our complicated past."

A Taste of Paradise

CONNIE MASON

LEISURE BOOKS NEW YORK CITY

A LEISURE BOOK®

March 2006

Published by

Dorchester Publishing Co., Inc.
200 Madison Avenue
New York, NY 10016

ISBN 0-8439-5464-7

Printed in the United States of America.

Visit us on the web at www.dorchesterpub.com.

A Taste of Paradise

Prologue

London, April 1831

"Please, Chris, don't stop," begged the woman writhing beneath Captain Christian Radcliff.

"Never," Chris gasped from between clenched teeth as he thrust hard, withdrew, and thrust again and again into the wet warmth of Lady Amanda Dartmore. If Chris had anything close to a mistress, it would be Amanda, a nobleman's wife bored with her elderly husband.

Soon they were both thrashing and moaning amidst the twisted bed sheets, each seeking the ultimate pleasure. Chris collapsed in a boneless heap, his breathing harsh and tortured.

"Must you leave London so soon, Chris?" Amanda asked breathlessly. "It's a rare man who sees to a woman's pleasure as well as his own. Believe me when I say I've been with enough men to know that most of them are selfish lovers."

"Sorry, Amanda," Chris said, pushing to his feet.

"I'm leaving England in a few days, perhaps for good. My visit this time is of short duration. But if I return, you'll be one of the first to see me."

Amanda clung to him. "Dartmore is old and feeble. He won't live much longer. I was hoping you and I . . . If I didn't have a husband, would you marry me?"

Chris shook himself free of her questing hands and rose from the bed. "You are married, so your question is moot."

Chris planned to sail to Jamaica within the week. Aware that he wouldn't have another woman anytime soon, he had taken Amanda twice tonight while her husband slept soundly in another chamber, but now it was time to leave and bid his brother good-bye. He hadn't lied to Amanda when he'd said he might never return to England; convincing his brother that this was a good move wasn't going to be easy.

Legs outstretched, powerful body tense despite his outward calm, Christian sprawled in a chair in his brother's comfortable study, facing the earl's considerable wrath. Justin, the Earl of Standish, scowled at Chris over his tented fingers.

"Damnation, Chris, what do you mean, you're leaving the sea to become a gentleman planter in the West Indies? Isn't it time you stopped your adventurous life and returned home where you belong? You should be looking for a bride and thinking about setting up your nursery."

"My adventures have earned me an excellent living. The *Intrepid* belongs solely to me. My trading ventures have made me a rich man. My inheritance from Grandmother has made me an even richer one. When I left England seven years ago, I never imagined I would own my own ship, or become rich."

Chris had always relished adventure and the thrill of danger. The challenges and risks he had faced as a sea captain made him feel alive and vital. Pitting his wits against the elements was more exhilarating than anything Society had to offer. But now it was time to turn to something new, something entirely different and challenging in new ways.

"So why are you giving up that life to become a planter on the other side of the world?" Justin snapped.

"Hardly the other side of the world," Chris corrected, "and I'll still visit England from time to time to confer with my factor." His handsome features grew pensive. "I owe England nothing. Society hasn't been kind to me, if you recall."

"Time glosses over all sins. The incident that caused you to flee English shores has become but a distant memory."

Chris's voice hardened. "*I* haven't forgotten, Justin. How could I forget killing my best friend?"

"It was an accident, Chris. The girl played you for a fool. She was using you to make Desmond jealous. She only appeared to favor you to bring Desmond up to scratch. She was young, and so were you and Desmond. You were too infatuated with her to think clearly."

"Perhaps, but because of her I killed my best friend in a stupid duel that would never have taken place were we not both deep in our cups. Desmond had already discharged his pistol and missed . . . deliberately; I shot wide to the right, intending to miss him. I had no inkling he would stagger into the bullet's path as I fired."

"Precisely what I've been trying to tell you," Justin argued. "It was an accident. No one cares anymore. You can return home and take your place in Society."

Chris shoved his fingers through his thick dark hair as he struggled for a reply. "I care. Society no longer interests me. That life was lost to me when I fell in love with a frivolous beauty and fought a duel with my best friend for her attention.

"I'll never forget the appalled look on her face when I told her I had killed Desmond. That was the moment I realized she had been playing games with men's lives. She never wanted me. It was Desmond's money she wanted. She led me on to make him jealous. I cannot believe how gullible I was back then. I will live with the guilt until the day I die."

"We all make mistakes, Chris. You admitted yourself that the last seven years have been profitable ones. All is well that ends well."

Chris pushed himself from the chair and walked to the window, his gait that of a man who had spent years navigating a pitching ship's deck. "How can you call an innocent man's death a good ending? Nothing has changed to absolve my guilt. I deprived Desmond's parents of their heir. I hold myself just as guilty as the faithless chit. Lord knows I've tried to banish the girl from my memory."

"It's just as well," Justin said. "If you recall, her family was impoverished; they came to Town in hopes of snagging a rich husband for her. They could scarcely afford her Season. After the duel and the scandal that followed, the family retreated to the obscurity of their Essex manor. Her parents have since died, and she hasn't been seen in polite Society since the duel. The girl was but seventeen at the time. By now she must be married to some country bumpkin and living in poverty, the mother of several brats. Serves her right, I say."

Chris turned away from the window. "Be that as it

may, I will always carry the guilt of Desmond's death." Though it hadn't been easy, Chris had done his best to forget the girl. The whole affair left a bad taste in his mouth and a pain in his gut.

Chris grew angry every time he remembered the trusting young man he had been. The girl he'd once thought he loved might have been too young to know her own mind, but she was old enough to tease and entice.

"Help me understand your need to move to the West Indies, Chris. Why this sudden urge to leave the country of your birth for good? At least as a ship's captain you returned regularly to England to discharge or take on cargo."

Chris placed his palms on the edge of the desk and leaned forward, his blue eyes fervent with determination. "I won a sugarcane plantation in a game of chance in Kingston, Jamaica. The owner, a buccaneer who had recently won it at cards himself, had no use for it and threw it into the pot. I won the pot and became the proud owner of Sunset Hill, a rather large plantation and distillery.

"When I visited Sunset Hill, I knew becoming a planter was something I would enjoy. And I love the island. It's as close to paradise as I'll ever get. I have the money to replace aging machinery and make repairs to the house, and I own a ship to carry my purchases to Jamaica. Truthfully, the challenge has energized me, and I cannot wait to return to the golden shores of Jamaica. English winters leave much to be desired."

"I don't like it," Justin growled. "Jamaica is known for its frequent slave uprisings. How do you know such a thing won't happen on your plantation?"

"That won't happen because I'm going to free my

slaves and pay them wages to continue working the fields and distilling rum."

Justin shook his head. "Freeing your slaves may be dangerous. The other plantation owners won't be pleased, no matter how pure and noble your intentions. Is there nothing I can do to change your mind?"

"I appreciate your concern, Justin, but I'm determined."

"What about the *Intrepid*? Will she still ply the trade routes under another captain?"

"Aye, Dirk Blaine, my first mate, will captain the *Intrepid*. The ship will carry rum and other commodities such as sugar, tobacco and coffee beans to foreign ports. The *Intrepid* will not sit idle in port."

Justin sighed and threw up his hands. "Apparently you cannot be dissuaded. All I can tell you is to visit often and take care of yourself. With the recent slave uprisings and the history of earthquakes and hurricanes, Jamaica will present challenges you may not have anticipated."

"I am prepared to take on new challenges," Chris maintained.

"Then there is nothing more I can say but wish you well. How soon will you depart?"

"A week, give or take a day. My ship is being provisioned as we speak, and everything I wish to take with me has been purchased and is being stowed away in the hold."

Justin rose. "Then you'd best come with me and bid your sister-in-law good-bye. Grace and I see you too seldom. Perhaps you will return in late fall to help me welcome our child into the world. It would mean a lot to Grace if you showed up for the christening."

Chris slapped Justin on the back. "A child! Congratulations, old boy. I'll make it my mission in life to return for the blessed event."

They left the study together. While Justin worried about his brother's future, Chris contemplated his new and exciting venture, a challenge he was eagerly looking forward to.

Chapter One

"I've come to collect my money, Caldwell. I cannot wait until your financial situation improves," the thickset man with thinning hair argued. "I've booked passage to Jamaica aboard the *Morning Star*. She sails in five days. I've been away from my plantation too long to delay my journey. If you don't settle your debt now, I'll summon the watch and have you carted off to debtor's prison. I'm sure I'm not the only man in Town who holds your vowels."

Rayford, Viscount Caldwell, had the sudden urge to thrash Sir Oscar Rigby soundly and send him packing. However much he hated it, he had to paste a pleasant smile on his face and try to placate the man.

"Now, now, Sir Oscar, there's no need for threats. You'll get your money."

"When?"

"As soon as I'm able to repair my finances."

"That will never happen, Caldwell. Everyone knows your pockets are empty. The amount you owe me is not inconsiderable. I can use the blunt to buy more slaves."

The argument continued unabated. Threats flew back and forth. Voices rose to a wild crescendo, until even the three servants Caldwell could scarcely afford disappeared into the lower regions of the run-down town house.

Sophia Carlisle descended the stairs of the town house her stepbrother had rented, drawn to the study by the sound of angry voices. She had a good idea what the argument was about. Not a day went by without someone appearing at their door, demanding payment for one of Ray's gambling debts or the foppish clothing he'd purchased for himself.

Sophia froze on the bottom landing as the study door burst open and a short, stout man with nondescript features and a red face charged forward. He saw Sophia and came to an abrupt halt.

"Who are you, my dear?" the man asked.

Sophia did not care for the man's familiar manner and was about to tell him so when Rayford appeared behind the brash stranger.

"Sir Oscar, this is my stepsister, Miss Sophia Carlisle. Sophia, please greet Sir Oscar Rigby, a . . . er . . . business acquaintance of mine."

Rigby reached for Sophia's hand and brought it to his mouth for a wet kiss. Repressing a shudder, Sophia snatched her hand away.

"Your sister, eh?" Rigby said, sending Caldwell a speaking glance. "Perhaps I was a bit hasty in my demands. Shall we return to your study to resume our discussion? I'm sure we can come to an arrangement that both of us can live with."

Sophia backed away, wanting no part of Ray's business dealings. If he hadn't gambled away her dowry along with his wife's modest fortune, they wouldn't be in such dire straits now. She'd hoped that when Ray married Claire he'd give up his wild ways and settle down, but that had not happened.

Sophia wished herself back in their rundown manor house in the country, where she could keep herself busy helping the people in their little village. This scheme of Ray's to bring her to London to find a wealthy husband had been doomed to failure from the beginning. They had been in Town nearly a month and not one invitation had arrived, and Ray had found no one to sponsor her at Almacks or any other Society function.

"Sir Oscar," Sophia said, nodding curtly, "I shall leave you and Rayford to your negotiations. I'm needed in the kitchen to confer with Cook."

Rigby watched Sophia walk away, his gaze riveted on the seductive sway of her hips. He watched until she had disappeared through a doorway before reentering the study. Caldwell followed him inside and shut the door.

"Your sister is stunning," Rigby said. "Why hasn't she married?" He tapped his chin, deep in thought. "Hmmm, Sophia Carlisle; ah, yes, now I remember. There is a bit of scandal associated with her name. She fled Town in disgrace some years back. I overheard a bit of gossip about her at one of the gambling hells shortly after you and Miss Carlisle returned to Town but paid it little heed."

Caldwell shrugged off Rigby's words. "It was a minor incident that happened years ago. Forget Sophia. You spoke of an arrangement. I'm anxious to hear the details."

"First, tell me if you can lay your hands on the five hundred pounds you owe me."

"No, but if you give me more time—"

"No more time. I already told you I'm leaving London shortly. But there is another way you can repay your debt without it costing you a penny."

Caldwell's face lit up. "Just tell me how and it's yours."

Rigby rocked back and forth on the balls of his feet, excitement combined with anticipation clearly evident in his leering grin. Lacing his hands behind his back, he preened before Caldwell like a strutting peacock.

After a suspenseful few moments, he blurted out, "I want your stepsister. Give me one night with her and I will destroy your vowels. If you refuse, I'll go straight to the magistrate and have you thrown in debtor's prison."

Caldwell gaped at Rigby. "You want Sophia?"

"Indeed I do. I want her in my bed for one night. She's far superior to the female slaves available to me on my plantation and the whores I've frequented in London."

Caldwell began to pace. "I brought Sophia to London to find her a husband. Give me time to arrange a profitable match and you'll have your five hundred pounds in cash."

Rigby shook his head. "That's not acceptable. Is your sister untouched?"

"I have reason to believe she is."

Rigby's eyes glazed over. "How fortunate for me. Is

it a deal, Caldwell?" Caldwell hesitated. "I might even offer a little extra if she pleases me," he added.

"Sophia will never agree. She's grown stubborn and fractious of late. I have little control over her."

Rigby shrugged. "It's up to you, of course, whether or not you force her to obey. You could remind her that your wife will have no husband if you go to debtor's prison."

Caldwell winced. He didn't care a fig about Claire. He had left her in the country because she would hinder his activities in Town.

Well, there was no help for it. Sophia would have to swallow her pride and face the inevitable. She was on the shelf. No man would offer her anything but an improper proposal, he now realized. Selling Sophia's favors was the only viable solution to mending his finances.

After Rigby had his night with Sophia, Caldwell intended to offer her favors to other men. Perhaps one would even keep her as his mistress. It wasn't as if Sophia would suffer as a rich man's plaything. She would be kept in style, have servants to wait on her, jewels she could sell later, and live a life of luxury. It wasn't a bad life, and Caldwell would make sure he shared in the profit. All he had to do was convince Sophia.

"Sophia will do as I say," Caldwell assured Rigby.

"I thought you would say that. I will call on Sophia tomorrow night. Make sure she knows what I want from her."

"Don't come until after ten; that's when she usually retires. I'll give the servants the night off and leave the house when you arrive. But I'll want my vowels returned before you visit her room."

13

The agreement made, Rigby took his leave, strutting off like a cocky rooster. Caldwell remained in his study, planning Sophia's ruination.

Sophia emerged from the kitchen when she heard the front door close. While she had no idea what the obnoxious Sir Oscar wanted with Rayford, she knew instinctively that it involved money. The man made her skin crawl. She headed for the study, intending to speak to Ray about leaving London.

"What did that man want?" Sophia asked as she strode into the study. "You'd do well to stay away from men of that ilk."

Caldwell sent her a sullen look. "You don't even know him."

"You're right, and I don't want to. There's something I'd like to talk to you about."

"And I have something to discuss with you, so speak your piece first, and then I will speak mine."

Sophia felt nothing but disgust for her stepbrother. Ray's mother had been her father's first wife. She had brought her son from a former marriage with her. Rayford had inherited the title of viscount at an early age.

After Ray's mother died, Sophia's father married her mother. She had been their only child. Unfortunately, her father had grown so fond of his first wife's son that he made Rayford Sophia's guardian. Ray was an unrepentant gambler and indifferent provider, and her father had been no better. Both Ray and her father had put their own needs before those of the family, leaving the women who depended on them destitute. Sophia could barely stand Ray and knew the feeling was mutual.

"It's time to return home," Sophia said. "There's nothing to be gained by remaining in London except accumulating more debt. We both knew that trying to find me a husband was doomed to failure."

"Why did you agree to come to London if you thought it was futile?"

She looked away. She had had several reasons, but only one she was willing to admit. "I wanted to prove to you once and for all that I'm unmarriageable. I wanted you to stop hounding me about snaring a rich husband to benefit your empty pockets. Let's put all this foolishness behind us and return home. You should concentrate on providing your estate with an heir."

"Why do I need an heir to a bankrupt estate?" Caldwell snarled. "*You* could save us if you put your mind to it."

"You're going to have to get yourself out of this one, Ray."

"Why should I put myself out for you when you're the reason the family has fallen so low?"

Guilt rode Sophia. She'd spent years trying to forget the event that had sent her fleeing from London. But one thing she had never forgotten was the man she had fallen in love with when she was seventeen.

"Our family would be fine today if you hadn't gambled away everything but our home and land. It's time to leave London, Ray. The estate still brings in rent and money from crops. You could make it prosper if you tried harder."

"I'm not a farmer and never will be," Caldwell contended. "No, Sophia, you're the only one who can save me from debtor's prison."

"Me! How do you figure that?"

"I've lost more than I intended at the tables. My creditors are hounding me. One man in particular is demanding immediate repayment of the debt I owe him. He has threatened to send me to debtor's prison if I don't come up with the blunt."

"You're an irresponsible fool, Ray," Sophia spat. "Debtor's prison is too good for you. Even though Claire and I never saw eye to eye, I pity her."

"I've received an offer for you that could help repair our financial difficulty."

Sophia stared at him, mistrusting anything he said. "What kind of an offer, and from whom?"

"Hear me out before you refuse. Your cooperation could save our family."

"You never cared about anyone but yourself," Sophia charged.

"I married that cow Claire, didn't I? Do you think I would have offered for her if I didn't need her blunt?"

"Blunt you managed to squander in a relatively short time."

Caldwell cleared his throat. "Sir Oscar—"

"Never say that toad offered for me!" Sophia spat. "The answer is no, no and no."

"Sir Oscar said he will tear up my vowels in exchange for a night in your bed," Caldwell continued over Sophia's objection. "He was quite taken with you."

"How dare you! You should have challenged him for the insult, or at the very least showed him the door."

Caldwell's mouth flattened; his eyes became cold as ice. "You always were a troublesome chit. It's not as if you're a sought-after deb. You're on the shelf, and even if you weren't, you're tainted by scandal."

"I won't do it, Rayford. I don't need your support. I received a very good education. I can support myself as a governess if need be."

"What about Claire? Would you leave her without support? The estate is bankrupt."

"I won't do it, Ray, not even for Claire. She has her parents, while I have no one. I'm not going to prostitute myself for you or anyone else. I'm going to place an ad in *The Times* tomorrow, advertising my services as a governess."

Turning on her heel, she swished past Caldwell and out the door.

Sophia spent the rest of the day avoiding her brother, and when he joined her for dinner that night, he didn't bring up the subject of Sir Oscar, much to Sophia's relief. She retired directly following the meal and didn't see Rayford again until dinner the following night.

"I gave the servants the night off," Caldwell said when Sophia finished eating and excused herself.

Sophia stared at him. It was so unlike Rayford to be generous that she could scarcely credit it. "Did they request the night off?"

"The maid asked permission to spend the night with her mother, so I decided to give Jeeves the night off, too. And of course, Cook always returns to her family after dinner is prepared and served."

"I bid you good night, then," Sophia said. She paused at the door. "By the way, my ad should appear in *The Times* tomorrow."

Since Rayford didn't react to the news as she'd expected, Sophia shrugged and left him sitting at the table. She went directly to her room, where she busied herself with various chores until her eyes began to droop. Then she undressed, washed, cleaned her teeth and pulled on a linen nightdress that had turned transparent after countless washings. Her final act before climbing into bed was to build up the fire with the last of the coal in the scuttle.

Squirming beneath the quilt to find a comfortable position, Sophia wondered if she would receive any replies to her ad. Aware that it would take a day or two for replies to reach her by return mail, she fell asleep looking forward to achieving full independence from Rayford. His despicable request that she prostitute herself on his behalf had been the last straw. Her disgust for him had finally reached the point of no return.

As sleep claimed Sophia, she had no idea that Rigby had arrived and was being welcomed by Caldwell.

"Is she waiting for me?" Rigby asked eagerly.

"Not exactly," Caldwell muttered. "She's probably sleeping. I'm leaving it up to you to tame her. She refused to cooperate, but I don't see that as an impediment. She always was a stubborn chit. A man of your experience should be able to handle one small reluctant woman."

Rigby, decked out like a dandy and smelling strongly of perfume, appeared pleased by Caldwell's compliment. Puffing out his chest, he said, "Point out her room so I can get on with it."

"In a moment. The servants are gone, and I am about to leave myself. But first, I'll have my vowels."

"Do you think I'm stupid? You'll have them tomorrow, after I've had my night with your fetching sister. If you think to trick me, there will be hell to pay. I'm an unforgiving man with a long memory."

"No tricks, I promise," Caldwell said. "Sophia's chamber is upstairs, the first door on the right. I wish you a pleasant good night. I don't intend returning until tomorrow morning, at which time you can give me my vowels."

After Caldwell's hasty exit, Rigby started up the stairs, all but drooling over the prospect of bedding Sophia. He'd had a whore or two while visiting London, but they were hags compared to Miss Sophia Carlisle. If she turned out to be a virgin, he'd count his bargain with Caldwell well worth the monetary loss.

It wasn't as if he were a pauper. He had made a fortune in the slave trade out of Jamaica.

Sophia stirred in her sleep. Not fully awake, she lay still, listening for whatever had disturbed her. When she heard footsteps in the hallway, she assumed it was Rayford seeking his bed and rolled over, hunkering down into the warm feather bed. Then she heard the door open and the latch fall back into place as it closed.

She sat up, squinting into darkness alleviated only by the dying embers in the grate. "Rayford, is that you?"

No answer was forthcoming.

The footsteps advanced, moving closer to the bed. "Rayford! What are you doing in here?"

Sophia felt a shimmer of panic when a man emerged from the shadows and passed before the hearth, his stout body outlined in the flickering light. She knew instantly that it wasn't Rayford, for the short, stout figure couldn't possibly belong to her tall, slim stepbrother. When she finally realized who had invaded her room, she opened her mouth and let loose a piercing scream.

"We're alone in the house, so there's no one here to hear you, my dear," Rigby said as he struck a light to the candle on her nightstand.

Stunned, Sophia stared at him. His mouth was slack, his eyes bright with lust. "Get out!"

"Oh, no. I'm paying dearly for you and I won't be denied."

"If you're talking about your unholy bargain with my stepbrother, I want no part of it. Rayford can rot in prison, for all I care. Now get out before I summon the Watch."

Rigby reached for the quilt and stripped it away. "I'm not going anywhere, my dear. Take off that nightdress so I can see what I'm paying for."

For a moment, Sophia's brain had shut down, but now she was thinking clearly, her mind searching for a way to escape Sir Oscar's nefarious plans for her. She was alone in the house, with no one but herself to rely upon.

Rigby reached for the hem of her nightdress.

"Wait!" Sophia cried. "I won't make it easy for you if you try to rape me. Wouldn't it be a much more pleasant experience if I came to you willingly?"

Rigby gaped at her. "You'd do that?"

Never in a million years. "Of course." She summoned a smile. "After all, my compliance would benefit my family." She nearly gagged over her next words, for she knew Rayford cared little for her. "I'm very fond of my stepbrother."

"I own I am surprised," Rigby replied. "Caldwell led me to believe you would object."

He discarded his jacket and cravat and would have shed his breeches and boots if Sophia hadn't raised a hand, stopping him. "Wait! Let me help you."

Trying her seductive best, though she knew little

about seduction, she climbed out of bed, allowing a bit of ankle and calf to show beneath her nightdress. Taking note of the way Rigby stared at her ankles, she sidled up to him and began unbuttoning his shirt. His eyes nearly popped out of his head when she pulled his shirt halfway down his arms, imprisoning them at his sides.

"Sit down, Sir Oscar, so I can remove your boots."

His arms still captured by his shirt, Sophia led him to a chair. "What about my shirt?" he asked.

"Not yet," Sophia purred. "We'll do this my way or not at all. Sit down and let me tend to your needs."

By now Rigby was panting with lust. "This waiting is killing me." Nevertheless, he sat down in the chair Sophia indicated.

"We have all night," Sophia reminded him as she thought of all manner of vile things she'd like to do to Rigby and Ray.

Sophia moved behind Rigby. He swiveled in the chair to find her. "What are you doing? Stay where I can see you."

Sophia's lush lips pursed in a fetching pout. "Turn around while I take off my nightdress. If you peek, I won't finish undressing you."

His eyes glazed over. "I had no idea you enjoyed playing sex games. Caldwell made no mention of your . . . unconventional nature."

"Rayford doesn't know everything," Sophia said, rolling her eyes. "Turn around, Sir Oscar."

Rigby had become so excited he was literally bouncing in the chair. Though clearly reluctant, he did as Sophia asked. "Don't take too long. I'm hard as a rock and ready to burst."

The moment Rigby turned his back on Sophia, she

grabbed a long, tasseled rope from the drapery at the window and flung it around his bulky body, wrapping it around him twice and knotting it behind the chair.

"What's this?" Rigby blustered. "I don't like this kind of game."

"Neither do I, Sir Oscar. I can't believe you had the audacity to think I would go along with the plan you hatched with Rayford. I'm not for sale, sir. You can tell that to Ray when he returns home and releases you."

Sophia turned away to find her clothing. She didn't intend to be there when Rayford returned. She dressed quickly behind a screen, disdaining a corset and several petticoats in her haste to leave. Rigby was struggling with his bonds and cursing violently when she emerged. She should have gagged him but decided to ignore his foul language instead.

Sophia dragged her valise from beneath the bed and packed only the necessities, leaving the bulk of her clothing behind. She could only carry so much.

Sophia doubted that Ray had left enough money in the strongbox in his desk to get her back home, but she knew where she could find what she needed. She turned to look at Sir Oscar, wondering how difficult it would be to lift his purse. Difficult or not, she had to do it.

"What are you going to do?" Rigby asked when Sophia approached him.

"I need money," Sophia said bluntly. "In which pocket do you keep your purse?"

The moment Rigby lunged forward, Sophia knew she had misjudged his strength as well as her ability to tie knots. The rope gave, and he burst free. Sophia didn't wait as he pulled his shirt up over his arms and grabbed his coat; she turned and ran, forgetting her valise, her wrap, and all thought of money in her haste to escape the enraged man.

Sophia flung open the door and raced for the stairs. Rigby was close on her heels. He lunged for her, catching the sleeve of her dress. It ripped in his hand.

"I've got you, bitch!" he crowed. "You won't get away with this. I'll fetch the Watch. It's a raw night; you wouldn't get far in this weather anyway. I'll have you brought up on charges of robbery and assault."

Sophia prayed for a miracle. It arrived when her sleeve tore away, freeing her. Rigby lost his balance and tumbled headlong down the stairs. Sophia scrambled after him. Reaching for the vase resting on the hall table, she crashed it on his head as he started to rise. She didn't wait to see if it had knocked him out as she flung open the door and sprinted into the dark night. But Sir Oscar must have had a hard head, for she heard him stirring behind her.

Sophia ran. Ran as far and as fast as she could. In the distance, she could hear footsteps pounding after her. Sir Oscar? It had to be.

Her chest ached, her legs were ready to collapse beneath her, but she refused to give in to weakness. All her life she'd been dictated to. She was told whom to let court her, whom to favor even though she yearned for another. Now she would take care of herself.

Sophia could hear voices behind her. Apparently, Sir Oscar had found the Watch. If she didn't find a hiding place soon, they would toss her in Newgate and throw away the key. Gulping in a lungful of cold air, Sophia stopped to get her bearings. She'd run so long and so far, she had no idea where she was.

The pungent scent of salt and rotting fish wafted to her on the frigid air. She began to shiver, wishing she'd had time to grab a wrap before fleeing. While she was running, she hadn't felt the cold, but she was aware now of the biting sting of sleet. England was experiencing an exceptionally cold spring this year.

Glancing about, she found herself in a narrow street lined with warehouses and saloons. Lights twinkling at the end of the street lured her in that direction. She began running, and then she realized she was near Southwark quay. The lights had come from saloons nestled together near the docks. She hesitated, glancing furtively behind her as she tried to catch her breath.

Driven by desperation, Sophia ducked into an alley. A few minutes later, Sir Oscar and the Watch barreled past her, but she knew it wouldn't be long before they retraced their steps and found her.

Stepping gingerly from the alley, Sophia saw nothing but saloons and warehouses on either side of the street. Then she heard Sir Oscar's voice, harsh and grating in the stygian darkness. "We've got her cornered." Turning, she ran into the nearest saloon.

Conversation stopped the moment Sophia entered the dingy, smoke-filled common room smelling of stale gin and unwashed bodies. A barmaid stopped her headlong flight toward a rear door.

" 'Ere now, wot are you doing? You don't belong in a place like this."

"I need help. I'm being pursued. Please, will you hide me?"

The brassy-haired tavern wench glanced toward the kitchen. "Mr. Tate don't want no trouble with the Watch. He'd turn you in faster than you can blink your eye. Wot 'ave you done?"

"Nothing. I've done nothing. Please help me. I need to get away."

The barmaid regarded Sophia for the space of two heartbeats. "How far away?"

"As far away from London as I can get."

The barmaid leaned close. "You can't hide here. Mr. Tate will return from the kitchen soon. If he sees you, Lord only knows what he'll do. I've seen him sell innocents to whorehouses. But since you look like a lady wot's in trouble, I'll pass on a bit o' information that might help."

Sophia darted a glance at the door. "I am desperate. Anything you can do for me will be appreciated."

"Most of our customers are seafaring men. Their ships are docked at Southwark quay. Perhaps you can buy passage on one sailing on the midnight tide, if you ain't too fussy about where you end up."

Leave England? That wasn't exactly what Sophia had in mind. And she didn't have a farthing to her name. But what if she hid aboard one of the ships and crept off once the danger was past? It was worth a try.

Sophia was still making up her mind when a commotion near the front door caught her attention. "Oh, my God, they're here!"

"This way," the barmaid said, grasping her arm and pulling her through a door. "This door leads to the alley out back. Good luck."

Sophia didn't waste a moment as she fled out the rear door into the alley. She emerged from the alley and ran down the street toward the quay. She felt a rush of relief when she saw three ships berthed along the quay. Only one ship, however, had its gangplank run out.

"There she is!" she heard Rigby call out. She raced

toward the ship with its gangplank resting on the pier. She paused at the end of the gangplank and glanced upward, then ducked into the shadows when she saw the night watch pacing the deck. She waited, uncertain what to do, and then she saw the watchman walk to the ship's stern and peer over the railing.

Dragging in a calming breath, Sophia darted up the gangplank and crouched behind a mast. She froze when she heard Sir Oscar hail the watchman. "Ahoy, the watch!"

The watchman leaned over the railing. "Aye, what do you want?"

"Did a woman come aboard your ship a few minutes ago?"

"A woman? No, sir, no one came aboard. She couldn't get past me even if she tried."

"Did you see which way she went? We followed her here."

"No, sir, I ain't seen anyone, and I've been here all night."

Rigby spat out a curse. "Let's go. She can't have gotten far."

Sophia nearly collapsed with relief when she heard their receding footsteps. That still didn't solve her dilemma, however. A far greater problem suddenly arose when sailors began boarding the ship in groups of twos and threes. When they greeted the watchman with jovial remarks, Sophia realized the crew was returning from shore leave.

Frantic, she turned about, searching for a hiding place until the coast was clear to leave. She spotted an open hatch and a ladder leading downward. Without hesitation she scrambled down the ladder and ducked inside a cabin whose door was ajar. Breathing hard, she leaned against the door, safe for the moment.

She'd scarcely had time to catch her breath when she heard footsteps outside the door. She backed away, her gaze darting about for a hiding place. She spotted a sea chest but decided it was too small for her to hide in. Frantic, she dived beneath the oversized bunk just as the door opened, rolling until she came up against the bulkhead.

A light flared. Sophia could see nothing of the cabin's occupant but a pair of muscular legs encased in expensive boots. She was wet and chilled to the bone, and her teeth began chattering so loudly she had to forcibly clamp them together. Hugging herself for warmth, she watched as the cabin's occupant bent over a brazier and fed coal into it. She shivered, waiting for the heat to reach her.

She offered a silent prayer of thanks when she felt warmth seeping into her chilled bones. After a little while, it became so cozy beneath the bunk that Sophia's cyelids drifted shut despite her best efforts to stay awake.

Chapter Two

Sophia awakened to murky daylight and a gentle rocking motion. She started to rise and bumped her head on a hard object located scant inches above her. She let out a yelp, then clamped her hand over her mouth when she recalled where she was and why. When she sensed no movement in the cabin, she rolled to where she could peek out without being seen.

The cabin appeared empty. How long had she slept? Long enough to be hungry, she decided when her stomach growled in answer to her question. Had the cabin's occupant slept in the cabin last night without her knowing?

Sophia scooted out from beneath the bunk and examined her surroundings in the light of day.

Since the cabin was fairly large, Sophia assumed that it belonged to the captain. She knew she had to leave before he returned. With luck, she could get off the ship without being seen. But her hopes were dashed when she glanced out the porthole and saw water, lots and lots of water.

The unwelcome knowledge of what had happened slowly seeped into her brain. The ship had weighed anchor and entered the channel while she slept. Where was the ship bound? China? India? America? No! She wanted to go home. She had to find the captain at once and demand that he turn back.

Sophia heard voices outside the door. Not yet ready to face anyone, she dove under the bed, intending to remain there until she found the words to address the man who held her fate in his hands. But if she waited too long, she feared she'd find herself journeying somewhere she had no intention of going.

The door opened, admitting a man Sophia assumed was the captain. He moved about the cabin a few minutes before stopping before the desk and spreading out a map. His hand brushed against a cup. Liquid splashed from it as it hit the deck and rolled under the bed. Remarkably, it didn't shatter. Sophia held her breath, praying the captain wouldn't decide to rescue the cup.

She heard his footsteps approaching. Squeezing her eyes shut, she prayed harder, but to no avail. She heard a sharp intake of breath followed by a curse. She opened her eyes and met the startled gaze of Christian Radcliff, a man she remembered very well, a man who had every reason to hate her.

"What the hell! Who are you and what are you doing on my ship?" he roared. "Come out of there!"

Apparently, he hadn't recognized her yet. She scooted as far away from him as she could get, but he had long arms. He reached her with little difficulty, dragged her none too gently from beneath the bunk and yanked her to her feet. She heard a ripping sound and realized the remaining sleeve of her dress had been torn off.

Sophia gazed into Chris's enraged countenance and nearly fainted as her past came rushing back to her. His was a face she would never forget. She'd known that Christian Radcliff had gone off to sea after the duel, but she'd heard little of him since.

"You!" Chris snarled. "What are *you* doing aboard my ship? I thought I was rid of you years ago, Sophia Carlisle."

Sophia swallowed the fear gathering in her throat and tried to brazen it out. "Hello, Chris."

He narrowed his eyes. They were the same mesmerizing blue she remembered. "I asked you a question. What are you doing aboard my ship?"

"I didn't know this was your ship. As to what I'm doing here, I needed to escape the Watch, and your ship was handy."

"What have you done now?"

"It's a long story. I was running from the Watch and found myself near the docks. I snuck aboard your ship to escape, intending to leave before the ship sailed."

He let his keen gaze roam over her, obviously coming to his own conclusion when he noted her filthy, torn gown. His voice held a note of disgust. "You look like a cheap doxy."

Her chin rose slightly. "How dare you insult me! None of this is my fault. If you will kindly turn the ship about, I will be more than happy to leave."

"It's too late."

"What?"

"You heard me, Sophia, it's too late to turn about. I fear you're stuck aboard the *Intrepid* until she reaches Jamaica."

"Jamaica! No, I don't want to go there. Please, Christian, return me to London."

"Sorry, Sophia, this is my ship, and you're stuck here. Once we reach Jamaica, I'll send you home on another ship." He stared at her breasts. "You've changed."

Sophia crossed her arms over her chest. "So have you."

He eyed her narrowly. "Where is your husband?"

"I'm not married."

"Engaged?"

"Not even close."

"A rich man's mistress?"

"No, damn you!" Sophia sputtered.

He shrugged. "It's a natural assumption. You were going to sell yourself to Desmond."

"That was Father and Rayford's doing. You know I preferred you. I had no choice. I was too young and inexperienced to fight them for the man I wanted."

"Stop it! I don't want to hear about who you did or did not prefer. It's the result of your actions that's important."

"I'm sorry about Desmond. I know you hold me responsible for his death."

He turned away from her. "I blame myself." He whirled back to face her. "Damnation! What devil tempted Fate to bring you back into my life?"

Her chin rose defiantly. "It's not as if I planned this."

"Are you living in London now?"

"No, I've only been in Town a few weeks."

"From whom were you running away?"

Sophia grimaced. "Men."

Chris gave her a wry grin. "Why don't I believe that?"

Sophia shrugged. "It's the truth."

Chris searched her face, pausing at her lips before abruptly looking away. "Are you hungry?"

"A little."

"I'll have my cabin boy bring hot water and something for you to eat. You look like you could use a good wash. Don't leave this cabin," he warned. "I can usually control my crew, but you're a bit too fetching to pass their notice. I'll return later."

There came a knock on the door.

"That will be my cabin boy," Chris said. "Come in, Casper."

A towheaded lad of eleven or twelve bounded into the cabin and skidded to a halt when he saw Sophia. His mouth dropped open as he stared from her to Chris.

"You can close your mouth, Casper," Chris said. "It seems we have a stowaway. Miss Sophia Carlisle will be traveling to Jamaica with us. Sophia, this is Casper—he will be seeing to your needs during our voyage."

Casper darted a glance at Sophia, then lowered his gaze. "Miss," he said shyly.

"Bring a jug of hot water for Miss Carlisle," Chris said. "I'm sure she'd welcome a bath. Then see if you can rustle up some food from the galley. Oh, yes, and bring more charcoal for the brazier. We won't hit warmer waters for another two weeks."

"Aye, Captain," Casper said, darting another glance at Sophia before ducking out the door.

"You should be set for a while," Chris said coolly. "I'll return later; we can talk about your circumstances then, and what's to be done with you."

He stared at her a full minute before stalking off.

Sophia shivered. Chris Radcliff was definitely not the man she remembered. Desmond's death had changed him in countless ways. He was no longer the charming young man she had fallen in love with.

Sophia's last memory of Chris was of the day he told

her he'd killed Lord Desmond in a duel over her favors. She had been so stunned she'd been unable to think, let alone speak. He kept staring into her eyes, she recalled, as if begging her to absolve him of guilt. When she remained mute, he had walked out the door and out of her life. She hadn't seen him again until today. She'd often regretted that she hadn't told him how worried she'd been that he would go to prison for participating in an illegal duel—or that she loved him. She had retired to the country soon after the scandal, and he had gone to sea. This was the first time she'd seen him in seven years.

Intuitively Sophia realized that Chris still bore the guilt of killing Desmond. She had learned afterward that both men had been in their cups and arguing over her favors. The duel had been the result of a friendly argument that had turned lethal. No one was truly at fault.

Sophia hadn't blamed Chris for Desmond's death. At seventeen, she had reveled in the attention of two handsome men and would have married Chris had it been her choice. But her stepbrother and father had insisted that she marry money in order to repair their depleted finances, even though it was Christian Radcliff she loved.

A knock on the door roused Sophia from her reverie. Casper entered at her bidding, carrying a jug of steaming water in one hand and a bucket of charcoal in the other.

"You'll find clean washcloths and towels in the cupboard, miss," the boy said. "Cook is preparing your breakfast; I'll bring it after I finish here. We still have fresh eggs and bacon. In a couple of weeks the food won't be as appetizing, so take advantage of it while you can."

"Thank you, Casper," Sophia said. "Have you been with Captain Radcliff long?"

The lad lost his sunny smile. "Three years, miss. When my mum and pa died of fever, no one would take me in. The captain found me begging on the streets and brought me aboard the *Intrepid*. He had just purchased the schooner and was making his first voyage as captain of his own ship. I've been with him ever since. The captain wanted to send me to school, but I refused. I won't leave him, miss. He wouldn't know what to do without me."

Sophia smiled at the boy. It was unusual to see such loyalty in one so young. "The captain is lucky to have you."

Blushing, Casper ducked his head and busied himself feeding charcoal into the brazier. After Casper left, Sophia poured hot water into the bowl, found the washcloths, towels and soap in the cupboard and washed her hands and face. She glanced at the door, walked over and latched it, and then shed her dress, stockings and shoes. If she couldn't have a full bath, an all-over wash would have to suffice.

Sophia finished her bath, brushed her hair with Chris's brush and picked up her gown to inspect it. She grimaced in disgust; it was dirty and torn beyond repair. But what choice did she have? She doubted Chris kept women's clothing aboard his ship.

Her gaze fell on his sea chest. She flung open the top, smiling when she found one of Chris's shirts lying on top of a pile of clothing. She pulled on the garment. Its long, flowing sleeves fell below her fingertips and covered her legs almost to her knees. She dug deeper into the chest and retrieved a pair of canvas trousers. After holding them up to her, she knew there was no way she could make them fit without scissors, needle and thread.

A search through the cupboards turned up nothing remotely resembling a mending kit.

"Miss," Casper called through the door. "Your breakfast is ready."

"Just a minute," Sophia answered. Grabbing a blanket from the bunk, she wrapped it around herself and unlatched the door. "Put it on the desk, please, Casper."

Keeping his eyes averted from her bare feet, Casper placed the tray on the desk and scooted out, closing the door behind him. The food smelled delicious, and Sophia was starving. Pulling a chair up to the desk, she dropped the blanket, sat down and dug into a plate of eggs, golden brown bacon, thick slices of bread spread with butter and a pot of tea.

Christian strode to the quarterdeck and took the wheel from Dirk Blaine, his first mate. Blaine must have realized from Chris's dark visage that he was in no mood to talk, for he handed the wheel over and took off.

Chris couldn't stop obsessing about finding Sophia in his cabin. The shock of seeing her again after seven years hummed through him. She'd resembled a disreputable tramp when he'd pulled her out from beneath his bunk. She must have been damn desperate to venture out on a cold, wet night without a wrap. His gut told him she was withholding more information than she was telling him.

During the next three weeks or so it would take to reach Jamaica, what in God's name was he going to do with the woman who had caused him more anguish than he had ever known? A woman aboard the *Intrepid* could cause a riot. The best way to keep his men from fighting over her favors, Chris decided, was to publicly lay claim to her himself, thus placing her off limits to his crew.

"Captain, might I have a word with you?"

It was Blaine, and the look on his face spelled trouble. "What is it, Mr. Blaine?"

"There's a rumor going around that you have a woman in your cabin."

Chris scowled. He suspected Casper was to blame for talking out of turn.

"The rumor is correct," Chris acknowledged. "The woman belongs to me. Pass the word that she's off limits to the crew."

Blaine stared at Chris, a puzzled expression digging a furrow between his brows. Since he and Chris had been friends a long time, he didn't hesitate to speak his mind. "You've never brought a woman aboard the *Intrepid* before, captain."

"As long as I'm the captain of this ship, I can do as I please," Chris barked in a tone he rarely used with Blaine.

The moment the words left his mouth, Chris wanted to call them back. Sophia had only been aboard the *Intrepid* a few hours and already she was causing problems.

"Aye, sir," Blaine responded, snapping a salute. "I'll relay your orders to the crew."

"Mr. Blaine, forgive me for being abrupt. I've got a lot on my mind."

"I imagine you do, Captain," Blaine replied cheekily.

"Take the wheel. There's something important I need to do."

"Aye, Captain," Blaine said, grinning broadly. "Take

your time. Important matters require a great deal of attention."

Since Chris wasn't sure how Blaine meant that, he ignored the gibe. Of one thing he was certain: Sophia wasn't his responsibility. When they reached Jamaica, he would give her money and send her back to England and out of his life forever.

It didn't surprise Chris when he found himself standing outside his cabin a few moments later. Without bothering to knock, he opened the door and stepped inside. He halted abruptly, slamming the door shut with his foot when he saw Sophia sitting at his desk, dressed in one of his shirts, devouring a heaping plate of bacon and eggs.

She dropped her fork and glared up at him. "I didn't expect you back so soon."

Her eyes were still as green as he recalled, as green as the thickly forested Jamaican hillsides, and her hair was a lustrous brunette. His gaze settled on her lips. They were more lush than he remembered. Definitely kissable lips. Suddenly he was incapable of looking at her delicious mouth without thinking about all the sinful ways she could use those full lips. He stifled a groan. He was mad! Utterly and irrevocably mad! He didn't want to think of Sophia in that way. He wanted to hate her.

Directing his eyes elsewhere was even more provoking, he decided as his gaze drifted down to her breasts. Rosy nipples, clearly defined beneath the fine lawn of his shirt, teased his already aroused senses. She hadn't been so well endowed seven years ago. He hardened instantly.

"My shirt looks better on you than it does on me."

Sophia crossed her arms over her chest. "It was all I

could find. My gown is badly in need of washing and mending."

Spying her gown lying on the floor, Chris picked it up and held it between his thumb and forefinger. His nose wrinkled in disgust. "I'm afraid this garment is beyond repair."

Without asking her permission, he strode to the porthole, unlatched it and tossed the gown into the churning water. Sophia leaped to her feet.

"You had no right to do that!"

"I beg to differ with you. As captain of this ship, I can do whatever I please."

Sophia knew she was in trouble when Chris's gaze settled on her exposed legs. This man was no longer the smitten boy she remembered. This was a man hardened by life, a complete stranger who knew what he wanted and was prepared to take it.

"Very fetching, Sophia."

Sophia resumed her seat at the desk, pulling her legs up beneath her. "Do you know where I might obtain needle, thread and scissors, Captain? Since you took it upon yourself to dispose of my gown, I'll need to fashion something decent to wear from the garments in your sea chest."

"I'm sure Casper can turn up something. But I find the shirt more than adequate. You've nothing to fear from me, Sophia. You no longer tempt me as you once did," he lied. "I lost interest in you the day I killed Desmond."

Sophia winced. His words hurt. Chris had been a different person then. He was harder now, weighed down by guilt. It seemed he lived in a hell of his own making.

"Finish eating," Chris said.

Sophia set her plate aside. "I'm finished. About the needle and thread . . ."

Chris pushed himself away from the bulkhead and ambled over to her. Placing his hands on the desk, he leaned forward until they were nearly nose to nose.

"Why are you worried about clothing? I just said you were unappealing to me." He paused, then asked, "How many men have you had in the past seven years?"

The insult was too much for Sophia to bear. She drew her arm back and slapped him. He reared backward. It took him a moment to react, but react he did. Grasping her upper arms, he hauled her up and pulled her over the desk, sending dishes and cutlery flying. Then he flung her on the bunk and fell on top of her.

"Don't ever strike me again," he warned through clenched teeth. "If you were one of my men, I'd have you flogged."

Sophia began to shiver uncontrollably, and not from cold, for the cabin had grown quite warm. This man held her life in his hands. If he wished to have her flogged, no one would stop him.

"You insulted me," Sophia said with more bravado than she felt. She pushed at his chest. "Get off me. I'm unappealing, remember?"

"I lied. I may not like you, but you feel damn good beneath me. We're going to be at sea several weeks and I'll be without female companionship. Since you aren't going anywhere soon, I see no reason why I should deny myself. I didn't invite you aboard, if you recall; you came of your own volition."

"I didn't know it was your ship!" Sophia cried. "Yours was the only ship with its gangplank run out. I intended to sneak ashore before the ship sailed."

Sophia gave herself a mental shake. The man was too mesmerizing by half. A tension she could only attribute to sexual awareness shimmered between them.

She went still beneath him, afraid to move for fear of the consequences. Chris was staring at her with an intensity that made her wonder if he intended to ravish her. She gazed at his beautiful mouth, vividly recalling the stolen kisses they had shared so very long ago. It was difficult to remember this was not the same young Chris she had once known.

He locked gazes with her. Chris couldn't deny Sophia was a beauty, with her delicate, fine-boned face, pearly white skin and voluptuous body. The years had been very good to her, fulfilling the promise of youthful loveliness.

He levered himself up on his elbows. "From whom were you running, Sophia? Seaman Horton told me he was hailed by a man and questioned about a young woman he was looking for. The story you told me coincides with Horton's."

Hard as he tried, Chris couldn't tear his gaze off her. He couldn't deny his attraction to Sophia despite his unwillingness to be ensnared again.

"What are you looking at?" Sophia asked sharply.

"You're even more beautiful than I remember."

"I'm surprised you want to remember me at all."

"I don't, dammit! But you've made it difficult for me to forget."

"Get off me; you're heavy."

"There's the little matter of paying for your passage. Now is as good a time as any to collect the first installment."

She pounded his chest. "Stop! I'm a virgin!"

Chris reared back, laughter rolling from his throat. "Now, why don't I believe that? Were you running away from a lover?"

"No, of course not, I—"

Her sentence died abruptly when Chris lowered his head and settled his lips on hers. He was just settling in for a long kiss when he felt a sharp pain. He reared backward, scarcely able to believe she had bitten his lip.

"Minx, why did you do that?"

"I expect to be treated with respect. You're no better than other men who tried to take from me what I wasn't willing to give."

Chris froze. Had someone tried to harm Sophia? Why *had* the Watch been chasing her?

"Let me be, Chris," Sophia cried. "I don't know you anymore. Who are you?"

"I'm not the gullible young fool I was seven years ago. It's obvious to me you're in trouble. You wouldn't be here if you weren't. Tell me."

"I . . . can't."

"I forget," he said harshly; "you don't trust me. I'm the man you cast aside because I wasn't heir to an earldom."

"No, it wasn't like that!"

Her denial incited his most primal instincts. He made a raw growl deep in his throat, lowered his head and captured her mouth with his. This time she didn't try to stop him when he plunged his tongue deep into her mouth, or when he cupped a firm breast in his hand and tweaked her nipple between his thumb and forefinger.

Chris smiled inwardly, thinking he was finally going to have what had been denied him seven years ago. But it wasn't to be. Sophia reared upward, causing him to lose his balance. The final insult came when she pushed him off the bunk. Unwilling to be thwarted by a mere woman, Chris reared up from the deck and flung himself on top of her. He didn't for one minute believe she was still virginal after all this time.

"Why are you pretending to be outraged?" Chris asked, his own anger rising.

"I'm not pretending."

"So you say."

Reaching down, he edged the bottom of her shirt upward and planted himself firmly between her thighs. "Relax, I'm not going to hurt you. Have you had a bad experience with a man? Is that why you're so skittish?"

Sophia gave a bark of laughter. It hadn't been all that long since Sir Oscar had attempted to ravish her.

One by one Chris released the buttons on her shirt, baring her breasts. He felt a rush of sensation as he stared at the creamy skin of her breasts and stomach. Perfection was the word that came to mind. She arched upward, trying to escape. Pure primal savagery ripped through him at the thought of plunging his aching cock into the woman who had caused him years of anguish. He raised himself slightly and unfastened his breeches. His cock burst free, hard and throbbing and more than ready to impale Sophia Carlisle at long last.

Chris drew a slow breath, trying to calm his lust. He was a large man and he didn't want to hurt her.

"Is this your way of punishing me for Desmond's death?" she cried.

He went still. "No, Sophia, this is for seven years of living in hell."

He kissed her shoulders, her breasts, and then caught a rosy nipple between his lips and suckled her. He heard her sharp intake of breath and smiled. "Your breasts are beautiful, perfect. Don't fight me; I'm not going to hurt you."

He continued to lave her nipples, first one and then the other, as he slowly smoothed his hands up the insides of her thighs. Her eyes were closed, she seemed resigned, a fact for which he was immensely grateful. He had worked up an inexplicable need for the unwelcome stowaway Fate had tossed into his bed.

With one hand he parted the nest of curls at the apex of her legs; he felt the muscles of her thighs clench in response. When he slid his fingers over the pulsing warmth of her wet cleft, she whimpered. He almost burst out laughing. It didn't take much for the pretend virgin to turn into an experienced wanton.

He parted her with his fingers and guided his cock to her entrance. He would have driven himself to the hilt if something in her eyes hadn't stopped him. Fear? Shock? Disgust?

Instead, he entered her slowly. She was tight. Too damn tight. He tried to ignore that stunning fact as he pushed deeper, and then his cock reached a barrier he hadn't expected. Damnation, he had wanted to believe the worst of her! He stared down at her, his mouth agape, eyes narrowed in disbelief. He had been with too many women not to recognize a virgin. The little minx hadn't lied.

Cursing violently, he pulled out and lifted himself off of her. She tugged her shirt as far over her legs as it would stretch and scooted off the bed. He tried not to notice the tears streaking her cheeks, or the lips swollen from his rough kisses. He had lost control. That wasn't like him. It seemed that seven years hadn't been enough time for him to forget his fascination with Sophia Carlisle.

Sophia had taught him that women were heartless creatures who valued money over love. Fortunately, he had learned his lesson well. Desmond's senseless death had made Chris value physical pleasure over emotional attachment. He had vowed to avoid becoming emotionally involved with a woman again, and he meant to live by his rule.

He glanced at Sophia. She was biting her bottom lip and staring at him as if he were some kind of ogre.

"Don't worry," he bit out. "You're still technically a virgin."

"I told you, but you didn't believe me," Sophia spat. "Now will you turn the ship about and return me to London?"

Chris laughed. "Not a chance, Sophia. The *Intrepid* is sailing to Jamaica and so are you. It's time you told me the truth about why you stowed away aboard my ship."

Sophia shook her head mutely. At one time Chris had professed to love her, a love Sophia had wholeheartedly returned but hadn't been free to accept. Lord Desmond had been the wealthy husband her family wanted for her. Though Chris's brother was an earl, Chris had little money of his own. He was dependent upon his brother for support and thus forbidden to her, or so her father and Rayford had insisted.

Sophia wondered how many duels Chris had fought over other women while she had been shunned by Society and forced to hide in shame in the countryside. He was a splendid man, impossibly handsome, strong and powerful. He could have any woman he wanted. Why did he still blame her for something that had happened years ago?

"Well, I'm waiting for an answer."

Smarting over his heavy-handedness, Sophia snapped, "You wouldn't be interested in my problems."

"You're right, women are nothing but trouble. Keep your secrets," he snorted as he stormed out of the cabin.

Chapter Three

Casper brought Sophia a needle, thread and scissors when he returned a few hours later with her lunch. He lingered near the door, staring at her as if he wanted to say something but was afraid.

Sophia smiled at him. "Is there something you wish to say to me?"

"The crew says you're a . . . Are you really one of . . . those women?" He shifted nervously from foot to foot, refusing to look at her.

"I am a lady, Casper. Does that answer your question?"

"Aye, I knew it!" Casper crowed. "That's what I told the crew. They believe you were brought aboard for the captain's pleasure. I told them you were a stowaway. That's right, isn't it?"

"Indeed it is," Sophia replied. "I stowed away without your captain's knowledge, although I've known Captain Radcliff for many years. You can tell that to anyone who asks."

Apparently satisfied, Casper took his leave. Later that afternoon, Sophia found a pair of trousers in

Chris's sea chest that looked too worn to be of much use to him and began altering them to fit her. Though she wasn't an expert with a needle, she had learned to do simple tasks since her family had fallen upon hard times.

As daylight faded, she had to light a lantern in order to put in the final stitches. She was just pulling the trousers on when Chris returned to the cabin. He took one look at her and burst out laughing.

"You look ridiculous."

"Go ahead and laugh," Sophia retorted, "but at least I'm decent."

His gaze, hot and avid, lingered on her breasts. "Are you?"

Aware that the transparency of Chris's fine lawn shirt offered scant protection, Sophia crossed her arms over her chest. That simple act caused her newly fashioned breeches to slip over her trim hips and fall around her ankles.

Chris shook his head. "Your sewing skills leave much to be desired. I'd lend you a belt, but I'm sure it would wrap twice around your waist."

He tapped his chin, grinned, and then picked up the scissors.

"What are you going to do?" Sophia asked.

"Cut a strip from the hem of the shirt. You can use it as a belt."

"I can do it myself," Sophia said when he knelt before her and raised the hem a bit.

"Would you deprive me of the pleasure of looking at your legs?"

He began cutting. Sophia squeaked in dismay when he grasped her thigh beneath the shirttail to hold her steady.

"Don't move," he warned.

His hand slid higher.

"Stop that! I didn't give you permission to take liberties."

"You're lucky I haven't done more than take liberties," Chris muttered. "This is my ship. You're at my mercy."

He stood, handing her the narrow strip of cloth he had snipped from the hem of the shirt. Immediately Sophia pulled up the breeches and threaded the material through the belt loops. Then she stuffed the shirt into the breeches and tied the makeshift belt at her waist. Chris stood back and gazed at her, an amused smile curving his lips.

"Do you feel better now?"

"Much better, except . . ." She glanced down at her breasts, aware that they were outlined beneath the shirt. This time when she crossed her arms, her breeches stayed firmly in place. "I need a jacket."

"One of mine, I presume."

Sophia returned to Chris's sea chest, rummaging around until she found a jacket fashioned of thick wool. "Do you mind?" she asked, holding it up to her chest.

"Not at all, but I have a better idea. I'll ask Casper to loan you one of his. It will fit you better than mine."

Aware of where his gaze lingered, Sophia pulled on the jacket and buttoned it over her breasts. It nearly swallowed her in its enormous folds. "I'll wear yours until Casper provides me with another."

"Pity," Chris muttered.

Now that she was decently covered, Sophia's courage returned. "What do you want?"

Chris's brows shot upward. "This is my cabin. This is where I take my meals and sleep."

"Where am I going to sleep?"

"You'll be sharing my cabin. I thought I made that clear."

"Be reasonable, Chris. You know that won't work, for obvious reasons."

Sophia turned away lest he see her dismay. It wounded her pride that he thought so little of her. He'd been wild in his youth, she recalled, but sweet and endearing. He'd sworn she was the love of his life. Ha, so much for love!

There came a knock on the door. Chris admitted Casper; he had brought their supper. The lad placed the tray on the desk and left immediately to fetch a bottle of port and one of his old jackets as Chris requested. Chris pulled two chairs up to the desk and seated Sophia with a flourish.

"Cook has prepared a veritable feast," he said, pointing out the various dishes of meat and vegetables. "I hope you like chicken. We brought live fowl and a few goats aboard to provide meat for the duration of our journey. The fresh vegetables will only last a short time and the flour will grow weevils, so eat hearty while you can."

"I love chicken," Sophia replied. He heaped her plate with succulent pieces of stewed chicken and vegetables and then filled his own. She caught him staring at her and sought to distract him. "Tell me about your ship."

"The *Intrepid* is a three-masted, square-rigged schooner. She's fast and dependable, and all mine. Though she carries twenty-four guns, we've rarely had to fire them. We can outrun anything afloat."

"Have you been a captain long?"

Chris bit into a piece of chicken and chewed thoughtfully. "I bought the *Intrepid* three years ago. Before that, I served aboard her for two years as first mate. The captain wanted to retire, so I found the funds to buy her. "

"So you've been plying the seas these past seven years."

"I enjoy the excitement."

"Are you carrying trade goods to Jamaica in your hold now?"

"Enough questions," Chris said. "Your food is getting cold."

Sophia bristled at his abruptness. Chris's moods ran hot and cold. He hated her, yet he wanted her. He had disappeared from her life without as much as a good-bye. She might still be a member of Society if Chris had offered for her after the duel instead of disappearing and leaving her to face the scandal and her family's wrath alone.

"Are you ready now to tell me who or what you were running from, Sophia?"

Sophia shook her head. "I've told you everything you need to know. Tell me about Jamaica."

"Ah, Jamaica. After experiencing the golden warmth of the island, you'll find the chill fog of England enormously unappealing. I did. That's why I'm settling permanently on my newly acquired plantation. I'm going to raise sugarcane and distill rum."

The conversation was momentarily interrupted when Casper arrived with a bottle of ruby port and a woolen jacket. Chris thanked him, and he left immediately. Chris handed the jacket to Sophia, then popped the cork on the port while she removed his oversized garment and thrust her arms into Casper's.

"Since fancy glasses aren't part of the ship's manifest, mugs will have to do," Chris said as he fetched two mugs from the cupboard and poured a generous portion of the red liquid into each of them.

Sophia took a sip, finding it mellow and pleasing to the taste. She continued eating until her curiosity could no longer be contained. "Why are you abandoning England for Jamaica?"

"I have no fond memories of England."

Sophia knew precisely to what he was referring but let the comment pass. "What about your family? I know you have a brother. Did he marry Lady Grace? He was courting her when I left London."

"Justin did indeed marry Grace. They expect a child in late fall. I have every intention of returning to London from time to time to visit my brother and his family. It's not as if I'm cutting all ties with England."

"I'd like to sever all ties with Rayford," Sophia muttered.

"You're referring to Caldwell, of course. Won't he be worried when he finds you've gone missing?"

"I doubt it. Can we find something more pleasant to discuss?"

Chris was reluctant to drop the subject. "I take it you're not fond of him."

Chris watched as Sophia drank deeply from her mug. He continued to stare at her while he drained his own mug.

"I don't want to talk about Rayford," Sophia said.

"What did Caldwell do to you, Sophia?"

Sophia stood. "I'm tired. Please leave so I can retire."

"You may retire any time you wish. But if you think I'm going to leave, you're dead wrong. Unless a crisis arises, I'm not leaving till morning. The bunk is plenty big enough for two."

Sophia felt her color rise. "I'm not going to sleep in your bed."

Chris shrugged. "You can sleep on the deck if you wish. But I warn you, it won't be as warm as the bunk."

Chris watched the play of emotion on Sophia's face. It went from disbelief to anger to determination. What a tantalizing woman she had become, but he had always known she would mature into a great beauty. No, he refused to let his mind explore further in that direction. He had put all that behind him years ago.

"You're safe with me," Chris said, "unless you decide you'd like an introduction to sexual pleasure. There could never be anything more than that between you and me."

"No, thank you," Sophia snapped. "Becoming intimate with you doesn't interest me."

Chris stalked her until he stood before her, his eyes probing deep into her soul. "I could make it interesting."

Their gazes collided. A simmering tension stretched between them. His features wore an expectant book, his expression dark with promise.

"I suggest that you use your powers of seduction on someone who will appreciate your efforts," Sophia sniffed.

Chris chortled. "You do tempt me, my lady, despite our complicated past."

Sophia tried to put distance between them, but Chris wasn't done with her yet. Reaching out, he dragged her into his arms. "I wouldn't mind becoming intimate as long as we both knew it was a temporary arrangement and nothing would ever come of it."

"Don't touch me."

"Too late," he whispered against her lips scant seconds before his mouth claimed hers.

She tastes like Paradise, Chris thought as he slanted his lips over hers. One taste wasn't enough. He wanted more of her. Prodding her lips with his tongue, he forced them open and plunged his tongue into her wine-scented mouth.

A groan formed deep in his throat. He wanted her. He wanted her violently. She tasted as ripe as a warm, sweet plum, just waiting to be plucked. Was Sophia experiencing the same sensations he was feeling right now? A dark, swift heat clenched his loins. Desire stabbed deep in his gut.

Damnation! He didn't want to desire a woman he had sworn to hate. She had boarded his ship uninvited, why shouldn't he take what he wanted from her? Sophia had ruined his life, she didn't deserve consideration from him.

A sound, half moan, half protest, slipped past her lips, giving Chris pause. Bedding Sophia would make him responsible for her, and he didn't want that. He had all the responsibility he could handle right now. If only she weren't a virgin, he'd have no qualms about tossing her on the bunk and thrusting himself into her hot center.

With a reluctant growl, he set her away from him. "Go to bed, Sophia."

Spinning on his heel, he stormed out of the cabin.

Sophia couldn't believe what had just happened. If Chris hadn't stopped when he did, she would have let him seduce her. He was as dangerous as Sir Oscar, only in a different way. This man, whether he meant to or not, could chew up her heart and spit it out without a thought for her feelings. He had hurt her once; it would be so easy for him to hurt her again.

Sophia's dismal thoughts were interrupted when Casper arrived with a jug of hot water. He bade her good night and carried the dirty dishes away with him.

There was no way she was going to sleep in Chris's bunk, Sophia decided. Lying beside him would present too great a temptation and invite another attempt at seduction. If Chris cared about her, it would be different, but he didn't.

Deciding that the deck would have to do, Sophia was relieved to find a spare blanket and pillow in the cupboard. After a hasty wash, she wrapped herself in the blanket fully clothed, lay down on the deck and tried to sleep. The deck was colder than she had expected. She scooted closer to the brazier, trying to soak up some of its warmth. A long time passed before she finally fell asleep.

Chris had intended to sleep elsewhere but changed his mind. Why should he put himself out for a woman who had broken his heart? He wasn't some green boy who couldn't control his sexual urges. He saw no reason why he and Sophia couldn't share the same bed without being intimate.

All was quiet when Chris entered his cabin. He glanced at the bunk, saw that it was empty and spit out a curse. Then he saw her lying on the deck, close to the brazier, which had little heat left in it. He approached her cautiously and leaned down to peer at her. Though she appeared to be sleeping, she was shivering uncontrollably.

Chris wasn't a mean-spirited person despite his rough exterior. He couldn't let Sophia suffer while he slept in comfort. Scooping her into his arms, he lowered her onto his bunk and pulled the covers over her. She was still shivering, Chris noted as he fed charcoal into the brazier. He hesitated but a moment before undressing and crawling into bed beside her.

Even in her sleep, Sophia gravitated toward the warmth of his body. Sighing in resignation, Chris clamped down on his lust and curled his body around hers. It wasn't long before her shivering stopped and she settled down into a peaceful sleep.

Chris was less fortunate. His body refused to relax. His erection made him all too aware of the desirable woman in his arms. The layers of clothing between them did little to disguise her delicious curves, or the fact that nothing but his conscience prevented him from using her for his own pleasure. He'd bedded women from all corners of the world, what made Sophia different?

Why wouldn't she tell him her reason for fleeing into the night?

It wasn't until his randy cock subsided and his mind shut down that he fell into a restless slumber.

Sophia woke to a feeling of warmth. Even the gentle rocking motion felt pleasant. She sighed and squirmed into a more comfortable position. The heaviness that lay across her breast and hips felt right somehow.

"If you don't stop writhing, all my good intentions will fly out the window."

Sophia's eyes flew open. It didn't take her long to realize she was in Chris's bunk, his body wrapped around hers, his hand on her breast and his leg flung across her hips. Sophia stiffened, her green eyes dark with outrage.

"How did I get in your bunk?"

"I carried you here last night. You were shivering when I returned to the cabin, and putting you in my bed was the only way I knew to warm you."

"You had no right."

"Sophia, let's get this straight. Whatever I do on my ship is my right. I didn't hurt you. All I tried to do was make you comfortable."

Sophia looked pointedly at his hand resting on her breast. "Why do you care if I am comfortable?"

"I suppose because deep down I am still a gentleman."

"Prove it. Remove your hand from my person."

Heaving a reluctant sigh, Chris did as she asked. Then he removed his leg and rolled out of bed.

"You're naked!" Sophia cried, shutting her eyes to hide her dismay. It had taken but one brief look to realize that Christian Radcliff was a stunning specimen of virile manhood. His power lay in his muscular torso and sinewy arms and legs. Nothing about him suggested weakness.

Sophia had always known he was exceptional, but seeing a mature Chris without benefit of clothing brought the full impact of his masculinity into focus. Dear God, he was magnificent!

"You can open your eyes now," Chris said. "I'm decent."

"You'll never be decent, captain," Sophia huffed.

"I wish I could stay here and trade barbs with you, Sophia, but duty calls." He pulled on his jacket and walked to the door.

Sophia jumped out of bed. "Wait! May I go topside today? I cannot abide being cooped up."

Chris stared at her so long, Sophia feared he would

refuse. To her relief, he nodded, albeit reluctantly. "Wait until I come for you. I want to prepare my men before I let you loose on them. They need to know that you are off limits. My crew follows orders and is well disciplined, but you're too damn attractive for your own good."

Sophia bristled. "It would be difficult to entice anyone dressed as I am." She whirled for his inspection. "I could pass for one of your crewmen."

Laughter lurked in Chris's eyes. "I sincerely doubt that, Sophia. Just be sure to stuff your hair under a knit cap. You'll find one in my sea chest."

He opened the door and was gone before Sophia could thank him.

The morning passed too slowly for Sophia's liking. While she waited for Chris to return, Casper had brought her breakfast, cleaned the cabin and performed other mundane chores.

Chris returned to the cabin shortly after she had lunched on bread and cheese. "Finally," Sophia said. "I thought you'd never come."

"A problem occurred topside," Chris said. "One of the lines on the mainmast became tangled. I had to climb up and untangle it."

"Why you? Shouldn't you leave the dangerous chores to your subordinates?"

"I never allow my men to do anything I'm not willing to do myself. Are you ready to go topside? Pull your hat down over your ears—there's a brisk wind blowing from the north."

"I'm more than ready. I don't mind the cold. Anything is better than staying in this cabin."

Chris opened the door, and she brushed past him.

He stood aside while she climbed the ladder to the deck and then followed. Sophia braced herself against the blast of icy wind that buffeted her. It snatched away her breath even though Chris had told her what to expect.

"Do you want to return to the cabin?"

"No, I'd like a tour of the *Intrepid*. I've never been on a ship before."

Sophia was surprised at how well Chris managed his crew and ship. He introduced her to Mr. Blaine, his first mate, and pointed out different parts of the ship, offering explanations as he went. When Sophia saw the mainmast, her mouth gaped open.

"Is that the mast you climbed?"

"It is."

"You could have been killed!"

"That's a bit dramatic, Sophia. I've been doing it for years and haven't fallen once."

"Once is all it would take to kill you. You always were headstrong and reckless."

Cocking his head, he sent her an odd look. "I could say the same about you."

Sophia sought to change the subject. Every time their past was brought up, Chris became sullen and unreasonable. "If you have something pressing to do, you can leave. I want to stand at the rail and watch the sea."

"I suppose you can't get into trouble if you stand here and behave yourself. If you get cold, feel free to return to the cabin."

Sophia nodded agreement and returned her attention to the sea, clapping delightedly when she spotted a school of frolicking porpoises.

"So that's our little stowaway," Blaine said when

Chris joined him a few minutes later. "How was she? I assume she spent the night in your bunk."

"She did, but not in the way you think, Mr. Blaine."

Blaine sent him a startled look. "Never say you didn't tup her."

"That's precisely what I'm saying, though I suggest you keep it under your hat. I want the men to believe Sophia is mine in every way."

Blaine wagged his head in disbelief. "I've never known you to pass up a good thing when it falls in your lap. Give her to me if she doesn't appeal to you."

Chris sent him a hard look. "Sophia is mine, don't forget it." Though Chris didn't like the way Blaine was regarding Sophia, he didn't want to reveal their past relationship. It was still too painful to talk about. "Don't you have something to do, Mr. Blaine?"

"I have a great deal to do, but I'd rather watch you stare holes into your stowaway. For pity's sake, Captain, if you want the woman, take her."

"I don't want her."

"Tell that to someone who will believe you."

There was no help for it. He had to tell his friend a bit of the truth. "Sophia isn't what you think. I knew her a long time ago. It didn't work out between us."

"Did you meet her in a bordello in London?" Blaine asked.

"Not even close," Chris replied. "Sophia is a virgin. She's running from someone but refuses to enlighten me as to why."

Blaine stared at Chris in disbelief. "She's a virgin? How can you be sure if you didn't tup her?"

"Don't you think I can tell when a woman is a virgin?"

"Of course, but wouldn't you have had to—"

Chris's expression must have warned Blaine he was treading in dangerous waters, for he quickly changed the subject. "Do you still intend to ship her back to England once we reach Jamaica?"

"I do. Sophia is a responsibility I don't need, a woman I refuse to get involved with again. She's trouble, Blaine. She's *in* trouble."

"She's in trouble? How can you return her to England to face whoever is threatening her if you know she's in danger?"

"Whose side are you on, Blaine?"

"Yours, of course, Captain. I'm just saying I've never known you to throw a woman to the wolves."

Chris returned his gaze to Sophia, wondering why he was letting her plague him, why he felt the need to protect her. Blaine was right, it was going to be difficult to return her to a dangerous situation, but what choice did he have. These were unsettled times in Jamaica. According to reports, the slave situation on the island was primed to explode.

Slaves were threatening to revolt against their white masters; it wasn't a safe place for an Englishwoman right now. Though Chris knew there were women on the island, wives of planters and such, letting Sophia remain was out of the question. Besides, she had begged him to turn the ship around and take her back to England despite the mysterious danger that threatened her.

"I'm convinced Sophia can take care of herself. From what she told me, the danger involved her stepbrother. I doubt he will harm her. Women are inclined to make much ado about nothing."

"You know best, Captain," Blaine said. He peered up at the sky. "Looks like we're in for a blow."

Chris scanned the fluffy white clouds fleeing before a stiff wind. "We'll outrun it, but go ahead and make preparations in case I'm wrong."

Blaine took his leave. Chris returned his gaze to Sophia. As if aware of his scrutiny, she turned her head. Their gazes collided, held; then his slithered away. The next time he looked in her direction, she was gone.

Sophia returned to the cabin to escape the wind, which had changed abruptly from brisk to near gale force. Casper must have fed more charcoal into the brazier while she was out, for the cabin felt warm and cozy after being topside. She began to perspire in her woolen coat and removed it. She walked to the porthole and stared out at the turbulent waves. The ship had begun to dip and rise alarmingly. She felt a bit queasy and moved to the bunk to lie down.

Sophia felt too ill to eat dinner that night and told Casper to take the food away. "We're in for a bit of a blow, miss," Casper warned. "Captain said it wasn't a bad one, so there's no need to worry."

Sophia couldn't help worrying when Chris didn't return to the cabin that night. She heard the wind howling as rain mixed with sleet slashed against the porthole. Although she tried to sleep through the worst of it, her upset stomach plagued her throughout the ordeal.

When Sophia awoke the following morning, it was as if there had never been a storm. The sky was blue, the ship rocked on a gentle breeze, and her stomach had settled down. She sat up in bed just as Chris staggered into the cabin.

Sophia slid out of bed. "You look terrible," she said, eyeing the dark shadows under his eyes and the beginning of a beard darkening his cheeks.

"Thank you," Chris said curtly. He began shedding his wet clothing.

"What are you doing?"

"Now that the danger is past, I'm going to bed." He sent her a challenging look. "You can join me if you like. I don't suppose you got much sleep last night."

"I'm fine," Sophia said, turning away as he pulled off his breeches.

Sighing, he flopped down on the bunk and pulled the blanket up to his neck. He fell asleep almost immediately.

Sophia stared into his face. He was the handsomest man she'd ever seen. She'd thought so all those years ago and she still thought so. His hair, wet from his recent drenching, looked black instead of the dark brown she admired so much. While his lashes were indecently long, his bold features made a noble statement about his masculinity.

Sophia recalled the way women had swooned over Chris during her Season in Town, and how he had devoted all his time to her.

Damn him! Why hadn't he offered for her after Desmond's death?

Chapter Four

Chris awakened from an erotic dream to find light streaming through the porthole and Sophia lying beside him. She lay on her side, facing him, fully dressed but for the woolen jacket. He rose up on his elbow and regarded her with grudging admiration. Carefully he slid the blanket down to her waist. The fine lawn shirt she wore hid nothing from him; she might as well have been naked. The lush ripeness of her body sorely tempted him.

A slash of sunlight piercing through the porthole clearly revealed the outline of her upper body. Her breasts were round and deliciously full. The taut buds of her nipples thrust against the sheer material of the shirt, plump and inviting. He wanted to rip away the damn shirt and look his fill.

He wanted . . .

Sophia opened her eyes and scooted as far away from him as she could get. "What are you looking at?"

"You. You've grown into a stunning woman."

She pulled the blanket up to her neck and fastened her eyes on his face instead of his naked torso. "You slept nearly twenty-four hours. You were so exhausted, I knew you wouldn't stir, so I decided to sleep in the bunk too."

"You don't have to explain, Sophia. The bunk is far more comfortable than the deck."

"It won't happen again." She eased out of bed and gave him her back.

Chris knew she expected him to rise and dress, and he didn't disappoint her. "I'll wash and shave in Blaine's cabin so you can have some privacy," he said. "Casper should arrive soon with hot water. Perhaps you can talk him into bringing the washtub into the cabin so you can take a hip bath."

Sophia's face brightened. "Would he do that?"

"I'm sure he would. I'll have a word with him. I'm dressed—you can turn around. Just give me a moment to gather what I need and I'll get out of your way."

"Thank you."

He glanced out the porthole. "You can come up on deck when you're ready. It promises to be a pleasant day."

Sophia thanked him again and he departed.

"Captain said you wanted a bath," Casper told her when he arrived with her breakfast a short time later.

"Would you mind?" Sophia asked.

"No, miss. The captain asked me to fetch the tub for you, and I wouldn't think of disobeying him. I won't be long."

Sophia ate her breakfast while Casper dragged in the tub and filled it with hot water from the galley. He even left a bucket of warm water beside the tub for rinsing her hair. Sophia was so grateful, she wanted to kiss him. Fearing she might embarrass him, she resisted the urge.

"Anything else you need before I leave?" Casper asked.

"No, thank you. I know where to find towels and soap."

"I'll return for the tub later. Take your time, miss." Ducking his head, he scooted out the door.

Sophia fetched towels and soap and placed them near the tub where she could reach them. She undressed quickly and stepped into the bath, sighing contentedly as she lowered herself into the steaming water.

She scrubbed her body clean, dipped her head into the water, washed her hair and rinsed out the soap with clean water from the bucket. When the bathwater began to cool, she stepped out of the tub, wrapped her hair in a towel and dried herself with another. Unwilling to put soiled clothes on her clean body, she washed her shirt and breeches in the bathwater and placed them on a chair before the brazier. Then she wrapped herself in a blanket and waited for her clothing to dry.

When Casper returned for the tub, he averted his gaze from her blanket-clad form. "I can string a line and hang your clothes topside, miss. They'll dry faster outside in the breeze than they will inside the cabin. I can return for the tub after I've hung your clothes."

"Thank you, Casper, that's kind of you."

Casper gathered up her shirt and breeches and left.

Feeling chilled after her bath, Sophia fed charcoal into the brazier and pulled the chair close to the heat. That was how Chris found her, toasting her toes before the spreading warmth.

"Did you enjoy your bath?" he asked.

"Immensely, thank you. I washed my clothes, and Casper took them outside to dry."

"I saw them hanging on a line. They should dry in no time."

His gaze slid over her thinly clad form. Sophia hugged the blanket tighter around her. Though no skin was showing, Chris's penetrating gaze made her feel naked.

"What are you looking at?"

He dragged his eyes away. "I was picturing you the first time I saw you, wearing a satin-and-lace ball gown."

Sophia flushed and looked away. "Casper said he would return for the tub, but I doubt he can manage it on his own. Can you summon someone to help him?"

Chris sent her a hard look, as if aware that she was deliberately changing the subject. "I'll see to it immediately."

Sophia breathed a sigh of relief. She didn't want Chris to think back to the duel. It would only bring back unpleasant memories.

Chris took two steps toward the door, then swung around to confront her. "It's not going to work, you know."

"What are you talking about?"

"Your attempts to distract me when I venture too close to the past. Nothing you can say will ease the guilt I harbor over Desmond's death."

He stormed out.

Later, wearing clothes that smelled clean and fresh, Sophia went topside to bask in the sunshine. She was surprised when Mr. Blaine, Chris's first mate, stopped to talk to her. They exchanged pleasantries for several minutes, and then he moved on.

During dinner that evening, Chris mentioned the exchange. "What did Blaine say to you, Sophia? He's quite taken with you, you know."

Sophia paused with the fork halfway to her mouth. "Mr. Blaine seems like a pleasant man. We exchanged but a few words. I seriously doubt he is interested in me. He was merely satisfying his curiosity."

She continued eating, doing her best to ignore Chris's intense scrutiny. She wanted to cringe every time he looked at her as if he wished she were anywhere but on his ship.

"The air seems to be growing warmer," she remarked.

"You'll notice the difference more once we reach southern waters."

"How soon will that be?"

"Another week, if all goes well."

Sophia finished eating and pushed her plate away. She cleared her throat, stared at her folded hands and said, "I think we should consider different sleeping arrangements."

Chris's mouth flattened. "Whose bunk would you prefer sleeping in? Mr. Blaine's, perhaps?"

Sophia rose abruptly, her hands clenched into fists at her sides. "What are you accusing me of, Captain? You and I aren't even friends. So why are you acting as if you care?"

Chris shrugged. "I don't care, but since I've already told my crew that you belong to me, we're going to continue sharing a cabin and a bunk. What we do or don't do in my bunk is no one's business. Whether you believe it or not, I will be immensely relieved the day you board a ship for your return to England."

He unfolded his large frame from the chair and headed out the door. "Take your time preparing for bed. I need to take a new reading to keep us on course."

That night set the pattern for many nights to come. No matter what argument Sophia used, Chris refused to sleep elsewhere. What really disturbed her was the fact that she enjoyed having Chris's body beside her at night far too much. The only concession he made to her was rising before she did and leaving the cabin to her until he returned in the evening.

As the days slid past, boredom set in, forcing Sophia to take note of those around her. Mr. Blaine spoke to her with increasing frequency. He often stopped and visited while she stood at the rail. Little by little, other crewmen dared to pass the time of day with her. A grizzled sailor must have noticed her restlessness, for he offered to teach her to tie knots in his spare time.

Sophia eagerly accepted, spending long hours each afternoon sitting on a pile of ropes beside Seaman Mapes, learning his skills. Another sailor let her help mend a torn sail.

The days began to grow too warm for the wool jacket Sophia wore, but she didn't dare take it off. One day Casper noticed sweat running down her forehead and suggested that it was warm enough now to discard the wool jacket and knit cap.

"You don't need those heavy clothes now, miss," Casper said. "The closer we get to Jamaica, the hotter it's going to get."

"I agree, the jacket and cap are a bit much," Sophia replied somewhat wistfully, "but not wearing them would attract too much attention. The captain wouldn't like it."

"But, miss, I don't understand why . . ." His words fell off as comprehension dawned. He ducked his head. "Oh . . . well, I'll see what I can do." He trotted off.

Sophia smiled and returned to the knot she had been working on. Not thirty minutes later, Casper returned with a short-sleeved, open-necked canvas shirt, much like the one the sailors had donned once they reached warmer climes. Sophia exclaimed in delight. The material was not transparent, and it was bulky enough to mask her femininity.

"You're a lifesaver, Casper," Sophia exclaimed. "I can't wait to put it on and soak up some of this delightful sunshine."

The next day, and every day after that, Sophia wore the canvas shirt when she went topside. Since Chris offered no objection to her new shirt, Sophia decided to discard the cap. She braided her black hair into one long braid and let it dangle down her back.

On most days she stretched out on coiled ropes on deck and dozed in the sun. Chris was right. English weather could not compare with day after day of sunshine and tropical breezes. Sophia's skin began to take on a golden tint. If her mother were alive, Sophia knew she would be horrified. She would force Sophia to remain indoors with a bleaching solution of lemon juice on her face and arms. But Sophia didn't care if the color of her skin made her look unattractive. There was plenty of time to worry about that during her return voyage to England.

Suddenly a shadow fell over her, blocking out the sun. "The sun is turning your skin. You should move into the shade. English ladies aren't supposed to tan— it's unfashionable."

Sophia squinted up at Chris. She held out a sun-bronzed arm. "I had no idea my skin would tan so well. Does the color offend you?"

"Many things about you offend me, but I don't want to get into that now. I thought young Englishwomen were taught to shun the sun. You should have a bonnet."

"I suppose most women protect their skin from the sun, but I'm not most women. I'll never be able to enjoy this kind of warmth again, and I intend to take advantage of it while I can."

"Caldwell won't recognize you if you allow yourself to get much darker."

"That suits me just fine. I have no intention of seeing Rayford ever again. I'm old enough to make my own way in life."

"How will you support yourself?"

"I received a good education. I can hire myself out as a governess."

Chris's lips twitched. He wanted to laugh out loud but restrained the urge. He couldn't imagine a Society matron with eyes in her head hiring someone as attractive as Sophia. She would have a hard time protecting her virtue from the males in the family. Why that thought bothered him he didn't know, except that Sophia was becoming a bigger problem than he had expected. Instead of causing dissension among his crew, she was becoming their little pet.

"What do you find amusing?" Sophia asked. "Do you doubt my intelligence?"

"Never," Chris averred. He dropped the subject. "You should be able to see Jamaica in a few days."

Sophia's eyes searched his face. "I hate the thought of returning immediately to England without seeing something of the island. I'm dreading another three or four weeks at sea."

"What are you saying, Sophia? Don't you want to return to England?"

"Of course I do," she maintained. "What would I do in Jamaica?"

"There is nothing for you in Jamaica, Sophia. I've already told you, there is no place for you in my life. You're my past, Jamaica is my future. I refuse to take responsibility for you."

Anger roiled deep inside Sophia. She leaped to her feet, hands on hips, facing him squarely. "You were never one to accept responsibility, were you, Chris? Instead of accepting things and making them right, you ran. You can keep running, for all I care. Forget about me. You're very good at that."

Spinning on her heel, she flounced off.

Sophia knew the moment the words left her mouth that she had made a terrible mistake. She didn't dare look back to see if her outburst had angered Chris as she clambered down the ladder. All she wanted was to reach the safety of her cabin.

There were only a few times in his life that Chris had been rendered speechless, and this was one of them. Damn Sophia to hell! How dare she play with his emotions! She was the one who had rejected him after the duel that took Desmond's life.

Had Sophia known that the *Intrepid* belonged to him when she chose his ship on which to hide? What was her real purpose in stowing away? Was it to bedevil him? Did she still want to punish him for killing Desmond after all these years?

"Captain, are you all right? Did something happen between you and your lady?"

"Something happened a long time ago," Chris spat.

"Sophia is a fortune hunter who enjoys playing one man against another. She's poison, Dirk, put on this earth to torment me. Believe it or not, long ago I fancied myself in love with her."

Blaine eyed him curiously. "What happened?"

"I've tried my damnedest to forget Sophia and almost succeeded, until she turned up on the *Intrepid*. There are things in my life I'm not proud of, things that happened during my misspent youth. Sophia is responsible for the most difficult time I have ever had to face."

"If Miss Carlisle is all that you said, I'm surprised you didn't return her to England immediately."

There was no mirth in Chris's laugh. "I've spent the better part of seven years trying to forget what I did because of Sophia. I told myself she meant nothing to me, that it didn't matter if she was on board, but I was wrong."

"Care to talk about it?"

Chris walked over to the railing, gripping it so hard his knuckles turned white. "Because of Sophia, I killed an innocent man, my best friend, in a drunken duel that never should have happened. The whole fiasco was a stupid mistake, and that's all I'm going to say."

"You said Sophia was in trouble."

A thoughtful expression crossed Chris's features as he directed his gaze at the water churning beneath the ship. "Trouble seems to follow Sophia. Once, I believed she cared for me, Dirk, but it was my friend Desmond she chose to wed."

"What are you going to do now?"

Chris whirled, his face contorted with rage. "I'm going to do exactly what I planned to do from the beginning. Bid the minx good riddance and book her passage on the first ship sailing out of Kingston Bay for England. I hold Sophia partly responsible for a man's death. No one will ever know how much guilt I've suffered since the day Desmond died in my arms."

"You shouldn't be so hard on yourself, or on Miss Carlisle. She must have been young when you first knew her."

"Don't diminish her guilt in the disaster, Dirk. I'm a changed man emotionally and mentally since that fickle minx lied to me about her feelings. She made me believe she loved me, and then refused to speak to me after the duel. Damnation, Dirk, I didn't mean to kill Desmond. We were both foxed. What had started as friendly competition ended with his death. I still can't forgive myself for killing my best friend."

Blaine regarded his friend with concern. "Take my advice, Captain—let it go."

"Your advice has been noted and duly rejected," Chris replied. "If you'll excuse me, I have a little matter to discuss with the lady."

Steeling himself for a confrontation with Sophia, Chris scrambled down the ladder and paused a moment to gain control of his temper before entering the cabin. His gaze found Sophia immediately as he opened the door and stepped inside. She was seated on a chair, looking small and vulnerable. But her defenselessness did not dampen his anger.

"You're as much to blame for Desmond's death as I am," he said with quiet menace.

Sophia leaped to her feet. "I'm not the one who killed him."

"So you *do* blame me."

73

"The only thing I blame you for is running off when I needed you. You let me face the scandal alone."

His mouth flattened. "I should dump you in the sea and let you swim back to London. A man died because of you. That man was my friend. You led us both on until a duel for your affections seemed the only way to gain your hand."

The color drained from Sophia's face. "I never intended for it to end in tragedy."

"Then why did you keep us both dangling? Why did you tell me you cared for me?"

"I was seventeen, Chris! I was enjoying my first Season even though I knew I had to wed someone soon. You were my first choice, but I knew I couldn't have you. My family was desperate for money."

"If that was true, why didn't you tell me that my circumstances put me out of the running for your hand? Why did you tell me you loved me?"

Sophia refused to meet his eyes. She was not proud of the way she'd handled the situation. She hadn't meant to provoke a duel; she'd just wanted as much time with Chris as she could get before wedding Desmond.

"I intended to tell you why I had to wed Desmond, but you became impatient and took matters into your own hands. Dueling over me was stupid. Why did you disappear after Desmond's death?" she dared.

Grasping her shoulders, Chris gave her a little shake. "Why? Because you refused to speak to me afterward. You looked at me with horror and disgust. You gave me no choice but to remove myself from your life."

Oh, Chris, I was too stunned to speak. And I was worried sick that you would be arrested and imprisoned. "I don't suppose you'd understand." She shook her head sadly.

"In the meantime, you've done all right for yourself, so why revisit the past?"

Chris gave her a self-satisfied smirk. "Judging from what I know of you now, you didn't do all right. You're still unmarried, and in trouble."

"Damn you! You left me to face the scandal on my own. Father whisked me away to the country, and I never heard the end of it from him and Rayford. They made life miserable for me. Not a day went by without them reminding me that I'd failed in my duty to my family. Marrying wealth was no longer possible after the scandal."

"I'm sorry to hear that."

Sophia bristled. His apology held a note of mockery. The Chris she'd once known had changed from a charming youth to an unfeeling, cynical man.

Sophia had mourned losing Chris after he walked out of her life. Over the years, she had kept him in her thoughts. Though Sophia knew that arguing with him was feeding the flames of his temper, she couldn't help it. Chris had hurt her. Because of him she had been banished from Society, treated with contempt by her family and shunned by her friends. After her father's death, Rayford had become her guardian and tormentor. What would Chris say if he knew Ray had tried to sell her innocence to repay a gambling debt?

That, Sophia decided, was something she'd never tell Chris. He'd probably laugh and tell her it was no more than she deserved.

"I'm not as heartless as you believe," Chris maintained. "I said I'd send you back to England, and so I will, but after that, you're on your own. Women like you always land on their feet."

Her dismayed expression showed that his words had pierced her. She was the one who should be angry, she was the one who had lost the most: her reputation and the man who could have helped her family rise above poverty.

Chris's fingers tightened on her shoulders. God, she was lovely. Seven years hadn't dimmed her beauty. He recalled how much he had loved her, how desperate he'd been to make her his despite his lack of funds. If only she could have waited for him until his grandmother had passed away and left him her fortune. But Sophia had been too eager for a title to wait.

Sophia tried to shrug off his hands. He refused to release her. Her shoulders shook, her silence more telling than her words. He knew he had hurt her and had no idea how to fix it, or if he even wanted to. He wanted to shake her and kiss her at the same time. Kissing her won out.

Roughly he dragged her against him. Lowering his head, he captured her mouth. His kiss was not gentle, nor was it meant to be. He kissed her until she went limp and moaned into his mouth. Then he pushed her away, a stunned expression on his face.

"No! I'm not going to let you tempt me again."

He needed to put space between them. He no longer wanted to know what kind of trouble had brought her aboard his ship, or the danger she would face upon her return to England.

"I never—"

He held up his hand. "I don't want to hear it. You're going to get your wish. I'm moving out of the cabin for the remainder of the voyage. You won't have to deal with my presence any longer. I'll send Casper for my things."

During the last days of the voyage, Sophia felt alone and isolated. She missed Chris in so many ways. Even the crew must have suspected that something was amiss between her and Chris, for they began avoiding her. Mapes rarely made the time to entertain her with his knot-tying tricks, and, though Mr. Blaine sent her pitying looks, he no longer sought her out for conversation. Casper, bless his heart, still saw to her needs and treated her no differently than before. She saw little of Chris, for he kept his distance and was careful not to make eye contact with her.

Several days after her volatile encounter with Chris, Casper rushed into the cabin to tell her that land had been sighted. Sophia hurried topside, shielding her eyes against the glare of the sun as she searched the horizon. Then she saw it—an emerald-green jewel basking in the sun beneath a cloudless blue sky. Above the land mass rose a line of forested mountains.

Sophia raised her face to the sun, eager to set foot on land and explore the island. She hoped she wouldn't have to return to England immediately, for Jamaica intrigued her. She wanted to see more of the island before returning home to an uncertain future.

"Miss, Captain said to tell you we'll dock in Kingston Harbor tomorrow morning."

Sophia smiled at Casper. She was going to miss the lad. "I suppose you're going to remain aboard with Mr. Blaine when the *Intrepid* leaves Kingston."

"Oh, no, miss, I'd never leave the captain. Me and him, we belong together. I'm going with him to Sunset Hill."

"Sunset Hill?"

"Aye, miss, that's the name of his plantation. I

haven't seen it yet, but if it's good enough for the captain, it's good enough for me."

Sophia returned her gaze to the green island rising majestically from the sea. *Sunset Hill*, she reflected, silently repeating the name. In her mind's eye she saw a splendid manor perched atop a hill. She saw herself sitting on a veranda, sipping a cool drink and watching the sun slowly sink into the ocean.

She nearly laughed aloud. That pleasant dream would never come to pass. Likely she'd find herself shut away from Society, marking time as a governess.

"I almost forgot, miss," Casper said, shattering her impossible dreams. "The captain said you were to remain with the *Intrepid* until he made arrangements for you to go ashore."

Sophia nodded and returned her attention to the island, attempting to recapture the pleasant imaginings of a life that could never be hers.

Sophia slept little that night; she was too excited about going ashore. Shortly before daylight, she heard noises indicating that the ship had reached its destination and was preparing to dock. Since she couldn't go back to sleep, she got up to watch the process through the porthole. Casper arrived soon after with her breakfast of bread, cheese and tea.

"How long before anyone can go ashore?" Sophia asked.

"The captain went ashore soon after the ship docked," the lad said. "Once the crew unloads the hold, they will begin shore leave. But the *Intrepid* won't stay in port long. She's due to leave day after tomorrow for Charleston in America with a cargo of rum and sugar. I have to go now, miss. I'm needed topside."

Sophia was too excited to eat. Instead, she followed Casper out the door and up the ladder to the deck. Her first sight of Kingston Harbor was one that would be etched in her memory forever. Men, their black skin glistening with sweat, were engaged in all manner of activity, while women of various shades roamed the streets in brightly colored dresses and turbans. She was also able to pick out white men and women on the crowded streets, garbed in typical English clothing.

Beyond the wharf, piled against lush green hills beneath a brilliant blue sky, lay the town of Kingston. Sophia couldn't seem to get her fill of the unfamiliar sounds and sights. Her eyes devoured the color and sweep of the harbor, listening intently to the cries of seabirds and the musical chanting of the slaves. Sophia remained at the rail a long time, savoring the sights and sounds and wondering what it would be like living in a tropical paradise like Jamaica.

"I've made arrangements for your return to England."

Chris! He stood beside her. She hadn't heard him approach. "Arrangements? What kind of arrangements?"

"You'll be staying at the King's Arms until the *South Wind* arrives. She's due in a week or so. She'll remain in port two days to take on cargo, then return to England. I've already paid for your passage."

He shoved a large bundle at her. "I purchased clothing for you so you won't cause a scandal when you check in at the inn. Go below and change. I'll wait topside for you."

Sophia clutched the bundle to her chest. "Chris, I'm sorry for what happened in the past. Please believe me—I never meant to intrude into your life again."

Without waiting for a reply, Sophia turned and walked away.

Chris watched her disappear down the ladder, conflicting emotions warring inside him. He hadn't wanted to see Sophia again . . . ever. She belonged in the past, one he wanted to forget.

Once he parted from Sophia today he would never see her again. It was for the best, he decided. His guilt left no place for Sophia in his life. Until he could forgive himself, he could not forgive her. Their meeting again had been a fluke, a quirk of Fate.

As Chris had learned early in life, Fate was a cruel mistress.

Chapter Five

The moment Chris saw Sophia in one of the two gowns he had purchased for her, he knew he had chosen well. She looked exceptionally lovely in a yellow-sprigged muslin gown with short puffed sleeves, modest oval neckline and fitted waist. Abruptly he frowned, uncomfortably aware that the color emphasized her sun-bronzed skin. He shouldn't have allowed her to bask those endless hours in the sun. He'd seen quadroons in New Orleans with lighter skin than hers.

"I'll leave you some money to buy a bonnet and parasol," Chris said. "I'm rarely called upon to purchase female clothing, so you may need a few personal items I've neglected to include. You can find what you need in the marketplace in Kingston. If you're ready, I'll escort you to the inn and see you settled in."

Sophia hugged the package carrying the second gown Chris had purchased for her against her chest. "I'm ready. You've been more than generous, considering everything that's happened between us."

He gazed at her for a long, suspenseful moment and

then looked away. "I don't hate you, Sophia. I suppose I never did, though I tried to tell myself otherwise. I wish you well in your future endeavors as long as they don't include me. You've caused enough anguish in my life."

Chris could tell by the way Sophia stiffened her shoulders that he had hurt her ... again. Unfortunately, it couldn't be helped. Sophia would bring him more problems than he was prepared to handle if he allowed her to creep under his skin and into his heart.

Aware that Sophia was waiting, Chris gestured toward the gangplank. "After you."

Chris followed her down the gangplank, overwhelmed with guilt and wondering why. It wasn't as if he owed her anything.

"This way," Chris said when they reached the quay. "The inn is within walking distance of the harbor."

"What is the name of those mountains rising above the town?" Sophia asked.

"The Blue Mountains. The Maroons make their home there."

"What are Maroons?"

"Not what but who. They are escaped slaves who established independent communities in the mountainous interior of the island. Besides Maroons, there are some ten thousand free people of color in Jamaica. The entire population consists of thirty thousand white masters to three hundred thousand slaves. It's not a good situation. There have been many uprisings in Jamaica's past. The militia cannot seem to prevent the uprisings despite all their attempts in recent years."

"How awful!" Sophia cried. "People shouldn't be enslaved. Can't the British government do something to stop the situation?"

Chris gave a bark of laughter. "Slavery is still legal in most parts of the world. Still, my brother is joining a group of men in the House of Lords to push through a bill outlawing slavery."

As they walked down King Street, the chief thoroughfare, Sophia exclaimed over some of the wonders she saw. "What is that building?" she asked, pointing to a large, ornate structure.

"That's the Church of St. Thomas, one of the oldest buildings in Kingston. The town has many fine houses, most inhabited by British plantation owners or slave traders. Kingston is a stopping-off place for slaves arriving from Africa."

Sophia shuddered and turned her thoughts in another direction, namely the sights, sounds and smells of this tropical paradise. The scent of lush vegetation, sago palms, giant ferns and wild orchids bombarded her senses.

The afternoon air was hot and humid and fragrant with unfamiliar odors: ripe bananas, fish, and baked goods wafting from a small bakery they had just passed. Sophia stopped a moment to watch a barefoot woman with skin the color of coffee. She wore a brightly colored scrap of material wrapped around her body and balanced a basket on top of her head. A naked, brown-skinned boy trotted after her.

Sophia was so interested in the activity around her that she wasn't aware they had reached the King's Arms until Chris said, "Here we are."

Sophia glanced up at the square two-story building. The sign above it proclaimed it the King's Arms.

"This is the best Kingston has to offer," Chris said as he guided her inside. "While it's not up to London standards, it's all we have."

"Ah, Captain Radcliff, welcome back. The room you engaged is ready."

"Thank you, Ludlow. This is Miss Carlisle. She'll be staying with you until the *South Wind* departs."

Ludlow stared at Sophia through narrowed eyes. "Is Miss Carlisle English? You didn't say. She looks Spanish or . . . Are you sure she isn't—"

Chris stiffened. "I assure you, Ludlow, Miss Carlisle comes from good English stock. Her brother is a viscount."

Sophia couldn't imagine why the innkeeper was staring at her so strangely. Was it because she wasn't wearing a bonnet or gloves? Were the rules of Society strictly adhered to in Jamaica?

"If you say so, Captain. I don't want any trouble," Ludlow demurred. He handed Chris the key to Sophia's room. "Number five, up the stairs and down the hall on the left."

Chris offered the key to Sophia. "I expect Miss Carlisle to be treated like the lady she is, Ludlow. I'm paying you well to see that her needs are met until she boards the *South Wind*."

"As you wish, Captain," Ludlow sniffed.

"I'll hold you to that," Chris replied as he ushered Sophia to the staircase.

Sophia watched as he reached in his pocket, retrieved a packet of papers and a heavy purse and handed them to her.

"You'll need these documents to board the *South Wind*. She's due in port in a few days. The purse contains gold coins. They're yours to purchase whatever you deem necessary," he said. "You may take your meals in the inn's dining room or your own chamber, whichever you prefer."

"Chris, I—"

Chris held up his hand. "Stop, Sophia, don't say anything. You owe me nothing. This is good-bye. I wish you well. I'm sure Caldwell will forgive you for running off. Whatever trouble you're in can't be that bad."

Sophia remained mute. If she spoke, she feared the quiver in her voice would reveal her inner turmoil. How could Chris wash his hands of her so easily? He didn't seem to care about her problems. She was nothing to him—he'd made that clear.

Chris stared at her for a long, tense moment. Sophia waited for him to say something, but he remained mute, his expression unreadable, his eyes shuttered.

"Damn you," he hissed. Then he spun around and stormed off.

Sophia dashed a tear from the corner of her eye as she watched Chris walk out of her life forever. She didn't regret having encountered him again after seven years. Her weeks aboard the *Intrepid* had brought them together unexpectedly, and she would never forget their time together.

Without knowing it, Chris had provided Sophia with a means to escape the uncertain fate that awaited her in London. With the money he had given her, she could start a new life. Chris had paid her room and board, she needed nothing else, neither bonnet nor parasol. She would hoard the gold coins and use them to live her life free of Rayford's influence.

Sophia ascended the stairs to her room. It was small but clean, and the bed linens looked fresh. She had scarcely closed the door behind her when she heard a discreet knock. She opened the door to a handsome, dark-eyed young woman of color. She was dressed in something bright that couldn't properly be called a gown.

"Master Ludlow sent me to unpack for you, mistress," she said in a singsong voice that sounded pleasing to Sophia's ear.

"I don't have much, just the gown I'm wearing and another," Sophia replied.

The woman's gaze found the package that Sophia had placed on the bed. "I can iron the wrinkles out for you, mistress."

"What is your name?"

"Kateena."

Sophia studied the woman's dark features. "Where are you from, Kateena?"

"Africa, mistress. I was stolen along with my parents and brought here on a slave ship."

"You're a slave? I'm sorry, Kateena."

Kateena gave Sophia a strange look, as if surprised by her compassion. "My master freed me and my family shortly before he died two years ago," she explained. "I am now a free woman of color." She removed the gown from its wrapping and shook it out. "I will take your gown with me, mistress."

"Thank you, Kateena."

Since Sophia had time to kill until suppertime, she decided to do a little exploring. As much as she hated the thought of spending any of her precious money, she needed to buy a comb and hairpins.

Mr. Ludlow directed Sophia to the marketplace, where almost anything and everything was for sale. She purchased a bone comb and several hairpins from a vendor and continued on her way.

She walked to the eastern limits of the town and discovered a fortress currently occupied by British troops.

She learned from a soldier that it was called Rockford and had been built in the late seventeenth century. On Duke Street, she stared in awe at Headquarters House, an architectural showplace and the seat of government.

Sophia would have liked to explore further, but dark clouds gathering overhead cut her aimless wandering short. Besides, she didn't need to see everything in one day. According to Chris, several days remained before the *South Wind* arrived. Plenty of time to explore.

Sophia ate a solitary dinner in her room that night. She didn't feel comfortable eating alone in the dining room and had asked Mr. Ludlow to have her meal brought up to her.

That day began the pattern that lasted until the *South Wind* arrived in port eight days later. Sophia happened to be exploring the shops lining the docks when she saw the ship sailing into the harbor. Sophia had paused to watch when a sudden, unexpected thought occurred to her. She loved what she'd seen of Jamaica thus far and didn't want to return to England. She hurried back to the inn, planning her future in Jamaica as she walked. But she needed to speak to Mr. Ludlow before making a decision.

"You really shouldn't walk about without a bonnet, Miss Carlisle," Ludlow scolded when she returned to the inn. "You look like a . . . Well, never mind, you'll be returning to England soon. I just heard the *South Wind* has arrived."

"I was wondering, Mr. Ludlow, about the English families living in Jamaica. Do any of them have young children?"

"Many of them do. Why do you ask?"

"Do you know of any that would be interested in acquiring an English governess? I am well educated, and I've fallen in love with the island. I'd love to stay if a position became available to me."

Ludlow stroked his chin. "Well, now, let me think. Offhand I can name three or four families living nearby that would welcome the chance to hire an English governess for their young ones. Have you spoken with Captain Radcliff about it?"

Sophia's mouth flattened. "What I do is none of his concern. If you could put me in contact with those families, I would be eternally grateful."

"What about the *South Wind*? She won't stay long in port."

"I understand that ships arrive regularly in Kingston Harbor. If a position doesn't become available, I can always book passage on another ship."

"Well, I suppose it wouldn't hurt, and I would be doing someone a favor. You do seem quite knowledgeable despite your rather . . . dark appearance."

Sophia glanced down at her tanned arms. She knew her face held the same golden hue, for she'd inspected it in a mirror. "I fear I've been careless about exposing myself to the sun. The hot, sun-washed days are part of the magic of the island. Everything I've seen here so far enthralls me."

Ludlow leaned close. "Don't be fooled, miss. All is not what it seems. The slave situation is poised to erupt into a nasty confrontation. You'd be wise to return to England while you can."

"I'll take my chances," Sophia replied.

"Very well, I'll send word of your availability to some families of my acquaintance. I'm sure a position can be found for you. But Captain Radcliff only secured your room and board until your ship leaves. Can you afford to remain while you seek employment?"

"I have money," Sophia said, optimistic about finding employment soon. She didn't want to go to Chris for help should her plan fail.

"Very well, Miss Carlisle, I will do my best to help you."

Sophia left the inn in a jubilant mood and hurried to the booking agent's office, where she presented her ticket and asked for a refund. After a good bit of grumbling, the agent refunded her the amount of the ticket in full.

The first thing Sophia did after leaving the booking agent's office was to visit the marketplace and buy a reticule to keep her money in, a wide-brimmed straw bonnet, a parasol and gloves. If one wanted to be a governess, one had to look like a lady. As for her tanned skin, she wasn't worried, for she knew the color would fade in time.

As Sophia returned to the inn, she noticed people streaming from the docking area, followed by porters bearing their luggage. Some were headed toward the inn. She paid them scant heed as she returned to her room. Her future looked brighter for the first time in a long time. If she was going to start a new life, it might as well be in a place far away from Rayford and his evil machinations.

Despite being busy from dawn to dusk, Chris still found time to think about Sophia. He'd begun to wonder if sending her back to England without discovering what or whom she feared had been the right thing to do. Something or someone had sent her fleeing into the night without even a wrap for protection against the elements, or money in her pocket.

On more than one occasion since arriving at Sunset Hill, he had nearly tossed caution to the wind and rushed back to Kingston to see how Sophia was faring. But just as he prepared to leave, a new emergency always seemed to arise to stop him. Being new to his position as plantation owner, Chris had much to learn and master, and just as many problems to solve. If not for Mundo, his overseer, he would have been lost.

Today, one of his neighbors, Lord Wombly, had stopped by on his way home from Kingston to tell Chris that the *South Wind* had arrived and was slated to leave Kingston Harbor in two days. Chris wanted to ask him if he'd seen Sophia in town but stifled the urge. As the day progressed, Chris had to forcibly restrain himself from racing pell-mell to Kingston to see Sophia one last time before she disappeared from his life forever.

Several days after the *South Wind*'s scheduled departure, a matter concerning the deed to Sunset Hill arose that necessitated a trip to Kingston and a visit to Headquarters House. With a list of goods to be purchased at the local market in hand, he left Sunset Hill with Mundo driving a wagon behind Chris's horse.

Anxious about the governess position she hoped to obtain, Sophia approached Mr. Ludlow a few days after the *South Wind* departed without her.

"Have you heard from any potential employers, Mr. Ludlow? I'm quite anxious to begin my duties as a governess."

"I have indeed, Miss Carlisle. The answers to two of my inquiries arrived just this morning. Lord Castor and Mr. Humbart are both interested but can't come to interview you immediately due to pressing commitments at home."

"How long do you suppose I'll have to wait?"

"Not long, I suspect. English governesses are sought after in Jamaica."

"Thank you, Mr. Ludlow, I appreciate your help. It's such a pleasant day, I think I'll take a stroll."

"Don't forget your bonnet, Miss Carlisle," Ludlow chided. "I don't think you realize the importance of protecting your fair complexion from the sun. If Captain Radcliff hadn't told me you came from English stock, I would have thought . . ." He shrugged. "Take my word for it, Miss Carlisle, tanning as deeply as you have is not recommended."

Sophia nodded solemnly, but for the life of her she couldn't imagine why anyone would care about her complexion except her mother, and that dear woman had long since gone to her grave. She did, however, return to her room for her bonnet before leaving the inn. She was proceeding out the door when she ran headlong into a thickset man who was entering the inn.

The man swept off his hat and bowed deeply. "Forgive my clumsiness, ma'am."

"Oh, no, it was entirely my fault, sir." When Sophia tried to step around him, the man grasped her arm and whirled her about.

"You!" he gasped. "Well, well, well, this *is* my lucky day. I don't know how you got here, but justice will finally prevail. Caldwell cheated me out of five hundred pounds, and you caused me a great deal of trouble, not to mention pain. I still bear the scar from your vicious attack."

Stunned beyond coherent speech, Sophia tried to escape Sir Oscar's punishing grip. Fate was still conspiring against her. How else could she explain Sir Oscar's presence in Jamaica? How had he learned her whereabouts? Had he followed her across the sea?

"What do you have to say for yourself, Sophia?"

"Release me at once!"

"You belong to me. I paid dearly for you, and you're not escaping me again."

People were beginning to stare. Mr. Ludlow, his face a picture of concern, hurried over to see what was causing the ruckus.

"Is there a problem, Miss Carlisle?" he asked anxiously.

"There is indeed," Sophia huffed. "This bully has just accosted me."

Ludlow glanced at Sir Oscar. "Oh, it's you, Sir Oscar. Welcome back to Jamaica. We have missed you."

"You know this man?" Sophia asked, unable to believe this was happening to her. If Rayford were here now, she would gladly kill him.

"Of course. Sir Oscar owns one of the largest plantations on the island. He has been visiting England and on the recently returned *Morning Star*."

Sophia wanted to pinch herself to make sure she wasn't dreaming. If this was really happening, it was more frightening than any nightmare she had ever had.

"Do you know this woman, Ludlow?" Sir Oscar asked.

"Indeed. Miss Carlisle is seeking a position as governess. I'm aiding her in her search."

Sir Oscar stared intently into Sophia's face. With a calculating gleam in his eye, his gaze traveled down her bare arms before returning abruptly to her face. His sly smile warned Sophia that he was up to no good. His next words proved it.

"I fear my slave has fooled everyone with her fine

manners and diction. I bought her shortly before I sailed to England. She was born on the island of Barbados, the product of a white father and slave mother. Her father was fond of her and had her educated."

"He lies!" Sophia cried. "Do not listen to him, Mr. Ludlow. I swear I am not who he says."

Ludlow looked torn. Sir Oscar was an important man on the island, and crossing him was not a good idea. Furthermore, Ludlow had seen many slaves lighter in coloring than Miss Carlisle.

"Captain Radcliff secured a room for her," Ludlow maintained. "She arrived in Jamaica aboard the *Intrepid* and was to leave on the *South Wind*."

"The *South Wind* has already sailed, has she not? Why didn't the woman leave?"

"She hoped to secure a position as a governess," Ludlow ventured.

"This is ridiculous," Sophia spat. "I am Sophia Carlisle, my brother is Viscount Caldwell."

"Can you prove it?" Sir Oscar asked.

"Can you prove I am not?" Sophia shot back.

"Indeed I can, Selena. I have papers to prove that I bought you from Lord Tyler-Wilford's heir."

"My name is not Selena! I am Sophia Carlisle! You're lying. Someone please summon the authorities."

"Miss Car . . . Selena, if Sir Oscar says you are his property, I see no reason to refute him," Ludlow said.

"Come along, Selena," Sir Oscar commanded with a smirk. "It was naughty of you to take advantage of my absence by running away and pretending to be someone you're not."

"Mr. Ludlow, help me! Send for Captain Radcliff. He'll tell you the truth."

"Don't bother, Ludlow," Sir Oscar advised. "I'm

sure she fooled the captain just as she did you with her fancy speech and manners. She's a sly little wench."

"Oh, no, you are mistaken, sir. Mistress Carlisle is exactly who she says she is."

Sophia sent a grateful smile toward Kateena, the only one who dared to come to her aid.

"Shut up, girl; you don't know what you're talking about," Sir Oscar growled.

"But you haven't seen her like I have," Kateena argued. "Her skin—"

Turning on Kateena, Sir Oscar backhanded her, sending her flying. "No one cares about your opinion, wench! Ludlow, control your slave."

"Kateena, if you don't keep out of this, you'll find yourself without work," Ludlow warned. "Kateena works for me for wages," he explained to Sir Oscar. "She's a free woman of color."

"I don't care what she is. If she interferes with me or my property, I'll bring charges against her."

Kateena picked herself up from the floor and approached Sophia. "What can I do for you, mistress?"

The purpling bruise on Kateena's face made it obvious that Kateena's defense of Sophia would only lead to more violence, more injuries. Sophia wouldn't allow it.

"Nothing, Kateena. I can take care of myself. Thank you for speaking up, but I fear that defending me will only bring harm to you."

Kateena shrank away, her distress palpable.

Sir Oscar began pulling Sophia away from the inn. "Come along, Selena; my carriage awaits outside. If you behave, you'll not be punished."

For all that Sophia dug in her heels, it did her little good. With a wave of his hand, Sir Oscar summoned the slaves waiting beside his carriage to help wrestle her into the conveyance.

"No, please, I'm an Englishwoman! Sir Oscar is lying. I don't belong to him. Don't let him take me away."

Her plea was met with stony silence. Her struggles were subdued, and the carriage rattled off down the street, on the way to hell. Or so Sophia assumed, for anywhere Sir Oscar lived had to be hell.

Somehow, some way, she had to get word to Chris. Surely he wouldn't allow this travesty, would he?

Please, God, don't let Chris abandon me.

Chris finished his business at Headquarters House and was ready to return home to Sunset Hill. Mundo, driving the wagon with the newly purchased supplies, had already departed. As Chris wheeled his horse along Duke Street, the devil inside him made him turn toward the King's Arms. Despite his resolve to wash his hands of Sophia, he wanted to make sure she had boarded the *South Wind* as planned, and that her stay in Kingston had been uneventful.

Chris dismounted in front of the King's Arms and walked inside. He was taken aback when a serving girl ran up to him and fell on her knees. "Captain, sir, you have to help her. He took her away; there was nothing I could do."

Chris's eyes looked into the woman's chocolate-brown eyes, and his heart plummeted. Her plea could only refer to Sophia. Damnation! What kind of trouble had the woman gotten herself into now?

"What is your name?"

"Kateena, sir."

He lifted her to her feet. "Tell me what happened, Kateena."

"Sir Oscar came and took Mistress Carlisle away. He said she was his slave. Tell them it ain't true, Captain."

"Kateena, I thought I dismissed you. Why are you bothering Captain Radcliff?"

"She's not bothering me, Ludlow. What is amiss here? Did something happen to Miss Carlisle?"

"Ah, my lord. I fear we've both been hoodwinked by that impostor. She's really a slave named Selena and she belongs to Sir Oscar Rigby. I know this comes as a shock, but—"

"Fool!" Chris shouted. "How could you have been so gullible? I admit Miss Carlisle should have guarded her skin against the tropical sun, but she is indeed an Englishwoman, albeit a foolish one. I've known her and her family for many years."

Ludlow turned a sickly green. "Dear God, if what you say is true, I've done the woman a grave injustice."

Chris made a chopping gesture with his hand. "This is no time for regrets. Although I don't know Rigby personally, I understand his plantation lies just north of mine. How many days ago did he take her?"

Chris had heard a great deal about Rigby's cruelty to his slaves, especially female slaves. If he hurt Sophia, or subjected her to his brand of brutality, Chris vowed to kill him.

"Why, they drove off in Sir Oscar's carriage not an hour ago."

That surprised Chris. He'd assumed the reason Sophia hadn't boarded the *South Wind* was because Rigby had claimed her first. "But Miss Carlisle was supposed to leave with the *South Wind*."

"She didn't want to return to England. She said she'd

fallen in love with Jamaica. She hoped to find a governess position with an English family."

Sophia didn't need to return to England to find trouble, Chris thought, trouble had found her.

Spinning on his heel, he left the inn. If he expected to intercept Rigby before he reached his plantation, there wasn't a moment to lose.

Sophia cringed in the corner of Sir Oscar's carriage, his leering smile turning her insides to jelly. Of all the ships she could have chosen on which to hide, why did she have to pick one sailing to Jamaica? Though she recalled Rayford telling her that Sir Oscar owned a plantation in the West Indies, he hadn't specifically mentioned Jamaica. What a cruel twist of Fate.

Suddenly Sir Oscar laughed—a not particularly comforting sound. "Good things come to those who wait. You're the last person I expected to see in Jamaica, but a welcome sight nonetheless. Your negligence in letting your skin tan worked to my advantage. I had no difficulty convincing Ludlow you were an escaped slave."

He tore off her bonnet and ran his hands through the richness of her black hair. Sophia jerked away. "Don't touch me!"

"I'm going to do much more than touch you, Sophia. I'm going to chain you to my bed and keep you there until I've had my fill of you."

Reaching out, he dragged her against his chest. Sophia screamed as he grasped her head between his pudgy hands and tried to kiss her. His strength, far superior to hers, won out. But Sophia wasn't ready to become his victim. Clamping his lip between her teeth, she bit down hard.

Sir Oscar made a gurgling sound in his throat and thrust her away. "Bitch! You'll pay for that."

He raised his arm as if to strike her. But before the blow fell, the carriage rolled to a stop and the door burst open. Rigby was dragged bodily from the carriage and shoved roughly to the ground.

Sophia gave a cry of gladness. "Chris! Thank God."

Chapter Six

His face a mask of fury, Chris stood over Rigby, who lay sprawled inelegantly in the dirt. Rigby's two slaves stood nearby, doing nothing to aid their master. Attacking a white man could mean their death.

"Who are you?" Rigby sputtered.

"Your worst nightmare," Chris growled. "If you've hurt Sophia, you're a dead man."

"I'm fine, Chris," Sophia called from inside the carriage.

Rigby pushed to his feet and dusted himself off. "Whoever you are, you have no authority to interfere. Selena is my slave, she belongs to me."

"The woman you call Selena is Miss Sophia Carlisle, and well you know it. If there ever was a Selena, which I seriously doubt, Sophia is not she."

Sophia stepped down from the carriage. "Sir Oscar knows full well who I am, Chris."

"Then why did he . . ." Confused, Chris shook his head. "I understand none of this. Why did Rigby tell Ludlow you were his runaway slave?"

"I'll explain everything, Chris. Just take me away from here," Sophia pleaded.

Chris turned the full force of his scowl on Rigby. "I am Captain Radcliff. Miss Carlisle traveled to Jamaica aboard my ship. She's no more a slave than I am. If you bother her again, I'll see you punished to the full extent of the law."

"Captain Radcliff," Rigby said disparagingly. "Aren't you the new owner of Sunset Hill? I understand you won the plantation in a game of chance."

"That's correct."

"A gambler," Rigby sneered. "You have no authority to challenge my rights to this woman. She belongs to me."

Chris shot a look at Sophia, one brow raised. "Is that true, Sophia? Do you belong to Rigby? Are you married to him, perchance?"

"Married! To that perverted creature? Not in this life or any other."

Grasping Rigby's coat lapels, Chris gave him a rough shake and backed him against the carriage. "Listen carefully, Rigby. I don't care what kind of hold you think you have on Sophia—it's not going to work."

"I have proof that I bought Selena before my visit to England," Rigby shouted, sounding desperate.

"Like hell! I have a full complement of sailors who will attest to her presence aboard the *Intrepid*."

Rigby smirked. "I understand the *Intrepid* left port some time ago. You're going to have a difficult time proving anything."

Chris's temper was hanging by a slim thread. "Lift your skirts, Sophia. Show Rigby your legs."

"What?"

"You heard me. The only way you can prove to him that you're not a mulatto is by baring some white flesh. Your legs will do. No higher than the knee, please."

Sophia stared at Chris for several heartbeats before lifting her skirts to her knees, baring flawless, white flesh.

"You can lower your skirt now, Sophia. I think Rigby has seen enough."

Rigby ogled her legs. "Very nice," he complimented.

Another word out of that smug bastard and Chris was going to rearrange his face for him. "I don't *ever* want to hear another word about Miss Carlisle being anything but an English lady. Do you understand?"

"You've made your point, Captain."

"Good. Now get out of here. If you bother Miss Carlisle again, next time you won't get off so easily," Chris bit out. The threatening look on Chris's face must have finally gotten through to Rigby, for he slowly he began to sidle away.

"What about her?" Rigby asked, pointing to Sophia. "What are you going to do with her?"

"I'm taking Sophia to Sunset Hill. If you have any ideas concerning her future, put them to rest."

Once out of Chris's reach, Rigby grew bolder. "Are you making her your whore?"

Fists knotted at his sides, Chris advanced two long steps to reach Rigby's side. "What did you say?"

Rigby fell back a step and quickly protested, "What am I to think? What will anyone think? Believe it or not, the rules of conduct in Jamaica are no less strict than they are in England. We plantation owners live by a code that cannot be breached. Eventually the news of Miss Carlisle's living arrangements will reach London.

She'll be ruined when she returns, and if she remains, she'll be shunned by our tight-knit group of English settlers."

"It doesn't matter, Chris," Sophia assured him. "I've been an outcast from Society for years and have no intention of returning to London."

"If you're still hoping to find a position as a governess, you may as well forget it," Rigby announced. "I'll make sure no one hires you."

"Miss Carlisle has no need of employment," Chris snarled. "Did you not understand me? If you speak one word of disparagement against Miss Carlisle, I'll forget I'm a gentleman and stomp you into the ground. Now get out of here, and don't let me catch you anywhere near Sunset Hill."

Rigby looked as if he wanted to say something more, but he must have thought better of it, for he scrambled into his carriage. His slaves clambered into the driver's box and sent the carriage hurtling down the winding road.

Once they were out of sight, Chris directed his scowl at Sophia. "You have a great deal of explaining to do, Sophia. You've told me nothing but a pack of lies from the beginning, and this time I want the truth. I'm taking you back to the inn for your things and then to Sunset Hill. Someone has to keep you out of trouble. You can await the next ship sailing to England at my plantation."

Sophia squared her shoulders. "I'm grateful for your help, but I'm not returning to England, Chris. There's nothing there for me."

"Your family—"

"Father and Mother are dead, and Rayford is so

deep in debt he was willing to sell my virtue to the highest bidder. I intend to remain in Jamaica and seek gainful employment."

"We'll see about that, Sophia," Chris ground out. Grasping her waist, he lifted her onto his horse and mounted behind her.

Chris maintained an angry silence. Rather than argue, Sophia took advantage of his silence to admire the scenery. She'd been too frightened to notice anything while inside Sir Oscar's carriage. They were plodding along a narrow rutted road through rolling hills. The Blue Mountains rose majestically above the city of Kingston, which stretched out on a flat plain between the bay and the mountain ridge.

Chris said, "Sunset Hill lies between Kingston and the Blue Mountains. At one time Port Royal was the main seaport, as well as a notorious pirate stronghold. Several earthquakes destroyed the city, and the British Navy cleared out the pirates. There are still a few pirates about, however, and it's not all that unusual to see a pirate ship or two put into port."

Sophia merely nodded. Her attention was centered on rows of ramshackle huts nestled in small clearings hacked out of the flourishing jungle and fields of sugarcane. She exclaimed in wonder at colorful birds flitting overhead and the occasional snake slithering along the edge of the road.

It wasn't until they reached Kingston that Sophia spoke directly to Chris. "I will be perfectly safe at the inn. Mr. Ludlow is helping me find a position with an English family."

"Forget about finding employment. Kingston is a small town. I understand Sir Oscar created a scene at the inn. Word will spread; whether or not Rigby's accusation is believed is beside the point. It's the notoriety that will keep you from obtaining gainful employment. Your only alternative is to return to England."

Sophia's mouth grew firm. "I am *not* returning to England."

"I say you are. But until another ship arrives in port, you will stay at Sunset Hill as my guest. You cannot remain at the inn; it's no longer safe."

"You cannot force me to return to England," Sophia stubbornly asserted. "There has to be a way for me to earn my keep in Jamaica."

Chris drew rein before the King's Arms, dismounted and handed Sophia down. He gazed down at her, his grin not at all comforting. "Oh, there is a way, but I doubt you will like it."

Sophia didn't have to ask what Chris meant. She had lived with Rayford too long not to know. "I will never do *that* to earn my keep."

"We'll talk about this later." Placing a hand on the small of her back, he guided her toward the inn.

After a few steps, Sophia stopped in her tracks. "Look, that's Kateena coming out of the inn! Kateena!" she called, "Where are you going?"

Kateena stopped, saw Sophia and gave a cry of gladness. "Mistress, you're safe! I hoped the captain would find you."

Sophia noted the basket Kateena carried on her head and repeated her question. "Where are you going?"

Kateena refused to meet Sophia's gaze. "I no longer work at the King's Arms, mistress. Master Ludlow said I was too bold and let me go. My parents are getting old and need my support, so I must find work soon."

"Oh, Kateena, I'm so sorry," Sophia commiserated.

"Life is so unfair. I wish I could employ you, but I can't even find employment myself."

Chris cleared his throat. "As it happens, Kateena, I'm interested in hiring free people of color to work on my plantation. I could use a housekeeper. I already have a cook, so your duties wouldn't include cooking. And you could serve Miss Carlisle while she is a guest at Sunset Hill."

Sophia beamed at Chris. "You would do that?"

"I just said so, didn't I? If my offer meets with your approval, Kateena, we can discuss wages."

Tears leaked from the corners of Kateena's velvet brown eyes. "You are a saint, master. I will accept whatever wages you consider fair."

When Chris mentioned an amount, Kateena's eyes widened. Then she fell on her knees, grasped Chris's hand and brought it to her forehead. Embarrassed, Chris lifted her to her feet and handed her off to Sophia.

"I'll wait out here, Kateena, while you help Sophia gather her things. Then we'll check with the shipping agent about booking passage for Sophia on the next ship bound for England."

"I'm not going, Chris," Sophia maintained. "Save yourself the trouble." She spun on her heel. "Come along, Kateena."

Hands on hips, Chris watched them walk into the inn. What in God's name was he going to do with Sophia? Stubborn woman that she was, he doubted she'd change her mind about returning to England. And until she told him the truth about why she had fled London, he wouldn't force her aboard a ship.

He'd been wrong not to delve deeper into the danger Sophia had fled from. Now that it had caught up with her, he could no longer ignore it. He shook his head. What were the odds of Sophia meeting Rigby, a man she had reason to fear, here in Jamaica?

"Captain Radcliff, you look flummoxed."

Chris greeted the man who had just joined him. He had met Lord Chester previously; he was his closest neighbor and owner of Orchid Manor. "Lord Chester, I didn't see you approach. Forgive my distraction."

Chester leaned close. "Did you hear what happened inside the King's Arms today? The slave Selena must have been a good actress to have fooled both you and Ludlow. I was appalled. And to think we considered hiring her as a governess."

"It was a misunderstanding, Chester," Chris explained. "Miss Carlisle is English through and through and my guest at Sunset Hill. She is no more slave than I am."

Now it was Chester's turn to look perplexed. "Ludlow said she arrived at the inn without a chaperone, and that you claimed she traveled aboard the *Intrepid*. Rather unusual, that."

Chris gnashed his teeth. Gossip was the same the world over. It didn't take long to spread, especially if it involved an innocent young woman. And Chris knew better than anyone that Sophia was untouched.

Chris's next words surprised even himself. The devil must have prompted him—he could think of no other reason. "Miss Carlisle is my betrothed. She's staying at Sunset Hill until our wedding. I've just hired a housekeeper, so there will be another woman besides the cook in the house."

Chester's face lit up. "A wedding! Excellent! My wife will be delighted to hear that. There's so little to celebrate these days, what with all the trouble over the slaves and all." He slapped Chris on the back. "Congratulations, old chap. How soon can we expect an invitation?"

"You'll be the first to know," Chris hedged.

"Excellent. Now I have something of import to tell you. Since you are new to the island, you should know that 'Daddy' Sam Sharp, the self-proclaimed preacher and leader of the Maroons, has been inciting passive rebellion. He's been seen on Mr. Humbart's plantation, speaking with the slaves. That's what comes of educating slaves."

"I don't expect any trouble at Sunset Hill, Lord Chester," Chris said. "I intend to free my slaves and pay them wages."

"You what? Damnation, man, you're going to come to grief if you free your slaves. We need them to work our land. You'll regret breaking ranks with the rest of us. If I were you, I would think twice before acting rashly."

"I've already thought about it, and my mind is made up. The paperwork is already being drawn up."

"Well, don't say I didn't warn you. I must be on my way. I still have business to conduct before returning home. I hope we can meet your betrothed soon. I know Agatha will be thrilled to make her acquaintance."

Chester, a tall, distinguished man of middle years, continued down the street. Chris stared after him, stunned by his own stupidity. Not about declaring his intention to free his slaves, but for declaring Sophia his betrothed.

What in the hell was he going to do now?

He didn't have time to figure it out as Sophia and Kateena emerged from the inn. Sophia had donned a straw bonnet and carried a parasol.

"I told you I didn't have much to pack," Sophia said.

"I didn't have a valise, so Kateena placed my things in her basket."

Chris searched her face. "Are you sure Rigby didn't hurt you?"

Sophia shook her head. "No, he didn't, but I'm sure he would have. Thank you again, Chris."

"I couldn't let him hurt you, Sophia." He scratched his head, a perplexed look on his face. "I hadn't thought about how I'm going to get you and Kateena to Sunset Hill. I don't own a carriage. If it meets with your approval, Sophia, I can take you on my horse and send Mundo back with the wagon for Kateena."

"If it's agreeable to Kateena," Sophia answered, "it is fine with me."

"That is acceptable to me, Captain," Kateena said. "I will visit my parents while I'm waiting. They will want to know about my new employment and where I can be reached if they need me."

"Then it's settled," Chris said. He clasped his hands around Sophia's slim waist and lifted her onto his horse. Then he mounted behind her. "Where should Mundo pick you up, Kateena?" he asked as he settled in the saddle.

"I will wait for Mundo at my parents' shack behind the fish market."

Chris nodded as he guided his horse into the traffic on King Street. At the end of the street, he headed north out of town.

"How long will it take to reach your plantation?" Sophia asked.

"An hour or so. Atlas is carrying two, and I don't want to overtax him in this heat."

"I could have waited for the wagon with Kateena."

Chris shook his head. "No, I don't trust you. Trou-

They followed a lazy bend in the road, and then Sunset Hill came into sight. Sophia was still sleeping when Chris reined Atlas through the gate. She awoke when Casper ran up to take the reins.

"Miss Carlisle! I thought you'd left Kingston aboard the *South Wind*."

Chris dismounted and handed her down. "It seems Miss Carlisle wished to stay in Kingston."

Casper beamed. "Is that true, miss? Are you going to stay at Sunset Hill with us?"

Sophia blinked. "Casper, it's good to see you again. I won't be staying long. I'm looking for employment."

Chris turned Sophia toward the house. "You'll find it much cooler inside. The heat must seem stifling to someone unaccustomed to a tropical climate. I'm sure Chandra will have something cool for you to drink."

"Captain, you're back!"

Mundo, a dark-skinned, muscular man, came loping up to Chris, his face a mask of worry. "When you didn't return to Sunset Hill when you were expected, I thought something had happened to you. I was about to round up men to search for you."

"I'm fine, Mundo. I was delayed, that's all. I brought back a guest. Miss Carlisle will be staying with us for a short time. I also hired a housekeeper. You're to return to Kingston in the wagon and fetch Kateena. You'll find her at her parents' home behind the fish market."

"I'll leave immediately, Captain."

"Mundo seems well-spoken," Sophia said as Chris guided her up the stairs onto a wide veranda that ran the entire length of the two-story manor house. Floor-to-ceiling front windows with shutters thrown wide to admit the breeze and white frothy curtains billowing in the opening made her feel as if she had come home.

"Mundo has been educated," Chris replied. "I freed him immediately after I took possession of Sunset Hill. He now works for wages. I rely heavily on him for the everyday running of the plantation. As you might guess, I know little about raising sugarcane and distilling rum, but I'm learning fast."

Chris opened the door and ushered Sophia inside. She stepped into the spacious foyer, duly impressed by everything she saw. She only caught a glimpse of the parlor as Chris led her into a combination library/study and invited her to sit down. A servant appeared almost immediately.

"Chuba, please ask Chandra to prepare something cool for our guest and to bring it herself. I wish to speak with her."

"Yes, sir, Captain," Chuba replied.

"Is Chuba free too?" Sophia asked.

"Not yet, but he soon will be, and so will Chandra."

"Your home is very nice, Chris."

"It wasn't when I first saw it. Extensive renovations were completed while I was in England. Most of the furnishings were brought over from England. Unfortunately, the previous owner was more interested in gambling and drinking than he was in running his plantation. He didn't need the income, you see, and neglected Sunset Hill in favor of other pursuits. I hope to change all that."

A discreet knock sounded on the door.

"Come in, Chandra."

A short, rotund woman, her face a wreath of smiles, entered the room carrying a pitcher and glasses on a tray. "You wanted to see me, master?"

"Please, Chandra, call me Captain. I don't feel comfortable being addressed as master."

Chandra's skin was smooth as silk and the color of rich coffee. She bobbed her turbaned head and set the tray down on a nearby table. Then she turned to Sophia, her black eyes wide with curiosity.

"Miss Carlisle will be our guest for a time, Chandra. I thought she might enjoy the room at the front of the house. It faces the bay, and the view is quite spectacular."

Chandra smiled shyly at Sophia. "Welcome to Sunset Hill, mistress. Your room will be ready soon. While you're waiting, enjoy the lemonade and fresh-baked gingerbread." She turned to leave.

"Wait a moment, Chandra. You have enough to do without adding to your burden, so I've hired a housekeeper. Kateena will also act as personal maid to Miss Carlisle. I sent Mundo to Kingston to fetch her."

"It's about time," Chandra said, her boldness surprising Sophia. "You need someone in charge, someone to make this old house a home. The old master didn't care what happened to Sunset Hill, but I can tell that you do."

"I care a great deal, Chandra. If I have my way, Sunset Hill will become home to all of us. Eventually I'll hire more servants, but until I do, I hope you and Kateena can carry on here."

"Humph! Don't see why not. As long as Kateena doesn't interfere with my cooking, I won't interfere with what she does."

Sophia smiled as Chandra quit the room. "I'm surprised you didn't reprimand your servant for her boldness."

"Chandra always speaks her mind. I find it refreshing. As for the other house servants, there's only Chuba. The field workers rarely have reason to come into the house or speak their minds about anything. They've been downtrodden most of their lives. I hope to change that at Sunset Hill."

Chris poured two glasses of lemonade and handed one to Sophia. She took a long, cool swallow. "Delicious," she pronounced as she helped herself to a generous piece of gingerbread.

Sophia heard Chris sigh and glanced up at him. He was standing over her, hands crossed over his chest, looking far too handsome for her peace of mind despite his scowl.

"Is something wrong, Chris?"

"A great deal is wrong. You've put this conversation off for the last time. Tell me everything, Sophia, and start from the beginning."

Sophia drained her glass and returned it to the tray. "I'm really tired, Chris. Can't this wait? The heat has drained me."

Grasping her shoulders, Chris pulled her to her feet. "No excuses this time, Sophia."

Sophia looked up at him. His eyes, usually as blue as the sparkling waters of Kingston Bay, had turned dark as midnight. She stared at his lips, desperately wanting to lean up and kiss their fullness. Her lips parted. She moistened them with the tip of her tongue.

Chris gazed down at Sophia, for a moment forgetting what he had asked her. The woman was a menace, he thought. He couldn't think straight when he was around her. Was she trying to entice him with her dewy lips and dreamy eyes? Well, it wouldn't work. She had drawn him into her web once, but it wasn't going to happen a second time.

Chris nearly lost the ability to think when her tongue darted out and she moistened her lips. Her tricks were as old as Eve, he thought. But despite his normal iron willpower, his head began to lower. Before he could stop himself, he was kissing her. Kissing her like a drowning man reaching for his last breath of air. To make matters worse, Sophia kissed him back, opening her sweet mouth for his tongue. She tasted like heaven. He should stop now. His head knew that, but the rest of him wasn't paying much attention to logic.

He wanted to bed Sophia.

His body ached with the need. He wanted to delve deep into her hot mouth and never surface. He wanted to tear off her clothes, pull her to the floor and rid her of her virginity. Chris had never had a virgin before, had never wanted one until now.

Releasing her lips, he clasped his hands about her waist and lifted her, setting her atop the desk. She blinked at him in surprise.

"What are you doing?"

He parted her knees and stepped between them. "What I've wanted to do since I first saw you aboard the *Intrepid*. What I've fought against every step of the way." Lowering his gaze, he reached for the top button of her bodice. "I'm going to make love to you, and then you're going to tell me everything I want to know."

Sophia scooted back. His fingers released the next button. She caught his hand; he freed it and continued on to the third button.

"Chris—"

"Not now, Sophia."

His mouth found hers again, nibbling, kissing, teasing, until, senses whirling, she grabbed him and kissed him back. Consumed by raging heat, Sophia felt his mouth leave hers and drift down her neck to her breasts. He found her nipple; she shuddered when he drew it into his mouth.

She probably would have let him continue if he hadn't suddenly released her and reared back.

"Damnation, this is unacceptable! I can't let this happen to me again. I killed my best friend because of you. Why did you return to torture me with memories better left forgotten?"

Yanking the edges of her dress together, he redid the buttons and lifted her down from the desk.

"Chandra will show you to your room."

Spinning on his heel, he quit the room. Reaching for a candleholder, Sophia hurled it at him. It hit the door and crashed to the floor.

Chapter Seven

Sophia stood on the balcony outside the bedroom assigned to her and stared over the tops of lofty trees at Kingston Bay, sparkling diamond-like beneath a broiling sun. Chandra had fetched her from the study after Chris's abrupt departure and brought her here. The view from the spacious room was spectacular, just as Chris had said it would be.

As much as she would like to stay at Sunset Hill, Sophia knew she couldn't. Not as long as Chris held her responsible for Desmond's death.

Sophia was confused, however. If Chris disliked her, why had he tried to seduce her? Chris wanted her; she had felt desire in his kisses, seen his body swell with it. Yet he had found the willpower to resist her.

Sophia felt she had no choice but to leave his home as soon as she found employment. She couldn't allow her emotions to become engaged more than they already were, for he had the power to destroy her.

Sophia was still gazing out at the view, pondering her options for the future, when Kateena arrived.

"The captain said to tell you that dinner will be served promptly at seven," Kateena said. "If you're hungry before then, I'm to ask the cook for something to hold you over."

"Thank you, Kateena, but I can wait for dinner."

Kateena joined her on the balcony. "Oh, mistress, how beautiful! You're a lucky woman. 'Tis obvious the captain cares for you."

Sophia gave a bitter laugh. "You misread the situation." She turned away from the balcony. "I'd like to rest, Kateena. Why don't you go down to the kitchen and get acquainted with Chandra? I'm sure you two will get along famously."

"I'll just hang up your dress first, mistress." She shook out Sophia's spare dress. "You should ask the captain to buy you a new wardrobe, since you seem to have so little. There's a talented seamstress in Kingston. She's a free woman of color who I know would be happy to make up a few frocks for you."

"What I have is sufficient for my needs," Sophia said curtly.

Kateena took no umbrage at Sophia's brusque reply. "I'll take your dress to the kitchen and press it. After I meet Chandra, I'm to report to the captain. He's going to tell me what is expected of me at Sunset Hill. Can I do anything for you before I leave?"

"No, thank you, Kateena, there's little I require. I've done for myself most of my life. But you can bring a pitcher of warm water when you return. I'd like to wash the road dust off before I go down to dinner."

Sophia stretched out on the bed after Kateena left, finding it so comfortable she promptly fell asleep.

* * *

Chris paced his study while he waited for Kateena. What he and Sophia had nearly done a short time ago was unacceptable. Why couldn't his body accept that making love to Sophia wasn't a good idea?

Make love to Sophia.

Just thinking about it brought a certain part of his body to attention. What was wrong with him? Why couldn't he control himself around her? He needed to go to town sooner rather than later to inquire about passage to England for her. Before she left he intended to give Sophia money to live independently from her brother.

A scratch on the door fractured his thoughts. "Come in."

Kateena entered and curtsied.

"Ah, Kateena, I've been waiting for you. You must be curious about your duties at Sunset Hill."

"Yes, sir. I'll try hard to please you."

Chris smiled. "It won't take much to please me, Kateena. You'll have charge of the household. I've asked two women who normally work in the fields to come in each day to do the cleaning, under your supervision, of course."

"I understand," Kateena said.

"I'd like you to see to Miss Carlisle yourself. There isn't anyone else here qualified."

"Will she be staying permanently at Sunset Hill?" Kateena dared.

"Good God, no! This is a temporary situation. I have nothing further for you, Kateena; you may leave."

When Kateena didn't move, Chris asked, "Is there something else, Kateena?"

Kateena opened her mouth, then promptly closed it.

"You may speak freely, Kateena. I respect everything my people have to say."

"It's about Miss Carlisle, Captain. It's not fitting."

Chris counted to ten before asking, "What isn't fitting?"

"Miss Carlisle is a lady, sir. Her lack of wardrobe is—please forgive me—shameful. She doesn't even have a decent petticoat."

"I know little about women's apparel."

"If you allow me, Captain, I can help. I know of a dressmaker in Kingston, a free woman of color, who would be grateful for the work. She has materials too, purchased from your very own warehouse."

"Very well, you may accompany Sophia to Kingston at her convenience to purchase what she needs."

Apparently satisfied, Kateena curtsied and left Chris to brood in silence.

Despite his reluctance, Chris seemed to be involving himself deeper and deeper in Sophia's life. He had rescued her from Rigby and had just agreed to purchase clothing for her. She should be on her way to England, damn it! Instead she was in his house, tempting him beyond redemption with her seductive eyes and enticing mouth.

Chris moved to the sideboard, poured a generous splash of rum from his own distillery into a glass and sat down to think. He sipped appreciatively of the dark liquor as he pondered the impossible situation in which he now found himself.

Sophia awoke from her nap feeling refreshed despite the humid breeze blowing through the open French doors. She rose, checked the hour on the small clock sitting on a nearby table and saw that it was six o'clock. Dinner was in one hour.

Sophia reached for the water pitcher. Just as she lifted it to pour water into a bowl, someone scratched on the door. "Come," she called.

"I thought you might enjoy a bath, mistress," Kateena said, easing into the room. "The water is already heated, and Chuba is waiting outside the door with the tub."

Delighted, Sophia said, "You're a treasure, Kateena. By all means, have Chuba bring in the tub. A bath is just what I need."

The tub was set up and water carried in to fill it. Shortly thereafter, Sophia lowered herself into the warm water, scrubbing her skin with soap that smelled deliciously of jasmine. After Kateena washed and rinsed Sophia's hair, she held a drying sheet aloft for her to step into.

"I pressed your dress, mistress," Kateena said. "I'll help you into it after I fix your hair. You'll want to look your best tonight."

Though Sophia saw no reason to look her best, she let Kateena fuss with her hair. Nothing she could do would impress Chris, she knew. The sight of her only reminded him of a tragedy he had struggled to forget.

At two minutes to seven, Sophia was dressed in a light green linen dress with a square neckline and high waist, her raven hair swept off her neck and piled atop her head. Since she had no petticoats or hoops, the gown closely hugged the soft curves of her figure, but there was nothing to be done about that. Dragging in a deep breath, Sophia descended the stairs. Chuba met her at the bottom and escorted her to the dining room.

Chris and Casper were waiting for her. "Casper, how grand you look," Sophia exclaimed. The lad had dressed for dinner in dark brown trousers, a tan jacket and a snowy white shirt.

"You look grand, too, miss," Casper said shyly. "I'm ever so glad you're here."

Sophia smiled but said nothing, aware that Chris wasn't as pleased as Casper to have her at Sunset Hill. Casper continued to chatter as Chris came around and pulled out her chair. Sophia nodded her thanks, trying to concentrate on Casper instead of Chris's handsome face and the muscular form clearly delineated beneath his buff trousers and brown jacket. Though his clothing could not be described as formal dinner wear, it seemed entirely proper for an informal dinner in tropical Jamaica.

If not for Casper's boyish enthusiasm, dinner would have been a dismal affair despite the outstanding array of food Chandra had prepared for their enjoyment. They dined on spicy jerked pork and fried plantains, neither of which Sophia had had the pleasure of eating before, sweet potatoes and various vegetables. And for dessert Chandra had made a luscious flan, a type of custard topped by caramel sauce.

Chris said very little during the meal, although he did direct a frown at Sophia from time to time. She had no idea what he was thinking, but it didn't take a genius to guess that he was wishing her elsewhere.

"Is it all right if I take a stroll outside?" Sophia asked after the meal. "It's such a lovely night. I know there must be a garden, for the scent of flowers in the air is strong."

"I'll show you the garden, miss," Casper offered. "It's a bit overrun with weeds but still pretty—if you like that sort of thing."

"And you don't?" Sophia teased.

Casper blushed. "Flowers are for women. We men have more important things on our minds, don't we, Captain?"

Sophia could tell that Chris was suppressing a laugh when the corners of his mouth twitched. "Indeed, lad, we men couldn't care less about flowers and such. But if you don't mind, I'd like to show Sophia the garden myself. I have a matter of importance to discuss with her."

Casper's disappointment was so apparent that Sophia said, "Another time, Casper. And it would please me if you'd call me Sophia."

Casper glanced from Sophia to Chris before nodding. "I'd like that. Good night, Sophia, Captain."

"Good night, lad. Why don't you read another chapter in the book of geography I gave you? Your reading skills need improving, as does your knowledge of the world."

"Aye, Captain," Casper said. He gave a smart salute and marched off.

"Casper is a delightful boy," Sophia said. "He's lucky to have someone like you to care for him."

"I'm lucky to have Casper," Chris replied. He offered his arm. "Are you ready for that walk in the garden?"

Sophia steeled herself for her confrontation with Chris. The time had arrived; she could no longer put it off. She placed her hand on his arm. "As ready as I'll ever be."

Chris ushered her through a pair of French doors that opened onto a veranda and down a short flight of stairs. The grass felt lush beneath her slippers as they walked down a path overgrown with a tangle of flowers and weeds and bordered by tall palm trees swaying in the breeze. In the light of a full moon, it was a beautiful spot, even though the jungle was trying to encroach upon the garden.

"This is almost how I envision Paradise," Sophia said, sighing wistfully. "I've never seen such a brilliant night."

Chris stared at her, her beauty luminescent in the moonlight.

"Do you have any idea how beautiful you are?" His voice was gravelly; revealingly deep.

Sophia ignored the compliment as she walked slightly ahead of him. Chris couldn't take his eyes off her. She moved as if she were made of shadow and mist, floating on a gentle breeze. He shook his head to rid it of disturbing thoughts and cleared his throat. Two steps brought him beside her.

"You know it's time for answers, don't you, Sophia?"

"I suppose you're right. What do you wish to know?"

He led her to a bench beneath a palm tree and seated her. "Tell me everything. Start from the beginning."

"The beginning," Sophia repeated. "Very well. As you know, the duel and Desmond's death created a scandal of major proportions. As a result, I was shunned by Society. The *ton* held me responsible for the duel and its tragic aftermath."

Chris nodded. "They had good reason to blame you."

Sophia gulped back her hurt. "It wasn't the outcome I intended. Nevertheless, Father waited a few days to see if you would offer for me, and when you didn't, he banished me to the country. He was convinced that I was unmarriageable, and Rayford supported his decision."

"How long did you stay in the country?"

"I didn't return to London until just recently. Father died two years ago, and Ray gambled away his wife's dowry and what little Father left us. That was when Ray decided that I should come to London to try once again to find a rich husband."

She took a deep breath and continued. "I didn't want to return to London. I was safe in the country, you see. Besides, I'm twenty-four and couldn't compete with young debutantes. After a few weeks, Rayford realized there was no hope of snagging a rich husband and decided on another course."

She fell silent, staring down at her clenched fists resting in her lap.

"Go on. What happened next? Where does Rigby fit in?"

Sophia hated to remember Rigby's lascivious attack or her brother's duplicity.

"Continue, Sophia. So far you haven't told me anything I hadn't already guessed."

"Ray lost over five hundred pounds to Sir Oscar Rigby during the short time we'd been in London. Sir Oscar wanted his money before he returned to the West Indies and threatened to send Ray to debtor's prison if he didn't settle up."

She glanced at Chris. "Are you sure you want to hear the rest?"

"Very sure."

"Ray struck a deal with Sir Oscar. He sold that vile man my virginity in exchange for his vowels. He asked me to oblige Sir Oscar and I refused. I thought that was the end of it. But the following evening Ray dismissed the servants, admitted Sir Oscar into the house and then left. I had no idea what those two scoundrels had cooked up until Sir Oscar entered my bedroom and tried to assault me."

"The bastard!" Chris bit out.

"I struggled, of course," Sophia continued. She paused, recalling that horrific moment. "I tricked him into believing I was agreeable and managed to tie him to a chair. I dressed quickly and ran. He escaped easily enough and followed, but I managed to push him down the stairs and hit him with a vase, though that didn't stop him for long. I fled into the night with him hard on my heels. Somewhere along the way he'd summoned the Watch.

"I ran and ran but couldn't seem to escape them. I had no idea where I was going and found myself near the river. I ducked into a saloon to throw them off my trail and learned that several ships were docked at Southwark quay. I left the saloon and found the quay easily enough, but the *Intrepid* was the only ship with its gangplank run out. I had no idea she was yours when I sneaked aboard. I was desperate to escape Sir Oscar. Had he caught me, I would have ended up in Newgate . . . or worse."

She darted a look at Chris. He seemed to be staring into space. But the look on his face was not comforting. Sophia took a deep breath and said, "Now do you understand why I don't want to return to England? Rayford is desperate for money; he will sell me again to any man who meets his price. The next man might succeed where Sir Oscar failed."

"Where did you intend to go when you ran out of the house?"

"Anywhere Rayford couldn't find me. I intended to find work, even if I had to serve drinks at the lowliest inn or scrub floors. I didn't want to remain dependent on Ray for my livelihood. If and when I lose my virginity, I will choose the man."

Chris looked up at her, his face stark with an emotion she couldn't read. "I can understand your reluctance to return to England, Sophia, but . . ."

"But what?"

"Go farther back than that. Go back seven years. Make me understand why you told me you loved me, then accepted Desmond's proposal."

"I did love you, Chris."

"No, you didn't. You enjoyed having the attention of two men, teasing us with your wicked-as-sin eyes and lying mouth. Why did you do it?"

His eyes seemed to beg her for an honest reply, but Sophia hesitated. What good would it do? He already thought the worst of her. He had broken her heart once; she wouldn't allow it to happen again.

"Perhaps I did enjoy the attention of two handsome men," Sophia lied. "I was young and, yes, foolish, and could see no harm in it."

"No harm!" Chris spat. "How in God's name can you say there was no harm in Desmond's death?"

"I can't, but I wasn't the one who killed him," Sophia whispered. Chris's stricken look made her wish she could call back her words.

He stood abruptly and stalked off.

Chris stormed back to the house, entered his study and slammed the door. Sophia's words had cut him deeply. Neither he nor Desmond had intended to kill the other. It was simply a friendly feud over a woman they both desired.

Chris walked to the sideboard, splashed a tot of rum into a glass and sank into a comfortable chair. What was he going to do about Sophia? After listening to her story, he understood why she didn't want to return to her brother's keeping. But after that fiasco at the inn with Rigby, finding employment in Kingston was out of the question.

Mired deep in his own misery, Chris struggled to keep memories of Desmond at bay. Had Fate led Sophia to his ship? Why did he still care about her welfare? Before he knew it, he had finished that first tot of rum and poured another. The alcohol burned all the way down his gullet and into his stomach but did nothing to ease his dilemma.

Chris had no idea how much time had elapsed since he'd left Sophia in the garden. Sometime later he heard her enter the house and climb the stairs to her room. And still he sat. The longer he sat, the more rum he consumed, and the alcohol seemed to affect him in a strange way. The anger and pain he had felt earlier slowly dissipated, replaced by lust for the woman who had caused his distress.

His gut clenched with the need to bed Sophia.

Sophia felt as if she carried the world on her shoulders. She hadn't meant to hurt Chris. She had waited in the garden for him to return, but when he hadn't, she'd sought her bed. But sleep eluded her. She wasn't tired in the least after her long nap earlier in the day. Besides, it was too hot to sleep.

She had left the French doors to the upper-floor balcony open to let in the breeze and felt a waft of coolness touch her feverish skin. She closed her eyes, trying to summon sleep, when she heard footsteps pause at her door and then continue on.

Chris!

Was his room nearby? She hadn't inquired and hadn't had time yet to explore the house. Her mind wandered. Should she leave Sunset Hill tomorrow? Obviously, Chris didn't want her around to dredge up painful memories. Finally her mind shut down and she slept.

A slight noise awakened her. She sat upright in bed. The sound came from the balcony. She saw a shadow move though the French doors. She opened her mouth to scream but quickly closed it when she recognized Chris's muscular form limned by the brilliant moonlight. She watched him approach, large, dangerous. Moonlight silvered his hair, rendering his face harsh in its stark light. She smelled sulfur as a light flared in the oil lamp.

Sophia blinked at the sudden light and pulled the sheet up to her neck. "What do you want?"

He sent her a strange look, as if surprised to find himself in her bedroom. "I came to apologize." His words were slightly slurred.

Sophia peered closely at him. "You're foxed."

He shook his head. "I never drink to excess. Not anymore."

Sophia didn't believe him. "Go away."

"Not until I apologize for walking away from you in the garden tonight."

He wanted to apologize? "Chris, it's late. Can't this wait until tomorrow?"

"Yes, it could, but I can't."

He settled on the edge of the bed. "Everything you said is true. I held the gun, I fired the pistol, but the bullet wasn't supposed to hit Desmond."

"I know you hold me responsible and that my presence here in your home makes you uncomfortable."

Chris plowed his fingers through his hair. "You're right, Sophia, you do make me uncomfortable, but not precisely in the way you think. You tempt me despite my best intentions. I can't trust myself around you, but becoming involved with you again is out of the question."

Sophia nodded. "I'll leave Sunset Hill, but I'm not returning to England."

Sophia touched his arm. He stiffened, as if her touch revolted him. When she started to retreat, he groaned and pulled her to him so tightly she could barely breathe. Then his mouth claimed hers. His kiss tasted of unbridled, unfulfilled passion, and Sophia realized it had been simmering inside him all along, unacknowledged, unrequited. Then his tongue swept inside her mouth, thrusting deep. She tasted rum. Moments later, he was lying beside her without her knowing how it had happened.

Sophia tried to push him away. Knowing how he felt about her, she couldn't let him to do this. If he disliked her now, he would despise her in the morning. No matter how much he denied it, Sophia knew he was foxed and would accuse her of leading him on once he sobered.

When Chris paused to take a breath, Sophia seized the moment to offer a protest. "Chris, you don't want to do this."

"Oh, aye, I do. Very much." He inhaled deeply. "You smell like flowers. Though I may be damned forever, Sophia, I need to be inside you."

His words shattered Sophia's resistance. She had dreamed of this moment since the first day Chris had walked into her life. Now she was keenly aware of his body next to hers, of her breasts pressed firmly against his chest, his manly scent, the roughness of his skin.

The passing years had not dimmed her memory of the man she had fallen in love with.

But Sophia did not want Chris this way. He wanted her body, but he didn't care about the person she was. And no matter what, he still intended to force her to leave Jamaica against her will.

Suddenly Sophia became aware of a new torment. Chris had lowered the sheet and was slowly raising her shift, baring her body to his avid gaze. A harsh sound gurgled from his throat as he put his hands on the insides of her thighs, spreading them.

Sophia nearly jumped out of her skin when Chris opened her with his thumbs, baring the most vulnerable part of her. With slow deliberation he lowered his head. Before Sophia realized what he intended, she felt his hot breath teasing her intimate flesh.

"Chris, what . . ."

The moment his lips brushed against her, Sophia cried out. The shock immobilized her, and the tingling sensation that followed made her squirm with unnamed pleasure. Her core pulsed, vulnerable, aching with a need she couldn't express. When he flicked his tongue against her, she moaned, her hips moving reflexively against him. He grabbed her hips to steady her as he explored the virgin recesses of her body, his tongue laving every intimate crevice.

When he drew the sensitive nub of her desire between his teeth, Sophia began thrashing her head from side to side, her hands flailing against his arms. She bucked her hips, searching for something, anything to ease the sensual torture. She felt as if she were tottering on the edge of an abyss, gripped by pleasure so intense it stole her breath.

Sophia wasn't prepared when she fell into a dark hole of splintering pleasure, the bliss so razor-sharp it shattered her. She cried out, lost in the throes of climax, her fingers clutching his head. Then she went limp, her labored breathing fracturing the tense silence.

"What just happened?" she gasped.

"I've just given you your first climax."

Sophia was confused. She knew about mating and how it was accomplished, but beyond that she was ignorant.

"Something wondrous happened inside me. Did you feel it?"

"Not yet, but I will." He rose and tore off his trousers and shirt.

Sophia stared at him. He was magnificently fashioned, with broad shoulders, slim hips and waist, powerful legs and thickly muscled arms. Her gaze slid down the length of him, stopping briefly at his engorged sex. She colored and looked away. But curiosity drew her gaze back to that mysterious part of him which jutted out of a nest of dark hair between his thighs.

Chris swelled longer and thicker beneath Sophia's perusal. Desire swelled in his loins, pulled low at his gut. He had tried his damnedest to stay away from her, but after a few tots of rum all he could think about was bedding her. He told himself his need was sharper because he hadn't had a woman for weeks, not because he was obsessed with the green-eyed temptress gazing at him as if he were some kind of ancient god.

Even if he took Sophia as his body demanded, this night wouldn't change his mind about sending her home to England, he told himself. She had sneaked aboard his ship, incited his lust and forced him to protect her from Rigby. He hadn't wanted any of those things to happen. He had considered himself well rid of Sophia Carlisle years ago.

"Chris . . ."

He gazed down at her. Her eyes were luminous in the lamplight. He wanted to arouse her again. He wanted . . . he wanted . . . to be inside Sophia.

His hand moved between her thighs, parted them, eased a finger deep inside. He felt her stiffen. She gasped his name as her hands rose to clasp his shoulders. He bent his head, taking the rigid peak of her breast fully into his mouth, nipping and suckling as his finger stroked inside her. She moaned softly.

Chris lifted his head and gazed at her. She was beautiful, more beautiful even than the seventeen-year-old girl he had fallen in love with. Though time and circumstances had killed his love for her, he still appreciated her beauty. He moved slightly, pressing his erection against her hip as he continued to suckle her breasts.

"Sophia," he whispered hoarsely as he moved fully over her and slowly thrust his thick erection inside her. He heard her gasp and eased back, but not for long. His body clamored for completion. He slid a little deeper, his clenched jaw the only outward sign of his restraint. When he felt her tighten around him, drawing him deeper, his control snapped.

He thrust powerfully with his hips, breaking through her virgin barrier, sinking into her depths. She gasped, and he knew he had hurt her. "I'm sorry, Sophia. I'll make it good for you, I promise."

He waited a moment, allowing her body time to adjust to his size before moving, slowly sliding and plunging, sliding and plunging, deep, deeper.

Sophia sucked in her breath as the pain gave way to something far more pleasurable. She moved her hips, tentatively at first, then timing them to meet his plunging loins in perfect harmony. The friction was astonishingly arousing, vibrantly wanton. The pleasure of it drove her wild. She thrashed madly beneath him, reaching, needing, wanting.

She could feel the strength of his desire growing inside her and the power of his body moving on top of her. When he rose slightly and slipped his hand between their bodies, the fire, white-hot, consuming, built within her again and roared out of control. The whimpering she heard came from her own throat. Then pleasure overwhelmed her as a wave of scalding heat flashed through her.

Her body seized, shuddered, and then she cried out. Somewhere in the deep recesses of her brain she heard Chris call her name, felt his member convulse, felt his heat spilling into her.

Panting, Chris collapsed against her, his face pressing into the hollow of her neck. Gathering her into his arms, he rolled to his side. "Did I hurt you, Sophia?"

Sophia pushed him away. "Why did you do it?" Her voice trembled with an emotion very close to anger. "You don't like me, remember?"

Chris rolled to the edge of the bed and sat up, resting his head in his hands. "I haven't had a woman since before the *Intrepid* left London."

Chris knew the excuse was a lame one, that what he had done was inexcusable. His head felt fuzzy, his mouth dry. Was he foxed? Had Sophia driven him to drink? It was the first time he could recall having more than a drink or two since Desmond's death. It was the only excuse he could think of. Or at any rate, the only reason he was willing to admit.

"You used me!" Sophia charged. "You needed a woman and I was handy."

Chris knew there was more to it than that but refused to say so. "You're right, I was foxed, but this changes nothing. You're leaving as soon as I can sort out your problems and book passage for you. I'll do all I can to keep you safe from your brother. I'll give you money so you can live independent of him."

Flexing her knees, Sophia kicked him out of the bed. He fell on his rump with a thud. "I'm willing to leave this house, Captain, but not Jamaica. You can keep your money; I am perfectly capable of taking care of myself."

"You'll do as I say," Chris growled as he gathered his clothing and stormed out of the room.

Chapter Eight

Sophia found sleep impossible after Chris left. Tears streamed down her face as she tried to make sense of his actions. No matter how hard she tried, she couldn't figure out what he wanted. He seemed to blow first hot and then cold. He wanted her, yet he didn't.

How could Chris not realize that she loved him? That she had never stopped loving him?

Ribbons of purple dawn streaked a leaden sky when Sophia finally fell asleep. She didn't awaken until a clap of thunder rattled the shutters. Startled, she sat up in bed, surprised to see rain pouring from the sky. She lay back down, seeing no reason to get out of bed. She was staring at the rain beating down on the balcony when Kateena entered the room.

"Good morning, mistress."

"I don't know what's good about it," Sophia complained.

Kateena flashed a smile. "This is Jamaica, mistress. The rain will stop soon, the sun will come out, and the day will be glorious."

Sophia wasn't at all interested in the day, glorious or otherwise. "I suppose."

"Your bathwater is heating in the kitchen."

Sophia perked up immediately. "Thank you, a bath is just what I need."

An hour later, Sophia descended the stairs and proceeded to the dining room. She was ravenous and asked for eggs, ham and toasted bread. Due to the late hour, she dined alone.

"Is Captain Radcliff still in the house?" she asked Chuba.

"No, mistress, he and Casper left for the distillery hours ago."

"In this rain?"

"There was trouble in the distillery; Mundo summoned the master early this morning."

Chuba poured Sophia's tea and left. The thrum of rain against the windows reminded her of England, making her realize how little she missed her home. She wondered if there was any place in the world she would be happy. If things were different between her and Chris, Jamaica would be the Paradise she had always dreamed about.

Sophia finished her breakfast and wandered into Chris's study, perusing the bookcases lining the wall. She chose a book on world history and settled down in a comfortable chair near the window to read.

Chris spent the entire day in the distillery. The rain had stopped shortly after noon, and the sun now rode high in the sky. Sweat dampened his shirt and dotted his brow as he labored beside his slaves.

The rich scent of rum permeated the air, making Chris slightly ill. After last night, he doubted he would imbibe again anytime soon. What had he been thinking? Making love to Sophia hadn't been the wisest thing he had ever done. Had he the sense God gave him, he would have steered clear of her room last night. Nothing good could come of his indiscretion.

After solving the problem in the distillery, Chris rode out to the cane fields to check the crop. Everywhere he looked, slaves were busily employed. But he could sense their discontent; tension was thick in the air, as if they were merely biding their time. Chris hadn't told them he intended to free them, and wouldn't until their freedom actually became a fact. If his efforts failed, he didn't want them to be disappointed. He intended to return to Headquarters House in a few days to see if the remittance papers had been processed.

Meanwhile, Chris had created another problem for himself. What was he going to do with Sophia? She adamantly refused to return to England, and he couldn't blame her. Perhaps, with his recommendation, she could find a governess post in Spanish Town or Ocho Rios. He discarded that notion as soon as it was born. He was uncomfortable sending her off on her own.

Chris didn't return to the house until dinnertime. Staying busy kept his mind and body occupied. He worked feverishly during the next several days, leaving the house early and returning late. He saw Sophia only during dinner and retired to his study immediately after the meal. He deliberately avoided rum and late night wanderings. He refused to become involved with her again.

When Chris first met Sophia at her come out, he had

been entranced by her angelic beauty and lively spirit. So had Desmond. The last thing Chris wanted now was to fall into her trap again. Once bitten, twice shy: the adage expressed his sentiments perfectly.

Chris liked his life just the way it was. He had his plantation and distillery, and women to assuage his needs were at his disposal in Kingston.

Despite his mental rejection, Chris couldn't forget how good Sophia felt in his arms, her innocent passion, her alluring scent; the way she shattered beneath him. Damn! He went hard just thinking about her. Desire pulsed through him. Heat surged to his groin. Clamping down on his lust, he turned his mind in another direction.

Sophia was bored. She needed something besides Chris to focus on. The weather had been hot and sultry for the past few days. There wasn't much one could do during the heat of the afternoon but fan oneself and think. Unfortunately, her thoughts never strayed far from Chris.

She had figured out why he was acting so cool and remote toward her. He was afraid of her. Afraid he might develop feelings for her. If he wanted her to leave, why didn't he just tell her instead of letting her remain in limbo?

When Chris returned early from the fields one day, Sophia learned from Chuba that he was expecting visitors. Sophia was sitting in the parlor reading when she heard voices in the foyer. She paid them little heed until Chris and his guests entered the room.

Since no guests had arrived at Sunset Hill since her arrival, Sophia was surprised to see Chris usher a distinguished-looking man and a handsome woman into the parlor. Despite Chris's frown when his gaze found her, the visitors seemed delighted to see her.

"I brought my wife so she could meet your betrothed," the man said. "They can get acquainted while we conduct our business."

Sophia rose, visibly startled. Betrothed?

"Ah, there she is," the woman said. "Welcome to Jamaica, my dear. I hope you'll allow me to help plan your wedding. A celebration is just what we need to take our minds off all this nastiness with the slaves."

"No, you must be mis—"

"Sophia, please make your curtsy to Lord and Lady Chester," Chris said. "My lord, my lady, meet Miss Sophia Carlisle."

Sophia made a halfhearted curtsy, confused by the sudden turn of events. What in the world was wrong with Chris? "Lord and Lady Chester, I'm pleased to make your acquaintance."

"Please, my dear, call me Agatha," Lady Chester said. "We English have a tight-knit community on the island, and we don't always adhere to protocol."

"Now that the ladies are acquainted, we can retire to your study and get down to business," Lord Chester said. "The unrest among my slaves is becoming troublesome. I'm calling on Wombly tomorrow to discuss the situation. We neighbors must stick together."

Sophia sent Chris a pained look. She knew nothing about a betrothal. It wasn't fair to let the Chesters believe she was his bride-to-be. But Chris's shrug was all she received. It looked as if she was on her own with Lady Chester.

"I'll have refreshments sent in," Chris said.

"Enjoy your visit," Chester added. "I'm sure you

ladies have a great deal to discuss, what with planning the wedding and all."

"Captain Radcliff is so handsome," Lady Chester gushed. "Have you known him long?"

"Over seven years," Sophia answered truthfully.

"I can understand why he brought you to Jamaica to be wed. It's a perfect spot for a wedding. Will any of your relatives be attending the ceremony?"

"I have no relatives. My parents, Viscount and Viscountess Carlisle, died several years ago."

Agatha clapped her hands. "You're highborn—how delightful! I don't know Captain Radcliff well, but I understand his brother is the Earl of Standish. Have you no brothers or sisters?"

"No, my lady," Sophia replied. She didn't count Rayford because they didn't share the same blood, and both her parents had been only children.

"You are to call me Agatha, remember? And I shall call you Sophia. Such a lovely name. Now then, Sophia, have you set a date for your wedding?"

"Er . . . no. Chris and I have only just arrived at Sunset Hill. We're just getting settled in."

The tea cart arrived, allowing Sophia a few moments to collect her thoughts. Whatever was Chris thinking? How could he let people believe she was his betrothed? She knew he had no intention of tying himself to a woman who provoked memories he'd rather forget. He might lust for her, enjoy making love to her, but his heart was in no way engaged.

Over the rim of her cup, Sophia watched Lady Chester sip her tea and munch on a small frosted cake.

"This is delightful," Agatha cooed. "I love my children, but I do enjoy an afternoon away from them now and again."

"You have children?"

"Indeed. Two lively boys of six and eight." She set her cup down and leaned toward Sophia. "Tell me, what was that little ruckus with Sir Oscar Rigby at the King's Arms all about? Why were you seeking employment as a governess? I'm just dying of curiosity."

Though Sophia had expected the question, she still wasn't prepared for it. "It was a case of mistaken identity." She held out her arm. "As you can see, I tan rather easily, and Sir Oscar mistook me for . . . someone else. As for the governess position, I thought it would keep me occupied until Chris and I were ready to wed. He has a great deal to learn as a new plantation owner, and I didn't want to become a burden to him."

Agatha sent her a skeptical look. "How could you ever become a burden to your fiancé? It all sounds rather mysterious, if you ask me."

Sophia took another sip of tea while she considered her answer. Relief flooded through her when Chris and Lord Chester returned to the parlor.

"Tea, gentlemen?" Sophia asked, grateful for the interruption.

Both men nodded, and Sophia poured.

"Captain Radcliff, Sophia and I were discussing her quest for employment. I vow I was surprised."

Chris looked at Sophia, as if expecting her to answer. When she didn't, he cleared his throat and said, "Sophia likes to be useful. As Mr. Ludlow will attest, I put an end to her quest rather quickly. I moved her from the King's Arms to keep her safe from men like Rigby."

"I'm ashamed to count Rigby as one of us," Chester acknowledged. "Things neither of us would approve of go on at his plantation. He abuses his women slaves and works the men until they drop from exhaustion. If there is a revolt, his plantation will be the first to come under attack."

"Oh, dear God, John, do you really think it will come to that?" Agatha cried, clutching her throat.

"Now, now, Agatha, don't fret. This is all speculation."

Agatha rose abruptly. "I have reason to fret. The children are home alone with the maids. Perhaps we should leave." She turned to Sophia. "We'll discuss wedding arrangements at a later date, my dear. Have your handsome captain bring you to Orchid Manor soon."

"I'll let you know what the other plantation owners decide, Radcliff," Lord Chester said as he escorted his wife out the door and into their carriage.

"All this talk of revolt is serious, isn't it?" Sophia asked as she waved the Chesters off.

"I won't lie. It's serious enough for the plantation owners to band together for their own protection. But I hope it won't come to that. But if it does, Sunset Hill will remain safe, my slaves will be free, so they will have no reason to revolt. Repairs on the slave quarters are under way. I wanted my people to know I have their best interests at heart. I'm hoping they will remain to work for wages once they are freed."

Chris turned away. Sophia stopped him with a hand on his arm. "Oh, no, you don't. Kindly explain why the Chesters believe we are betrothed. You should have corrected them instead of leaving me to deal with Lady Chester's questions."

"Come into the study," Chris said. "We need to talk."

"Indeed we do," Sophia replied, preceding him into the chamber.

"Sit down, Sophia."

"I prefer to stand, thank you."

"As you please." He paced away, then spun around. "I claimed you were my betrothed to save your reputation. Lord Chester heard about your confrontation with Rigby and actually believed what the innkeeper said about you. I set him straight, but in the process was forced to tell him you were my betrothed."

Anger swamped Sophia. "Forced? You lied! Now you have to fix it."

"There's no fixing this, Sophia. I suppose we will have to marry. You have a choice. Either marry me or return to England. If we break this sham engagement, you will never find work here. You're living in my home; therefore a wedding is expected. If you leave, your reputation will be in shreds."

"Humph, it won't be the first time. Besides, we both know you don't want to marry me."

Chris shrugged. "What I want is no longer important, it's what people expect. Fate brought us together again, and we have to make the best of it."

Sophia searched his face. "That doesn't mean we have to marry. You don't even like me."

"Be that as it may, you are living in my home and I am responsible for you. We will wed, Sophia, sooner rather than later."

Sophia couldn't believe it. Did Chris actually think she would agree, knowing he didn't want her? She couldn't bear loving Chris, living with him, and not having her love returned. "No, Chris, I won't marry a man who doesn't want me."

"Not want you? Oh, I want you, Sophia. Never doubt it. One night in your bed was scarcely enough."

His words stunned Sophia, even if she didn't believe him. A man wouldn't leave her to languish in boredom if he wanted her. He wouldn't ignore her or refuse to make small talk at the dinner table. He wouldn't treat her with disdain and try to send her away.

Sophia wanted to believe Chris cared for her. Dear God, she wanted it desperately. She wanted to reach up and kiss him, wanted to feel his mouth moving on hers. She yearned for his touch, for his sweet caresses. She wanted him to make love to her again and really mean it.

Sophia licked her suddenly dry lips and gazed into his eyes. "Prove you want me, Chris."

At first she didn't think he would react. Then something seemed to snap inside him as he slid his hands into the dark strands of her hair and pulled her head back, crushing his mouth down on hers.

The kiss wasn't gentle, but Sophia didn't care. At least he was showing something for her besides apathy. He kissed her fiercely, plundering her mouth with his tongue, cupping her bottom and hauling her against him. She felt the swelling thickness of his sex beneath his trousers and suddenly recalled where they were.

She made a strangled sound of protest in her throat and tried to push him away. Reluctantly he broke off the kiss and held her away from him, his fingers digging into her shoulders.

"Can you still say I don't want you?" he bit out. "Never doubt it, Sophia, I do want you and we will marry."

Sophia couldn't think, much less speak. Her lips felt

swollen, her flesh bruised. She felt unbalanced, unfocused. She could only stare at him, mouth agape. Chris released her, spun on his heel and strode off.

Sophia had no idea what had just happened. Why did Chris want to marry her when he had told her countless times that he didn't want her in his life? Why did he care about her reputation when he had helped ruin it?

Chris was angry at himself, but even angrier at Sophia. It was his fault for mentioning Sophia and marriage in the same breath to Lord Chester, but he wouldn't be in this predicament if Sophia hadn't stowed away aboard his ship.

He told himself that marrying Sophia didn't mean he had to care about her. He had a plantation and a distillery to run, slaves to care for. Sophia wasn't necessary to make his life or his happiness complete.

Chris entered his study and slammed the door. He sank into a chair and stared at the paperwork on his desk, unable to focus on the work at hand. He knew he was lying to himself. In one respect he did need Sophia. He needed her body next to his in bed, his arms around her. He needed her kisses. He went hard just thinking about making love to her. Would there ever be a time he wouldn't want to be inside her?

Of one thing Chris was certain: He would never let Sophia know how badly he needed her. From this day forward, Chris promised himself, he would guard his heart and remain emotionally detached. If he didn't, Sophia would wrap him around her little finger, just as she had seven years ago.

* * *

Several days elapsed without Chris mentioning marriage again to Sophia. In fact, he seemed even more remote than usual. She was so certain he had given up the idea that she decided to ask him to take her to town so she could inquire of Mr. Ludlow if he had received any replies to her inquiries about a governess post.

One night over dinner, Sophia told Chris, "I'd like to go into town tomorrow. Mundo could take me and Kateena in the wagon, if it's all right with you."

He seemed not to hear her.

"Chris—"

"I heard. I'll take you to town myself. You need a new wardrobe. I won't have it said that I'm miserly with my betrothed."

Sophia gave a huff of exasperation. "I thought you realized that marriage between us is impossible."

"Why would you think that?"

"Your actions speak for themselves. You barely acknowledge me, let alone talk to me."

"I've got a lot on my mind," he hedged.

"Are you still worried about a revolt?"

"That, among other things. You can see to your wardrobe in Kingston while I visit Headquarters House. I'm anxious to free my slaves before matters get worse than they already are. I've already lost four men. They ran off in the dead of night to join the Maroons in the mountains."

"Are you going to report them missing?"

"No. They'll be free soon and can do whatever they please. Can you be ready at nine tomorrow morning? You can ride one of my horses and Kateena can ride with Mundo in the wagon."

"I'll be ready," Sophia said, "but I won't accept your

charity. You know I can never repay you for anything you buy me."

"You'll be my wife soon. I'm supposed to provide you with a suitable wardrobe. Why are you fighting the issue?"

"Why? Because marriage isn't what you want from me."

"That's beside the point." He rose. "It's useless to argue about this, so you might as well resign yourself to our marriage. I have," he added as he strode from the dining room.

Sophia wanted to throw something at him. The man was impossible. He was determined to have his way with or without her approval. No matter; Sophia had plans of her own. She was determined to find employment, no matter where in Jamaica she had to travel to find it.

The wagon was waiting when Sophia and Kateena walked out the front door the next morning. Kateena smiled shyly at Mundo and climbed in beside him. Chris arrived moments later, leading two horses. He seated Sophia atop a mild-mannered bay mare, then mounted his own coal-black Atlas.

"Mundo will drop you and Kateena off at the dressmaker's shop and then continue on to the general store to pick up supplies. Let's go," Chris said as he reined his mount down the lane.

"Do you know the dressmaker's location?" Sophia asked as she caught up with Chris.

"Kateena gave me directions earlier. The dressmaker's name is Wanda. We should arrive thirty minutes or so ahead of the wagon."

Sophia nodded and said nothing more. What could she say to a man as hardheaded as Chris? If she didn't love him so much, she would wed him, but she couldn't endure a loveless marriage.

When they reached Kingston, Chris led her down a narrow lane off King Street and reined in before a small shop with a simple sign that said "Dressmaker" hanging over the door. It was unpretentious in the extreme but welcoming with its blue-and-white-striped awning stretched across the front.

Chris dismounted and lifted Sophia down. He held the door open while she entered ahead of him. A tall, dark woman of indeterminate age greeted them at the door. She was dressed casually in a colorful island dress with a *tignon* covering her head.

"What can I do for you, sir?" she asked in a sing-song voice that seemed to have a melody all its own.

"Are you Wanda?" Chris asked. When the woman nodded, he said, "I am Captain Radcliff and this is Miss Carlisle, my bride-to-be. Kateena from the King's Arms recommended you. She said you were an excellent seamstress."

Wanda smiled and bowed her head. "If your lady is in need of a dressmaker, I will do my best to please her."

"My betrothed requires a complete wardrobe, including a wedding gown," Chris replied. "She'll need the wedding gown and half the initial order in two weeks. Can you manage that?"

Wanda's sparkling black eyes exuded confidence. "I can indeed, Captain. I employ several free women of color and have taught them myself."

"Very good. After we choose patterns and materials, I shall leave Miss Carlisle in your capable hands. Kateena will join her shortly."

Sophia spent the next hour poring over patterns and materials with Chris, all in lightweight materials to accommodate the Jamaican climate. When Kateena joined them, she added her opinion when asked, but Chris seemed to know what he wanted to see Sophia wearing and chose styles that pleased him. Sophia voiced her preferences from time to time and tried to stop Chris at three gowns, but he ignored her.

Once six gowns had been commissioned, Chris said, "I'll leave the choice of undergarments to your discretion, Sophia. Try to remember you'll have little use for the numerous petticoats and steel corsets that are all the rage in England." He turned to leave. "If you'll excuse me, ladies, I have business to conduct at Headquarters House. Wait here until I return. We still have to find a shoemaker."

The fittings were pure torture, despite the anticipated pleasure of having new clothes. Rayford had ordered the first new gown Sophia had had in years, prior to their return to London. Before that, she had turned hems, added ruffles, done anything to make an old gown look new. Since she had been rarely out and about in public, Rayford had seen no need to replenish her wardrobe.

When Wanda announced she had everything she required to begin her work, Sophia was relieved that Chris hadn't yet returned. She would have a chance to visit Mr. Ludlow at the King's Arms. She asked Wanda to tell Chris she would meet him at the inn and departed with Kateena in tow, leaving her horse behind for Chris to collect.

"The captain told you to wait for him at the dressmaker," Kateena scolded.

"I need to speak to Mr. Ludlow, and this is my only chance."

Kateena clucked her tongue but said nothing more.

"There's Mr. Ludlow," Sophia said as she approached the innkeeper.

"Miss Carlisle, how nice to see you again. I hear you're to wed Captain Radcliff. Congratulations."

"Thank you. I wondered if you've heard anything further from families interested in hiring an English governess for their children."

"Mistress!" Kateena gasped. "Why do you need to work? You are to marry the captain."

"Can't the captain provide for you?" Ludlow asked.

"My fiancée doesn't need employment, and I can provide for her very well, thank you."

Chris.

Sophia whipped around, paling when she saw the look on Chris's face. He was furious. His brows were drawn together in a frown, his eyes narrowed.

"You were supposed to wait for me at the dressmaker's," Chris said, anger burning through him. He'd assumed Sophia had resigned herself to their marriage, so why was she asking about employment? Bloody hell! Didn't she know he was trying to do the right thing? He had lost control and taken her virginity. Since there was nothing but an uncertain future for her in England, and he had ruined her, she had no choice but to marry him.

"I wanted to speak to Mr. Ludlow before returning to Sunset Hill," Sophia replied.

"We'll discuss this at home. If you wish, we can invite Ludlow to our wedding. Come—we still have to order footwear for you."

"But—"

"Sophia," he said roughly, "I said it's time to leave."

"Very well, if you insist."

Chris felt ready to explode as he watched Sophia precede him out the door, head held high, shoulders proudly squared. Did the woman know no fear? Did she want Rigby to carry her off again? When Chris had seen Rigby leaving Headquarters House a short time ago, his heart had nearly thudded to a halt. He had concluded his business quickly and returned to the dressmaker. When he learned that Sophia had left against his orders, fear for her safety pierced through him.

Then, when he had walked into the inn and heard her asking about employment, fear turned to blinding rage. Despite her lack of options, Sophia didn't want to marry him. She'd rather take her chances on a precarious future as a governess than become his wife. So much for all those pretty words she had whispered in his ear seven years ago. They had meant nothing . . . less than nothing, just as he had always known.

"Your horse is outside," Chris growled. He nodded to Kateena. "So is the wagon."

Kateena climbed onto the wagon beside Mundo while Chris lifted Sophia onto her horse, then mounted Atlas. Chris's anger continued to simmer as they ordered slippers and boots at the cobbler's shop and rode back to Sunset Hill.

When they reached the manor house, Chris spoke for the first time since leaving Kingston. "In my study. Now!" He stormed into the house, expecting her to follow.

"What is this about, Chris? Why are you so angry? I merely wanted to inquire if any replies to my request for employment had arrived."

"Why are you dead set against our marriage?"

"Because it's not what you want."

"You never did love me, did you?"

She lowered her eyes. "Does it matter now?"

"It doesn't matter at all." Lies, all lies. Of course it mattered. He didn't know why, but it did.

Sophia turned her back on him. "You needn't marry me because you took my virginity. I can take care of myself. I don't want a loveless marriage, Chris. What if we wed and have children? Will you love the children we have together?"

Chris grasped her shoulders and turned her to face him. "You may already be carrying my child."

He knew by the shock on Sophia's face that she hadn't thought of that. "It was just one time. I don't think—"

"You don't know. It's very possible."

His hands tightened on her shoulders, slid down her arms, grasped her hands and yanked her against him. Then his mouth slammed down on hers. He went hard the moment his lips touched hers. He had deliberately maintained his distance after he had relieved Sophia of her virginity, but abstinence had only sharpened his need for her. He could wait no longer. Sweeping her into his arms, he sank into a chair with her in his lap.

"What are you doing?" Sophia gasped.

"Making love to you. Help me lift your skirts out of the way."

"Here? Now? In your study? Anyone could come in."

Chris surged to his feet with her in his arms. "Very well." He carried her though the door and up the stairs.

"Where are you taking me?"

"To your bedroom, if that meets with your approval."

"Kateena will return soon."

"We'll lock the door. Protest all you want, Sophia, but I mean to have you."

"Why?"

Chris didn't know why. Even if he did, he wouldn't tell her. What he did know was that he ached to be inside her, trembled with need for her. Because of his pride, he had denied himself too long. He would show Sophia that making love to her meant no more to him than assuaging his body's needs. That thought made him chuckle bitterly.

He was fooling no one but himself if he believed making love to Sophia meant nothing to him.

Chapter Nine

Sophia closed her eyes as Chris drew her into his arms and kissed her. Not a gentle, seductive kiss but a deep, soul-destroying kiss, an aggressive, ravishing kiss that curled her toes and filled her with need. Her knees went weak and she slid her arms around him to keep from melting into a heap at his feet.

"Tell me you want me," Chris whispered against her lips.

Sophia shook her head. She wanted to deny her need for Chris, wanted him to believe she could resist him. To her utter dismay, when she opened her mouth to reject him, her lips said, "I want you."

A deeper kiss followed, fierce, abandoned, possessive. She moaned a protest deep in her throat when he broke off the kiss. Dizzy from his sudden burst of passion, she faltered and would have fallen if he hadn't reached out and steadied her.

"Take off your clothes," he said raggedly.

She blinked. "What?"

"Why should we deny ourselves when this is what we both want?"

Sophia must have moved too slowly, for he brushed her hands aside and worked the buttons on the front of her gown. The material parted, exposing the soft swells of her breasts. He groaned as he cupped the firm mounds in his hands, teased and caressed them, stroked his thumbs across her nipples. The tips peaked and distended. The throbbing nearly drove Sophia mad with wanting. Her body was no longer hers as she pressed herself against him; it belonged to Chris, to do with as he wished.

His hands left her breasts, pushed her gown down her shoulders and slid it past her hips. It pooled at her feet in a colorful froth. Her chemise went next, and then her stockings and shoes. She swayed against him. He swept her into his arms and carried her to the bed.

He gazed down at her, his eyes dark, intense, hungry. Sophia raised her eyes to his and released a slow, shallow breath. A shiver ran through her. Never had a man looked at her like that. His face was stark with need, his eyes shadowed, enigmatic, haunted. Was he still plagued by guilt? Her mouth went dry as she watched him remove his clothing and boots

Her gaze slid over his body, tall, dark, lean. Broad shoulders, wide, deep chest, slim hips, taut belly, heavily muscled thighs and long, lean legs. Her eyes settled on his erection, rising forcefully against his stomach.

His eyes smoldered with dark fire. "Despite our past history, never doubt that I want you, Sophia," he said.

Sophia didn't doubt his lust, but she wondered how long a marriage based only on physical attraction could last. Would Chris continue to blame her for the death of his best friend? Could she accept him on those terms?

Sophia's thoughts fractured when Chris joined her on the bed. Her body thrummed to life as his hand slid over her belly, through the tight, dark curls at the juncture of her thighs and cupped her intimately. His head lowered to suckle her breast as his fingers parted her, exploring the slick folds of her cleft.

Sophia whimpered and arched against his questing lips and probing fingers. She was on fire. She wanted to touch him, caress him, breathe in his scent.

"Touch me," he said, as if reading her mind.

She raised her hands to his chest, learning the texture of his skin, savoring the ripple of tendons over each rib. Her senses came alive. Nerves flickered, unfurled, tightened in anticipation. His muscles tensed beneath her touch. His groan encouraged her to venture further. She guided her hands over his hips to his hard buttocks, pressing him more fully against her.

She felt his sex jerk against her thigh. Her nerves were tightening while her body softened. She yelped in dismay when Chris flipped her over on her stomach, pushed her tumbled mass of black hair aside and nuzzled her nape. Then he kissed an agonizing slow path down her spine, stopping to fondle the taut mounds of her bottom.

"What are you doing?" Sophia asked as he nipped her playfully. Though she liked what he did, she didn't know where it was leading.

"Don't be impatient," Chris growled. "I'm not going to hurt you. There are many ways to make love. I intend to teach you all of them."

He pushed her knees up so that her bottom was

raised. Never had she felt so exposed and vulnerable. His heat scorched her as he pressed himself against her. He bent over her, kissed her neck, her back, then grasped her breasts in both hands and teased her nipples. She stiffened when she felt his sex penetrate her.

"You're still so tight," Chris whispered against her ear. "It won't hurt this time, I promise."

He slid into her velvety folds, teased a ragged moan from her throat and felt her relax. Flexing his hips, he slid in all the way. She was hot, wet; he felt her stretching to accommodate him. She felt so damn good, Chris had to force himself to remain still lest he spill immediately.

Sophia gasped and wriggled her hips against him.

"Don't," he warned. "Wait until I regain control. Do you realize how good you feel?"

"I hope as good as you feel to me."

Her words pushed him close to the edge. Flexing his hips, he began to move, pushing deep, then withdrawing, again and again, faster, ever faster. Blood thundered through his veins as he pounded inside her, his hands grasping her hips to hold her still. His climax hovered so close he feared he would burst. But he gritted his teeth and hung on.

"Chris . . ."

Her passion served to inflame him. He didn't know if he could wait much longer. "Come to me, Sophia. I need you now."

Her eyes widened, her body stiffened, and then she screamed. He absorbed the full power of her release and matched it with his own. He kept thrusting until her tremors subsided and she went boneless beneath him. Then he rolled off and collapsed beside her, panting harshly.

He glanced at Sophia. Her eyes were closed; a tear slipped from beneath her eyelid and trickled down her cheek.

"Did I hurt you?"

She shook her head. "Not physically."

He rose up on his elbow, watching her closely. "What is that supposed to mean?"

"After Desmond's death I gave up on marriage. But I secretly vowed that if I ever found a man who would have me, it would have to be a love match. You don't love me, Chris."

Unable to reply, unwilling to admit to uncharted feelings, Chris left the bed and began to dress. Guilt rode him, though he had no idea why. He was marrying Sophia for her own good. Their marriage would save her from her brother's evil machinations as well as from men like Rigby. Chris didn't have to love Sophia to marry her. All he was required to do was treat her well and protect her. Those things he was quite willing to do.

"Your silence speaks volumes about your feelings for me," Sophia choked out.

"Very few people marry for love," Chris replied. "You need my protection; why can't that be enough?" He strode to the door.

"Chris, wait!"

He turned. "What is it?"

"Why won't you let me seek employment? If something turns up in Spanish Town or Ocho Rios, I see no reason not to accept the post. I'll be far enough away that you won't have to set eyes on me again."

"Forget it, Sophia. If the slaves revolt, you won't be safe anywhere but at Sunset Hill. As of today, my slaves are free. The only way you can remain in my home, under my protection, is to become my wife."

"Is that why you went to Headquarters House today?"

"Yes. I signed the papers today. Everything is legal and binding. I'm going to ask Mundo to arrange a meeting with the field hands and their families tonight. I intend to ask them to remain as paid workers."

"Will I see you at dinner this evening?"

"Probably not. I'll eat in the kitchen with Mundo before the meeting."

Chris left Sophia lying in bed, even though his body was far from sated. Would he ever get enough of her? As he mounted Atlas and rode to the distillery, he wondered if marrying Sophia would ease his guilt over Desmond's death, or cause him to remember his friend every time he looked at her. He sighed. When he made love to Sophia, Desmond ceased to exist.

He told himself it was Sophia's ripe body that enthralled him, her passionate response to his lovemaking, the sweetness of her kisses. That was what made him want her for his wife.

Love wasn't an issue between him and Sophia. It could never be part of their relationship. Their marriage would be based on mutual lust and Sophia's need for protection. Any stronger emotion would compromise his principles. The last thing he wanted was to forget Desmond, the friend he had killed in the name of love.

That evening Chris waited in an open field near the distillery for the workers to arrive. Torches placed in strategic places illuminated the area. As the slaves approached the meeting place, Chris searched their faces. Most appeared defeated, some angry, others just plain weary.

"They don't know what to expect," Mundo said. "They barely know you. The previous master left the plantation in the hands of cruel overseers."

"I dismissed those men as soon as I realized what was going on. I don't believe in slavery, as you well know, nor do I condone cruel and inhuman punishment."

Mundo began counting heads. When all fifty men and women had arrived, Chris stepped onto an overturned barrel and raised his hands for quiet. The rumble of voices ceased as fifty pairs of black eyes gazed up at him. Chris couldn't help wondering how he would feel if he were in their shoes.

Frightened, he supposed; wary and helpless certainly. Slaves existed at the whim of their white masters, who held the power of life or death. Insurrections had occurred many times during Jamaica's troubled history. All had been quashed by the militia at the cost of countless lives.

"Sunset Hill cannot exist without you," he began, looking from face to face. "While I need each and every one of you, I don't want you as slaves. I'm asking you to work for me as free men. I want you to work for me because you want to, not because I own you and you have no choice."

Blank stares met his words. Did they not know what he was offering? Were they so oppressed that they couldn't grasp the concept of freedom?

"As of today, you are all free men and women. This very day, each of you will receive a document freeing you from the yoke of slavery."

It started as a murmur and soon escalated into a crescendo of sound, rising ever louder. A woman wailed and fell to her knees. Others followed suit. A large man whose ebony skin glistened in the torchlight stepped forward.

"Are we really free, master? All of us?"

Chris nodded. "Every last one of you. I hope, however, that you will continue to work for me for wages. You are the blood and guts of Sunset Hill. I cannot prosper without you. There's work available for the women at the manor house, if they so desire. I've placed Chuba in charge of the hiring."

What happened next was like an explosion. The former slaves were all talking at once, some singing, others lifting their arms, praising God. A few remained skeptical.

"They want to celebrate, Captain," Mundo said.

"Let them. Give them tomorrow off to decide if they wish to stay and work for wages. Impress upon them that they will have improved quarters and can come and go as they please as long as they put in a full day's work for a full day's pay. Report back to me tomorrow night, after they have made their decisions."

Chris returned to the house. Chuba met him at the door.

"They know, Chuba. Now it's up to them to decide what they wish to do."

"I speak for everyone when I say thank you, Captain. From the day you walked in the door, I knew you would be different from other white masters."

Chris clapped Chuba's shoulder. "In order to make this plantation successful, I need men willing to work. But I won't force anyone to stay, nor punish anyone who wishes to leave."

"It is inevitable that some will choose to leave."

"I expect it, but they will be replaced by free men of color." He glanced around. "Where is Miss Carlisle?"

"She ate supper alone in her room and is still there."

Chris forced himself to walk past Sophia's door

without stopping, but Sophia must have heard his footsteps, for she flung the panel open.

"Chris, what happened?"

"I told them they were free."

"How did they take it?"

"Listen—do you hear the drums? They're celebrating."

"Will they stay?"

"Most of them, I hope. I suspect there are some who will join the Maroons in the mountains. Freedom is a heady experience; some might not know how to handle it."

"You're a good man, Christian Radcliff."

Chris stared at her. "I killed my best friend; most people would call me a murderer. Good night, Sophia." He walked away.

Shaking her head, Sophia retreated inside her room and closed the door, starkly aware that the passing years hadn't healed Chris. Desmond's death had left him raw and hurting inside. Chris had forgiven neither himself nor her, and it seemed he never would. How could his wounds heal with her living in his home to remind him of that tragic day?

Sophia saw little of Chris during the following days. It was a busy time of year for planters, and it seemed there was always something needing his attention. As Chris had predicted, about two-thirds of the freed slaves remained to work for wages, while the remaining third left. Until replacements could be found and hired, Chris was left shorthanded.

Summer had arrived with a vengeance. There was little difference in temperature between night and day;

both were hot and humid, making sleep uncomfortable. Chris said nothing more about a wedding, and Sophia didn't press him. Yet, for some unexplained reason, he refused to let her leave. He hadn't attempted to make love to her again, either. Sophia existed in a vacuum, feeling neither wanted nor loved. Paradise wasn't nearly so wonderful with no one to share it with.

Two days later, Sophia was sitting in a window seat in the parlor, reading a book, when she heard Chuba admit a visitor.

"Captain Radcliff is at the distillery," she heard Chuba say. "I'll send someone to fetch him immediately. Please wait for him in the parlor."

"Others will be arriving," the visitor said. "Tell Radcliff to hurry along; it's important."

Sophia froze. That voice! She started to flee through the door, but it was too late. Sir Oscar Rigby had already entered the room. He stopped abruptly when he saw her. The smile he gave her did not reach his eyes.

"You're still here. I did wonder, you know. I looked for a wedding announcement, but obviously Radcliff has no intention of marrying his whore."

"What are you doing here?" Sophia asked, doing her best to ignore his insult.

"I have business with Radcliff. Have you written to your brother since you arrived in Jamaica?"

"That's none of your business."

"It is now. I wrote to him."

"How dare you!" She glanced at the door, wondering how long it would take Chris to arrive from the distillery. "Please excuse me; I have business elsewhere." Head held high, she walked past him.

Rigby grasped her arm and swung her around to

face him. "You owe me, missy. One way or another, I'm going to have you. I know it's too much to hope that you're still untouched, but it doesn't matter. Caldwell still owes me a gambling debt. You were supposed to repay it with your body, and I have every intention of collecting."

Sophia struggled to free herself from Rigby's punishing grip. "You're hurting me. Let me go."

"You heard my fiancée, let her go."

Chris's voice held a note of menace. Sophia was sure he would have done Rigby serious damage if the older man hadn't released her.

"What are you doing here, Rigby? Didn't I warn you about annoying Miss Carlisle?"

"It's not your fiancée I've come to see, it's you," Rigby replied, sending Sophia a disparaging look. "The others will arrive soon."

"The others? What's this about, Rigby?"

The "others" arrived before Rigby could answer Chris's question. Lord Chester, Mr. Wombly and Mr. Humbart from neighboring plantations were ushered into the parlor.

"Gentlemen," Chris greeted. "To what do I owe the pleasure?"

"We need to talk, Radcliff," Chester said.

"It sounds serious."

"It is. We heard you freed your slaves."

"Ah," Chris said, "so that's what this is about."

"You had no right!" Rigby charged.

Chris angled a glance at Sophia. "Before you leave, my dear, I would like to make known to you Mr. Wombly and Mr. Humbart. You already know the other two gentlemen. Wombly, Humbart—Miss Carlisle, my fiancée."

Sophia recognized a dismissal when she heard one and promptly excused herself.

Chris made sure everyone was seated before offering the men refreshments. They accepted a tot of rum all around, then got down to business.

"What you did affects all of us," Chester charged. "Our plantations cannot survive without slave labor."

Chris counted to ten before speaking. "I disagree. I cannot abide slavery in any form and followed my conscience."

"How many of your slaves agreed to work for wages after you gave them their freedom?" Wombly asked.

"About two-thirds."

"Two-thirds, bah!" Rigby spat. "You're a fool, Radcliff. This is a busy time—how will you replace them?"

"I posted notices in Kingston, advertising for free men of color willing to work for wages."

"Any takers?" Humbart asked.

"I hired five men just yesterday and expect more to show up."

"What you did was irresponsible," Rigby argued. "You've caused problems for all of us planters. Word has spread. Our slaves are restless. They grow more agitated than ever."

Chris shrugged. "Whose fault is that? If you treated your slaves like human beings, there wouldn't be unrest among them. You could free them as I did mine."

"Insufferable bastard," Rigby muttered.

"There will be none of that, Rigby," Chester warned. "Keep your animosity to yourself. None of us like what Captain Radcliff did, but we have to live with it."

"I'm not going to free my slaves," Rigby maintained.

"Nor I," Wombly agreed.

"My plantation has to support my growing family," Humbart added. "I cannot manage without slaves."

"I cannot tell any of you what to do. Each of you must live with your own conscience."

"Pretty words, but I don't buy them," Rigby spat. "You're a hypocrite, Radcliff. Doesn't living with a woman who's not your wife prick your conscience? If you intended to wed Miss Carlisle, you would have done so by now."

"See here, Rigby," Chester chided, "you have no right to insult a man in his own home."

"I'm just saying what the rest of you are too polite to say," Rigby retorted.

"This is getting out of hand," Wombly observed. "We came here to discuss slavery, not the captain's fiancée."

"Agreed," Humbart injected.

"Gentlemen," Chris began, "there is nothing further to discuss. My slaves have been freed, and that's the end of it."

"Captain Radcliff is right, gentlemen," Chester conceded. "The deed is done; nothing will change it. I suggest we return home and see what develops. Perhaps in time we, too, will see the wisdom in freeing slaves."

Chris inclined his head. "Thank you, my lord. I didn't think my simple act would arouse such a firestorm."

"It's not all that simple," Rigby muttered. "There's going to be trouble, mark my words."

"I agree," Chris said. "But it's been coming for a long time. Though I haven't been a plantation owner long, I can taste rebellion in the air. That's why I acted

167

so swiftly in freeing my slaves. I wanted to save Sunset Hill."

"We can handle anything the slaves bring on," Rigby bragged. "Rebellion is a way of life in Jamaica, but nothing has ever come of it. The slaves eventually return to their white masters and life goes on."

The men rose as if on cue. "It's time we left, Captain," Chester said. "Sorry to have disturbed you. We're all a little concerned, but who wouldn't be? We have families to protect."

"I understand," Chris replied.

"Your fiancée hasn't been to visit my wife," Chester continued. "Agatha said to be sure to tell Miss Carlisle that she is eager to help plan her wedding." He sent Chris a stern look. "There *is* going to be a wedding, isn't there?"

"Indeed. I thought a fall wedding would give me time to settle in here and Sophia the opportunity to grow accustomed to the climate. Jamaican summers can be brutal."

Chester and the others took their leave, but Rigby lingered in the doorway. "I know you're not going to marry her, Radcliff. She's good enough for a whore but not for a wife. Tell you what. I'll take her off your hands. Name your price."

His face as dark as a storm cloud, Chris thundered, "Get out! Don't ever darken my door again."

"Come now, Radcliff, you can't blame a man for wanting what he's owed. Tell you what. Give her to me for a week to settle Caldwell's debt and you can have her after I've finished." He leaned close and whispered. "We'll keep this between us, just you and me. No one else need know."

Rage exploded inside Chris. The man had no principles, no morals. He was lower than an insect. There was only one way to deal with a reprobate like that. Clenching his fist, he sent it flying into Rigby's face. Looking stunned, Rigby staggered and tumbled to the ground, howling like a banshee as blood spurted from his nose.

"Chuba!" Chris roared. The servant appeared immediately. "Escort Sir Rigby into his carriage and send it on its way."

Turning on his heel, Chris walked away. If he remained a moment longer, he would stomp Rigby into the ground and damn the consequences. To his chagrin, he found Sophia standing in the foyer.

"What did those men want?" she asked. "What did Rigby say to anger you so?"

"Come into my study, we'll talk there." Sophia preceded him into the study; he closed the door behind them. "Sit down, Sophia. Would you like something to drink?"

Sophia shook her head and dropped into a chair. "Those men were angry because you freed your slaves, weren't they?"

Chris inclined his head. "I did what my conscience demanded. If they don't like it, that's their problem. But that's not why I wanted to talk to you. What was Rigby saying to you in the parlor when I interrupted?"

"He doesn't frighten me, Chris."

"That's not what I asked. I could almost cut the tension with a knife. If I'm not mistaken, he had his hands on you."

"Very well; he tried to stop me from leaving the room. He said he wrote to Rayford, telling him where to find me."

Chris's eyes narrowed. "What else?"

Anger flashed in Sophia's green eyes. "He said he intended to have me. I disagreed with him."

"That does it!" Chris growled. "Clearly, the man is a menace. He won't dare threaten you after we marry. Tomorrow we'll call on Lady Chester. She offered to help plan our wedding, and you're going to accept her offer. I'm sure a small affair can be arranged. Shall we say four weeks?"

Sophia gasped. "You want us to marry in four weeks?"

"Didn't I just say so?"

"Chris, you don't have to do this."

"Yes, I do," he replied.

"I can protect myself."

The uncompromising set of his jaw remained firm. "That's beside the point. Everyone expects us to marry."

Didn't the contentious woman know she had no choice in the matter? Both her fate and his had been sealed the day she set foot on his ship. Like it or not, they would wed.

Sophia shook her head. She remembered with stark clarity the day Chris had told her he had killed Desmond. He had looked at her as if he never wanted to see her again. As if he couldn't stand the sight of her. Then he had disappeared. She had suffered through the scandal, and abandonment by the man she loved, with her head held high. She wasn't a sniveling, helpless female. She had thwarted Sir Oscar Rigby once, she could do it again.

Her mind wandered back in time, to the irresistible young man Chris had been. She had wanted him from the beginning, even knowing she couldn't have him. Nothing she had said to him had been untrue. But at seventeen she had been too young to realize she was setting the scene for a tragedy.

"Why is marrying me repugnant to you?"

Repugnant? Dear God, if he only knew. "Very well, I'll marry you, Chris, but never say I didn't warn you."

Was that relief she saw in his eyes?

"Warn me about what?"

"I'm trouble. You said it yourself."

"I think I can handle your kind of trouble."

Sophia stared at him, picturing his powerful body in her mind's eye, all hard planes and bronzed skin. No matter how hard she tried, she could not purge his naked image from her mind, nor could she banish the fluttering in her belly every time they were together. He would be shocked if he knew how desperately she wanted him. She would never expose her vulnerability to him, however, unless he reciprocated her feelings, which Sophia seriously doubted would ever come to pass.

Sophia dug deep in her soul for an answer to her dilemma. What were her choices? Instead of marrying Chris, she could return to England. She discarded that notion as soon as it was born. She could continue her search for employment. As if anyone would hire her, she thought wryly.

She could marry Chris and make the best of their life together.

"Stop thinking about a way out of this, Sophia. If I can tolerate a marriage between us, so can you."

Head held high, she faced him squarely. "Very well, Chris, I'll marry you. I still say it's a devil's pact we're making, but I'm game if you are."

Chris reached for her hands and pulled her out of the chair. "We'll always have this, Sophia." Then he kissed her, and her doubts fled like leaves before the wind.

Her mouth opened beneath his. His tongue slipped inside, fencing with hers; his teeth nipped the tip of her tongue. Her breath faltered, nearly stopped when he clasped her face in both hands and thrust his tongue deep inside her mouth.

She groaned and melted against him. Chris was right, the attraction between them was raw and immediate; perhaps it would be enough.

She prayed it would be.

Chapter Ten

Despite that soul-destroying kiss in his study, Chris did not visit Sophia's room that night. The following morning, Kateena told her that there had been a fire in the cane fields, and that Chris had left the house shortly after she retired.

Chris was eating his breakfast in the dining room when Sophia entered. He raised his head. "Good morning."

"Good morning," Sophia replied as she took her seat and waited for Chuba to pour her coffee. She ordered eggs and toasted bread, took a sip of scalding coffee and studied Chris over the cup rim. He looked tired and disheveled, as if he hadn't slept or changed his clothes.

"Kateena said there was a fire last night. I hope it wasn't serious."

"Any fire is serious," Chris said. "But fortunately, this one was discovered in time and little damage was done."

"Any clues how it started?"

Chris set down his fork and looked at her, his face grim. "The fire was deliberately set."

"What? Who—"

"I don't know, but I have my suspicions. I've arranged for guards to patrol the fields at night."

"You look exhausted. Did you get any sleep last night?"

"No. I just returned from the fields."

"You should lie down."

"I'm fine, Sophia, don't fret. I'll be ready to leave for Orchid Manor after I bathe and change. Will eleven o'clock suit? I sent word ahead of our impending visit. Wear your new riding habit."

"Why the rush? We can go tomorrow, when you're feeling more yourself."

"You're not going to talk me into putting this off, Sophia. If you intend to remain on the island, we'll do what is expected of us. I can't see another alternative; can you?"

Sophia sighed. There was no alternative. "I'll be ready when you are."

Chris nodded and devoted himself to his breakfast. Sophia's food arrived, and she, too, fell silent. Her marriage to Chris was really going to happen, whether either of them wanted it or not.

Chris was waiting in the foyer when Sophia descended the stairs at precisely eleven o'clock. The dressmaker had done herself proud with Sophia's wardrobe. The riding habit had been one of the first outfits to arrive. It was made of green linen, the color complementing her eyes and the creamy gold of her fading tan. She wore a bonnet to protect her face from the summer sun, and her feet were shod in new half boots. Several pairs of slippers to match her gowns had also arrived during the past two weeks along with the boots.

"You look lovely," Chris complimented.

"Thanks to you," Sophia replied. "I've never owned so many gowns in my life. As you well know, my family was not affluent."

Chris looked away. Replying would only dredge up memories he preferred to forget. Her family's lack of finances was what had prevented Sophia from accepting Chris's offer.

"Shall we go? We've been invited to take lunch with the Chesters."

The stable lad was waiting in the courtyard with two horses, Chris's Atlas and a white mare Sophia was to ride. Chris helped her mount.

"Her name is Queen. She rather looks like one, don't you think?"

"She's beautiful," Sophia said, patting the mare's neck affectionately. "Rayford sold all our horses, including Calico, the mare Papa bought for me."

"Queen is yours," Chris said as he mounted Atlas. "Consider her a wedding present."

Sophia patted Queen's neck and spoke softly into her ear. "Thank you," she told Chris. "I love to ride."

They rode west beneath the shadow of the Blue Mountains. The heat was oppressive; not a breeze rustled the trees that grew tall and lush on either side of the narrow road. Soon they came to open fields where bushes bearing red berries grew in profusion.

"What kind of plants are those?" Sophia asked.

"Coffee. It grows extremely well on the mountainsides. Chester prefers it to sugarcane. I'm thinking of devoting a few acres to coffee in the near future, and maybe growing some tobacco."

Orchid Manor was a study of contrasts. Though the land and manor house were carefully tended and maintained, the same couldn't be said for the slave quarters. They were run-down and in need of repair. Conversely, the manor house was grand in the extreme.

"Lord Chester should be more mindful of his slaves," Sophia said as they approached the house. "I'm surprised he isn't embarrassed by the pitiful condition of their quarters."

Chris nodded grimly. He appeared as disapproving as she was. "Perhaps I will discuss the matter with Chester while you consult with Lady Agatha about the wedding."

A lad ran up to take their reins as Chris dismounted and handed Sophia down. A tall, dignified servant opened the door to Chris's knock and bowed them inside. Lord Chester came out of his study to greet them.

"I heard about the fire, Radcliff. How did it start?"

"It was deliberately set, but did little damage."

"I knew freeing your slaves was a mistake. They can do anything they want now without fear of reprisal."

"My workers didn't start the fire," Chris said.

Chester frowned. "Whom do you suspect if not your workers? My guess is that they were ordered to set the fire by 'Daddy' Sam Sharp. Everyone, including you, is in danger, even though you freed your slaves."

Agatha descended the stairs at that moment and greeted her visitors warmly. "I'm so pleased you could come," she said, grasping Sophia's hands. "My husband tells me we have a wedding to plan. You and I shall adjourn to my private sitting room while the men have their rum and cigars in the study. We'll meet them again on the veranda for luncheon."

Sophia followed Lady Chester up the stairs. She didn't know where to look first in the sumptuous home. The foyer was as grand as any she'd seen in England, all black and white marble. The wide staircase led to the second floor and a multitude of closed doors. Agatha opened a door midway down the hall and invited Sophia inside.

Dainty white furniture and pale green and cream curtains at the windows made the sitting room appear cool and inviting. Agatha invited Sophia to sit on a wicker sofa covered with colorful cushions, and sat down opposite her in a matching chair. She laced her fingers together and asked, "Would you like tea, my dear?"

Sophia shook her head. "No, thank you, I had a late breakfast."

"Then let us get down to business, shall we? I take it you've set a date."

"Four weeks from last Saturday. Will that be enough time?"

Agatha clapped her hands. "Oh, yes. I think you should be wed in the Church of St. Thomas in Kingston. Reverend Townsend will officiate, and my husband and I will host the reception at Orchid Manor after the ceremony."

It sounded as if Lady Chester had planned everything already. "That's not necessary. Sunset Hill—"

"—is too small. Besides, Lord Chester and I want to do this. We've already discussed it. Captain Radcliff is new to the island, and even though Jamaica has been one of his ports of call for many years, he doesn't know the people that we do. Planters from as far as Spanish Town and Ocho Rios will wish to attend. It will be a grand affair, my dear."

"I don't know what to say."

"Don't say anything. Just leave everything to me. I'll send out the invitations and inform Reverend Townsend of the time and date for the wedding. Now, what will you wear?"

Things were going so fast Sophia could hardly keep up. "Chris has commissioned a wardrobe for me. Almost everything has been delivered. There is a peach lace gown that would be perfect."

Agatha clapped her hands again, something she seemed to do a lot. "Wonderful! You can have your choice of flowers, but I suggest roses and orchids. Both can be found in abundance here. Leave everything to me. I do believe I was born to plan weddings." She sighed. "This is so romantic."

Agatha and Sophia continued to discuss the wedding, or rather Agatha did and Sophia listened. Sophia felt as if her world were spinning out of control. From the moment she'd stepped onto Chris's ship, she had been at Chris's mercy. For years Rayford and her father had dictated her life, and now it was Chris.

"My husband will walk you down the aisle," Agatha continued, "and I shall act as your attendant."

"I thought about having Kateena as my attendant," Sophia remarked.

"My dear," Agatha said, clucking her tongue in disapproval, "that simply won't do. Your Kateena is a servant, a former slave, a woman of color. The scandal of it would sweep the island like wildfire; it just isn't done. I'm sure Captain Radcliff would agree with me on this." She sighed heavily. "You have much to learn about the way things are done on the island."

Though Sophia wasn't happy about it, she accepted Lady Chester's edict.

Meanwhile, Chris was receiving similar advice from Lord Chester. "Agatha has decided that your wedding will be held at the Church of St. Thomas in Kingston. Since your bride has no male relatives, I will walk her down the aisle. Lady Chester and I will hold the reception at Orchid Manor."

When Chris started to protest, Chester held up his hand. "No, no, it's all settled. Agatha won't accept refusal. It will be our pleasure to host your wedding."

"That's very generous of you, my lord, but entirely unnecessary, especially since we disagree on the subject of slavery."

Chester waved aside Chris's objection. "Your wedding has nothing to do with your views on slavery. You must live with the consequences of your decision, as I must live with mine."

"Not everyone would agree with you," Chris said darkly. "One man in particular was very vocal about his disapproval."

"You're referring to Sir Rigby, I presume."

"You presume correctly. Matters of a personal nature have made me and Rigby enemies. I suspect him of firing my cane fields. Though I don't know him well, I believe him to be a vindictive man."

"Yes, well, you're right about Rigby. Few people like him. He treats his slaves like dirt and administers excessively cruel punishment for minor infractions. Though I know nothing about the animosity between you and Rigby, I suggest you watch your back."

"I have every intention of doing so." Chris paused. "While we're on the subject of slavery, I noticed your own slave quarters are in deplorable condition."

Chester cocked his head. "Actually, that fact was just brought to my attention. I intend to correct the problem immediately. I'm not a cruel man, Radcliff, just a busy one who tends to put off matters that don't seem important."

"The success of your plantation depends upon your people; I suggest you pay more attention to them and their needs. I don't mean to preach, Chester, but human beings are human beings, no matter the color of their skin."

Chester chuckled. "I'd best take care lest you make a believer of me." He slapped Chris's back. "If I'm not mistaken, that's the bell summoning us to luncheon."

The men joined the ladies on the veranda overlooking the garden, where a table had been set up for luncheon. The garden was ablaze with color—pale orchids, vibrant roses, hibiscus and bougainvillea. The lush plants were a testimony to the care of countless servants and Jamaica's tropical climate.

Sophia thoroughly enjoyed the meal, which consisted of fresh fruit, cold meats, an assortment of cheeses, delicate fish simmered in cream sauce, and fancy frosted cakes as light and delicate as a feather.

"The heat is brutal," Agatha said, fanning herself. "I should be accustomed to it by now, but summers have always been a trial to me. Shall we go inside where it's cooler?"

"I don't want to overstay our welcome," Chris said, "so Sophia and I will take our leave. Perhaps another time."

"Indeed," Agatha said. "I'll need to confer with your bride-to-be a time or two before the wedding. I'll send word to Reverend Townsend today, concerning the date and time of the ceremony."

"No need for that, my lady," Chris replied. "I will take care of it myself."

"Oh, pooh," Agatha said, pouting. "You're much too busy for that. As I told Sophia, I will handle everything. All you need do is turn up at the church on time." She tapped her chin. "I've been thinking— perhaps Sophia should move in with us until you are wed. We don't want any nasty talk about . . . well, you know."

Chris's expression hardened. "No, I don't know. I see no reason for Sophia to leave Sunset Hill. In fact, I won't hear of it."

"But . . . but . . ." Agatha sputtered.

"Leave off, Agatha," Lord Chester said kindly. "I'm sure Captain Radcliff knows what he's doing."

Sophia nearly collapsed in relief. She didn't want to leave Sunset Hill. She'd begun to think of it as home. She loved the view from her veranda, the magnificent sunsets, and everything else about the plantation. Besides, she would miss Chris. She couldn't make him love her if she had to live apart from him. Even four weeks was too long.

"Very well, then," Agatha said grudgingly, "if that's how it must be. We'll be in touch soon."

Chris and Sophia took their leave.

"Is it all right with you that Lady Chester is planning our wedding?" Chris asked as they reined their horses away from the mansion.

"It's probably for the best," Sophia replied. "We are

both new to the island. Lady Chester wants to make our wedding a grand affair, and although I would prefer a small gathering, her way will allow us to become acquainted with other planters."

Chris nodded. "I've had business dealings with a few of the men, but I don't know them or their families well. Freeing my slaves hasn't gained me any friends, but I'm certain they will attend a wedding hosted by the Chesters. People will come out of curiosity if for no other reason."

Lady Chester visited Sunset Hill frequently to confer with Sophia during the following weeks. A week before the wedding, Chris told Sophia at breakfast that he was taking her to Kingston to meet Reverend Townsend. The arrangements had been completed and everything was in place for the festive affair Lady Chester had planned. The only thing left to do was meet the reverend. Sophia was nervous. She couldn't believe she was going to marry Chris. She hadn't had a long conversation with him of late, or the opportunity to ask how he felt about their impending nuptials. He still made love to her nearly every night, but he usually left her bed before she could initiate a discussion, and he usually left the house early and returned late. Would it be this way after they were wed?

"The *Intrepid* is due to arrive any day now," Chris remarked between mouthfuls of food.

"Where has she been?" Sophia asked curiously. Any day Chris wished to converse with her was a good day.

"She carried rum to Charleston and then returned to England to pick up the carriage I ordered before I left London. I'm hoping the *Intrepid* will arrive in time for our wedding. I'd like Mr. Blaine and the crew to attend the celebration."

"I'd like that too," Sophia said. "What time should I be ready to go to Kingston?"

"Is an hour too soon? We'll take the wagon; Chandra gave me a list of staples to purchase in town."

"I'll be ready," Sophia said.

After Chris left for the distillery, Sophia summoned Kateena to help her dress for her trip to town.

"Are you excited about your wedding, mistress?" Kateena asked. She sighed dreamily. "The captain is so handsome, and he truly loves you. You're a lucky woman."

Sophia went still. "Why do you think he loves me?"

"I have seen the way he looks at you."

"He and I are rarely together, so how can you possibly know how he looks at me?"

"You do not believe me? Ask any of the servants and they will confirm what I have observed."

"I'm sure you're mistaken," Sophia contended. "Our history is long and complicated."

Kateena shrugged. "If you say so, mistress."

Sophia was ready and waiting when Chris brought around the wagon. Chuba helped her onto the bench beside Chris, and soon they were on their way. The day was hot and sultry; the threat of rain hung heavy in the air. Summer was the season of thunderstorms and something far worse. Kateena had explained about hurricanes, those violent storms spawning fierce winds that blew houses apart and uprooted trees.

Sophia swatted at the flying insects that swarmed around her bonnet, grateful for the veil that kept them off her face. She considered Jamaica a paradise, but the island did have its drawbacks. Nothing in life was perfect, not even in Paradise.

Kingston was teeming with people. Vehicles clogged King Street, making travel slow and difficult. Finally Chris pulled up before the Church of St. Thomas and set the brake. He leaped lightly to the ground and handed Sophia down. They approached the rectory together. A servant answered the door and invited them to wait in the parlor. The reverend arrived a short time later.

"Captain Radcliff"—Townsend, a tall, thin man in his mid thirties, greeted them affably—"and Miss Carlisle, welcome to Jamaica. Lady Chester has told me all about you. You are the happy couple I am to wed Saturday next. Yours will be the first marriage in St. Thomas since my arrival three years ago. Most of the planters arrive in Jamaica with wives and family in tow. And the bachelors usually return to England to marry."

Chris and Sophia made small talk and took tea with the reverend. After an hour, they took their leave.

"I am looking forward to performing your nuptials," Townsend remarked as they said their good-byes. "It's refreshing to see a young couple so in love."

Sophia shot a glance at Chris. He appeared discomfited. As for herself, she recalled Kateena's words earlier and wondered what the servants saw that made them think Chris loved her. Perhaps they judged Chris's feelings by what they saw in her. Were her eyes misty with love when she looked at Chris? Did she hang on his every word, follow him with her eyes?

"Where are we going now?" Sophia asked as Chris guided the wagon into traffic.

"To the docks to see if the *Intrepid* has arrived. Afterward, we'll visit the marketplace. Then I thought we would have lunch at the King's Arms, if that meets with your approval."

Sophia's eyes glowed. She hadn't spent this much time with Chris since . . . She couldn't recall when. "I'd like that."

The *Intrepid* hadn't arrived. "I was hoping to find her in port," Chris said, clearly disappointed. "I wanted to take you to the church in style."

Touched, Sophia laid her hand on his arm. "It doesn't matter, Chris." He didn't shake off her hand, which Sophia considered a good sign.

The visit to the marketplace was pleasant, the combination of sounds, sights and smells uniquely Jamaican. After Chris made his purchases, they headed to the King's Arms for lunch. Mr. Ludlow greeted them enthusiastically and told them he had received an invitation to their wedding and would attend. Sophia had insisted that Lady Chester invite the innkeeper.

Sophia thought lunch went well. They didn't discuss anything controversial, which made the outing all the more enjoyable. After lunch, they left the King's Arms for their return to Sunset Hill.

"Thank you for this day," Sophia began. "I wish every day could be like this."

"We will have good days and bad days, Sophia. It's inevitable, given our past."

His answer didn't satisfy Sophia. She sighed and broached the subject they both had avoided all day. "I know you're a reluctant bridegroom, and I'm truly sorry it turned out this way. There is still time to cry off."

"Stop talking nonsense, Sophia," Chris replied curtly. "We both know ours isn't a love match, but we are adult enough to muddle through this marriage."

Curbing her sudden jolt of anger, Sophia said, "Muddle through? I don't want to muddle through. I want a real husband, Chris. If you can't be what I want, then cry off now."

Chris reined the horse to a stop on a deserted stretch of road and glared at her. Sophia glared back. "I thought we'd worked through this," he bit out. "You needed protection and I offered it. Once we are wed, you will never have to worry about Rigby or Caldwell again."

The words that came out of Chris's mouth hurt. Why didn't he understand that their marriage meant so much more to her? All her life she'd looked forward to marriage as the culmination of all her dreams, a union that would provide a wealth of love and need. A need Chris didn't intend to fulfill.

"I mean it, Chris. Don't go through with this marriage if you intend to ignore me or find another woman to give you what you need."

"Dammit, Sophia, you ought to know by now that I want you in my bed. If you want sex, I will give it to you unstintingly. If you need protection, I will be there for you. What more do you want?"

Love. "I don't want you to feel trapped. Marriage is more than the need for protection or sex on demand. How can you possibly want me when you have shown so little interest in me these past weeks?"

"You think I don't want you? How can you believe that when I'm in your bed most nights?" Chris said angrily. "Perhaps I've done too good a job of controlling my lust."

As if to prove his words, he pulled her against him.

"Chris, I—"

He swept away her words with his lips and tongue, his kiss demanding and thoroughly intoxicating. He tangled his fingers in her hair, moving her head so that their lips meshed fully. Shivers of pleasure danced along her scalp and down her spine.

The heat of her body set his on fire. She moved against him, and if they hadn't been in the middle of a public road, he would have dragged her beneath him and thrust himself into her sweet heat.

He broke the kiss with a ragged groan. "This is neither the time nor the place."

Sophia's expression nearly unmanned him. Did she care for him that much? Should he trust what he saw in her eyes? He took several deep breaths, willing his erection to subside.

"Is there ever going to be a time and place?" Sophia challenged. "You say you want me, but all I see is a man who constantly fights his attraction to me."

He picked up the reins, and the wagon jerked forward. "A man needs to protect himself, Sophia."

"From what?"

Chris muttered under his breath something she didn't understand.

"Prove you want me, Chris," she challenged. "Make love to me when we reach Sunset Hill."

Chris hardened instantly, his hands tightening on the reins. "You know I can't. The plantation is shorthanded right now, and this is a hectic time of year. Can't you wait until tonight?"

Chris saw the light die in Sophia's eyes and immediately regretted his words. He knew that hurricanes arrived without warning this time of year, and that volcanoes were always a threat. So much could happen before the cane was harvested. Chris had to work night and day until the wedding to bring in the crop.

Sophia grew quiet, too quiet. "I'm sorry, Sophia. I don't mean to sound harsh, but the reality is I'm a planter trying to make a success of things without slaves. I don't want to cry off. If I did, I would have done so before now."

Sophia lifted her face to his. Unshed tears wet her lashes. He looked away. Her next words made him cringe inside.

"I know why you won't cry off. It's so obvious. After we wed, you intend to withhold your affection in order to punish me for Desmond's death."

"Do you truly think I would do that?"

"I . . . don't know."

Neither did Chris. Did he want to punish Sophia for Desmond's death? He might have in the beginning, but things had changed. Now he was fighting tooth and nail to keep from falling under Sophia's spell. Chris wished he could forget that he had killed his best friend, but the guilt would always remain whether or not he married Sophia.

Rain clouds threatened Sophia's wedding day. Though she knew it wouldn't make Chris love her, she wanted to look her very best. After Kateena had dressed her, she gazed into her bedroom mirror. The peach lace gown had short sleeves and frothy layers that revealed the darker peach underskirt. A matching ribbon caught the gown high under her breasts, while the skirt skimmed the gentle swell of her hips. The mirror told her the color complemented her creamy complexion. Her tan had faded, leaving her skin with just a hint of gold.

"You look lovely," Kateena sighed as she piled Sophia's hair atop her head in a froth of curls. "The loveliest bride I've ever seen."

"Thank you, Kateena. What time are the Chesters supposed to arrive?" Since they had a carriage and Chris did not, the Chesters had offered to take her to Kingston in theirs.

"You have plenty of time."

They heard a commotion in the foyer. Sophia sent Kateena to find out what was happening.

"The captain's ship arrived in port," Kateena explained when she returned. "There is a brand new carriage sitting in front of the house."

Sophia was genuinely pleased. "I'm glad. Chris wanted the *Intrepid*'s crew to attend the wedding, and now they can."

A few minutes later, Chris brought her the news himself. Kateena answered his knock but wouldn't let him inside to speak to Sophia.

"You can't see your bride, Captain. It is bad luck."

"Sophia, can you hear me?" Chris called.

"I hear you, Chris. Kateena told me your ship has arrived."

"Blaine delivered my new carriage. I'm driving it to the church. Lord and Lady Chester will arrive soon for you. I'll meet you at the altar."

"Yes, at the altar," Sophia replied. She heard his steps retreating and wanted to run after him. Wanted to feel his arms around her, wanted him to reassure her, tell her their marriage wouldn't be the farce she expected.

Of course, she didn't.

Sophia arrived at the church with the Chesters. Judging from the number of carriages and horses parked around the church, Sophia knew that the Chesters' friends had arrived in force.

"Oh, what a wonderful turnout," Agatha gushed. "Are you ready, my dear? Don't forget your bouquet."

"As ready as I'll ever be," Sophia replied, clutching her bouquet of roses and orchids as if they were a lifeline.

"Then take my dear husband's arm and let us commence."

Lady Chester was the first to enter the church. She lingered in the vestibule until the reverend motioned the wedding party forward. Sophia watched her start down the aisle, and then felt a tug on her arm as Lord Chester stepped out smartly. She glanced toward the altar and faltered when she saw Chris.

Formally dressed in black and white, his powerful body looked taut and fit beneath his clothing. His handsome face showed little of his thoughts. Her own thoughts were emotionally charged. Soon Chris would be hers, all hers. Though his proposal had stunned her, he hadn't begged off, and soon they would be husband and wife. Was this what Chris really wanted?

Sophia scarcely recognized anyone in the crowded church except for the members of Chris's crew. She smiled at them in passing and took a measure of comfort in their presence. Then she was standing next to Chris as Lord Chester melted away. She sensed Chris's tension, but when she looked into his eyes, she saw a spark of something she couldn't read, something that gave her a glimmer of hope.

Reverend Townsend began the ceremony. Sophia tried to listen, but her mind kept wandering. She answered when it was expected of her, and then she heard the reverend ask, "If anyone knows why this couple shouldn't be wed, speak now or forever keep your peace."

"Stop the wedding!"

The entire congregation turned toward the door. Two men stood backlit in the opening.

"Who are you, sir?" Reverend Townsend asked.

"I am Sophia Carlisle's guardian; she doesn't have my permission to wed."

Rayford! Sophia couldn't believe her eyes. What was he doing here? She felt Chris's arm encircle her and took comfort in it. Then she recognized Sir Oscar Rigby standing behind Ray, and she sagged against Chris.

Chris's arm tightened as he leaned down and whispered in her ear, "Chin up, Sophia. They can't hurt you."

Sophia desperately wanted to believe him.

Chapter Eleven

"Please continue the service, Reverend Townsend," Chris commanded.

Caldwell started down the aisle. "I am Viscount Caldwell, Sophia Carlisle's guardian, and I demand to be heard."

The murmur of the congregation rose in volume, earning a stern look from the reverend.

Sophia shrugged out of Chris's protective embrace to confront her stepbrother. "You are not my guardian, Ray. I am past the age of guardianship. You cannot dictate my life."

From behind him, Rigby hissed into Ray's ear, "Stop the wedding now, Caldwell. The woman belongs to me. Pay your debt or go to prison."

Chris pushed Sophia behind him. "You heard my fiancée, Caldwell. She is old enough to do as she pleases. And it pleases both of us to wed."

"Sophia is a wanted woman in England," Caldwell said in a voice only Chris could hear. "She attacked Sir Oscar for no reason and left him for dead."

Chris smiled at Sophia, his opinion of her rising. "How very clever of her. Fortunately, this is not England, is it?"

"I can press charges here," Rigby maintained. "This is English territory, after all."

"Try it and you're a dead man," Chris growled. "Now step back, both of you, and let the good reverend continue the ceremony." He turned his back on Caldwell and Rigby.

Though Sophia thought it a bad idea to turn her back on either man, she trusted Chris as she faced the reverend.

"Is Viscount Caldwell your guardian?" Reverend Townsend asked.

"No, I am no longer under his guardianship," Sophia asserted. "I am four and twenty years old. Please continue, Reverend."

"Very well, then. By the law vested in me by the Church of England, I now pronounce you husband and wife." He smiled at Chris. "You may kiss your bride."

Sophia's breath faltered as Chris turned her toward him, raised her chin with his thumb and forefinger and kissed her full on the mouth. If his kiss was meant as a display of possession, Chris succeeded admirably. She heard someone curse—probably Rayford—and more than a few titters from the congregation. And still Chris continued to kiss her. When he finally released her mouth, her knees wobbled like jelly and she had to hang on to Chris to keep from falling.

With an arm around her waist, he hurried her down the aisle to the front of the church amid a scattering of applause. They paused briefly to receive congratulations from the congregation, and then Chris handed her into his new carriage.

"Excuse me a moment," Chris said. "I need to speak to Blaine before we leave." He conversed briefly with the new captain of the *Intrepid*, then returned to the carriage. With a signal to Mundo, the carriage jolted forward.

"I'm sorry," Sophia said. "Ray was the last person I expected to see in Jamaica. Sir Oscar told me he had written to Ray, but I have no idea how he came by the money to travel to Jamaica."

"It wouldn't surprise me if Rigby asked his factor in England to pay Caldwell's passage. He would do it just to bedevil us. Blaine told me Caldwell arrived aboard the *Intrepid*."

Dismayed, Sophia groaned. Why was Chris staring at her? Did he blame her for the interruption of their ceremony? The intensity of Chris's gaze made her squirm in her seat. What was he thinking?

"Rigby must want you badly," Chris finally said. "He thinks he owns you."

Sophia snorted. "It's rather late for that. I'm a married woman now."

"Nevertheless, he still wants you."

"That's his problem," Sophia sniffed. She grew serious. "Can he press charges against me in Jamaica?"

"He probably could, but I won't let it happen. You're safe now, Sophia. Our marriage is legal; it would serve no purpose to press charges. He has nothing to gain from it."

"Satisfaction," Sophia murmured. "He's a vindictive man; I'm not sure our marriage will prevent him from trying to hurt me. He brought Rayford all this way to stop our marriage. But Ray is the one who owes him, not me. I had nothing to do with that gambling debt."

"Don't let it upset you. Lord Chester has a great deal

of influence with the governor of Jamaica, and he doesn't like Rigby. He'll support any claim you make in your defense, if it comes to that. Personally, I don't think it will. I don't make idle threats; I think Rigby knows that by now."

"Marrying me wasn't a good idea, Chris. I told you that, but you refused to listen. Why did you insist on marrying me when it isn't really what you want? I'm trouble—you said it yourself."

"Let it go, Sophia. We've already been over this. Think what would have happened if Caldwell took you back to England after Rigby got his money's worth out of you."

Sophia didn't want to think about Ray and Rigby anymore. She wanted to believe Chris loved her, even if he didn't. She wanted to believe her marriage was forever, and that Chris felt the same. Sophia knew she was only fooling herself, but the truth hurt too much, so she decided to live her life as if her marriage was based on love. And indeed it did, for she loved Chris dearly.

"We're here," Chris said as the carriage stopped in front of Orchid Manor. Chris handed her down, and they stood on the steps to greet their guests. First to arrive were Lord and Lady Chester.

"My dear, what a ghastly scene at the church," Agatha said. "Forgive me for saying this, but Caldwell cannot be a nice man."

"I cut my ties with my stepbrother the day I left England. I know exactly the kind of man he is."

"He forced me to invite him to your reception. Forgive me for not asking you first, but it all happened so fast."

Sophia gritted her teeth. Would she never be free of Rayford's machinations?

"I hope you didn't invite Rigby," Chris said. "That would be above too much."

"Indeed not," Lord Chester replied. "The man is an abomination."

"We won't keep you. Guests are waiting to greet you, and I must see that everything is in place for the reception," Agatha said as she and her husband continued past them into the house.

By ones and twos, people filed past the newlyweds, smiling and offering congratulations. Rayford was last in line, having waited until all the guests had entered the house.

"How dare you interrupt my wedding?" Sophia blasted. "Whatever were you thinking?"

"Sir Oscar paid my passage. Besides, I needed to escape my creditors. Rigby's offer couldn't have arrived at a better time."

"I advise you not to make trouble for my wife," Chris said with quiet menace. "The *Intrepid* will return to England soon; I'll be happy to arrange for your return passage."

Caldwell sneered. "You're not going to get rid of me that easily, Radcliff. I don't know how the two of you got back together after all these years, but I certainly intend to benefit from the match."

"How so?" Chris asked coolly.

"I need blunt."

"To repay Rigby the gambling debt you owe him, I assume. I understand you sold Sophia's virginity to Rigby, and that Sophia found a way to thwart your evil plan for her."

Sophia could tell by the tautness of Chris's voice that he was very close to tossing Ray out on his ear, and she didn't blame him.

Caldwell didn't back down from the accusation. "Sophia was contributing nothing to the support of the family. You're the one who killed her beau and ruined her chances of marrying well. You owe me, Radcliff. Since I'm in a magnanimous mood, I'm only demanding two thousand pounds for the privilege of marrying my sister."

"Get out!" Chris hissed from between clenched teeth. "You'll not get one farthing from me."

Lord Chester appeared in the doorway. "Are you two coming in? Everyone is waiting for the bride and groom. Are you coming, Lord Caldwell?"

"Unfortunately, Lord Caldwell has just recalled a previous engagement. He will be leaving immediately. Isn't that right, Lord Caldwell?"

Sophia waited with bated breath. Ray's face was turning a mottled shade of red. She'd seen that look before and knew he was furious. How furious remained to be seen. She also knew that Ray was a coward. If he intended to thwart Chris, he would do nothing overt, but wait to strike when Chris least expected it.

"I'm leaving," Caldwell said, "but you haven't heard the last from me."

"I'll count the days until I do," Chris replied sarcastically as he turned away, took Sophia's hand and led her inside.

Chris fumed in impotent rage. Though he tried to show a happy face during the wedding luncheon and reception that followed, he seethed inwardly. What galled Chris the most was the fact that Caldwell was demanding money from him. Caldwell was a fool if he thought Chris would give in to his demands.

Though Chris might not love Sophia, she was his wife and under his protection. Caldwell had treated her abominably. She wasn't a piece of flesh to be bought and sold.

Chris's gaze wandered over Sophia. She was so beautiful it hurt his eyes to look at her. If he wasn't careful, he would lose his heart to her all over again.

Was that what this wedding was all about? Chris wondered ruefully. Had he already lost his heart to the woman who'd broken it seven years ago? That thought made him cringe. He didn't want to fall in love with Sophia again.

"What are you thinking, Chris?" Sophia asked. "You're so quiet. People will think you are a reluctant groom."

He shrugged. "Let them think what they want. No one has to know about our past."

Sophia sighed. "You're never going to let me forget Desmond, are you?"

His answer was forestalled when Lord Chester offered a toast, followed by another from Dirk Blaine. By the time the toasts had ended, Chris was ready to leave the reception so he could have his wife to himself.

"It's time to leave," he whispered into her ear. "Wait for me in the foyer while I find Lord and Lady Chester and thank them."

A little woozy from rum punch and the heat, Sophia walked to the foyer. But the possibility of catching a cool breeze outside drew her through the door, held open for her by a servant. She breathed deeply of a freshening wind that blew in from the sea.

"Don't think you can escape me that easily," a voice growled.

Sophia stared into the gathering darkness, her eyes widening when Rigby stepped out from the shrubbery. "What are you doing here?" she demanded.

"I certainly didn't come to wish you well. I was a fool to believe Caldwell could stop the wedding. He's a weakling."

"I agree, you are a fool. Rayford has no control over me, and neither do you."

She shook her head to banish her sluggishness. Her scrambled brains and slow reaction showed the effects of drinking too many toasts raised to her and Chris's happiness.

"What do you want?" she asked. "There's nothing you can do now to hurt me."

"I beg to differ. I want revenge. You tied me up and then bashed me on the head after I fell down the stairs. I was bruised for weeks afterward."

"Apparently, I didn't put enough muscle into the blow. Did you expect me to let you assault me?"

"I paid for that right. Now I expect to get what I paid for. I'll forget what you did to me if you accommodate me. Either that or repay my five hundred pounds plus the blunt I shelled out for Caldwell's passage to Jamaica."

"Go to hell, Sir Oscar," Sophia said sweetly. "I'm not responsible for my stepbrother's debt." She turned away.

Rigby grabbed her arm. "You're not getting off that easily. Caldwell's pockets are empty, but your husband is flush with blunt. I know because I made inquiries."

"Let me go!"

"Take heed, Sophia. Either get me the blunt or find time for me in your bed," Rigby snarled as he pulled her against him. "I always did fancy you, you know. Caldwell told me about your past with Radcliff. Your marriage sounds ill-advised. Once Radcliff tires of your body, he'll toss you out."

He tried to kiss her; she twisted her head away from

his fleshy, wet lips and pushed desperately against his chest. Suddenly Rigby released her and backed away, staring at something behind her. It was Chris, angrier than she had ever seen him. His eyes were narrowed into glittering slits, his fists knotted at his sides.

Snagging Sophia about the waist, Chris pulled her behind him and lunged at Rigby. "You bastard! I warned you once to keep away from Sophia. Do you have a death wish, Rigby?"

Rigby backed away. It was easy to see he was only comfortable bullying women and cowards like Caldwell. "I merely wanted a word with your wife."

"You weren't invited to the wedding."

Chris grasped Rigby's lapels, pushing him backward until he stumbled down the front steps. Then Chris gave him an extra push that sent him tumbling to the ground, where he sprawled inelegantly on his back. He scrambled to his feet. Chris started down the steps after him. Rigby stood his ground for several seconds before turning and disappearing into the darkness.

Sophia's knees buckled, but luckily Chris was there to steady her. "What did he want?" Chris asked.

"Money," Sophia whispered.

Chris's mouth flattened. "More than that, I'll wager."

"Chris, take me home. I told you I'd bring you nothing but trouble. You shouldn't have married me."

Without responding, Chris swept her into his arms and carried her to his carriage. The night breeze felt cool against Sophia's hot skin. Sighing, she leaned back against the squabs, thinking about the spectacle Rayford had made of her wedding. And then Sir Oscar had ruined what was left of the day.

The coach traveled slowly over the rutted roads, giving Sophia too much time to ponder her marriage to

Chris. Her husband's continued silence bothered her. She didn't know what to make of it.

"It isn't your fault, Sophia."

His voice startled her. "What?"

"Nothing that happened today was your fault. I'll take care of Caldwell and Rigby. They won't bother you again."

He sounded cold, detached. Sophia shuddered. Not an auspicious way to begin a honeymoon. She exhaled slowly. Was there going to be a honeymoon? Chris had already had her in his bed, what more could she offer him?

The carriage reached Sunset Hill and stopped before the front entrance. Chris leaped to the ground and handed Sophia down. Chuba opened the door, grinning from ear to ear. Kateena stood behind him, smiling shyly at the newlywed couple. Neither had been allowed to attend the church wedding or the reception despite Chris's willingness to have them. It just wasn't done, Lady Chester had insisted.

"Go with Kateena," Chris said. "I'll join you later."

Sophia turned toward the stairs, her heart thudding against her ribcage. She wanted Chris to come to her tonight, but would he? Their marriage had been all but forced upon him, and this wouldn't be the first time they'd made love. Did he still want her?

Kateena opened the door to Chris's room and stood back while Sophia entered. Sophia saw at once that her things had been carried into his room and her nightgown laid out on the bed. Had Chris ordered the change, or had the servants taken it upon themselves?

Vases of fresh flowers filled the room; their scent, while strong, was divine. A decanter of wine and a tray of fresh fruit awaited them on the table. The door to the veranda had been thrown open, admitting a humid breeze. The scent of rain lay heavy on the air.

"Congratulations, my lady," Kateena said. "I hope your marriage brings everything you've ever wanted. There's fresh water in the pitcher; shall I help you bathe?"

Sophia smiled at Kateena, wishing her maid and friend could have attended her wedding. "Just help me undress; I can manage the rest on my own."

Kateena completed her duties and quietly left the room. Sophia walked naked to the washstand, poured water into the bowl and washed herself from head to toe with soap that smelled like jasmine. Afterward, she walked to the bed and picked up the nightgown, not recognizing the filmy garment as her own. Had Chris purchased it for her?

"Don't bother putting it on," Chris said as he closed the door behind him.

Sophia whirled, holding the nightgown in front of her to shield her nakedness. She hadn't heard Chris enter. "Did you buy this?"

He shook his head. "That's Lady Chester's doing. I prefer you naked."

He moved languidly toward her, removing the nightgown from her nerveless fingers and tossing it on a nearby chair.

"I didn't know if you'd want to make love to me."

"We're married; there's no reason to deny ourselves. We've already proven we're compatible in bed."

"I know, but—"

He leaned in close, brushing his lips against her ear. "You know I find you exciting. And I believe you feel the same about me."

Sophia bristled. "You don't know how I feel. You have no idea."

"Do you wish to tell me?"

"No. Not now; maybe never."

His hand slid up her arm. "It doesn't matter. We are husband and wife. Marriage is the best solution to your problem."

Chris could tell he hadn't said what Sophia wanted to hear, but it was all he was prepared to acknowledge.

Sophia reared away from him. "I never wanted to be an obligation."

Reaching out, he brought her against him. "It's done, Sophia. Let's make the best of it. Marriage to me won't be so bad. It will be what we both make of it."

Chris almost wished he could give Sophia what she wanted to hear, but he had no romantic prose, no flowery words. Though he had married her against his better judgment, he would protect her and keep her safe; that would have to be enough.

Sophia felt helpless, trapped between pride on the one hand and desperate, secret love on the other. She wanted Chris to love her. Wanted him to *make* love to her. She swayed against him.

Chris lowered her to the bed and began to undress. Sophia watched him. She had always admired his masculinity; the sight of his naked body thrilled her to the marrow of her bones. He was hard and vital, pulsing with power. She exhaled sharply when he stood naked before her, fascinated by the way his chest rose and fell with each breath, by the bulge of his shoulders where they met his upper arms and the sinuous flatness of his stomach.

Her gaze lowered to his loins, where his engorged shaft thrust upward against his stomach from a forest of dark brown.

"If you keep looking at me like that, this night will end sooner than we'd both like," he growled hoarsely.

She lowered her gaze. It was difficult not to look at him; he was magnificent.

Chris hunched down beside her, felt the tightening of his loins, the pain of muscles clenching, the pounding of his heart. Sophia excited him as no other woman. Raven-black lashes fell in a soft sweep over her cheeks; her hair spilled like dark silk over the pillow. He was dismayed to find he wanted her so badly after he had spent years trying to forget her.

He leaned over her and kissed her hard, his fingers playing lightly, teasingly over her flawless skin. She moaned and arched up against him.

"Chris . . . please . . ."

"Oh, I have every intention of pleasing you, love. This is going to be a long, pleasurable night for both of us."

Chris stilled. *He couldn't believe he had called Sophia his love.* He breathed a sigh of relief when Sophia didn't appear to notice his slip. Shifting his body lower, he kissed a path from her mouth to her breasts, lingering over her hard little nipples, suckling and nipping until she was writhing beneath him.

Sophia didn't know how much longer she could stand Chris's sensual torture. His kisses felt like pinpoints of fire as his mouth trailed down her stomach to her inner thigh. When she quivered in response, he held her hips in a gentle grip. He glanced up at her, his eyes glowing hotly in the dim light.

"I want to taste you."

She went rigid as he resumed his nibbling caresses up her inner thigh to a place that ached for his touch, crying out when his tongue found her dewy center. Her taut body was hot and explosive with need as he held her open with his thumbs and laved her with the rough pad of his tongue.

"Sweet," he murmured against her damp folds. When he thrust his tongue inside her, she jerked upward, crying out his name.

Her entire body clenched with anticipation as his tongue thrust into her slick heat again and again, and then he gently suckled the aching bud of her femininity. She whimpered and clutched at him, her fingers tightening reflexively in his thick hair. He continued his wicked, teasing assault, exploring the supple wet petals of her cleft, until the pleasure became too great to bear. Her heart beat wildly, her pulse pounded with desperate desire.

"Oh, God," she gasped. "I can't . . . I want . . ."

"Do it," Chris said, lifting his head from his succulent feast. "Take what you want."

"Don't stop," she wailed.

"Never!" His hands slid under her bottom, raising her against his mouth to savor her more fully.

Sophia began panting. Each slow, arousing stroke of his tongue was part heaven, part hell. He continued suckling her, lapping, drinking from her essence, tormenting her beyond endurance. When his probing tongue thrust deep inside her, she shuddered and shifted her hips, straining under the determined lash of his tongue, the relentless plundering of his mouth.

A scream built inside her, rising in her throat. She shuddered, thrashing her head from side to side, rising to meet the passionate assault of his tongue.

"I can't stand it," she panted jerkily.

"Come, then, don't hold back."

Unbearable pleasure brought forth a keening wail as she shattered. Bliss crested again and again as Chris continued his tender torture, until she collapsed in the breathless aftermath of her climax. Dazed and quivering, she was scarcely aware when Chris stretched his body over hers and gently began suckling her nipples, prolonging the tide of her pleasure until it finally ebbed, leaving her drained and limp.

When he finally lifted his head and looked at her, his face was hard, taut, like a man pressed to the limits of his endurance. Staring into her eyes, he spread her legs with his knees, flexed his hips and thrust hard and deep inside her. He lowered his head and kissed her, their mouths and tongues melding into one entity.

Suddenly he turned, bringing her on top of him, his cock still embedded deep inside her. Grasping her knees, he brought them up on either side of him, opening her fully to his hips.

"Ride me, Sophia. You're in charge—do as you please with me."

Scant moments ago, Sophia would have sworn she had nothing left to give, but Chris proved her wrong. He knew how and where to manipulate her body to make her yearn for more of his magical loving. She began to move on him, taking him deep, writhing against him. He caught her nipple between his teeth and bit down gently. She felt it clear down to the place where they were joined.

His body taut, his breath harsh in her ear, he urged her on with guttural words that brought her closer and closer to achieving Paradise.

"Now, Sophia, now!"

Sophia soared, reaching for the stars, and then she touched them. Vaguely she felt his body stiffen, heard her name whispered through the darkness, felt the warm gush of his seed.

"I love you, Chris." The words came without volition, torn from her by unrequited love and frustration.

Chris stared at her in horror, and then he slammed his mouth over hers, stopping her from saying anything more he didn't want to hear.

Chris went limp. Long moments later, he shifted Sophia beneath him, pulled out of her and rolled away. They were both breathing hard, their bodies shaking.

"Don't love me, Sophia."

"I'm sorry if I upset you. I thought . . . I hoped . . ."

"Hoped what? That I might return your love?"

"Would that be so terrible?"

"Have you forgotten our past? I'm a killer; I murdered my best friend. And you are the woman we dueled over. Guilt is the only emotion I am capable of."

Sophia stared at him. "But you made love to me as if you cared."

Chris searched his heart. It was not completely empty, but he didn't recognize what he found inside. He thought he knew what love felt like, for he had fancied himself in love with Sophia seven years ago. That feeling was definitely absent now. But there was something there, something he couldn't put a name to.

"Perhaps I do care," he mused. "I married you to keep you safe, didn't I?"

"Are you sure that's the only reason?"

Chris ignored her probing question. It opened him to the kind of hurt he never wanted to experience again. "Your nagging is becoming annoying," he said gruffly, pulling her beneath him. "The night is young. I can think of more pleasant ways to enjoy what is left of it."

His mouth settled on hers, and pleasure built, waned, built again until, exhausted and sated, they fell asleep.

Chapter Twelve

Chris had already left for the fields when Sophia awakened the morning following her wedding. She stretched lazily. Her limbs still felt weighted, her body flushed and languid. She had gotten little rest during their long night of loving. How could Chris have so much energy when she could barely move?

Kateena entered the room and began picking up discarded clothing. "Are you ready for your bath, mistress?"

"Tea first, Kateena, and a sweet biscuit. I'm famished."

Kateena left immediately to do Sophia's bidding. Sophia stretched again and smiled to herself. Chris had taken her to Paradise more than once last night, and though he hadn't said he loved her, her heart told her he cared deeply.

Kateena arrived with tea and a sticky bun. While Sophia ate, the tub was carried in and filled with water. She took a leisurely bath and dressed in an attractive blue dimity gown, one that Chris had commissioned for her. Then she went downstairs and waited for Chris to arrive for lunch.

Sophia lunched alone. Chris didn't return, nor did he send word about when to expect him. She ate dinner alone that night, too, all her dreams of a happy marriage crumbling. As Chris's wife, she expected to be informed about his comings and goings, not left in the dark, wondering when or if he would deign to return. Obviously, Chris intended to lead his life as if their marriage made little difference in the scheme of things.

That night, as Kateena helped Sophia prepare for bed, she said, "The men are working around the clock to get the cane cut and sent to the mill. Then it will be brought back to be turned into molasses and distilled into rum."

"I wonder why Chris didn't tell me that," Sophia mused. "I've been kept in the dark about every aspect of his life."

"I'm sure the captain meant no slight," Kateena soothed. "He's very busy, and new at this. He has a great deal to learn."

Chris didn't return to the house that night. Sophia fell asleep feeling lonely and wanting her husband. She awoke later to the smell of smoke and ran to the window. Her heart sank when she saw flames rising from the fields. She watched for a while, assumed the fire had been brought under control and went back to bed. When she awakened the following morning, she asked Kateena what had happened.

"It's normal to set fire to the fields before harvesting the cane to kill or chase off rats and snakes and get rid of trash and leaves," Kateena replied. "Mundo explained the process to me when I first arrived."

That's more than I learned from Chris, Sophia thought.

Chris arrived home late that night, exhausted, dirty and smelling of smoke.

"Are you all right?" she asked anxiously.

"Don't fuss, Sophia," Chris answered grumpily. "All I need is a bath and a good night's sleep."

"Did you sleep at all last night?"

"No, the fire had to be watched closely."

"Why didn't you tell me what was going on? I became worried when you didn't return home last night. Kateena had to explain the burning of the fields to me."

He removed his shirt, boots and breeches. "I didn't think you'd be interested."

"We're married, Chris. I'm interested in everything you do. I can't be your partner if you don't tell me what's going on."

"I'm tired, Sophia, leave off. Chuba is filling a tub for me in the shed off the kitchen. We'll talk after I've bathed."

He took his robe from the wardrobe and left before Sophia could reply. She knew he was tired, but didn't a wife deserve some consideration? Why was Chris treating her as if she had no stake in making the plantation a successful opperation? She had never been a wife before, but it seemed to her that she should be helping Chris in some way. Sighing, she sat on the bed and waited for her husband to return.

Chris knew he owed Sophia an explanation, but when he had left her bed yesterday morning he hadn't wanted to awaken her. He knew he might not make it home that night and had meant to send word later, but as the day progressed, more pressing needs took precedence. Sophia would have to learn that the plantation came first with him and always would.

Chris sank into the tub Chuba had prepared, feeling his tension drain away with the dirt and grime. The fire had nearly gotten out of control. Yet the fire had been necessary to clear the north field of rats and snakes so the cutting could begin. He didn't relish the idea of losing good men to snakebite.

Resting his head against the rim of the big wooden tub, Chris finally had time to think about his wedding night. Sophia's response to him had been magnificent. Though he had already experienced her passion, his wedding night had far exceeded his expectations.

He'd tried not to think about the words she'd cried out, unwilling to acknowledge how deeply her declaration had affected him. He didn't want Sophia to love him, and had told her so. He wanted to remember the pain of Desmond's death and the reason for it. Returning Sophia's love would somehow negate his guilt. He had lived with guilt so long, he couldn't imagine existing without it.

Nevertheless, Sophia was his wife and deserved a place in his life. But where did she belong besides in his bed? He didn't know, was too tired to think that far ahead. He finished his bath and climbed the stairs to his bed. Sophia was waiting for him. She looked ethereally beautiful in the candlelight. Unfortunately, he was too tired to do more than fall into bed and close his eyes.

"Chris . . ."

He sighed. "Go to sleep, Sophia. Don't expect more from me than I'm capable of giving. Planters like Lord Chester have slaves to do their work. And if he needs more workers, he simply buys them on the slave market. I pay my workers wages and toil beside them because there aren't enough free men of color looking for work. That means my days are going to be long and hard. I'm sorry if you can't live with that."

"I'm sorry, too," Sophia whispered as she turned away from him.

Chris tried to sleep, but as the arousing scent of Sophia's body reached him, his exhaustion drained away. He should have slept in another bed. He reached for her. She stiffened.

"I thought you were tired," Sophia said.

"I am, but I can't seem to relax."

"Perhaps you're not accustomed to having another body in your bed. Shall I leave?"

His arm curled around her waist. "No." He brought her beneath him. He was already aroused. What had seemed physically impossible when he returned from the fields suddenly became not only possible but necessary to his well-being.

With renewed energy, he slowly began to arouse Sophia, using long, slow kisses and heated caresses. He suckled her breasts, teased her nipples with his tongue until she moaned and writhed beneath him. He reached between her legs, found her wet and swollen. He fondled her slick folds and shoved two fingers inside her.

"Chris!"

"You're ready for me," he said hoarsely.

Unable to wait a moment longer, he rose up and thrust deep inside her.

Her moans set off a firestorm inside him as he jerked his hips back and forth, his sex plunging deep, withdrawing, again and again, faster, deeper. Perspiration gathered between them, their slick bodies gliding together in perfect harmony.

Chris couldn't recall when he had felt such power, as if he could go on forever, as if his body had no limitations, no boundaries. But when he heard Sophia scream his name and felt tremors rip through her body, his own body clamored for release. He thrust once, twice, and went rigid, emptying himself inside her.

He pulled out and sank down beside her, asleep before his head hit the pillow.

Sophia remained awake, her mind racing. Chris had made love to her despite his exhaustion. Though she didn't want to read too much into his change of heart, hope for their future soared.

The following days passed in a whirl of activity. The sugarcane had been taken to the mill to be cut and then returned to the distillery to be processed into molasses, rum and raw sugar. The machinery continued working night and day without stop. Since cane could be cut any time of the year, the procedure never ended. Chris slept away from the house more than in his own bed. There was no opportunity for lovemaking, and Sophia missed him.

To pass the time, she decided to take Kateena and Casper to Kingston for a day of shopping. Since Mundo was busy in the fields with Chris, Sophia asked Chuba to drive them to town in the carriage. Unfortunately, both Chuba and Casper had been recruited for work in the distillery. Sophia didn't let that stop her, however. She was perfectly capable of driving the carriage herself.

The weather didn't look promising. The sky had a threatening cast; purple and gray clouds hung heavy on the horizon, and the air held a strange air of expectancy. But Sophia wasn't about to let a summer storm stop her. The storm probably wouldn't arrive for hours, and she needed new ribbon for her bonnet and a few personal items.

Sophia found Kateena in the laundry room. When she told Kateena they were going to Kingston, the maid looked at her as if she had lost her mind.

"Have you noticed the sky, mistress?" Kateena chided. "I've seen the likes before, and it doesn't bode well. I think we should remain close to home."

"Why ever for? This is the tropics. Storms come and go all the time. If a storm does come while we're in town, we will simply seek shelter until it passes."

"You could be wrong, mistress. Hurricanes often come this time of year. One never knows when an approaching storm might carry fierce winds that destroy everything in their path. I've lived through several myself, some worse than others."

"How can you tell if it's a simple storm or a hurricane?"

"At this time of year we don't know until it arrives, that's what worries me."

Sophia pulled on her gloves. "A little weather isn't going to stop me. Are you coming or not?"

Kateena looked torn, but in the end she put on her bonnet and joined Sophia in the carriage. The ride over bumpy roads to Kingston was uneventful. The marketplace was teeming with shoppers of all colors and descriptions. Sophia waded into the crowd, admiring the array of goods offered in each stall as she strolled along. Somewhere between the cloth merchant's stall and the fruit hawker, Sophia and Kateena became separated.

Sophia made her purchases and was wandering aimlessly when someone snagged her arm and pulled her into a dark space between two stalls.

"Ray," she exclaimed. "I thought you'd returned to England. Your wife must be sick with worry."

"My wife left me," Rayford sneered. "She went back

to her parents before I left England. She said she was tired of living like a pauper." He snorted. "If Claire's father had given me the blunt I needed, I wouldn't be in financial straits."

"Good for Claire," Sophia applauded. "She finally found some courage. You can't blame her father for denying you when you've gambled away Claire's dowry and all the money he lent you over the years." She shrugged free of his grip. "What do you want?"

"Money, you stupid cow. Any other woman would have found a rich husband after her come out instead of causing a scandal and living off the largess of her brother. You've brought nothing but trouble to the family. You owe me."

"I owe you nothing but contempt," Sophia spat. "You tried to sell me. Good-bye, Ray. I need to find my maid and start for home." She glanced up at the sky. "The storm is closing in faster than I expected."

"You'll pay one way or another, Sophia," Rayford warned as she backed away from him, straight into the arms of Sir Oscar Rigby.

"Well, well, what have we here? I've waited a long time to find you alone."

Panic swept through Sophia. The marketplace was quickly emptying as the wind picked up and the skies darkened. No one paid her the slightest heed as Rigby and Rayford cornered her between them. Where was Kateena?

"Take her to the carriage," Rayford said. "I suspect her husband will pay dearly for her return."

"I wouldn't try it if I were you," Sophia warned. "Chris will make you sorry if you so much as touch me." *She hoped he would.*

"You're right," Rayford grumbled, "but that doesn't

mean I'm letting you off the hook. I need blunt. If you don't get it for me, I'll make sure Radcliff meets with an accident. Machetes are dangerous weapons in the hands of inexperienced men."

Sophia didn't bother to reply. She spun on her heel and ran. Rayford reached her first, stopping her in her tracks. The wind had picked up; it began to rain. The few people remaining in the marketplace were fleeing for cover. Where was Kateena?

"Mistress, there you are! We must leave immediately and find cover. I fear—"

Kateena came to an abrupt halt. "Are you in trouble, mistress?"

"My sister is not in trouble," Rayford said smoothly. "Wait for her at the King's Arms. I'll bring her to you in a little while. There's a matter of some importance I need to discuss with her."

"Don't leave, Kateena," Sophia cried. "I have nothing to say to my stepbrother."

"If you value your husband's life, you'll send your maid on her way," Rayford hissed in her ear.

Sophia weighed Rayford's threat against the consequences of complying with his wishes. After careful thought, she didn't believe Rayford had the power to hurt Chris.

"Find help, Kateena! Go! My stepbrother and Sir Oscar mean me harm."

Kateena turned and fled, the howling wind whipping her skirts about her legs.

"Damn you!" Rayford hissed. "I warned you, but you refused to listen. Bring five hundred pounds to me at the King's Arms in one week or else your husband will suffer the consequences."

The wind pulled at Sophia's skirts, tugged at her

bonnet, drowned out the sound of Rayford's voice. Above the conflict of wind and rain came the sound of pounding footsteps and voices raised in alarm.

"Dammit, the maid brought help," Rigby spat. "Let's get out of here. We'll deal with your sister another time." Bracing themselves against the wind, they took off.

"Are you all right, mistress?" Kateena asked when she reached Sophia. "They didn't hurt you, did they?"

"I'm fine, Kateena. Thank you for bringing help." She smiled at her rescuers and thanked them profusely. She even produced a few coins to give them.

"You were right about that storm, Kateena," Sophia said. "It's worse than I expected. We should return home immediately."

"It's too late," Kateena cried above the wailing wind. "We'd be blown off the road. We need to seek shelter immediately."

"No," Sophia protested. "If I don't return, Chris will worry. The storm's not too bad yet—I can make it."

Her bonnet was blown off her head; the pins were torn from her hair, whipping it around her face.

"The carriage is too light, it will be blown off the road," Kateena persisted.

"I'll leave the carriage behind and ride the horse home."

Kateena bit her bottom lip, torn between duty to her mistress and fear of the storm. "I've lived here longer than you, mistress; listen to me, please."

"If I start out now, I can arrive home before the worst of it." Bent against the pull of the wind, Sophia stumbled toward the King's Arms, where she had left the horse and carriage in charge of the stable boy. Kateena ran to catch up with her.

"Mistress, please—"

"Kateena, if you're worried, I suggest you see to your parents. Take them to a safe place to wait out the storm."

"I couldn't—"

"I insist. Go, Kateena. I can make better time without you. I've ridden horses all my life—can you say the same?"

Kateena shook her head.

"There you have it. Don't return to Sunset Hill until the storm passes."

Kateena looked as if she wanted to protest, but in the end Sophia's logic won out. Kateena turned and headed toward her parents' humble shack behind the fishmonger's shop.

Sophia reached the King's Arms just as a flash of lightning streaked across the sky. But she let neither the lightning nor the ominous green and purple sky stop her.

It took a great deal of persuasion to get the stable boy to lend her a saddle and place it on the carriage horse. His warnings about a hurricane echoed Kateena's, but Sophia refused to listen.

As Sophia rode away from the inn, she noted that the streets were deserted now and shopkeepers were boarding up their shops. Still not terribly worried, Sophia urged her reluctant horse through the stinging rain. Hampered by the muddy road and buffeted by the wind, she found the going slow. But the need to be with Chris during this time of danger kept her focused on her goal to reach Sunset Hill.

Halfway between Kingston and Sunset Hill, a swaying palm tree fell in her path. The horse shied, skittered, but through sheer will Sophia guided the frightened animal around the obstacle.

When the wind drove slashing rain into a sideways pattern and lightning flashed across the purple sky, Sophia experienced real panic. She could no longer see the road, which had begun to flood, couldn't even tell if she was going in the right direction. Her mount began to pull against the reins, shaking his head and trying to break away and flee into the jungle.

When the trees around her were uprooted, Sophia realized she had made a terrible mistake, one that could cost her her life. Another flash of lightning and crack of thunder caused her horse to rear. She lost the reins and hung on for dear life as the frightened animal bolted toward the mountains. Tree branches whipped across her face and tore at her skirt as her mount fled farther and faster, completely out of control.

A tree fell in the horse's path. The animal skidded to a halt, bucking wildly. Sophia went flying, landing in the mud. Her head hit a rock, and she knew no more. The horse, free of its rider, leaped over the fallen tree and galloped off.

Chris knew a hurricane was coming. He smelled it in the air, saw it in the darkening sky. He'd seen too many of them in his years at sea not to recognize the signs. Thankful that most of the cane had been harvested and turned into molasses and rum, Chris set his men to work piling the kegs of rum and molasses inside the brick distillery.

They worked against time as the wind howled and the trees bent double from the terrifying force of it. They worked steadily throughout the day, until the last keg was safely stowed inside the building. Then the workers scattered to see to their families. Chris, Chuba and Casper made their way to the house through slashing rain and winds so strong that Chris and Chuba had to hang on to Casper to keep him from flying away.

During the madness of saving the fruits of their labor, Chris still found time to worry about Sophia. He knew she had never experienced anything like a hurricane and hoped Kateena had been able to quiet any fears his wife might have.

When they reached the house, most of the windows had already been boarded up by the house servants. Chandra met him at the door, wringing her hands, her dark face scrunched up into a worried frown.

Chris's heart sank. He knew without being told that Sophia was the reason for the cook's anxiety. "What is it, Chandra? Is Sophia upset over the storm?"

"She ain't here, Captain," Chandra wailed. "The mistress drove the carriage to Kingston today and took Kateena with her. She hasn't returned, and I'm worried sick about her."

"She's gone?" The color drained from Chris's face. The force of the wind drove him inside. Calming his rising panic, he closed the door with Chuba's help and forced himself to think rationally.

"Sophia and Kateena wouldn't start back to Sunset Hill in threatening weather. I'm sure they're fine, Chandra. Kateena has lived in Jamaica long enough to know how dangerous a hurricane can be. They probably sought shelter at the King's Arms."

Despite his words, Chris's fears escalated. Sophia was wild and unpredictable. Kateena wouldn't be able to stop her from returning home if her mind was set on it. Sophia had proven her reckless nature time and again, but would she risk injury or death to return home?

"I'm going to ride to Kingston," Chris announced. "I won't be satisfied until I know Sophia is safe."

"I'm going with you," Casper chimed in.

"You're going to stay here where it's safe," Chris ordered sternly.

"Look outside, Captain," Chuba ventured. "The trees are bent double; some have been uprooted. You don't stand a chance of reaching Kingston. Wait until the hurricane passes."

Chris began to pace. "That could take hours. My gut tells me that Sophia needs me."

That feeling remained with Chris the rest of the day as the wind howled like a banshee and bullet-like pellets of rain pelted the window panes. He paced. He tried to eat. He cursed Sophia's recklessness. She shouldn't have left the house in threatening weather. True, Sophia had no idea what a hurricane looked like or the damage it could do, but common sense should have told her something was amiss when she saw the ominous sky.

Sometime during the long night a tree came crashing down onto a section of the veranda. Chris wasn't overly worried about his workers, for he knew they and their families would seek shelter in the sturdy brick distillery. Only Chuba and Chandra remained with him in the manor house—and Casper, of course, who had refused to leave Chris's side.

Toward dawn, the wind and rain began to subside, indicating that the hurricane had passed over the island, leaving mass destruction in its wake. Chris ventured outside to assess the damage. Several palm trees had been uprooted, part of the veranda was gone, and two wooden outbuildings had been leveled. The brick distillery had withstood the onslaught, but several of the workers' huts had lost roofs and two had been leveled. As for the cane fields, the stalks that hadn't been cut lay scattered upon the sodden ground.

They could still be salvaged if the men worked fast. Chris issued orders to Mundo to begin the cleanup and then went to the stables for his horse. Much to his relief, the stables were still standing, though a bit worse for wear. The stable lad stumbled out from one of the stalls to saddle Atlas. Moments later, Chris reined his mount toward Kingston.

The road was flooded, making travel difficult. Chris had to stop several times to remove debris from the road so he could pass. Twice, trees too heavy for him to move blocked the road. In each case he found a way around the obstacle, though the detours slowed him considerably. A trip that should have taken less than an hour took four.

As Chris rode down King Street, it became apparent that the town had received the brunt of the storm. Debris from mangled shops and dwellings littered the ground. Rain stood in the roadway. Amazingly, some buildings appeared unscathed. The King's Arms was one of the lucky few.

The scene inside the inn was chaotic. People who had taken shelter in the sturdy building were rushing out to check on the condition of their homes and businesses. Chris pushed his way through the frantic exodus until he spied the proprietor.

"Ludlow," Chris called above the din of voices.

Ludlow seemed startled to see Chris. "Captain, I'm surprised you were able to get through. The roads must be a mess. What can I do for you?"

"I'm looking for my wife. Can you direct me to her room?"

"Your wife? She isn't here, Captain."

A spiral of fear snaked down Chris's spine. "She couldn't have left Kingston already, for I would have encountered her on the road."

"I haven't seen your lady, Captain."

Chris felt as if the room were closing in on him. "But . . . that's impossible. I was told Sophia and her maid came to Kingston before the storm broke. Naturally, I assumed they sought shelter from the hurricane at the inn."

Ludlow shook his head. "I'd know if they were here."

"Master Ludlow," a small voice piped up. "I seen the lady."

Chris turned to the stable lad, his hopes soaring. "Speak up, lad. Tell me what you know."

"The lady left her carriage at the inn while she shopped in the marketplace. She returned just as it began to rain and asked me to unhitch the horse from the carriage and saddle it. I think she intended to return to Sunset Hill. She said something about wanting to reach home before the storm broke."

"She didn't make it," Chris whispered. "Oh, God, she's still out there somewhere. What about Kateena?"

"She wasn't with your lady," the boy replied.

Frantic, Chris rushed from the inn, mounted Atlas and rode hell for leather out of town. Sophia could be lying hurt somewhere, or, God forbid, dead. He intended to pull all his workers from the fields and organize a search party. Perhaps she had found shelter and was even now trying to get home.

Chris found Lord Chester waiting for him when he arrived home.

"I thought I'd come over to see how you fared during the hurricane," Chester said.

"As you can see, it could have been worse."

"I lost half my coffee beans and my tobacco barns, but nothing that can't be repaired or replaced."

"Did Sophia happen to seek shelter at Orchid Manor?" Chris asked hopefully. "She took the carriage to Kingston yesterday, and I can't locate her."

"Are you implying that Sophia was out during the storm?" Chester asked, aghast. Chris nodded. "My God, man, where could she be?"

"I don't know. I hoped, prayed that she had sought shelter at the King's Arms, but she wasn't there. I'm going to send out a search party immediately."

"Let me help. And I'm sure Wombly will want to join in the search. I'll contact him. The more men searching, the better chance we have of finding your wife."

"Thank you," Chris said sincerely. "We should concentrate on the area between here and Kingston. She started home on horseback but never arrived."

Chester left. Chris organized his workers into two groups and joined one of them. It was late afternoon when Chris found Sophia's mount. He was pinned beneath a fallen tree well off the main road, his leg broken, his eyes rolling wildly in his head. Chris found no evidence that Sophia had been with the horse when it had been struck. He put the poor animal out of its misery and widened the search.

Exhaustion and waning light halted the search. The men returned to their homes for a well-deserved meal and rest. But the search continued the following day and the day after that. The only sign of Sophia was a piece of material from her dress that one of Chester's slaves found near the foothills of the Blue Mountains.

How could Sophia have strayed so far from the road? Chris wondered. Had she become lost in the mountains? Was she even now trying to find her way home?

Where could Sophia be? The obvious answer was the most painful.

Sophia was dead.

Chris refused to stop searching, but after four days of fruitless tramping through the jungle, he released his men to make repairs on their homes and to gather the salvageable cane lying in the fields. He sent word to Chester and Wombly that the search was officially over, even though Chris continued looking.

Kateena had returned home to find the household in mourning. When Lady Chester arrived to express her condolences, Chris quickly set her straight. Until a body was found, he considered Sophia missing, not dead.

That night Chris dreamed of Sophia. He felt her in his arms, flushed with passion, her sweet body arched beneath his, her lush mouth gasping his name as he brought her to completion. The dream was so real, he woke up and reached for her, only to find the space beside him empty.

He missed her, dammit! He missed her vitality, her spirit. He missed knowing she was in his home, waiting for him in his bed. And that truly puzzled him. Nothing in their past suggested that Chris should want Sophia in his home, in his life.

In his heart.

Chapter Thirteen

Sophia opened her eyes to a world of pain and a sea of dark faces staring down at her. She groaned, blinked, and struggled to regain her wits. Her head pounded, the pain so debilitating she could barely string two thoughts together. Of one thing she was certain: This wasn't Sunset Hill.

"Lady, lady."

The woman hovering above her had skin the color of tobacco. Her slightly slanted eyes held a worried expression. "Are you awake, lady?"

Sophia nodded and wished she hadn't. Her arms felt like lead as she lifted them to her head. The woman pushed Sophia's hands away and replaced them with a cool, wet cloth.

Sophia tried to summon some moisture to lick her dry lips and failed. Immediately someone lifted her head and held a cup of water to her mouth. She drank thirstily until the cup was empty.

"Where am I?" she croaked. "What is this place?"

"You were found four days ago," the woman said in a

singsong voice, "lying on the ground near our campsite during the height of the storm. The men carried you to the cave in which we had taken shelter. After the hurricane passed, you were carried to my hut. My name is Udamma."

"I've been unconscious four days?" Sophia gasped, stunned. Her first thought was of Chris. "My husband doesn't know what happened to me."

"We would have notified him had we known who you were," Udamma said. "Fear not, lady; you are safe with us."

Sophia let her gaze wander over the people gathered in the small room. Udamma answered her unspoken question immediately.

"My people are curious about you." She spoke to them in a language Sophia didn't understand, and they drifted out the door.

"Many camps like ours thrive in the foothills of the Blue Mountains," Udamma explained. "We are called Maroons. Some of us are escaped slaves who no longer wish to live under the yoke of slavery. Others are free people of color. We live in freedom here, our physical and spiritual needs taken care of by 'Daddy' Sam Sharp."

"Thank you for your care of me, Udamma," Sophia said. "I'd like to go home to Sunset Hill now."

A smile appeared on Udamma's dark face. "You are Captain Radcliff's woman?"

"I am Sophia, his wife. Have you heard of my husband?"

"We know that Captain Radcliff freed his slaves, and we admire his bold action. How did you come to be on the road during a hurricane?"

Udamma helped Sophia to sit up. Her head spun dizzily and then filled with a dull ache. "I was returning home from Kingston. I suppose I was foolish to brave the storm, but I was anxious to return to my husband. I've never experienced a hurricane before. My maid warned me to take shelter, but I ignored her. It won't happen again, I assure you.

"Lightning and falling trees frightened my horse and I lost control. He threw me and ran off." She touched the bump on her forehead. "I must have hit something hard, for I knew nothing more until I woke up here."

"We didn't find your horse. We wouldn't have found you if one of our men hadn't been late seeking shelter in the cave and stumbled upon you."

"I'm sure my husband will reward you," Sophia said sleepily. Her eyes fluttered shut. "I don't know why I feel so tired."

"You are still healing, lady. Sleep. We will send word to your husband."

Disheveled, dirty, tired and disheartened, Chris was finally ready to accept that Sophia was dead. What he hadn't expected to deal with was Viscount Caldwell waiting for him upon his return from his fourth day of searching for Sophia.

"Speak your piece, Caldwell, and make it quick," Chris growled.

"My sister is dead, and I hold you responsible," Caldwell blustered.

"We don't know she's dead," Chris said, unwilling to admit what he had finally come to believe.

"How long has it been? Four days? That's a long time for a defenseless woman to be missing. For all we know, she's being held prisoner by escaped slaves, and Lord knows what they've done to her."

"We have no reason to believe that," Chris argued. "What is it you want from me, Caldwell?"

"Compensation for my sister's life," Caldwell ventured. "You owe me for failing to protect her."

Chris sighed, too bone weary for patience. "Are you saying you would have done a better job? You sold her to repay a debt, even though you knew Rigby intended to use and discard her. You're a mercenary bastard, Caldwell. Now get out of here, you're not getting one farthing from me."

He turned and strode off, ignoring Caldwell's vile curses. He had enough to worry about without Caldwell's interference. Losing Sophia had devastated him. He was too heartsick to deal with the damage done to his plantation or worry about the *Intrepid* being in the path of the storm.

Chris walked to the house, a defeated man with little hope left. Sophia was gone. Though his mind knew it, his heart refused to accept it. She was so young, so vital, so wonderfully alive. She had said she loved him. Why hadn't he been able to return the sentiment? His guilt, already ponderous, was now suffocating.

Kateena met him at the door. "No luck, Captain?"

Chris shook his head. "I fear—"

"No, don't say it!" Kateena cried. "My mistress isn't dead."

"I don't want to believe it, Kateena, but I don't have much hope left. I'm going to bathe, have something to eat and rest an hour or two before continuing the search. Wake me if I'm needed."

"Mundo and the workers are taking care of the repairs," Kateena said. "Don't you worry about the plantation, Captain, you've got enough on your mind."

Chris bathed, ate and sought his bed. Sleep came instantly. He was sleeping so soundly, he failed to hear Chuba pounding on the door.

"Captain, Captain, wake up!"

Chris shook himself awake, fear racing through him. "Come in, Chuba. What is it? Has Sophia's body been found?"

Grinning from ear to ear, Chuba shook his head. "No, Captain, just the opposite. The mistress is alive and well and being cared for by the Maroons. One of their people arrived with the news moments ago. He's waiting for you in the foyer."

Wide awake now, Chris scrambled into his clothing and flew out the door and down the stairs. "You have news of my wife?" he asked the man standing in the foyer.

" 'Daddy' Sam sent me. I am Santo. Your lady rests comfortably in my hut, being looked after by my wife."

"Why didn't you contact me before now?" Chris asked, holding his anger in check. "It's been four days, for God's sake!"

"We didn't know the lady or where she belonged," Santo explained. "One of our people found her lying unconscious in the jungle near our campsite and brought her to our shelter during the height of the storm. She'd suffered a head injury and regained consciousness just today. She told us her name and asked us to let you know where she is."

Chris sagged in relief. "She's with the Maroons? Is she all right?"

Santo inclined his head. "We would not harm the woman of the man who freed his slaves. We feared for her life when she failed to awaken, but she is strong and refused to die."

"Take me to her."

Chris followed Santo out the door. Noting that the man had arrived on foot, Chris took him to the stable and waited for the carriage to be made ready. He feared Sophia would be unable to ride.

Chris couldn't begin to imagine how Sophia had wandered so far off the main road, but he supposed it was easy to get lost during a storm of such magnitude. She shouldn't have been out in the first place. He should have protected her better. He wouldn't have been able to live with himself had he been responsible for Sophia's death.

When Sophia awoke, Udamma offered her food and drink. She sipped broth and ate sparingly of fruit and small pieces of pork. But she felt better for it and was able to sit up without difficulty.

"My man went to Sunset Hill to notify your husband," Udamma said. "The captain should arrive soon."

"Thank you," Sophia replied. "If I can ever do anything for you, you have but to ask."

"You can convince the other planters to free their slaves," Udamma said. "If they do not, there will be dire consequences. Rest now, lady; the journey to your plantation won't be an easy one. The men are preparing a litter for you."

"There is no need. I can walk."

"You can try but you won't succeed. You are very weak. You've had little to eat or drink in four days. Are you still in pain?"

"A bit, but it's not as bad as it was. And I'm feeling stronger."

"I will give you a powder to mix with water. Drinking it will ease the pain. It's a remedy made of ground roots of a plant that is well known to our people."

Sophia sent Udamma a wobbly smile and lay back down on the pallet. She closed her eyes, letting her mind drift. Would Chris be pleased to find her safe? Had he been searching for her? Would he be angry at her for venturing out in the storm?

Sophia knew she had been foolish to disregard the warnings about the approaching hurricane. But she had been bored and disgruntled at being ignored by Chris.

Before her mind closed down and sleep claimed her, she prayed that Kateena and her family had survived the hurricane. If anything had happened to Kateena, she'd never forgive herself.

Halfway between Kingston and Sunset Hill, Santo pointed to a barely discernible path through the jungle and told Chris to stop. Chris left the carriage on the road and followed Santo through the dense thicket on foot.

The path led to the foothills of the Blue Mountains. They trudged through thick underbrush for some distance until they reached a cluster of ramshackle huts nestled in the shadow of a mountain. Chris realized he was approaching the Maroon camp.

Santo led Chris directly to his hut and stood aside so Chris could enter. "Your lady is inside. Since she is still too weak to trudge through the forest, our men have constructed a litter and will help carry her to your carriage."

"I am most grateful," Chris replied.

Santo nodded and strode off. Chris stepped into the

hut and paused, letting his eyes adjust to the meager light as his gaze searched for his wife. He saw her lying on a pallet beneath the single window. She appeared to be sleeping.

A woman emerged from the shadows. "I am Udamma, Santo's woman. Your lady sleeps, Captain."

Chris's gaze fixed on the woman. "Have you been taking care of my wife?"

Udamma inclined her head. "It was my pleasure. She awakened from her stupor just today. She had suffered an injury to her head." She directed her gaze at the sleeping Sophia. "She will be fine, Captain. She just wishes to go home."

"Is it all right to awaken her?"

"Yes. I will wait outside and notify you when the men arrive with the litter." She slipped out the door.

Chris approached the pallet and dropped to his knees. Reaching out, he brushed a strand of hair from Sophia's forehead, his eyes widening when he saw the purple and yellow bruise there. She looked so pale, so defenseless. How could he have let something like this happen to her? He bent his head and brushed his lips against hers. She stirred and sighed.

"Sophia. Wake up. I've come to take you home."

Sophia's lashes fluttered. "Chris, you came. I want to go home."

"I know, love. That's why I'm here. Though everyone had given up on you, I continued to search. I refused to believe you were dead."

Sophia started to rise.

"No, don't get up. Wait until the men arrive with the litter."

"I can walk."

"Nevertheless, you'll be carried to the carriage in a litter. Dear God, Sophia, I've been worried sick, terrified that I'd stumble upon your body."

Sophia searched Chris's face. He did indeed sound worried and appeared exhausted. Dark circles rimmed his eyes, and his face was drawn. It looked as if he hadn't slept in days.

"How did the plantation fare during the storm?"

"There was some damage, but nothing that can't be repaired. We lost some cane and some dwellings, but it could have been worse."

"What about Kateena? I left her in Kingston. Did she get home safely?"

"She's fine, Sophia, don't fret. Concentrate on your own recovery."

Santo arrived and told them that two men were waiting outside with a makeshift litter constructed of two sturdy bamboo poles with a blanket stretched between them. Sophia started to rise, but Chris effortlessly swept her up from the pallet into his arms. He carried her outside and placed her on the litter.

"Thank you, Udamma," Sophia said when the woman appeared in the doorway of the hut.

Udamma nodded and smiled as the two litter bearers carried Sophia off down a slight incline and along a path through tall palms and tangled underbrush.

One of the litter bearers stumbled, jarring Sophia. "Are you all right?" Chris asked when she winced and moaned.

"I'm fine, Chris. The going is a little rough, but it's nothing I can't handle. How far are we from the road?"

"We still have a ways to go. Maroon encampments are chosen for their isolation. Thank God you stumbled into one. How did you wander so far off the road?"

"My horse became frightened and took off into the jungle."

"We found your horse but failed to find the campsite."

"No one knew who I was until I was able to tell Udamma my name. Apparently, you are well known to her and her people. She said if the other planters don't free their slaves, there will be trouble."

"I know that, and I think the others do too, but they believe they can handle a slave uprising. Perhaps they can, but lives will be lost."

Sophia couldn't bear the thought of anyone at Sunset Hill suffering. She fell silent, pondering the injustice of slavery and wondering where it would all end, and how many lives would be lost because of it. She must have dozed, for when she awakened, she was in Chris's arms, being lifted into the carriage.

"Did I sleep long?"

"No, not long. Does sitting up hurt your head?"

"Not enough to worry about. I'm growing stronger by the minute."

Chris spoke a moment with the litter bearers before climbing into the carriage and taking up the reins.

"I left the carriage at the King's Arms," Sophia said.

"Mundo brought it back to Sunset Hill after the road was cleared."

As the carriage clattered down the rutted road, Sophia was astounded by the number of trees felled by the hurricane. She'd never seen anything like it.

"How did the other plantations fare?" Sophia asked. "Are the Chesters all right?"

"They came though it fine; a little damage here and

there. This wasn't the first hurricane Jamaica has seen, and it's likely not the last."

Chris turned the horse down the road that led to Sunset Hill. Sophia could see the house in the distance. As they got nearer, she saw that part of the veranda had been destroyed, and that trees lay at odd angles on the ground.

"Oh, the veranda—"

"—can be rebuilt."

"My recklessness has kept you from your duties here," Sophia observed. "I'm sorry, Chris. I never meant . . ."

Sophia's sentence fell off when the front door opened and the household servants poured out to meet them. Chris drew rein at the front door; Kateena reached them first.

"Mistress, thank God! Everyone but the captain feared you were dead. He refused to give up."

Chris stepped down, walked around to the passenger side and lifted Sophia into his arms. Chuba hurried to open the door as Casper jumped up and down with excitement. Chris entered and headed for the stairs. Kateena followed close behind.

"Can I get you anything?" Kateena asked.

"Fetch tea and something for Sophia to eat," Chris requested. "I'd like a word with my wife in private, so take your time."

He carried Sophia into their bedroom, closed the door with his foot and placed her on the bed. Then he stood back and stared at her.

"I know you're angry, Chris."

"Anger is but one of the emotions I'm feeling," Chris acknowledged, "but I don't want to upset you with my emotions now. When you are rested, I want to know why you went to Kingston without telling me, and why you decided to return when the weather was so bad."

Chris was torn between holding Sophia in his arms and giving her a good shaking for acting irresponsibly. He had come close to losing his mind these past few days. The stress of not knowing what had happened to Sophia had affected everyone at Sunset Hill. He hadn't slept more than a couple of hours a night since she'd disappeared.

He couldn't talk to her now, he was too emotional. He turned away from her and walked to the window. "Is there anything you need?"

"You should get some sleep. You look terrible."

He spun around, smiling for the first time since finding Sophia. "I could say the same for you. The swelling on your forehead looks painful. I'll see if Chandra has something to bring it down. I'm sure your head must hurt."

"Udamma gave me a powder for the pain." She dug into her pocket and retrieved a small packet. "Give this to Chandra to mix up for me."

Chris took the packet from Sophia. And then, because he needed to, because he couldn't stop himself, he leaned over her, lowered his head and kissed her. He hadn't meant it to be more than a gentle touching of lips, but his good intentions flew out the window when her lips clung sweetly to his.

"God, Sophia," he groaned, going in for another kiss. Though it still wasn't the kind of kiss he wanted, craved, he satisfied his need by slipping his tongue inside her mouth for a quick taste of something he feared he had lost forever.

Sophia's arms slid around his neck, Chris's arms tightened around her, and who knows what might have happened if Kateena hadn't appeared with their refreshments. Chris bolted away from the bed.

"Take care of your mistress, Kateena. I'm going to give the headache powder to Chandra to prepare for you, Sophia, and then sleep for a couple of hours. We'll talk later. I'm mentally and emotionally exhausted right now."

"Now then, mistress, let's get you out of that dress and into a nightgown," Kateena said after Chris left. "Once you've eaten and rested, I'll have a bath prepared and try to comb the tangles out of your hair."

"Kateena, we've known each other long enough for you to call me Sophia."

"I couldn't. It wouldn't be right."

"It's right if I say it is. How about that tea? I haven't had a decent cup in four days."

"Right away . . . Sophia."

Chris went directly to his study and poured himself a large tot of rum. He flung his head back and drained it in one gulp. He hadn't been lying when he'd told Sophia he was emotionally drained. He felt wrung out, depleted. Though he hadn't wanted to admit it even to himself, he had begun to doubt he would find Sophia alive.

He'd been so busy searching, he hadn't had time to examine his emotions, to discover exactly how he felt about his wife. He had married Sophia because it had been expedient to do so. She was in trouble and needed rescuing. She was being threatened by both her stepbrother and Rigby, and if he hadn't stepped in, Lord knows how or where she would have ended up. Rigby could have claimed her as his escaped slave, and no one would have questioned him.

He poured another tot of rum and polished it off.

Then he sank down in a comfortable chair and closed his eyes. What precisely did he feel for Sophia? He lusted for her, craved her kisses, her sweet body, but he knew there was more, that his feelings went deeper. But he wasn't ready yet to explore the depth of his emotions. Was he capable of feeling love?

He fell asleep before he arrived at an answer.

Sophia was sitting up in bed when Chris visited her the following afternoon. "You're looking better," he said, studying her with an intensity that made her flush with pleasure.

"You're not. Didn't you sleep last night?" Though he had bathed and shaved, he still looked exhausted.

"I fell asleep in a chair in my study. I'm leaving the house as soon as we've had our little talk."

Sophia patted the bed. "Sit down, Chris."

Chris hesitated a moment before gingerly settling on the edge of the bed. He took her hand in his. "How do you feel?"

"Not too bad, considering. The headache powder worked wonders. I hope to leave my bed and go downstairs later today. Perhaps we can have dinner together."

"Isn't it too soon?"

"I don't like lying in bed."

"You almost died, Sophia."

"I might have died had the Maroons not found me."

"You were unconscious four days."

"Udamma said that was a healing time for me."

"Are you feeling well enough to talk?"

She sighed. "I already said I was sorry. I know I acted rashly, and I promise to do nothing in the future to worry you."

"Your brother was here. He accused me of failing to

protect you. For once he was right. I shouldn't have taken a wife while I have no time to devote to one."

"Since when have you listened to anything Rayford has to say?"

"Since I've had a chance to think."

"What exactly are you saying?"

He stood and walked to the window. "I don't really know."

Sophia eased out of bed and joined Chris at the window, surprised to find she wasn't the least bit dizzy. "It's a beautiful day outside."

He glanced at her over his shoulder. "You shouldn't be out of bed."

"Why not? I feel fine." She searched Chris's face, reading nothing but concern in his expression. How could she have been so stupid as to think he could love her?

"Hold me, Chris."

"Sophia—"

"Please, I've been so lonely. I know you don't have time for me, but I miss being close to you."

Chris stepped behind her and wound his arms around her. "Is that better?"

Her head fell back against his chest. "Hmmm, much better. When I was caught in the hurricane, I feared I'd never see you again."

He turned her in his arms and stared into her eyes. "Would that bother you?"

"I know you don't want to hear this, Chris, but my feelings haven't changed. No matter how you feel about me, I still lo—"

He stopped her words with a kiss, as if he didn't want to hear her declaration of love. Nevertheless,

Sophia tasted love in his kiss, sensed his desperate attempt to deny his own feelings. How long did he intend to resent her and blame himself for Desmond's death? How long would he deny what was in his heart?

"Damnation," he growled as he broke off the kiss and tried to pull away. Sophia's hold on him tightened.

"You're not well enough for this."

"I assure you I am fine. Make love to me, Chris. I need to feel alive again."

She could tell by the look in Chris's eyes that he was fighting a battle within himself. But in the end it was no battle at all. He was as hungry for her as she was for him. Her nightgown fell away as if by magic. She stood before him naked and unashamed as she reached for the buttons on his shirt and frantically worked them free.

Chris tore off his shirt and carried her the short distance to the bed. She slid down his body until her feet hit the floor. Chris dropped to his knees before her, kissing a path between her breasts and down her stomach to the nest of curls protecting her womanhood.

Sophia's knees nearly buckled when he parted her with his thumbs and teased the hard little nubbin he found there with his tongue. Sophia clung to his shoulders for support as he inserted two fingers inside her and licked along the dewy folds of her cleft. She was only moments away from climax when Chris rose abruptly.

"Nooo!" she wailed.

He gently pushed her onto the bed. "Roll over on your stomach, love," he urged hoarsely.

Sophia stretched out on her stomach, watching as Chris locked the door and then pulled off his boots and trousers and tossed them aside. He was already hard, his engorged sex jutting upward from between his muscular legs. Sophia reached for him.

"Not yet," he said, deliberately avoiding her touch. "Lie still and let me love you."

Sophia felt him leaning over her, his body hot, his breath even hotter. She jerked in response when his lips touched her neck, kissing and nipping gently as his mouth slowly moved down her spine, pausing to lavish attention on her firm buttocks. Her patience at an end, Sophia wanted to scream for him to hurry.

"Soon, love, soon."

She felt him shift behind her. Then he pushed her knees up and placed a pillow under her stomach. Open and vulnerable, Sophia waited for him to tell her what to do. She felt his mouth on her, felt his tongue enter her pulsating center. She squirmed and moaned, raising her bottom to give him better access.

"Chris, please." She wanted more than he was giving her.

She was nearly mad with need when he finally thrust his sex inside her. She wiggled her bottom and pushed backward against him, begging without words.

"I know," Chris gasped. "I feel the same way."

Grasping her hips to hold her still, he shoved hard, withdrew and shoved again, this time to the hilt. Sophia cried out as he thrust and withdrew, setting a frantic pace, driving her higher and higher. Leaning over her, he pushed her hair out of the way and kissed her neck. Then he lifted her breasts in each hand and alternately pulled and massaged her nipples.

Sophia felt as if her soul were leaving her body. The ache grew intense, stronger than she'd ever felt before. Her need was greater than reason, her pleasure soaring higher than mortal comprehension. Then she shattered.

Moments later, Chris joined her. Sophia heard him cry out, felt his final thrust and then the warm gush of his seed as he exploded inside her. He collapsed against her, causing her to crumple beneath him. They lay still, panting, limbs entwined, his weight pressing her down into the mattress. Then he rolled away, staring at the ceiling. Sophia shifted around to lie on her back.

"Are you all right?" Chris asked. "I didn't mean to be so rough. I can't seem to control myself when I'm with you."

"Is that a bad thing?"

He turned his head and looked at her. "The worst. You make me forget my guilt, and I'm not ready yet to forgive myself."

"Or me," Sophia ventured.

"I . . . don't know what I'm feeling right now; however, I can no longer find it in my heart to hold you responsible for Desmond's death, if that's any comfort to you."

Sophia considered his answer and decided she could live with it. She smiled and snuggled against him.

Chapter Fourteen

Except for the colorful and still somewhat painful knot on her forehead, Sophia felt like her old self again. A week had passed since Chris had made love to her. They had made love twice that night, and Sophia couldn't have been happier. The only thing she wasn't at peace with right now was her uselessness. She was of no use to Chris except in bed. She wanted to be his helpmate, someone he could confide in, someone who could help ease the burden of running the plantation.

Over dinner one night, Sophia voiced her misgivings about her place in Chris's live. "I'm bored doing nothing all day," she said as the last course was taken away. "I need something to fill the void. You are always so busy; there must be something I can do to help."

Chris considered her request and then shook his head. "I don't know what that would be, Sophia. Isn't taking care of the house enough for you?"

"The house runs itself. There's little for me to do except go over the menus with Chandra."

"You can't work in the fields, I wouldn't allow it. The same goes for the distillery. It's hard, dirty work."

"What about the books? I am a quick learner."

"My financial records are kept up to date by my solicitor in Kingston. Mundo keeps a daily accounting, and I take the results to Mr. Fenton weekly."

Sophia's shoulders slumped. There must be something she could do.

"Why don't you visit the Chesters? I'm sure Lady Agatha will tell you how she occupies her days."

"It's not the same, Chris. Agatha has children to keep her busy."

Chris searched her face. "Do you want children, Sophia?"

"It's bound to happen."

"That's not what I asked. Do you want my children?"

"Do you want me to bear your children?" Sophia shot back.

"I hadn't really thought about it before, but as you say, it's bound to happen."

He was evading the issue, Sophia knew. "Why are you being evasive?"

"I didn't think I was."

"I told you I lo—"

"Be careful, Sophia."

Since Chris didn't want to hear words of love, she began again. "I want children, Chris, your children. But until it happens, I need something to do."

"Most women would be happy to engage in ladylike pursuits such as embroidery, gardening, music and shopping."

"I'm not most women."

His blue eyes kindled. "I know." He pushed his chair

back and rose. "Shall we explore the difference in our bedroom?"

She couldn't resist that devilish smile of his, especially when it was directed at her. She placed her hand in his. "Very well, but this conversation isn't over."

Sweeping her into his arms, he carried her up the stairs. He did indeed hear the last of the subject from Sophia that night, for he kept her mouth far too busy to talk.

Lord and Lady Chester and their house guest arrived at Sunset Hill the following morning. They had come to inquire about Sophia's health.

"We didn't come sooner because we didn't want to interfere with your recuperation," Agatha explained. "You're looking marvelous, my dear, except for that ugly discoloration on your forehead, and I'm sure that will disappear in time."

"We've brought our niece," Lord Chester said. "Sophia, I'd like you to meet Lady Amanda Dartmore. She was just recently widowed and has come to Jamaica to get over her loss. She arrived yesterday on the *Lady Jane* out of Liverpool."

"Welcome," Sophia said. "I hope you enjoy your visit to Jamaica."

Sophia thought Lady Amanda very young to be a widow. She was petite and blond and round in all the places a woman should be round. The only unattractive thing about her was a certain hardness about the eyes. Her catlike gaze settled disconcertingly on Sophia as she offered a limp hand.

"I'd like to speak with your husband," Chester said. "Is he about?"

"Please make yourself comfortable in the parlor

while I send someone for him. I'm sure he'll be happy to see you. Will you stay for luncheon?"

"We'd be delighted," Agatha replied. "Wouldn't we, Chester?"

"I believe I can spare the time. Perhaps you can tell us about your ordeal, Sophia. I understand you were found unconscious by the Maroons."

"Later, dear; let dear Sophia send for the captain," Agatha scolded.

Sophia hurried from the room, uncomfortably aware that Lady Amanda had judged her and found her lacking. She wondered why. She sent a kitchen boy for Chris, ordered tea and returned to the parlor to await her husband.

The conversation faltered after the weather was explored. Lady Amanda jumped into the void. "I'm dying to know what happened to you while you were with those horrible Maroons." Her eyes gleamed. "Did they . . . did they harm you? I would kill myself if one of them touched me."

Sophia felt a slow building of anger. Lady Amanda knew nothing about the Maroons, yet assumed the worst. "They treated me very well. If not for them I would have died."

Amanda gave a delicate shudder. "I'm glad it was you and not me."

Fortunately, the tea tray arrived, allowing Sophia to drop the subject. Unfortunately, Amanda wasn't about to let it drop. While Sophia poured, Amanda asked, "What did your husband think about your sojourn with the Maroons?"

As Sophia struggled for an answer, Chris walked through the door.

"I am grateful for their care of Sophia," Chris said as

he joined the small group. He stopped in his tracks when he saw Amanda.

Glancing over at Chris, Sophia noted his stunned expression and wondered if he knew Amanda Dartmore.

"Christian!" Amanda squealed. "How wonderful to see you again! I've missed you."

Chris seemed to pull himself together. "Lady Amanda, I'm speechless. You're the last person I expected to see in Jamaica."

Agatha clapped her hands. "How wonderful! You already know one another."

Jealousy clawed deep into Sophia's heart when Amanda rose to her toes and kissed Chris's cheek. Was that a gleam of appreciation in his eyes? How well had he known Amanda? He certainly seemed to be devoting a great deal of attention to her.

Amanda seemed overly flirtatious and friendly for a newly widowed woman. She eyed Chris hungrily, as if she wanted to pounce on him and devour him. As for Chris, he appeared suitably embarrassed.

Finally he disengaged himself from Amanda. "Shall we retire to my study, Chester?"

The moment the men left, Amanda said, "If my dear departed husband had been as attractive as Christian, I wouldn't be so happy to be a widow."

Sophia was quick to notice how easily Amanda used Chris's given name.

"Amanda," Agatha chided, "you're embarrassing dear Sophia."

"Oh, pooh, Auntie, we both know I hated Dartmore; he was thirty years my senior. The marriage was arranged by my parents, I had no choice in the matter."

"I'm sorry your marriage was an unhappy one," Sophia said. "Have you known Chris a long time?"

Amanda's eyes gleamed. "Long enough."

Flustered, Agatha shot Amanda a startled look and abruptly changed the subject. The three women exchanged small talk until the men returned to the parlor for lunch. Sophia excused herself to see to the preparations and order a table set up on the patio overlooking the garden. When she returned, she noted that Amanda had Chris cornered and was conversing earnestly with him. The Chesters were noticeably absent.

"What happened to Lord and Lady Chester?" Sophia asked.

"They were summoned home," Chris said. "One of their children had sustained a minor injury, and Lady Agatha wished to return to Orchid Manor immediately."

"I preferred to remain and enjoy the company of people closer to my own age," Amanda explained. "Christian generously placed his carriage at my disposal. I hope you don't mind, Sophia. Chris and I have a great deal to discuss."

"Of course I don't mind," Sophia replied, resisting the urge to grit her teeth. They repaired to the patio. Sophia saw to the removal of two place settings and joined them at the table.

"Weren't you Sophia Carlisle before your marriage?" Amanda asked presently. She tapped her chin. "Now, why does the name sound familiar? Perhaps it will come to me."

"Drop it, Amanda," Chris warned. "How long ago did Dartmore pass? Were you with him when it happened?"

Amanda batted her eyes at him. Apparently, Chris and Amanda had been intimate friends at one time, Sophia deduced, and jealousy reared its ugly head.

Amanda sent Chris a beguiling smile. "You know

perfectly well Dartmore and I weren't close. I was in Town and he was in the country when he passed four months ago. Like most married couples, we found it expedient to live separate lives. That's the best plan, don't you agree, Chris?"

Sophia waited for Chris's answer. Would he prefer to live apart from her like Amanda and her husband?

"If that arrangement worked for you, then I'm pleased you and your husband found a measure of happiness in your marriage."

His noncommittal answer pleased Sophia.

Amanda batted him playfully. "I commend you on your diplomacy, Chris, but I found no happiness whatsoever in my marriage." She stared pointedly at him. "There were some advantages in being married to an older man, however, as I'm sure you're aware. Was yours an arranged marriage? You never mentioned you were getting married when you visited me in London before you sailed off to Jamaica."

Chris could almost taste the hostility between Amanda and Sophia and wondered if his wife suspected that he and Amanda had been lovers. He had to warn Amanda to keep their past to herself.

"One might call our marriage arranged, but not in the way you probably think," Chris said truthfully. "I chose to wed Sophia, but neither of us expected to end up married to each other. It's complicated."

Amanda looked confused. "I don't understand."

"Perhaps Chris can explain," Sophia said, rising abruptly. "Please excuse me, there's something in the kitchen I must attend to. I'm sure my husband will entertain you in my absence."

Chris stared after Sophia, aware of her displeasure. What had she expected him to say? Did she want him to declare his undying love? Avow that theirs was a love match?

Amanda grasped his arm. "I would enjoy a stroll through your garden, Christian. It's lovely. I've never seen such an array of flowers. The colors are magnificent."

"It's grown rather wild, but Sophia and I like the untamed look."

Amanda licked her lips, rose on her toes and kissed him on the mouth. "Untamed, yes; you always were one to enjoy the taming of wild things. We were good together, weren't we, Chris?"

"That was a long time ago, Amanda."

He guided her along the winding garden path, only half listening while she chatted about anything that popped into her head. When they reached the place where the jungle encroached upon the garden, she stopped and pushed her breasts suggestively against his arm.

"I might be convinced to remain in Jamaica," she purred, "if you gave me a tiny bit of encouragement."

Chris pushed her away. "I'm married, Amanda. Why did you come to Jamaica?"

"I came for *you*, obviously. I had no idea you were married." She glared up at him. "You don't love your wife; you as much as admitted it. Besides, if I remember correctly, there is a scandal associated with her name."

Chris scowled. "Shall we change the subject?"

She moved closer to Chris, until he could smell the musky scent of her lust. He felt as if he were being stalked by a predator. Not only was Amanda a beauty, but she was an enthusiastic lover. Some things a man never forgets. His cock gave an involuntary jerk, and he cursed his body's involuntary response to her sexual overtures. It wasn't as if he wanted Amanda; he just couldn't stop his spontaneous reaction.

"You've always known how I feel about you, Chris. Just say the word and we can be lovers again."

"Amanda, you are an alluring woman, but I think you should set your sights elsewhere. I don't need a lover, I have a wife."

She laughed. The grating sound set Chris's nerves on edge. "I've already set my sights on someone, do you have any objections?"

"None at all, as long as it isn't me."

Reaching up, Amanda wound her arms around Chris's neck and pulled him down for a kiss. Her lips were soft, lush, the promise in them apparent. Chris fell into the kiss reluctantly, wondering why this she-devil had picked him to torment when London was full of men.

When she came up for air, she sent him an enticing smile. "It *is* you, Chris." Then she pulled his head down for another kiss.

A bush rustled. "Excuse me—am I interrupting something?"

Chris pushed Amanda away, searching his mind for an explanation.

"Oh, no, Sophia, you're not interrupting," Amanda purred. "I was just enjoying the garden and your husband's company. We *are* intimate friends, after all." She sent Chris a seductive smile. "I hope to continue our . . . conversation at a later date."

Chris groaned inwardly. He couldn't be alone with Amanda again. The woman was a troublemaker, and he had enough trouble for one lifetime.

Chris did the only thing he could think of to get himself out of an uncomfortable situation. "It's time I returned to the distillery, ladies. We lost valuable time during the hurricane and its aftermath, so every hand is needed. It was a pleasure seeing you again, Lady Amanda. My carriage will be waiting to take you home whenever you are ready. Sophia, I'll see you at dinner tonight."

"The pleasure is all mine, I assure you," Amanda replied. "I'll see you again soon, Chris."

Turning on his heel, Chris made a hasty exit.

Amanda regarded Sophia with cool composure. "I suppose you saw your husband kissing me."

"It seemed to me that you were doing the kissing," Sophia shot back. "How well do you know Chris?"

"Intimately, if you know what I mean."

Sophia bristled. "I don't care what you were to Christian in the past. Keep away from him. I'm not going to stand by idly while another woman seduces my husband."

"I know men, and believe me when I say Chris is ripe for seduction."

"I'll thank you to stay away from him in the future."

"Stay away? Indeed no. I'm finding Jamaica to my liking. Shall we return to the house? It's time I left."

As far as Sophia was concerned, it was past time. How had Chris become involved with a wanton little vixen like Amanda? Why were the Chesters not aware of her wicked nature? Was she the only one who saw Amanda for what she really was? Now she knew why a woman of Amanda's sophisticated tastes would leave the comforts of London for Jamaica. She had followed Chris.

* * *

Sophia postponed dinner when Chris failed to return to the house and she finally ate alone. She retired immediately afterward. Lady Amanda's visit had left her exhausted and feeling inadequate.

Kateena was brushing Sophia's hair when Chris entered the bedroom. He must have just bathed, for his hair was wet. He dismissed Kateena with a wave of his hand. She bobbed a curtsy and left.

"I'm sorry about dinner. A piece of machinery broke down and I couldn't leave until it was fixed. I ate leftovers from the kitchen when I returned."

"Would you like to explain about this afternoon?"

"If you're referring to that little episode in the garden with Amanda—"

"Little episode? Is that what you call it? The woman followed you to Jamaica to continue your affair. You were kissing her. What does that say about our relationship?"

"You're making too much of it, Sophia. For your information, Amanda kissed me. And I didn't invite her to Jamaica. I said good-bye to her in London and thought that was the end of it."

"Did you enjoy the kiss?"

Chris flushed. "Not exactly."

"What *exactly* did you feel?"

"Surprise, mostly. Amanda was the last person I expected to see at Sunset Hill. You believe me, don't you?"

Sophia turned away. "The evidence was pretty damning. I don't want you to be alone with your former mistress again."

"Hardly a mistress, Sophia. I only saw her during my occasional visits to London."

"She's a man-eater. I don't know what the Chesters

were thinking to invite a woman of loose morals into their home."

A smile turned up the corners of Chris's mouth. "You're jealous."

Hands on hips, eyes defiant, she glared at him. "You've given me sufficient reason to be."

Curling his arms around her waist, he brought her against him, bent his head and kissed her, little nibbling kisses on her mouth and down her throat. She arched her neck, breathing deeply of his essence, of the clean smell of soap. He held her close with one arm about her slim waist and pressed his face in the hollow between her breasts. His tongue flicked out and he licked her skin.

"You taste delicious."

Sophia's skin felt on fire. But she had to find the strength to stop him, no matter how difficult it might be. Breathless, shaking with suppressed need, she pushed against his chest. Chris backed away, cocking his head to stare at her.

"What is it now?"

"I want to discuss Lady Amanda."

"Later." He reached for her. This time she went willingly into his arms.

He bore her to the bed and began to make slow, sensual love to her, leaving no part of her body unattended. With hands and mouth and tongue, he aroused her until she lay quivering beneath him. But when he would have completed the act, she pushed him onto his back and lifted herself astride him.

Her blue eyes gleamed with wicked delight. "It's my turn to torture you."

She felt his body jerk in response and smiled. Then she lowered her head and licked his flat nipples. He let out a curse. She didn't let his pained expression stop her as she slowly and thoroughly kissed and licked down the length of his body. When she took his engorged staff into her hands and ran her tongue over the tip, he nearly bucked her off the bed.

"You don't have to do that, love," he gasped breathlessly.

She raised her head. "I want to."

She continued to lavish her undivided attention on his throbbing sex until he roared an oath, lifted her up and thrust hard and deep inside her weeping center. She tightened her muscles around him, savoring the feel of him stretching her, thrusting deep and fast inside her.

She panted. She moaned. She lifted her hips to meet his passionate assault. Then suddenly the tempest building inside her burst into a thousand bright stars of shimmering joy. Every muscle in her body contracted. Dimly she heard Chris shout her name, and then she closed her eyes to savor his release and the aftermath of her own.

Arms and legs entwined, Sophia relaxed against Chris. She could tell by his even breathing that he was nearly asleep.

"Chris."

"Hmmm?"

"What did Lord Chester wish to speak to you about?"

He sighed. "Can't it wait until morning?"

"No, you usually leave the house before I awaken."

"Very well, what do you want to know?"

"Lord Chester. What did he want?"

"Trouble has erupted on his plantation. His slaves are upset about the long hours they've had to work to restore the plantation after the hurricane and have retaliated in small ways. He's afraid the situation will only get worse."

"Did you tell him what Udamma said?"

"Telling planters to free their slaves is a waste of breath. In fact, they hold me responsible for causing dissatisfaction among the slave population because I freed my slaves when they didn't."

"That's ludicrous!"

"Tell that to Chester and the others. This situation was a long time in the making. I'm afraid it's going to come to a head soon."

"What do Lord Chester and the others intend to do?"

"Chester is sending Lady Agatha and the children to England on the first available ship. He thinks I should send you home with them."

Sophia shot up. "I'll do no such thing! Surely you're not considering it, are you?"

"I'm tired; can't we discuss this later?"

"We most definitely will not discuss it later."

"If you must know, I'm seriously considering it. You can stay with my brother and his wife until it's safe to return. Go to sleep; nothing is final yet."

Sophia lay awake long after Chris fell asleep. She wasn't going anywhere until she spoke to Lady Chester. Was this Chris's way of saying he wanted to rid himself of her?

The earliest opportunity Sophia found to visit Lady Chester was a week after her conversation with Chris. Three days of soaking rain had left the roads a quagmire, but three more days of sunshine had dried up the muck. Sophia and Kateena set out for the Chester plantation shortly after luncheon.

After days of being stuck inside with two lively children, Agatha was happy to see Sophia. Kateena visited with the servants while Sophia sat on the veranda with Agatha and Amanda.

"What brings you out this sunny day?" Agatha asked.

Sophia took a sip of fruit juice from a crystal goblet as she considered her answer. Upon entering the house she had noticed boxes and crates piled up in the foyer.

"Are you going on a trip, my lady?"

"Perhaps, but I'm not sure yet. I'm preparing just in case my dear Chester decides the slave situation is getting out of hand and sends us home to England."

"Oh, pooh," Amanda scoffed. "I'm not going anywhere. If Aunt Amanda leaves, I intend to remain and see to the household for Uncle Chester. What about you, Sophia? Will you be leaving Jamaica? If you do, rest assured that I will do my very best to take care of your husband in your absence."

Agatha sighed. "I've tried to convince dear Amanda to leave with me and the children, but she adamantly refuses." She spread her hands in defeat. "There is nothing more I can do."

"You'll be happy to know, Lady Amanda," Sophia said, "that I fully intend to remain at Sunset Hill no matter what. My husband's welfare comes before my own safety."

"How admirable," Amanda said sourly.

"I feel the same way, but neither of you have children to worry about. Their safety must come first. When Chester says it's time to leave, we will go."

"As well you should," Amanda agreed. "So should you, Sophia. What if you are carrying Captain Radliff's heir? Shouldn't you have a care for your health and welfare?"

"Amanda is right, my dear," Agatha concurred. "I know the captain would want you safe. He must have mentioned his wishes on the matter to you."

"Oh, indeed he did, but I have a mind of my own. I don't always do as he says. I am of the opinion that Sunset Hill will remain safe from marauders."

Agatha let out a gusty breath. "I admire your courage, but I must warn you that no one is safe in these troubled times. When slaves revolt, madness takes over. Plantations are burned and people are killed indiscriminately. It happened before, late in the last century."

"Nevertheless, I'm not leaving Chris," Sophia insisted, sending an unspoken message to Amanda.

"Then you and dear Amanda can keep each other company," Agatha maintained, "unless I can convince Amanda to leave the island when the time comes."

Agatha shot from her chair when a child's scream echoed through the house. "Oh, dear, it's one of the children. I must go; I'm sure dear Amanda will entertain you in my absence."

Amanda studied Sophia through narrowed cat's eyes. "I finally remembered why your name sounded familiar. Though I don't recall the details, the scandal you caused set London on its ear several years ago."

"You have a good memory, my lady, but you have little room to talk. I doubt your reputation is as pristine as Lord and Lady Chester believe. I assume you and Chris were lovers at one time," she said bluntly.

"We were intimate friends," Amanda purred. "Make of that what you wish."

"I know exactly what to make of it."

"I know enough about you to go to your husband with the facts. He might not be as forgiving as you think. He may send you away after he hears me out." Amanda's smug voice set Sophia's teeth on edge. "And I will be here to relieve his loneliness."

Sophia stifled a smile. Amanda didn't know as much as she thought if she wasn't aware that Chris had been involved in the scandal himself.

"Be my guest, my lady. Tell my husband whatever you wish. Nothing you can say will cause a rift in our relationship."

Lady Agatha returned. "Motherhood has its rewards, but it's also trying. Are you looking forward to providing your husband with a family, Sophia dear?"

"I hope to have children one day," Sophia replied.

"You've been married several weeks; perhaps you're already increasing."

Sophia was saved from replying when a servant arrived to announce that Captain Radcliff had arrived.

"Chris is here?" Sophia said, half rising from her chair.

"Remain seated, Sophia. I'll invite him to join us, then send for Chester."

Agatha gave the appropriate orders. Sophia noted with some irritation that Amanda fluffed her blond hair and tugged at the neckline of her bodice in anticipation of Chris's arrival.

Chris strolled onto the veranda, stopping abruptly when he saw Sophia. "Sophia—I had no idea you were here."

"Obviously," Sophia muttered darkly. Had he come to see Amanda?

"Chuba said you and Kateena had taken the carriage, but I assumed you had gone to Kingston."

"Please sit down and join the conversation, Captain," Agatha invited. "Chester will be here directly."

"Something has happened," Sophia said when she noted the worried expression creasing Chris's brow. "What is it?"

"Please do tell us, captain," Agatha said. "I'll hear it from Chester sooner or later."

"I'd prefer to wait for Lord Chester."

"I am here," Chester said as he joined them. "What is it, Radcliff? Have you news?"

"Are you sure we should discuss this in front of the ladies?"

"If this is something that will affect all of us, then please speak freely, Captain," Agatha said.

"Very well. I received word that marauding slaves burnt a plantation near Spanish Town. The violence could spread down here."

"That settles it," Chester asserted. "My family will leave Jamaica on the *Mary Deare*. She's due in port next week."

"Oh, pooh, Uncle, I'm not afraid," Amanda scoffed. "I shall remain and see to things here while Auntie takes the children to safety."

"You should leave with your family, my lady," Chris said. "I'm sending Sophia to my brother until the danger is over."

"You can try," Sophia warned, "but it will do you no good. I'm staying, Chris."

"We'll discuss this at home, Sophia."

Though Chris appeared determined, Sophia refused to be coerced into something she didn't want to do. And she most definitely didn't want to leave him.

"I think you should leave, Sophia," Amanda said,

breaking the tense silence stretching between Chris and Sophia.

"Why should you remain behind when I cannot?" Sophia shot back.

"I'm the logical choice to see to the men. Auntie has her children to protect, and you may be carrying your husband's heir."

Chris's head shot up. "Sophia, is that true?"

"It's time I left," Sophia said, rising and smoothing out her skirts. "I'll find Kateena while you and Lord Chester discuss this latest development."

"I'm going with you. From now on, I don't want you leaving the plantation without a guard."

"Chris, really—"

"He's right, my dear," Lord Chester concurred. "Things are fairly quiet for the time being, but one never knows. Rest assured that my family will be aboard the *Mary Deare* when she leaves Kingston."

Chris and Sophia took their leave. Once Kateena joined them, there was no opportunity to continue their argument.

Riding beside the carriage on Atlas, Chris pondered Amanda's startling words. Was Sophia carrying his child? If so, he had to convince her to return to England. Chris's emotions were bewildering. How did he feel about becoming a father? He searched his heart for an answer and was surprised at what he found. He hadn't felt anything so emotionally exhilarating in more years than he cared to count.

Chapter Fifteen

Three days later, Rayford arrived at Sunset Hill after Chris had left the house for the distillery.

"I've come to bid you good-bye, Sophia," Rayford said.

"You're leaving?"

"Sir Rigby offered me employment as his overseer, but I refused. I might have accepted if I hadn't learned what he and other plantation owners are planning. I wanted no part of it. I'm not putting my life in danger for them. I've booked passage aboard the *Mary Deare*. Most of the planters are sending their families home, and I wondered if you were going with them."

Sophia's mind was focused on what Rayford had said about the plantation owners' plans. "What do you mean? What are the plantation owners planning?"

"You mean your husband hasn't told you about the militia?"

"What militia?"

"Rigby and some of the other planters have formed

a militia. They intend to flush the Maroons out of the foothills and kill as many of them as they can find."

"No! That's inhuman. When is the attack supposed to take place?"

"Soon, I think. They believe Sam Sharp is behind the recent problems they have been having with their slaves. They think he's inciting the slaves to act against their masters. I know nothing about slavery and care even less. Why should I place my life in jeopardy when none of this means anything to me?"

"I think you should go home, find gainful employment and beg Claire to take you back," Sophia advised. "Your unsavory vices are ruining your life. Associating with men like Sir Oscar was a big mistake."

Rayford's shoulders slumped. "I know that. He's a vindictive man. He won't let me rest until I redeem my markers from him."

"How do you intend to raise the funds to pay him? I'm surprised he's allowing you to leave, knowing you have no way of getting your hands on that kind of money."

Rayford looked away, but not before Sophia noted the guilty look on his face. "Tell me the truth, Ray."

"Be careful, Sophia—that's all I'm going to say. The man never gives up. The *Mary Deare* arrives in a couple of days, so I doubt I will see you again. I hope I'm gone from this cursed place before violence erupts." He spun on his heel and strode off.

"Damn you, Ray, you always were a coward!" Sophia called after him.

But Sophia didn't have time to waste on her stepbrother. She had to warn the unsuspecting Maroons before the militia struck. She considered sending for

Chris but decided against it. He probably knew what the planters intended and had purposely kept it from her. If he wasn't going to do anything about it, she would.

Sophia told no one where she was going as she headed to the stable. The stable lad saddled her mare without asking her destination. It wasn't his place to question the mistress.

Though Sophia wasn't sure she could find Udamma's hut in the foothills, she had to try if she wanted to prevent a massacre. She rode along the main road until she reached what she guessed was the halfway mark between Sunset Hill and Kingston. Then she turned her mare into the jungle, riding but a short distance until the underbrush grew too dense to continue. She dismounted, tied her mount to a tree branch and set off on foot toward the foothills.

She walked quite a while before she spied the footpath she'd been looking for. Her face glistened with sweat as she swatted at insects buzzing around her head. She wished she had worn long sleeves but hadn't thought that far ahead in her rush to leave. Abruptly the footpath disappeared. With a start, Sophia realized she had wandered off the trail and was hopelessly lost. She couldn't see the mountains for the trees.

Nevertheless, Sophia trudged on. The shimmering sun rose high in the sky; it filtered through the trees, burning her face and arms. She took a step, heard a rustling sound ahead of her and froze. A man carrying a cudgel stepped out of the brush, blocking her path. Sophia stifled a scream. The man was tall and huskily built, his dusky face covered by a beard.

"What you doin' here, lady?"

Sophia swallowed the lump of fear lodged in her throat. "Can you take me to Udamma? It's important."

The man narrowed his eyes. "Who are you, lady?"

"Sophia Radcliff."

"Captain Radcliff's woman?"

"His wife, yes."

"Why do you want to see Udamma?"

"I must speak with her. It's a matter of life or death."

She must have convinced him, for he nodded and said, "Follow me."

They trudged through the forest for what seemed like hours before reaching the Maroon campsite. Udamma was carrying water from a nearby stream when she spotted Sophia.

"Mistress, what are you doing here? Has something happened? Are you in trouble?"

"No, but you are."

"Come inside and rest, mistress. After you have refreshed yourself with a cup of cool water, you can tell me what is troubling you."

Sophia entered the hut and was offered the only chair. She took it gladly and accepted a cracked cup filled with cool water. She drained the cup and handed it back to Udamma.

"I've come to warn you, Udamma. You must alert your people immediately."

Udamma's dark brow furrowed. "Warn us about what, mistress?"

"The planters have formed a militia and are preparing to raid Maroon campsites. They blame Sam Sharp for inciting rebellion among their slaves."

"Daddy Sam preaches passive resistance. He would never condone violence."

"That's not what the planters think. The raid will come soon; you and your people must flee into the mountains. I'm sure you have hiding places where no one can find you."

"We do, mistress. Are you sure about this?"

"Very sure. They will bring firearms, Udamma. Do your people have weapons?"

Udamma shook her head. "We only have cudgels and sharpened sticks."

"The militia have guns and pistols that fire bullets. Many people will be killed."

"You came all this way to tell us we are in danger?"

"You saved my life—I could do no less."

Udamma grasped Sophia's hand and squeezed. "Thank you. If you are ready, someone will lead you back to the road."

"I left my mare in the forest near the road, but I'm not sure I can find her again."

"Lemuel, the man who brought you here, will take you to your horse. Trust him—he won't hurt you."

Sophia took her leave. Lemuel guided her through the jungle, and after a few false starts they found her horse grazing contentedly. When Sophia turned to thank Lemuel, he had disappeared. Sophia led the horse to the road, mounted and prepared to set off toward Sunset Hill. But before she could get started, she had the bad luck of spotting Sir Oscar Rigby, who happened to be on his way to Kingston.

"What the devil . . ." Rigby blustered as he came abreast of her. "What were you doing in the forest?" A crafty look came over his face. "Never say you were meeting a lover."

Sophia kneed her mount, but Rigby grabbed her reins.

"Not so fast. You didn't answer my question. If you were meeting a lover, I want equal time. Caldwell was of no use to me where you are concerned. I regret bringing him to Jamaica. The bastard hasn't two farthings to rub together; I'll never get the blunt he owes me."

"My stepbrother's debt has nothing to do with me. Let go of my reins."

Rigby lunged at her. Sophia arched away, struggling to regain control of the reins. If she'd had a riding crop she would have used it. Unfortunately, she hadn't thought to bring one.

Rigby grabbed for her again. "Hold still, damn you! All I want to do is talk to you. Perhaps we can reach an agreement on terms for payment of Caldwell's debt. I'm not difficult to please." His face hardened. "I also have friends in England. Word from me can bring an end to your stepbrother's worthless life."

"Blackmail won't work. I'm not responsible for Rayford's debts."

Rigby finally managed to catch her skirt. He would have hauled her off her horse if another rider hadn't come galloping down the road. Sophia heard the rider call her name. It was Chris. Relief shuddered through her. Rigby released her instantly, dug his heels into his mount's flanks and fled in the opposite direction.

Sophia waited until Chris caught up with her. "What in God's sweet name are you doing out here alone? Was that Rigby I saw riding off?"

"It was."

"Are you mad? Or are you deliberately looking for trouble?"

"Chris, we need to talk." She wanted to know if he was aware of the militia and if he intended to warn the Maroons.

"Indeed we do, but not here." He reined Atlas around, expecting Sophia to follow.

Chris fumed all the way home. He'd been furious when he learned Sophia had left Sunset Hill without informing him or telling Kateena where she was going. Had he known she intended to ride out alone, he wouldn't have allowed it. If she'd wanted to go to Kingston or visit neighbors, she should have taken her maid and a guard. By the time they reached Sunset Hill, Chris's anger had simmered into full-blown rage.

"Upstairs," he growled when they entered the house. "Now!"

He preceded her up the stairs, opened the door and stepped aside so she could enter, then slammed the door behind him.

"Will you kindly explain why you insist on putting your life in danger? Didn't I tell you not to leave the plantation without protection? Never have I known a more stubborn, rash or irresponsible woman. You attract trouble like a magnet."

Sophia stamped her foot. "Will you stop berating me long enough to listen? I have reasons for what I did."

"Was one of them meeting Rigby?"

Sophia's mouth dropped open. "Why ever would you think that?"

"Chuba told me your stepbrother called on you today. What did he tell you to send you out on your own?"

"That's what I've been trying to explain. Rayford told me the planters have formed a militia and plan to raid the Maroons. Did you know about it?"

"No, I did not, and I strongly suspect they deliberately kept me in the dark. They know I would try to stop them."

"Thank God. I hoped you weren't involved."

"So where were you? Why didn't you tell me about this instead of tearing off?"

"There wasn't time. Ray didn't know when the raid would take place, except that it was going to be soon. I had to warn Udamma."

"You what? You could have been . . . What if . . . ? You little fool!"

Grasping her shoulders, he hugged her against him, his arms tightening until the breath whooshed out of her.

"I'm sorry," he said, loosening his hold but not letting her go. "You should have let me take care of it. Acting rashly could have brought you to harm."

"Would you have ridden out to warn the Maroons?"

"Of course—did you doubt it?"

Sophia looked away. "I was afraid that you knew about the raid and weren't going to do anything about it."

"I didn't know about it. Now tell me what happened. Tell me everything, starting with your meeting with Caldwell."

"Rayford is leaving Jamaica on the *Mary Deare*." She went on to tell him everything, including Ray's reason for leaving and the civilian militia Rigby had organized for the raid.

"How did you and Rigby happen to meet on the road?"

"It was accidental."

"What did he want?"

Sophia shrugged. "He was being his usual obnoxious self, demanding payment for Ray's gambling debt."

"And you are the payment he's demanding," Chris growled. "Will that man never give up?"

"Not until Rayford pays him, and at this point that doesn't seem likely."

Chris gave her a quick kiss and pushed her away. "I'm going to see Rigby. I want to know more about the raid he's planning."

Sophia clung to his arm. "Don't go. Rigby is a dangerous man. He'll stop at nothing to get what he wants."

"That's what I'm afraid of. He's made it plain that he wants you, and I intend to set him straight. Then I'm going to call on Chester and ask him why I'm the only planter who wasn't informed about the raid."

"You already know the answer to that."

"I want to hear it from his lips. I thought we were friends, but things haven't been the same between us since I freed my slaves." He gently extracted his arm from her grasp. "Don't leave the plantation, Sophia, not for any reason. Understand?"

"Udamma said the Maroons aren't inciting a rebellion. She said if there's trouble, it's the planters' fault for mistreating their slaves."

"Don't change the subject. I want your promise, Sophia."

"Very well, I promise to remain on the plantation. Besides, I believe the Maroons are seeking shelter in the mountains even as we speak. No one will find them if they don't want to be found. The raid will be an exercise in futility."

Satisfied with Sophia's answer, Chris left.

Chris was angry as hell. When he'd come upon Sophia and Rigby on the road he'd wanted to strangle the man, but Rigby had taken off before Chris could confront him. His anger at Sophia for leaving the plantation after he'd specifically forbidden her to travel abroad had been formidable. But when he'd learned the reason for her disobedience, his anger had slowly dissipated.

Then fear had kicked in. Placing herself in danger was a way of life with Sophia. Was he destined to spend the rest of his days protecting her from her impulsive acts?

Simmering rage rode Chris's shoulders all the way to Rigby's plantation. When he arrived and asked for Sir Oscar, the butler invited him to wait in the foyer while he announced Chris's presence to his master.

A short time later, Rigby lumbered out of his study, eyeing Chris with a hint of fear. "I didn't hurt your wife," he blustered. "We happened to meet on the road." His eyes narrowed slyly. "Did you know she had been wandering alone in the jungle? What errand do you suppose sent her there?"

"My wife's comings and going are none of your concern. I'm giving you one last warning, Rigby. Stay away from Sophia. She's not responsible for her stepbrother's debts."

"Perhaps," Rigby hinted snidely, "she was meeting a lover in the jungle. Reprehensible as it sounds, some women enjoy fornicating with randy bucks."

Chris grasped Rigby's throat, squeezing until the other man's eyes bulged. "You bastard," Chris hissed. "I'd squeeze the life out of you if I didn't need information you've been keeping from me." He released his hold. Rigby slumped, gasping for breath.

"One day you'll regret your attacks upon my person."

"I doubt it. All I require from you is information."

"I'm a veritable font of information. I know a lot about your history with your wife. Rayford wasn't at all reticent about relating the facts to me. What amazes me is that you married the woman responsible for the death of your best friend. I understand she provoked the duel, and that you took off afterward and left her to the scandalmongers."

Chris's hands clenched into fists. "You're treading on dangerous ground, Rigby. My private life is none of your affair. Tell me about the raid into Maroon territory you're planning."

Rigby paled. "Who told you about that?"

"Caldwell called on Sophia today. He told her he's leaving on the *Mary Deare* and why."

"The coward," Rigby bit out. "I offered him employment as a means of repaying his debt, and he refused. Seems he doesn't want to become involved in our problems with the slaves."

"Why wasn't I told about the raid?"

"We are all aware of your objection to slavery. Your foolish decision to free your slaves has placed us all in grave danger."

"I don't see how my affairs affect you or anyone else."

"Don't you? Our slaves are demanding freedom because of you. We have to act before things get out of hand. Incidents have already occurred. Rebellion is in the air."

"Why attack the Maroons?"

"They are the instigators. Sam Sharp is preaching insurrection. He has to be stopped."

"It is my understanding that Sam Sharp preaches passive resistance. Your militia will carry firearms; the Maroons own no lethal weapons. What you're planning is a massacre."

"Slaves don't know the meaning of passive. You

heard what happened at Spanish Town, didn't you? They didn't need weapons to destroy property and kill. That could be us if we don't take steps to prevent it."

"I want no part of your raid."

Rigby smirked. "That's why you weren't told. But don't think your plantation is safe. Your paid workers are as likely to join the rebellion as my slaves. Sunset Hill is no safer from death and destruction than my plantation or Chester's, or anyone else's."

"We'll see about that." Chris strode toward the door, halted and swung around. "Where is Caldwell now?"

"In town, waiting for the *Mary Deare* to arrive. If you were wise, you'd send your wife to England along with Lady Chester and her children."

"I'm surprised you're not leaving with them."

Rigby shrugged. "I may, if our raid proves unsuccessful. I don't care to be around when the Maroons retaliate, and I'm sure they will if we don't eradicate them."

"When will this raid take place?"

"As if I'd tell you," Rigby sneered. "Good day, Radcliff."

Chris stormed out. If murder weren't unlawful, he'd gladly see to Rigby's early demise.

Chris's next stop was Orchid Manor. The place was deserted but for servants. Upon Chris's inquiry, he was told that Lord Chester had taken his family to Kingston to await the *Mary Deare*. It seemed that someone had tried to set fire to the house the night before, but the fire had been discovered and doused before substantial damage was done.

"Where is Amanda?" Chris asked, recalling her vow to remain no matter what.

"She packed her bags and joined the rest of the family," Chris was informed. "The attempt to burn down the house frightened her."

Chris returned home in an apprehensive mood. The situation was extremely dangerous, thanks to the planters. If they had followed his example, none of this would be happening. Rigby had been right when he'd said no one was safe. Neither his plantation nor his wife would be spared if rebellion swept the island. It was a known fact that rabble-rousers created the kind of chaos that incited men to violence. Random death and destruction would surely follow.

Sophia was waiting for Chris when he returned. "What did you learn?"

"It's just as you said. Rigby wouldn't tell me when the raid would take place but hinted that it would be soon. I was deliberately kept in the dark because of my objections to slavery."

"What can you do?"

"Nothing; it's too late, anyway. You've already warned the Maroons. We can only hope they are well on their way to safety."

"What did Lord Chester have to say?"

"I didn't see him. He's taken his family to Kingston to await the *Mary Deare*. Lady Amanda decided to leave with them after an attempt was made to burn down their house."

Sophia exhaled slowly. "So it's started."

"It may well be the beginning of the end. Considering the situation, I think you should leave the island. Pack your things. I'll write letters to my brother and my banker. I want you to be able to draw on funds I have deposited in the Bank of England."

"Funds? I didn't know you had funds to draw upon.

I assumed the reason you were determined to make your plantation work was because your livelihood depended on it."

Chris laughed. "I'm wealthy, Sophia. My ship has carried cargo and plied the trade routes for many years. It has earned me and my crew a good living. Even if the plantation fails, I will still be rich. Though my brother inherited the title and estate from our father, I received a generous bequest upon the death of my grandmother and invested it wisely."

"I don't understand."

"I don't suppose you do. Sunset Hill presented a challenge, one that I embraced wholeheartedly. I love the sea, but I looked forward to making Sunset Hill profitable. It was a new adventure, and I always did relish venturing into unknown territory. It takes my mind off . . ." He fell silent.

Sophia knew exactly what Chris had been running from these past seven years. His guilt.

"Your wealth or lack of it makes no difference to me, Chris. I'm not leaving Jamaica."

"You *will* leave, even if I have to carry you aboard the *Mary Deare*. And I'm sending Casper with you."

"Why do you care whether or not I remain? It's my choice."

"It's *my* choice. You're my wife, and I intend to keep you safe. Don't argue, for you won't win. You're going and that's final. I'll send Kateena to help you pack. We'll leave for Kingston first thing in the morning. You can wait with the others at the King's Arms for the ship to arrive."

Sophia's mouth flattened. "If you make me leave, things will never be the same between us. I will never be a wife to you again." She turned away.

He swung her around to face him. "Don't make threats you'll regret, Sophia. You are leaving and that's final. My brother will take care of you until I send for you."

"The danger is as great for you as it is for me," Sophia charged. "If you don't need the plantation, come with me. We can live anywhere. I know you never wanted this marriage, but please don't send me away."

Chris stiffened. "Is that why you think I want you to leave? You're wrong, dead wrong. I married you to keep you safe, and you won't be safe here."

She backed away from him, his determination to send her away leaving an ache that would never heal. "Deny it all you want, but Desmond's death is still a raw wound inside you. Until it heals, we can't be together. I shall leave, but don't expect me to return. I knew our marriage was a mistake."

"Sophia, listen to reason. No matter what, we're still married. Nothing will change that. When I send for you, you'd damn well better return."

"Go to hell, Chris! When I leave Jamaica, I will live my life as I see fit. If you cared for me, you wouldn't send me away."

"You little fool! I'm sending you away to protect you."

"Protecting me—that's all it's ever been about. I want more than that. If I can't have what I want, what I need, I may as well leave and be done with this marriage and you. Excuse me—I've packing to do."

"I'll have the letters ready before we leave for Kingston tomorrow." He nodded curtly and stormed off.

Sophia opened her mouth to tell him she wanted neither his brother's protection nor his money, but she promptly closed it. She'd need money for lodging and expenses. She wasn't sure whether she wanted to buy a cottage in the country or rent a modest town house in a respectable neighborhood in London. She was through with living like a pauper, depending on Rayford for her sustenance. If Chris couldn't love her, he could at least support her.

Casper and Chris entered the dining room together that night. Sophia could tell by the look on Casper's face that he wasn't happy. In fact, he looked downright defiant.

"Is something wrong, Casper?"

Casper sent Chris a sullen look. "The captain said I have to go to London with you. He said you need my protection."

Sophia shot Chris a quizzical glance. Chris returned it with a warning look.

"I don't want to leave the captain, Sophia. He needs me. After you leave, he'll have no one."

"That's his choice, Casper, not mine. It won't be so bad. We can explore London together. Or maybe we'll live in the country. We can do anything we like."

"It won't be for long," Chris promised. "I'll send for you and Sophia as soon as the current situation is resolved. I may even come for you myself. I promised Justin I'd return to England for the christening of his heir."

"Truly?" Casper asked.

"You have my word. But you must promise to behave and give Sophia no trouble."

"I promise," Casper said, albeit reluctantly.

After the somber meal, Casper left to pack his belongings. Sophia excused herself immediately afterward. Chris rose and followed her up the stairs. Sophia entered their bedroom and turned on him.

"What do you want?"

He reached for her. She skittered away. "This is our last night before we part. It may be months before we're together again."

"More like never," Sophia retorted. "You can always ease your loneliness with Lady Amanda."

"She's leaving with Lady Chester. Besides, you don't mean that."

She searched his face. "Chris, do you love me?"

He hesitated. "Define love."

"If you felt it, I wouldn't have to describe it."

"I feel desire for you—that's always been an integral part of our relationship."

"Admit it, lust is the only emotion you're capable of where I'm concerned."

"I want to make love to you, Sophia. I can't let you go without a proper good-bye."

"Then don't let me go."

"That's not an option and you know it. Will you let me love you, Sophia?"

She shook herself free from the burning desire in his eyes. "Letting you *bed* me was never a problem; making you love me was."

With a groan, Chris reached for her and bore her to the bed. He was so eager for her he didn't bother undressing her. Instead, he shoved her skirts to her waist and knelt between her thighs. He unbuttoned his fly; his cock sprang free.

But instead of impaling her immediately, he bent his head and placed his mouth on her, feeding on her pink, succulent flesh. But he was too needy to linger on preliminaries. Sophia was leaving, and he wouldn't see her again for a very long time. This was their last night together. When she began to moan and raise her hips to meet his questing tongue, he rose up, balanced himself on his muscular arms and thrust inside her.

He captured her lips, his mouth devouring hers, his hands kneading her breasts. Needing to touch bare skin, he found the edges of her bodice and tore it open. Then he closed his mouth over her nipple and suckled. He felt her body convulse, heard the keening wail building in her throat. His mouth left her breast and returned to her lips, swallowing her cry as she shattered in his arms. He shouted his climax into her mouth and exploded.

"Was that good-bye, Chris?" Sophia asked when her breathing returned to normal.

"For now, Sophia, but not forever."

Sophia doubted that very much. Nevertheless, she didn't object when he undressed her and then himself and began to make love to her again. This time, his initial urgency appeased, he slowly built her passion and his until a firestorm of need roared through them, culminating in sweet surrender.

Chapter Sixteen

Sophia and Chris spent two nights at the King's Arms before the *Mary Deare* arrived. They had made love both nights; Sophia couldn't refuse him despite her anger, for it might be the last time she and Chris were together as husband and wife.

Sophia stood at the rail now, watching Chris grow smaller as the ship slipped her moorings and rode the wind across the bay. Their good-bye at the dock had been coolly polite in spite of their heated lovemaking the previous three nights. Her passionate response had done nothing to change his mind about sending her away.

Because of the limited quarters, Sophia was forced to share a cabin with Amanda while Agatha and her children occupied another. Rayford was given the first mate's cabin, which he shared with Casper, while the first mate bunked with the second mate.

During the long voyage, Sophia helped Agatha with the children and tutored Casper in geography and English. She kept as far away from Ray as possible; she spoke to him only at the evening meal, when all the passengers came together. To Sophia's dismay, Ray and Amanda had formed a close friendship. They were often together on the deck, their heads together, engaged in intimate conversation.

Sophia tried to fill the long days at sea with activity, but the endless nights were difficult. She missed Chris. Even though she had accepted that he could never love her, just being with him, making love with him, had made life bearable. Now she had nothing. Chris had sent her away, and what was left of her shattered pride would prevent her from returning when he sent for her—if he sent for her.

Chris hadn't wanted a wife. He especially hadn't wanted Sophia. Being with her kept his guilt over Desmond's death alive. He had used the potential slave rebellion as an excuse to send her away.

Sharing a cabin with Amanda was as bad as Sophia had suspected it would be, and she was grateful to Ray for keeping Amanda occupied much of the day. But at night she had to suffer Amanda's complaints of boredom, bad food and the damage the salt air was doing to her flawless complexion. Amanda bemoaned the lack of fresh water for bathing and needled Sophia about her sickly appearance.

"I intend to return to Jamaica when all this is over. Chris and I had scarcely time to renew our acquaintance," Amanda told Sophia one day as Sophia prepared to leave the cabin.

"Good luck," Sophia replied, walking away from Chris's ex-lover. She was heartily sick of listening to Amanda's bragging about her relationship with Chris.

Once the ship left the warm southern waters and entered colder climes, Sophia and the others spent less time on deck. Late-fall weather in England was usually rainy and cold, and no one had clothing warm enough to protect them against the cutting north wind. Sophia spent long hours by herself, pondering the past few months she'd spent as Chris's wife and wondering what the future held for her.

Fortunately, no storms appeared on the horizon to delay the *Mary Deare* and she arrived in London on schedule. As the ship slid into her berth in London Pool, Rayford cornered Sophia on the windswept deck.

"What are your plans now, Sophia?" he asked. "Will you return to the family home in Essex?"

"No, I have no fond memories of the family estate. I haven't decided where Casper and I will settle. Chris wants us to stay with his brother, and perhaps we will until other arrangements can be made."

"How will you manage on your own without the earl's support?"

"I have access to Chris's bank account."

An avaricious gleam appeared in Rayford's eyes. "Perhaps you can find it in your heart to lend me the blunt to start over. If I can pay some of my debtors and fix up the house, maybe Claire will return to me."

Lady Amanda came up to join them. "Are you ready to debark, Ray?" She wound her arm in his and batted her eyelashes.

"You should see Claire before you do anything stupid," Sophia advised. "Have you written to her since you left London?"

"She's the one who left me; I saw no need to write."

"I thought you wanted to borrow money to pay your debts and fix up the house."

"Ray has no need of a house," Amanda maintained. "He can stay with me."

"Is that true, Ray? Have you fallen so low that you'd let a woman support you?"

Ray scowled at her. "Amanda offered me a temporary place to stay until I get back on my feet, and I accepted. What's wrong with that?"

"You lied to me about needing money to fix up the house and win Claire back. You wanted money for your own selfish pursuits."

Rayford did not reply.

Sophia felt compelled to issue a warning, whether or not Amanda heeded it. "If you have money, Lady Amanda, Ray will drain you dry. He has a legal wife, so marriage is out of the question, if you're thinking along those lines."

"Oh, pooh," Amanda scoffed. "Ray's wife left him; as far as I'm concerned, he's free. Besides, he amuses me."

"For how long?"

"See here, Sophia, you have no right to interfere in my affairs." Ray said. "So what if I lied to you? You always were a selfish bitch. You never did anything I asked to help out the family."

"Like prostitute myself?" Sophia asked sweetly. Without waiting for a reply, she strode toward the gangplank, which had just been run out. Casper joined her, his face beaming with excitement.

"What are we going to do once we debark?" he asked. "Shall we find an inn?"

Dusk was quickly approaching. "Do you know of a respectable inn where we can stay while we decide where we will settle?"

He shook his head. "The captain and I usually slept aboard ship when we were in port. We never stayed in London long."

By the time their luggage arrived, darkness was descending. Sophia knew she had to make a quick decision. Amanda and Rayford had already hailed a hackney, and Lady Chester had sent word for the Chester coach to pick up her family.

"May we drop you someplace?" Agatha asked. "I do believe Amanda secured the only hackney available."

Sophia made up her mind. "Christian wanted us to stay with his brother, the Earl of Standish. Do you know him?"

"Not personally, but my dear Chester is acquainted with him. His mansion is not far from our town house on Berkley Square in Mayfair."

"Then Casper and I would be happy to accept your generous offer of transportation."

They chatted about a half hour before the Chester coach lumbered out of the darkness. The baggage was quickly loaded in the boot as the Chester family, Sophia and Casper settled inside.

"Are you expected, Sophia dear?" Agatha asked.

"No, there was no time to send word ahead. Christian gave me a letter of explanation for his brother. We won't be staying long, however, for I intend to find my own lodging."

"Why ever for?" Agatha asked. "None of us will be staying in London long. All this nastiness in Jamaica will be over before you know it, and we can return home."

Sophia said nothing. Casper could return, but she would not, even if Chris sent for her, which she seriously doubted. He didn't have time for a wife, and Sophia had been the last woman in the world Chris would have wed had he been given a choice. She had literally been thrust upon him.

Sophia sat in silent contemplation while Agatha

tried to control her exuberant children. Even Casper seemed excited, but that could be explained by his sudden freedom after the confinement of the ship. The coach rolled to a stop.

"Ah, here you are, Sophia. This is where Lord Standish and his wife Grace live."

The coach door opened and the steps were let down. Casper scrambled out first and gawked at the house. "Is this where we're staying? It's a bloody mansion."

"Watch your language, Casper," Sophia chided. "We'll stay here until we can find our own lodging. Don't let the size frighten you."

Sophia was somewhat intimidated herself. This was no mere town house. From what she could see of it, the Standish home was a gated mansion sitting well back from the street on a manicured lawn.

"Rather impressive, isn't it?" Agatha said from the coach. "Shall I send my man to announce you?"

"No, thank you," Sophia declined. "That won't be necessary."

If the earl turned her away, she didn't want anyone witnessing her embarrassment. The coach rattled off, leaving Sophia, Casper and their luggage sitting before the imposing gate guarded by a stone lion on either side.

"Well, Casper, I suppose we had best find our way to the door."

"What if the gate is locked?"

"Then you can climb over and announce our arrival. I've seen you scamper up the masts on the *Intrepid*. I doubt that little gate will hamper you."

Casper grinned. "I can climb that in no time at all."

"Let's see if it's locked first." She tried the latch; it opened at her touch. "It wasn't locked after all. Shall we find out if we're welcome?"

Casper picked up one of the valises.

"Leave the luggage, Casper. If we're not welcome, we won't have to carry it back. And if we are welcome, someone will fetch it for us."

She swung open the gate and strode resolutely up to the front door. Casper was but a step behind her. She grasped the brass knocker and banged it hard.

"That ought to bring someone."

Indeed it did. A stately butler opened the door a few moments later. "How may I help you, madam?"

"You can fetch the earl for me, if you please," Sophia said. "I carry a letter from his brother."

"Captain Radcliff? He is in Jamaica, madam."

"I know. Casper and I just arrived on the *Mary Deare*. We sailed from Jamaica nearly four weeks ago. I am the captain's wife."

"Wait here while I inform His Lordship of your arrival."

He disappeared into the far reaches of the mansion. Sophia studied her surroundings. Lord Standish must be fabulously rich, she decided, impressed by the marble foyer supported by tall columns and decorated with statues and valuable pieces of art. Several candelabras illuminated even the darkest corners. A marble staircase leading to the second floor rose magnificently before her.

A man who looked a great deal like Chris, only older, approached from the direction in which the butler had disappeared.

Sophia had seen Chris's brother a time or two during her Season but she'd never paid much attention to him, for he was already courting Grace. It was Chris who had caught her attention, and held it to this day.

"Sophia? Is Chris with you?"

"Chris is still in Jamaica, my lord. I carry a letter from him."

"Who is the lad with you?"

"Casper, Chris's ward."

"Ah, yes, Chris has spoken of him. You must both be exhausted after your long voyage. Shall we go into the parlor while I read Chris's letter? Then you can tell me what happened to bring you and Casper to London. Baxter, bring refreshments for Lady Sophia and young Casper. Better yet, take Casper to the kitchen. I'm sure Mrs. Humphreys can find something special for him."

Casper left with Baxter. Sophia watched the earl for his reaction to her. She knew Chris had written to him about their marriage and wondered how he would treat the woman who had caused his brother years of anguish. When he frowned at her, Sophia decided he didn't approve of her, and she really couldn't blame him.

"You are the last person I would have expected Chris to marry," he said.

"I know you don't approve of me, my lord, but for Casper's sake, I hope you will let us stay until I can make other arrangements."

"What the devil are you talking about? There has to be a good reason you are here, and I'm anxious to hear it—after I read Chris's letter, of course."

"Of course." Sophia dug in her reticule for the sealed letter and handed it to the earl. She waited for him to read it, having no idea what Chris had written.

"Good God," the earl exclaimed after he had read the letter through twice. "I had no idea things had gotten that bad over there. Chris was right to send you away. You are welcome to stay with us as long as you wish. You are Chris's wife, whether or not I approve, and you will be treated with the courtesy and respect due a lady of your standing."

"You're very kind, my lord," Sophia said. "But I intend to find lodging for Casper and myself as soon as possible."

"That won't be necessary. Chris asked me to look after you until the danger is past and he comes for you, and so I shall. He never explained in his last correspondence, however, how you two found each other after all these years. I saw him the day before he sailed, and he said nothing about you. In fact . . ." He hesitated. "Well, never mind what we discussed—our conversation is no longer relevant."

"I can well imagine what Chris said," Sophia muttered. "Our meeting was accidental. I thought Chris explained how it happened. Perhaps another time—"

"Of course, forgive me for prying." Baxter entered the parlor with a tray. "Ah, the refreshments have arrived. After you've eaten, Baxter will show you to your room. Dinner is at nine. We aren't having guests tonight; my wife is increasing and prefers quiet evenings at home. I'll introduce you at dinner; she's resting right now. Will you pour?"

Sophia poured tea for herself and the earl and munched on tiny sandwiches and biscuits. Casper joined her a short time later, grinning from ear to ear.

"Cook makes delicious gingerbread. Much better than Chandra's. But don't tell Chandra I said so."

Sophia smiled at the boy's ability to adjust. The earl rose and summoned Baxter. He arrived shortly.

"Have our guests' bedrooms been prepared?"

"They have, milord. A fire has been lit in both chambers to ward off the chill."

"Thank you, Baxter," Sophia said. "The transition

from hot to cold weather hasn't been easy. I appreciate the warmth of a fire."

"I can sleep in the servants' quarters," Casper injected.

"Indeed not," the earl said, affronted. "The house has a very pleasant nursery. And I intend to hire a tutor for you tomorrow. We can't have you slacking off on your studies."

"Casper has had no formal lessons," Sophia explained.

"Then it's about time. Where is your luggage?"

"We left it at the gate."

"I'll have it delivered to your rooms. Off you two go now. We'll see you both at dinner."

"Thank you, Your Lordship. Casper and I appreciate your hospitality."

"Please call me Justin, and I shall call you Sophia. You are my sister by marriage, after all."

"Do I have to have a tutor, Sophia?" Casper asked. "I don't need any book learning. The captain taught me all I need to know." He grimaced. "I'd rather sleep in the stables. I'm too old for the nursery."

"The nursery will be more comfortable than the stables," Sophia said. "Accept the present situation, Casper. It won't be for long."

Casper brightened. "That's right. I'm sure the captain will send for us soon."

Sophia said nothing. It hurt too much to think of Chris. She had begged him to let her remain in Jamaica, and he had denied her. Casper might return to Paradise, but she would remain in England. There was no longer a place for her in Chris's life.

Sophia was assigned a lovely room overlooking the garden. Amid much grumbling, Casper was taken to the nursery. Sophia's luggage arrived shortly afterward, along with a little Irish maid named Peg, a sweet-faced girl who couldn't be more than sixteen. Peg unpacked for Sophia and hung up her wardrobe, which Sophia saw at once was totally inadequate for late fall in London. She and Casper would need warmer clothing immediately.

"Will there be anything else, milady?" Peg asked. "His Lordship said I'm to be your maid."

"No, thank you, Peg. I'd like to rest until dinner. But you could check on Casper in the nursery, if you will. He's probably feeling lonely."

Peg bobbed a curtsy and left. Sophia lay down on the bed, her own loneliness nearly insurmountable. How was she going to exist without Chris? She had lived in a kind of limbo for seven years, until they had found one another again. Their meeting and subsequent marriage after all those years had been a miracle wrought by Fate.

Now Fate had struck again. Chris had sent her away and she was alone once more. Sophia fell asleep thinking about the only man she would ever love. A man who would never return her love.

Peg woke Sophia in time to dress for dinner. Adding a shawl to her dimity gown for warmth, she left her room and followed Peg down the stairs to the dining room. A footman opened the door and she swept inside.

"Sophia!"

Casper jumped from his chair and ran to meet her. "I thought you'd never come down."

"Where is everyone?"

"His Lordship just left to escort Lady Grace to the dining room. I don't like it here, Sophia. I miss the captain and everyone at Sunset Hill."

Sophia ruffled his hair. "I'm sure Chris will send for you soon. Until I can find suitable lodging for us, we must accept the earl's hospitality."

"I don't want a tutor."

Sophia didn't have time to answer; the earl and his wife had just entered the dining room. Sophia turned to greet the heavily pregnant woman.

"My lady, thank you for opening your home to us. I promise it won't be for long."

"Grace, my dear, this is Sophia, Christian's wife, and Casper, Chris's ward," Justin said.

"Welcome, both of you," Grace said kindly. "Please be seated. I swear I am always hungry these days."

They took their assigned seats. Servants began bringing food immediately. While they ate, Sophia surreptitiously studied the countess. Blond, petite and beautiful, she appeared to be at the end of her pregnancy.

"Why didn't Chris come with you?" Grace asked.

"There was trouble on the island, my lady," Sophia explained. "Most of the planters have sent their wives and families to England, out of harm's way."

"How dreadful. Even in England we've heard about the unrest among the slaves. Slavery is such a terrible thing."

"That's why Chris freed his slaves soon after he arrived at Sunset Hill." She toyed with the food on her plate. "I didn't want to leave Chris, but he insisted. I don't believe Sunset Hill is in danger."

The earl and his wife exchanged knowing glances. Sophia sensed their curiosity but didn't want to delve into her relationship with Chris in front of Casper. When she noticed him yawning, she suggested that he go to bed as soon as he finished dessert.

After Casper was led off by a footman, the earl suggested that they have tea in the drawing room. Sophia knew instinctively that the earl would ask questions. She also knew she would not lie to Chris's brother.

Once Grace was seated comfortably, her feet resting on a footstool, she said, "I must confess that both Justin and I were stunned by Chris's marriage."

"No more than I, my lady."

"Please call me Grace—we are sisters now. I don't mean to be nosy, but we saw Chris before he sailed and he said nothing about you or marriage."

"I'm not surprised. We met aboard his ship. It was strictly accidental."

"You were a passenger aboard Chris's ship? Funny—Chris didn't mention taking on passengers," Justin mused.

"I was a stowaway—I had no idea the *Intrepid* belonged to Chris."

"I see," Justin said, but apparently he didn't. "But marrying you, a woman he had reason to . . . er . . . dislike, a woman he wanted to erase from his memory, doesn't make sense," Justin continued relentlessly.

"Justin," Grace admonished. "It's not our place to pry. Sophia is Chris's wife. That's all we need to know. Sophia, dear, does Chris intend to come for you and Casper once the danger has passed?"

"I don't know. We parted on less than friendly terms. I'm not sure he'll want me to return to Jamaica, and if he does, I'm not certain I wish to return."

"Oh, dear," Grace said, clearly distressed.

"When are you expecting, my lady?" Sophia asked, abruptly changing the subject.

Grace laid a hand on her burgeoning middle. "In

four weeks, but it seems like forever. Late October or early November at the latest. Chris promised to return for the christening."

Sophia said nothing; she wasn't privy to Chris's plans. A great deal depended on the situation in Jamaica.

"Chris's letter asked us to make you welcome for the duration of your stay, and indeed we shall," Justin said. "Please consider our home yours."

Though grateful for the earl's hospitality, Sophia couldn't accept his generous offer. Not when she was undecided as to where she would settle permanently. She needed a home to call her own, and that wasn't necessarily at Sunset Hill with Chris.

To that end, Sophia said, "I know Chris wanted us to stay here, but I intend to find suitable lodgings as soon as possible. Chris gave me access to his bank account, so I won't be dependent on anyone."

"But, Sophia, we are your family," Grace said in a hurt voice.

Touched, Sophia said, "I know, and I shall depend upon you and His Lordship for many things, but I am not sure Chris and I can heal our differences. I don't want to impose on you at a time like this. Then there is Casper to consider. You know Chris found him living on the streets. He's not accustomed to luxurious surroundings. He's seen too much of the world, some of it sordid, and sailed with Chris too long to be treated like most children his age. Both Casper and I would be happier living on our own."

Justin shook his head. "I believe you are making a mistake, but I will honor your wishes. If you like, I will accompany you to Christian's bank and help you find appropriate lodgings."

"I'm glad you understand," Sophia replied.

"But, Sophia," Grace objected, "you and Chris married against all odds. You were fated to be together. I know Chris. He wouldn't have wed you unless he wanted to. What can possibly be wrong between you that cannot be healed?"

"It's a long story. Suffice it to say, our marriage was forced upon Chris. I'm not sure he wishes it to continue."

"But you love Christian; I can see it in your eyes when you talk about him."

Sophia lowered her eyes. "Unrequited love is a difficult cross to bear."

"Oh, Sophia, I'm sure Chris—"

Sophia gave Grace a sad smile. "I know you are aware of our history together, my lady. Chris still bears the guilt of Desmond's death. Unless he can resolve his guilt, our marriage is doomed. It should have never happened. I told him it was a mistake, and so it was."

Grace bowed her head. "I'm sorry."

"As I am, my lady."

Grace struggled to her feet. Justin rushed to help her. "I am tired. We will speak further in the morning, Sophia. I will give you the name of a dressmaker who can furnish you with a wardrobe appropriate for English weather. You have but to mention my name and she will put all her efforts into dressing you as quickly as possible."

"Thank you, Grace."

During the following days, Sophia spent a good deal of time at the dressmaker and finding clothing for Casper. They both shivered in their thin attire and were grateful when the first items of their wardrobe arrived. Sophia now had access to Chris's bank account and was taking Justin's advice about which parts of London would be appropriate for her to seek lodgings.

Within a month, she had rented a small, tastefully furnished town house on Russell Square that came with three servants. The rent was reasonable, since it was a less fashionable but still respectable area of London.

The day before Sophia was to settle into her new home, Grace went into labor, delaying Sophia's move. The midwife was sent for. While they waited, Sophia did her best to make Grace comfortable.

As the hours dragged on, Justin became frantic with worry. The midwife sent him away until he could calm himself, assuring him that all was going well. After Justin left, Grace clung to Sophia's hand, squeezing until Sophia feared her bones would break. About twelve hours after her labor commenced, Grace gave birth to a baby boy. The healthy lad began crying the moment he slid into the midwife's capable hands. Sophia had never seen anything more beautiful than that tiny scrap of humanity.

When Justin rushed in to see his wife and son, Sophia tiptoed out to give them privacy. She smiled and spread her hands over her stomach. It was quite possible that she had come away from Jamaica carrying Chris's child. A footman met her at the bottom of the stairs.

"Milady, a letter arrived for you today." He offered it to her on a silver salver.

Sophia accepted the letter and went into a small parlor at the back of the house to read it. It was from Chris. He must have sent it shortly after she'd left for it to have reached her so soon. She ripped it open and read the contents.

Chris wrote that the attack upon the Maroons never took place. It had been called off after an advance patrol informed the militia that the Maroons would be impossible to find. They had abandoned their campsites and moved into the mountains. No further instances of rebellion had occurred, and everything was back to normal.

The last part of the letter stunned Sophia. The *Intrepid* was bringing Chris to England to fetch her and Casper! He expected to arrive about three or four weeks after his letter reached her. He hoped to be in time for the christening of Justin's heir. Furthermore, he expected Sophia to return to Jamaica with him.

Nothing in Chris's letter raised her hopes for their future together. He hadn't said he missed her. There was no loving salutation or fond ending. Just Chris's edict scrawled across the paper, as if he expected her blind obedience. Had he learned nothing about her in all the time they had been together?

Three days after Grace gave birth, Sophia and Casper moved into their new lodgings.

Chris didn't regret sending Sophia away, for he had done it to keep her from harm. What he did regret was their bitter parting. Did she mean what she had said about not returning to Jamaica when the danger was over? Knowing Sophia, he was sure she had meant every word. But he wouldn't accept that. He had missed Sophia more than he imagined, more than he'd wanted to admit.

That was why he had written her the moment he realized it was safe for her to return. The ship that carried his letter had arrived in Kingston two weeks after Sophia had left.

Two more weeks after his letter was on its way, the *Intrepid* had arrived in Kingston. After the hold was loaded with rum, molasses and sugar, the *Intrepid* had sailed to England with Chris at the helm and Lord Chester as a passenger.

Chris wasn't concerned about his plantation during his absence for he had left Mundo in charge. All the cane had been processed, and there was nothing to do for a month or two except normal maintenance.

The *Intrepid* docked in the London Pool four weeks later, delayed several days by a violent storm. Chris hadn't seen Sophia for nearly three months and was the first one down the gangplank. Leaving Dirk Blaine in charge, he hailed a hackney and gave the driver his brother's direction. Then he sat back and tried to envision the kind of reception he would receive from Sophia and what it would take to convince her to return to Jamaica.

"Chris!" Justin exclaimed upon Chris's arrival. "Sophia said you were returning to London. And just in time for the christening. Come in, come in."

"Is Sophia here?"

It took but a few words from Justin to shatter Chris's hopes for reconciliation with Sophia.

"I'm sorry, Chris. Sophia moved to her own lodgings and took Casper with her. I don't think she felt comfortable here."

Chapter Seventeen

"Come inside, Chris," Justin invited. "We need to talk before you speak with your wife."

Chris followed Justin into the parlor.

"First things first. I have a son," Justin said proudly.

Chris slapped Justin on the back. "Congratulations! How is Grace?"

"I'm doing very well, thank you," Grace said from the doorway. "Welcome home, Christian. You're just in time for the christening a week from Saturday."

Chris bussed her cheek. "You look radiant, Grace. Motherhood becomes you. What did you name your son?"

"Theodore Christian. We call him Teddy."

"When am I to meet little Lord Teddy?"

"Soon, but first we need to discuss your wife," Justin answered. "Whatever possessed you to marry Sophia when you have refused to so much as speak her name ever since Desmond's tragic death?"

"You had best sit down for this," Chris said. "It's a long story."

Justin and Grace sat side by side on the sofa while Chris stood, legs braced as if he still rode the deck of a ship. "Did Sophia tell you anything about our meeting and marriage?"

"Very little," Justin said, "except that she stowed away aboard your ship. How did that come to pass?"

"Sophia was fleeing from a dangerous situation."

"Oh, my," Grace whispered. "Please continue."

"Her stepbrother had sold her virtue to a man to whom he owed a gambling debt. Sophia managed to escape her would-be ravisher and fled into the night. He called the Watch, charged her with assault and pursued her. When she found herself near Southwark quay, she sneaked aboard my ship."

"Oh, my," Grace repeated. "How horrible for Sophia."

"I always knew Caldwell was a bastard," Justin put in.

"I discovered Sophia on my ship the following day, too late to turn back," Chris continued.

"That must have been some meeting," Justin commented.

Chris plowed his fingers through his hair, recalling that day as if it were yesterday. "It was. I swear Sophia was put on this earth to torment me."

"So how did you end up married?" Justin wondered.

Chris paced as he spoke, revealing most but not all of the facts leading to his marriage to Sophia.

"So you really were forced into the marriage," Justin mused. "Sophia hinted as much, but I didn't know what to believe."

"How chivalrous of you," Grace said. "You married Sophia to protect her and then fell in love with her."

Chris stopped his pacing and stared at Grace. "Why ever would you think I love Sophia?"

"It's true, isn't it? Sophia loves you, she told me as much. The problem, as she sees it, is your inability to forgive yourself for Desmond's death."

"I'll carry that guilt to my death. Desmond's parents lost their son and heir. How can I forgive myself for that?"

"It's time to forget and forgive," Justin advised. "You can't be happy in your marriage until you do."

"Justin is right," Grace said. "Don't you want a family of your own and a wife who loves you?"

"I do, but I don't know if I deserve those things."

Grace gave an exasperated snort. "Honestly, Chris, you are the most stubborn man I've even known. Forgive yourself and get on with your life. Make up with Sophia—that's the best advice I can give you."

Justin was of a different opinion. "Grace is right about forgiving yourself, but whether or not you and Sophia can find happiness is debatable. You've made no effort to hide your contempt for her since that tragic day. I wouldn't recommend reconciliation unless you are certain you can get past Desmond's death. Why don't you stay here tonight and call on Sophia tomorrow? Have dinner with us and get acquainted with your new nephew."

Chris wavered, but in the end he declined the offer of dinner and a bed, although he did want to see his nephew. He followed Grace and Justin to the nursery. Grace picked up her son and presented him for Chris's inspection.

"Meet Lord Theodore Christian," Grace said, beaming.

Chris's admiration was genuine. Tiny Teddy was a handsome lad who yawned hugely and clutched Chris's finger with surprising strength. When he began rooting around for his mother's breast, Grace laughed and shooed the men from the nursery so she could nurse her babe.

Justin gave Chris Sophia's location as he walked his brother to the door.

Chris frowned. "My bank account was at Sophia's disposal; couldn't she find lodgings in a better neighborhood?"

"Sophia said the town house she rented suited her needs. When I saw she couldn't be swayed, I let her have her way. Your wife has a mind of her own, Chris, if you haven't discovered that by now."

"I know that better than anyone."

Justin wished him good luck. Chris knew he was going to need it as he mounted his horse and rode away. He was well acquainted with Sophia's stubbornness. But if the last three months without his wife had proved anything, it was the startling fact that he had missed her.

Sophia had been feeling ill ever since her move to her town house. Furthermore, she knew the reason for her malaise and was thrilled. Three months had passed since she had been with Chris, but she hadn't suspected she was increasing until just recently. She had wished for a child, but the signs of impending motherhood had escaped her notice. She'd been far too involved with Grace's lying-in and finding suitable lodgings to think about her missed courses.

One thing bothered her, however. If she hadn't been ill before, why now? Was something wrong with the babe? Her appetite was off, and she wasn't sleeping well.

Sophia wandered aimlessly about her bedroom, trying to decide whether to go for a walk or lie down and sleep. She was always tired these days.

Casper had accompanied his tutor on an outing and would be gone for hours. She wasn't expecting callers, for she hadn't been formally recognized by Society and probably never would. She was seriously considering moving to the country with her babe when her six-month lease was up on the town house.

Listlessly she picked up a book she had purchased on her latest foray to a bookstore, but she was so sleepy the words began to run together. She put the volume down and stretched out on the bed. She was asleep in minutes.

Chris almost had to force his way into Sophia's town house. The butler, who said his name was Dunning, had refused him entrance. Dunning said his mistress was indisposed and not receiving visitors. Even after Chris had identified himself as Sophia's husband, the man remained reluctant to let him enter. His patience exhausted, Chris brushed past Dunning and took the stairs two at a time. He found Sophia's room easily enough but stopped in his tracks when he saw his wife sleeping soundly, her face pale against the dark pillow of her hair.

He touched her cheek and whispered her name. She didn't stir. What was wrong with her? What had changed Sophia into this pallid imitation of his vivacious wife? She was sleeping so soundly he didn't have the heart to wake her. He tiptoed out of the room and closed the door behind him. As he started down the stairs, he heard voices in the foyer. They belonged to Dunning and another that he recognized immediately.

Chris continued down the stairs, wondering what Amanda Dartmore was doing here.

When he reached the bottom of the stairs, he demanded, "Why are you here, Amanda?"

Amanda squealed in delight and threw herself into Chris's arms. He tried to push her away, but she clung to him. "Christian! I was with Aunt Agatha when Uncle Chester arrived. He said he'd arrived aboard the *Intrepid*, and that you were in London, too. I came as soon as I could get away."

Aware that Dunning was staring at them, Chris dismissed the butler and peeled Amanda off of him. "This won't do at all, Amanda. I have a wife, in case you've forgotten."

"Oh, pooh, why should that bother you? Your marriage was no love match, so why should we deny ourselves? Remember how good we were together?"

"That was a long time ago."

Amanda threw herself at him, pressing her voluptuous body against his. "Not that long ago. This is London, not Kingston. Infidelity is expected among the *ton*."

"I'm not *ton*, if you recall. I'm not welcome in Society."

"Oh, pooh! That was then, this is now. Scandals come and go; few people remember what happened seven months ago, let alone seven years."

"It's over between us, Amanda; I thought I made that clear in Jamaica. Admit it and let us get on with our lives. You've taken lovers during my long absences— why this obsession with me now?"

She licked her lips and gazed up at him. "You're the best lover I've ever had, Chris. I couldn't wait for Dartmore to die. When he did, I traveled to Jamaica to tell you, and found you married. I had hoped we would wed and take up where we left off in London."

Stunned, Chris stared at her. "What ever gave you the idea we would wed if you were free? I thought we both understood that our relationship was based on pleasure, that commitment was neither wanted nor expected."

"Speak for yourself, Chris," Amanda huffed.

Before Chris knew what she intended, she grasped his head and pulled it down for a kiss. Her arms closed like vises around his neck, and her mouth clung to his lips with stubborn determination.

Chris heard a choking sound behind him and broke Amanda's strangle-like hold on him.

"Don't let me interrupt your reunion," Sophia said from the top of the stairs. "Have you tired of my stepbrother already, Amanda?"

Chris groaned. "Sophia, this isn't what it looks like."

Sophia started down the stairs but stopped before she reached the bottom. "What am I supposed to think when I find the husband I haven't seen for months kissing another woman in my foyer?"

"Chris and I are very old, very dear friends, I thought you understood that," Amanda sniffed.

"So I did. When did you dump Rayford?"

Amanda shrugged. "Ray was becoming annoying. His creditors began showing up at my door, threatening to throw him in debtor's prison if he didn't pay them. Besides," she added, "as amusing as he was, he expected me to provide the blunt to keep him solvent. I no longer wanted him around."

"How did you know Chris was in London when even I wasn't aware of the fact?"

"Sophia," Chris said, "I can explain."

Contempt colored Sophia's words. "An explanation isn't necessary. I have two good eyes in my head."

Chris groaned in frustration. "Please leave, Amanda."

"When can I expect you to call on me?" Amanda asked, smiling up at him.

"Never."

"Really, Chris, you don't have to be rude."

"It's the only way I can make you understand."

"Well!" she sputtered, gathering her skirts about her.

Chris held the door open, then slammed it behind her after she swished out.

Sophia felt her heart shatter as she watched Amanda leave. She had awakened earlier to the sound of voices echoing up from the foyer. Curious, she had risen from bed, washed her face, combed her hair and left her room. Once in the hallway, she had recognized Chris's voice. He had returned from Jamaica! Apprehension mixed with happiness had pulsed through her as she reached the top of the open staircase and gazed down into the foyer. But Chris wasn't alone. Amanda Dartmore was in his arms.

Anger had surged through her. When she saw them kiss, any hope Sophia harbored for a happy future with Chris evaporated. What she felt now was disappointment and hurt.

Chris started up the stairs. "Sophia, are you all right? You look so pale."

Sophia bristled. "How am I supposed to look when I find my husband kissing another woman?"

"If you'd looked closely, you would have seen that I wasn't participating in the kiss. Amanda was the last person I expected to see today."

"Today? What about tomorrow or the day after that?"

"This is ridiculous, Sophia. Why would I want to see Amanda at all? I made it abundantly clear in Jamaica that I wasn't interested in her."

"Obviously not clear enough."

She turned and started back up the stairs. Near the top, her foot tangled in her skirts, she tottered for a moment and then started to fall backward. She grasped frantically for the banister and found nothing but air. She closed her eyes and braced herself for the worst, folding her arms over her stomach to protect her babe. Then suddenly she was floating in air, cradled in Chris's strong arms.

She began trembling, too shaken to speak.

"I was right behind you, Sophia. I wouldn't have let you fall."

He carried her to her room and lowered her to her feet. She looked around, a puzzled expression on her face. "You carried me straight to my room. How did you know?"

"I was up here earlier. You were sleeping so soundly I didn't want to awaken you. Then Amanda arrived."

Sophia stiffened. She didn't want to be reminded of how badly it had hurt to see Chris kissing Amanda. "Forgive me for interrupting your passionate reunion."

"It wasn't like that, Sophia. I came straight here from Justin's house. I had no idea Amanda was with Lady Agatha when Lord Chester arrived home. He sailed with me aboard the *Intrepid*. Amanda took it upon herself to come here. How did she know where you lived?"

"From Rayford, I suspect."

"Has he been bothering you?"

"Not really. Amanda has been keeping him far too busy."

Sophia put some distance between them. Chris was

too attractive, too vitally alive for her peace of mind. On one hand she wanted to throw herself into his arms and on the other she wanted to flay him with the sharp edge of her tongue. The man was impossible. Impossibly handsome, impossibly arrogant, impossibly tempting. She couldn't bear any more hurt.

Chris reached for her. "This isn't the kind of homecoming I anticipated, Sophia. I hoped you'd be glad to see me."

She slipped out of his reach. "You sent me away, remember?"

"For your own safety."

"You should have waited to see if danger actually existed before getting rid of me."

He stalked her until she had nowhere to go to escape him. "The danger was very real. Fortunately, nothing came of it. I came to London to fetch you and Casper as soon as the *Intrepid* returned to Kingston Bay to take on new cargo. I thought we would remain in London until after the Christmas holiday. I want to give the crew several weeks' shore leave. They need to spend time with their families, and I promised Grace I'd stick around for little Teddy's christening and spend the holidays with them."

"Will you stay with Justin or find rooms of your own?"

Chris sent her a puzzled look. "I intend to stay right here with my wife. What makes you think I'd want it any other way?"

"Lady Amanda. Won't a wife hinder your . . . affair?"

He reached for her again and this time he caught her. "Dammit, Sophia, I have no interest in Amanda."

"You could have fooled me." She searched his face. "Have you forgiven yourself for Desmond's death? Do you still hold me responsible for the duel?"

"Why bring that up now?" He pulled her against him. "We haven't seen one another in months." His next words rumbled from his chest in a husky whisper. "I don't want to argue. I want to take you to bed and love you."

Sophia wanted that, too, even though she knew his need was driven by lust, the only emotion he was capable of. But before she could voice her reservations, he grasped her head between his hands and raised it for his kiss. As always, his kiss was pure magic, capable of making her forget her resolve, her name, her very reason.

She needed time to pull her ragged thoughts together. She broke off the kiss and looked into his angular face, burnished a deep gold by the Jamaican sun. His eyes, a startling blue, searched hers. Ignoring her reservations, she raised her hands to his chest.

Chris grinned, his eyes crinkling at the corners.

Unable to resist the magic of his kisses, Sophia slid her arms upward and stepped closer, locking her hands at his nape. She pressed herself against him and lifted her lips for another kiss.

Their lips met and fused. Hungrily. She felt his arms encircle her waist, close viselike about her as his mouth settled over hers. He deepened the kiss, his tongue tangling with hers.

Startled by her easy acceptance following her angry words, Chris shackled the demons still plaguing him after seven years and concentrated on his delectable wife. It had been too long since he had made love to Sophia. He molded her to him, urging her hips nearer, cupping the firm globes of her bottom and drawing her forcefully into the V of his braced thighs.

He eased back, aware of her hands on his chest, burning him, branding him, her fingers kneading. He was desperate to rid them of their clothing. Brushing her hands aside, he unknotted his cravat, then dragged the long strip free.

Dear God, if he wasn't inside her soon he'd go mad.

Hauling his shirttails free of his trousers, he pulled the constricting garment over his head without bothering with the buttons and tossed it aside. Then he spun her around and undid the laces on the back of her gown. Grasping the sleeves, he shoved the gown past her hips and lifted her out of it, kicking it away with his foot. Her shift followed. He pulled her into his arms, grateful that she wore neither corset nor drawers.

"I've dreamed of having you naked in my arms again."

"Are you sure it was me you dreamt about?"

Chris muttered a curse. "Don't spoil it, sweetheart. Forget the past and let me love you."

His hand slipped between them, cupping her breast. He weighed it in his hand and frowned. "My memory must be failing me. You're larger than I recall." Then he smiled. "I like it."

"Only because you imagine I'm someone else."

"I know precisely who you are. You're my wife, and I love making love to you."

He proceeded to prove his words as he bent his head and suckled her nipple.

Sophia caught her breath as he stroked and kneaded one breast while teasing the other with his tongue and teeth. She moaned out a protest when he released both breasts, dropped to one knee and clasped her waist.

"I need to taste you," he whispered, planting a kiss in the valley between her breasts before moving lower, over the slight bulge of her belly to the V between her legs.

Her legs started to buckle; Chris's strong arms about her were all that supported her. She clutched his head as his bold, hungry mouth rooted for the slick folds between her thighs. His thick hair flowed over her hands in a silken mass of brown; she couldn't resist stroking it.

His muffled voice sent tremors down her body. "You smell like Paradise and taste like honey. I've missed you."

Sophia did not reply. She had already offered Chris her love and had been rejected. Admitting how much she had missed him would serve no purpose.

Her silence didn't seem to bother him. Spreading her legs, he held the petals of her sex open with his thumbs and laved her with the rough pad of his tongue.

Her legs turned to jelly. She grasped his shoulders.

With effortless grace he scooped her off her feet and into his arms, leaving her weak and wanting. "Chris . . ."

"I know." He placed her on the bed and followed her down. Then he knelt between her legs, his mouth returning to her succulent flesh.

Sophia felt her passion escalating, hastened by Chris's intimate kiss. When his mouth found the hardening nub between her thighs, she went wild beneath him. She burned; she feared she would turn to cinder. The air in the room seemed heavier, hotter. A groan ripped from her lips. Her breath was coming in fast, desperate pants.

He slid one finger into her burning center, then another, going deeper, pumping them into her warm, silken heat. Sophia cried out, a soft, shaky plea. She was wet. Beyond wet. Her taut sheath sucked at his fingers.

He lifted his head.

She wailed a protest.

"Do you want me, Sophia?"

"Yes, damn you!"

He kissed her. She tasted herself on his lips.

"You want it as much as I do," he whispered against her lips

"My *body* wants you. It always did."

Chris shed his trousers and settled over her. His cock was as hard as stone. His senses were filled with the scent of her, the musky scent of sex.

"Tell me again you want me."

"Why are you tormenting me? I want you—does that make you happy?"

Happy scarcely described how Chris felt, but he was beyond replying. All he could think about was plunging his throbbing sex into her tight sheath and driving them both to completion. Roughly he turned her onto her stomach, raised her hips, pushed her legs wide with his knees and shoved his cock inside her. As he rocked himself back and forth inside her slick, wet warmth, he tasted Paradise. Beneath him, he felt Sophia begin to tremble.

She missed me, he exulted in a sane moment before he lost the ability to think.

When she began to buck beneath him, he held down her shoulders and began thrusting hard and deep, pumping rhythmically again and again, struggling to hang on until Sophia found her own Paradise.

Beneath him, Sophia screamed, a short, soft cry. Still clutching her shoulders, he drew out and drove in again. *This* was what he had missed. What he had wanted. Was it simply lust or . . .

His thoughts flew away and his world spun out of control. Vaguely he felt Sophia shudder and heard her cry out. Then he surrendered to the hunger driving him and fell into a sensual abyss. His seed exploded from his body into hers, and moments later he collapsed on top of her, limp and sated. He buried his face in her neck, inhaled her scent and murmured her name. "Sophia."

She stirred beneath him. He rolled away. She flipped over onto her back.

"I was too rough. I'm sorry."

"I'm fine."

He climbed out of bed and began to dress. She rose up on one elbow and watched him.

"Where are you going?" she asked.

He met her gaze and caught his breath. She looked so thoroughly loved, so adorably disheveled that he was sorely tempted to climb back in bed. Even her color seemed better. But he needed to return to his ship, collect his trunk and tell his crew that he was giving them extended shore leave.

"I have to return to the *Intrepid*. There's a great deal to be done before I am free to rejoin you. Is it all right if I bring Dirk Blaine home with me tonight for dinner? Can your cook manage all right?"

"Of course, but . . . I hope you're not planning to stay here. It would be better for both of us if you stayed with your brother."

Chris went still. "Why would I stay with Justin? You're my wife, and this is our home while we're in London."

Sophia inhaled a fortifying breath. "I don't want to live with you. In fact, I plan on moving to the country when the lease on this house expires. I was going to ask you to settle a sum on me so I can live independently of you. Then you'd be free to do as you please."

His response came out harsher than he intended. "You're spouting nonsense. Forget about living apart.

We're married. Where I go, you go." He strode to the door, reached for the latch and paused. Without turning around, he asked, "Did making love with me just now mean nothing to you? Not long ago you told me you loved me. Have you changed your mind?"

Sophia felt like crying. Making love with Chris had meant everything to her. She did love him, but she didn't know if her love would be enough for both of them. Though a life without Chris would be devastatingly empty, she couldn't live with him until he learned to forgive himself and her. Her hand flew to her stomach, where his child rested. She would always have a part of him no matter what happened between them.

He spun around and strode back to the bed. "Answer me, Sophia. Do you truly want us to lead separate lives?"

"I want to be with you, Chris, but I fear Desmond will always stand between us. Can you look at me without thinking about the duel that caused his death?"

He merely stared at her.

"I thought not. I cannot live like that, Chris. Can you tell me you love me and mean it?"

Chris wanted to . . . desperately. But the words stuck in his throat. Desmond hovered like a phantom between them. Chris wanted no other woman, but he couldn't tell Sophia he loved her. Their tragic past had built a barrier between them. He wanted Sophia in his bed, in his life, but confessing his love for her still seemed like a betrayal of Desmond's memory.

"I . . . care for you, Sophia. I wouldn't be here if I didn't."

"That's not enough, Chris. I want more. I *deserve* more. Until you can give me what I need, it's best that we live apart."

"Best for whom?"

"For both of us."

Chris kept his expression purposely bland. "Are you sure this is what you want?"

"It's not what I want but what I must do."

"Very well, then, so be it. You can contact me at the Thorn and Thistle if you have need of me."

It took all Chris's considerable control to walk away when what he really wanted was to be with Sophia, to make love to her until she begged him to stay. Either that or shake some sense into her.

What had happened to her during their brief separation? Had she found someone else? The rage boiling inside him made him want to howl. When he reached the bottom of the stairs, Dunning was there, holding the door open for him.

"If your mistress has need of me," he said curtly, "send word to me at the Thorn and Thistle."

He stormed out the door, vowing to search his heart until he found the answers he sought. Chris felt confident that if he succeeded in banishing Desmond's ghost, he would be able to tell Sophia he loved her.

Chapter Eighteen

Sophia didn't see Chris again until little Teddy's christening. There was such a crush of people at the house after the church ceremony that Sophia didn't find it difficult to melt into the woodwork. She had seen Chris from afar but had thus far managed to avoid him. She did notice, however, that Amanda was in attendance with Lord and Lady Chester. From her position behind a pillar, she saw Amanda approach Chris and gaze adoringly up at him.

"Are you hiding from Chris?"

Sophia started violently. She had been so engrossed in Chris's response to Amanda that she hadn't heard Grace approaching.

"I didn't know Lady Dartmore would be here," Sophia said.

"Lady Chester asked if she could bring her niece, and I couldn't say no. You met her in Jamaica, didn't you? Is there some reason you don't like her?"

Sophia glanced at Chris; he was still engaged in conversation with Amanda. Suddenly Chris looked up and met her gaze. The blood rushed to her head. His blue eyes were focused so intently on her that her whole body began to thrum with awareness. She looked away, but not before Grace noted the exchange.

Grace linked arms with Sophia and led her off. "I should check on Teddy. Come with me, we need to talk."

Sophia had no choice but to comply. At the foot of the stairs, she glanced over her shoulder at Chris and saw that he was watching her. Then she turned and followed Grace up the stairs.

Teddy was sleeping soundly. His nursemaid sat in a chair beside him, gently rocking his cradle. Sophia stepped close to the cradle, bent and placed a kiss upon his soft cheek.

"He's adorable," she said on a sigh.

"You and Chris could have a child if you both weren't so stubborn. We haven't seen much of Chris lately." She led Sophia out of the nursery. "I know you arrived at the christening separately; are you and Chris having problems?"

"We're living apart."

"Oh, Sophia, I'm so sorry. I know you love Chris, can't you work through this?"

"Chris doesn't love me. Desmond's ghost still stands between us. Until Chris absolves himself of guilt and opens his heart to love, I see no hope for us. I asked him to live elsewhere while he's in London."

"I think Chris *does* love you."

"I think so, too, but until he acknowledges it, our future looks bleak. I'm fully prepared to raise our child alone."

Grace grasped Sophia's arm and squeezed. "You're with child? Does Chris know?"

"I haven't told him. You must promise to keep my secret."

"But, Sophia, you have to tell him."

"No, Grace, I don't. I wasn't going to tell anyone what happened, but you deserve to know why I am opposed to telling Chris about the babe." She took a deep breath and exhaled slowly. "I found Amanda Dartmore in his arms in my own foyer. They were kissing. Did you know they once were lovers?"

"No, I didn't know. Forgive me for inviting her, Sophia."

Sophia patted Grace's hand. "There is nothing to forgive. You couldn't possibly have known. If you don't mind, I'd like to leave now."

"Of course. I'll have the carriage brought around to take you home. You came in a hired hack, didn't you?" Sophia nodded. "Promise you'll visit me tomorrow so we can discuss this further."

"Very well, if you insist."

"I do insist. Come."

They descended the stairs together.

"Wait here," Grace said. "I'll have a footman bring your wrap while I speak to Justin about the carriage."

Sophia's gaze immediately sought Chris. He was still standing in a corner with Amanda. Lord Chester had joined them. When Chris turned in her direction, she refused to meet his gaze. The footman arrived with her wrap and helped her into it. When Sophia looked Chris's way again, he was gone.

Jason appeared and informed her that the carriage awaited her. Sophia stepped out the door. The driver was holding the carriage door open for her. She entered the dark interior and settled on the seat. Immediately she sensed she was not alone. When she seized the door handle, a hand reached out and grasped her arm.

"Don't be afraid, Sophia. It's just me."

"Chris! You frightened me. Where is Amanda?"

Chris muttered a curse. "Amanda and I are not together."

"You certainly looked together."

Chris rapped on the roof and the carriage jerked forward. "This is the first I've seen of Amanda since that day in your foyer."

"What do you want, Chris? How did you know I was leaving?"

"Grace told me. I entered the carriage before it left the mews. Grace seemed to think we have something to discuss. Do we, Sophia?"

"That's up to you, Chris. You know where I stand in our relationship. You're the only one who can decide if we have a future together."

The carriage pulled up to Sophia's door. "Let me come in, Sophia. Then you can tell me what Grace thinks we should discuss."

The driver opened the door. "Not tonight, Chris. I really am exhausted."

"So nothing has changed," Chris bit out.

"You tell me. Has anything changed?"

"I—"

"No, Chris. Not tonight. Come day after tomorrow for tea. I promised Grace I'd call on her tomorrow."

"I'll walk you to the door."

"That's not necessary."

"Indulge me."

He left the carriage first and handed her down. Then he grasped her elbow and walked her to the door.

"You can go now. Dunning always waits up for me. I have but to knock and he'll open the door."

Chris pulled her into his arms. "I miss you, Sophia. I know we parted with angry words, but that's not how I wish it to end."

"I don't want that either, Chris."

"Then why can't we be together if it's what we both want?"

"Because I want more than you're willing to give. We've discussed this before, if you recall."

"Maybe I'm ready to give you what you want."

Sophia searched his face. Darkness prevented her from reading his expression. But what she did see gave her a glimmer of hope. Unfortunately, she hadn't been lying. She *was* exhausted, and in no condition to decide the future of her marriage.

Since Chris had returned to London, Sophia hadn't been sleeping well. After several sleepless nights, she might agree to any kind of arrangement Chris suggested, even if it didn't include love. She had to hold firm until she felt strong enough to deal with him. If Chris had banished Desmond's ghost and was ready to acknowledge his love for her, he could wait to tell her until she felt more like herself.

"Day after tomorrow, Chris, I'll be waiting for you."

Chris had no intention of leaving Sophia without giving her something to think about. During the past several days he had pondered long and hard about the relationship between them and how he would hate to return to Jamaica without her. A future without Sophia in it looked impossibly bleak.

Before she could rap on the door, Chris pulled her into his arms and kissed her. She tasted so sweet, felt so delectable in his arms that he never wanted to let her go. He felt her stiffen, and then she surrendered, melting into his embrace. His arms tightened, he deepened the kiss. He was on the verge of sweeping her up and carrying her back into the carriage when the door opened.

Dunning stood in the opening, unapologetic, his stance confrontational. "Good evening, milady, Captain."

Chris wanted to strangle the overprotective butler as Sophia pulled away from him.

"I'll see you day after tomorrow, Chris."

She disappeared inside. Dunning sent him a haughty look and closed the door in his face.

Cursing Dunning's ill timing, Chris returned to the carriage, instructing the driver to take him to his lodgings at the Thorn and Thistle.

Chris sulked in morose silence as the carriage carried him to the inn. Sophia hadn't given him time to tell her what was in his heart. He really did love her and wanted to tell her how much she meant to him. Seven years was too long to mourn a friend's passing. Desmond's death had been a horrible tragedy, but his long absence from Sophia had shown him that he would have no life at all without her. It was time for him to let the past go and give love a second chance.

Chris had also revisited Sophia's role in the tragedy and realized he had judged her unfairly. He and Desmond had been randy bucks, vying for the same woman. Sophia had been young and pressured by her family to marry money. Surely he was mature enough now to understand her position. His epiphany had been a long time coming, but he now knew what he wanted and why.

He wanted Sophia because he loved her. Perhaps he had never stopped loving her.

Sophia was on her way out the door the next day to visit Grace when Rayford arrived on her doorstep. She had seen little of him since her return to England and hadn't missed him.

"What do you want, Ray? I was on my way out."

"I need to speak with you, Sophia. It's important."

"Another time, perhaps. I just sent Dunning to find a hack. He should return soon."

"This is important, Sophia. I need your help. I want Claire back. Will you speak to her on my behalf?"

"I don't know what good I can do. You haven't exactly endeared yourself to your wife, or to me."

"I'm a changed man, Sophia, I swear it. I've even paid off my debts."

Sophia lifted her brows in surprise. "Wherever did you get the money? Never say Amanda gave it to you. The last I heard, she kicked you out."

"I . . . earned the blunt," Ray said, refusing to look at her. "Will you come with me now? I've rented a carriage. It's parked at the curb. Why wait for a hack when I have a conveyance at my disposal?"

"No, Ray, not now. Lady Standish is expecting me."

"Are you refusing to help me?"

Sophia sighed. She owed Ray nothing, but if he was serious and had paid his debts, perhaps Claire could keep him on the straight and narrow.

"Come back tomorrow morning, Ray. I'll be ready around ten. I'll do what I can for you, but don't get your hopes up. You've given neither Claire nor me much reason to trust you."

"Thank you, Sophia." He sent Sophia a sly smile. "By the way, I saw your husband with Amanda Dartmore the other day. He was just leaving her house. I thought you should know."

A hack came clattering around the corner. Dunning sat on the box with the driver. "Ah, here's your transportation. Until tomorrow, Sophia."

Sophia nodded numbly. Ray's words stung. Had he really seen Chris with Amanda? He could be lying. It was hard to tell with Ray. Would he lie to her after asking her to help with Claire? She didn't know what to think. But she intended to ask Chris about it tomorrow.

After the hurtful news Ray had just imparted, Sophia no longer felt like visiting Grace. She dismissed the hack and sent Dunning to find someone to deliver a message to Grace postponing her visit.

The following day, as Sophia considered her promise to accompany Rayford, she began to have second thoughts. Being alone with her untrustworthy stepbrother wasn't a good idea. When Peg entered her bedroom to make up the bed, Sophia said, "I'd like you to accompany me today, Peg. I'm going with my stepbrother to call on his estranged wife."

"What time should I be ready, milady?"

"Meet me in the foyer at ten o'clock."

"Very good, milady."

Peg was waiting when Sophia arrived downstairs. Dunning stood nearby to open the door. Rayford arrived at precisely ten o'clock.

"I shouldn't be long," Sophia informed Dunning.

"Tell Casper I'm looking forward to having lunch with him."

Dunning peered out the window. "A hack just arrived, milady. Could that be your stepbrother?"

Rayford stepped out of the closed black carriage with shuttered windows and waited at the curb. Dunning opened the door. Sophia walked down the stairs, Peg following close behind. Dunning watched a moment, then shut the door.

"You brought your maid," Ray said. "You don't trust me."

"Do you blame me? Let's just get this over with, Ray. Chris is coming over later."

Ray handed Sophia into the carriage. But when Peg started to enter behind her, Ray pushed the maid to the ground, jumped into the carriage and slammed the door. The carriage rattled off down the road at a fast clip.

"Dunning! Help!" Peg cried as she picked herself off the ground and raced toward the house.

Dunning opened the door. "What is it? Why aren't you with your mistress?"

"Something is wrong, Dunning. The carriage took off without me."

"Come in, girl, come in."

Shaking violently, Peg entered the house. "You have to do something, Dunning. Milady's stepbrother shoved me to the ground and fled with milady in the carriage."

"I have to think," Dunning said, looking every bit as distraught as Peg.

"Why would milady's stepbrother do such a thing to her?"

"I understand the man is a ne'er-do-well, a veritable cad. Perhaps he intends to hold her for ransom."

Just then Casper came running down the stairs, his tutor hard on his heels. "We heard a commotion. Has something happened?"

Wringing her hands, Peg said, "Milady has been kidnapped by her stepbrother. I was to accompany her, but he shoved me to the ground and took off with milady inside the carriage."

"The Earl of Standish must be told immediately," Dunning said.

"Someone should tell the captain," Casper insisted. "I'll go. Mr. Dexter has taken me to visit him at the Thorn and Thistle several times since he arrived in London."

He started out the door. "I'll go with you," Dexter said. "You shouldn't be running about London on your own."

"And I'll fetch the earl," Dunning said. All three men sped out the door, Casper and his tutor in one direction and Dunning in another.

Once Sophia regained her wits, she rounded on Rayford. "What is the meaning of this, Ray? What are you up to now?"

"I had to do it, Sophia. It was either obey him or go to debtor's prison."

Sophia's heart pounded with fear. "Him? Who are you talking about?"

"You'll find out soon enough."

Sophia decided she wasn't going to wait around to find out. She reached for the door handle, intending to jump out the door before the carriage picked up speed.

"Oh, no, you don't," Ray said, reaching for her and hauling her back against the squabs. "I don't want you to kill yourself. That wouldn't do at all."

"Where are you taking me?"

"Please understand my predicament, Sophia. You're not going to be harmed, I promise."

Sophia sneered. "Don't tell me you sold my favors again."

Ray refused to look her in the eye. "Claire won't take me back. Her father threatened me when I asked for money to keep myself out of debtor's prison. I was desperate. Then *he* arrived and offered to pay my creditors. He was a godsend, Sophia. I had no choice but to agree."

"Why me? London is full of whores willing to accommodate a man for a few coins."

"They're not you. Just do this, Sophia. What can it hurt? You're no longer a virgin."

"You vile bastard!" Sophia cried. She began beating on his chest and screaming for the carriage to stop.

Ray grasped her wrists in a bruising grip. "Be still. The driver has been paid to ignore any outbursts from you. My benefactor has seen to everything."

"Tell me his name, Ray. I want to know what I am facing."

"No, it is best that you don't know."

"Chris will kill you. Think about that before you carry out your nefarious plan."

"You and Radcliff aren't even living together," Ray said smugly. "He never wanted you, Sophia. If he had, he would have asked for your hand after Desmond's death. But he didn't. He ran off to sea and left you to face the scandal alone."

Ray's cruel words hurt, but he was right. Chris hadn't wanted her. He'd run off, leaving her alone. She knew now that guilt had driven him away, but nonetheless, his feelings for her hadn't been strong enough to keep him from fleeing.

"I have no idea how you two met again after all these years, but I knew your marriage wouldn't last when I learned about it. Do you really think Radcliff will care what happens to you?"

"Damn you! Let me out of this carriage! Your plot to sell me the first time didn't work, and it won't work this time either."

She lunged for the door again but stopped herself when she realized the carriage was barreling down the road much too fast. Her rash act could kill her child, a child she desperately wanted.

"I'm expecting Chris's child, Ray. Have you no compassion?"

Ray's stunned expression quickly faded, dashing Sophia's hopes. "I'm sure *he* won't care. You look no different to me."

"Tell me who *he* is, Ray. You owe me that much."

"I owe you nothing. You owe me. I kept a roof over your head when Society abandoned you."

Sophia tried to raise the shade as the carriage sped down the road, but it had been tied down, using complicated knots. She had no idea where she was being taken or to whom. Ray had no scruples, no morals. Whatever he did was for his own benefit.

Two hours later the carriage rolled to a stop.

"We're here," Ray said. He opened the door and stepped down.

Sophia peered out at a small shuttered cottage placed in a bucolic setting. There was nothing sinister about it, but she knew that what she'd find inside could very well place her life and that of her unborn child in jeopardy.

The cottage door opened. Ray hauled Sophia from the carriage and shoved her through the opening. Though it was too dark to see anything, she knew she was not alone.

A voice came out of the darkness. "You can leave, Caldwell. You can return for her in the morning."

Sophia gasped. She recognized the voice. "You!"

Chris wasn't at his lodgings when Casper and his tutor arrived.

"Maybe he's visiting the earl," Dexter said.

"If he is, Dunning will find him," Casper replied. "But I think we should wait here for him in case he's gone off on an errand."

They found an empty table in the common room and sat down to wait. Casper kept jumping up and pacing to the door to peer outside. He even counted the minutes in his head.

"Perhaps we should return home," Dexter suggested. "Dunning probably found the captain at the earl's house."

"Can we wait a little longer?" Casper begged.

Their patience paid off when Casper spotted Chris walking through the door soon after. "Captain!" he cried, rushing to intercept him.

Chris sent Casper a welcoming smile. He was always happy to see the lad, but wondered what he was doing here when Casper had visited him just yesterday.

He nodded to Dexter. "I'm surprised to see you. I thought Casper was to resume his lessons today."

"It's Sophia!" Casper cried.

Chris's heart slammed against his chest. Had something happened to Sophia? He prayed not. He had spent the last two days thinking about Sophia, missing her, chiding himself for being too stupid to recognize love when it hit him in the gut. He had been so consumed by guilt and misery that he had failed Sophia utterly. But he wasn't going to make that mistake again. He knew what he wanted and intended to make sure Sophia understood that he loved her, that she was the only woman he wanted, would ever want. They belonged together. He'd been miserable without her and hoped he wasn't too late to make things right.

Today Chris had intended to tell Sophia how much she meant to him. He had even purchased a wedding ring worthy of Sophia's beauty.

"Has something happened to Sophia?"

"I don't really know her reason for doing so," Casper explained, "but Sophia went off in a carriage with Viscount Caldwell. Peg was to accompany her, but Caldwell shoved Peg to the ground and jumped in the carriage with Sophia. The carriage took off immediately, and no one knows where Caldwell took her."

A cold sweat broke out on Chris's forehead. What kind of nefarious plan had Caldwell hatched for Sophia this time? Chris knew intuitively that Sophia's abduction involved money. He'd heard that Caldwell was just a breath away from debtor's prison.

"Go back home," Chris said. "I'll find Sophia."

"I want to help," Casper cried.

"You can help by returning home and keeping track of any messages that arrive. Caldwell might be holding Sophia for ransom. The man is desperate. I cannot imagine why she went off with him, knowing his penchant for mischief."

"Dunning went to inform the earl," Dexter ventured.

"Good. Perhaps he can learn something I cannot."

"Good luck," Casper called as Chris hurried off. "Bring Sophia back."

Chris intended to do just that. No one was going to take Sophia away from him. Not after he had finally buried his ghosts and opened his heart to love. He loved Sophia. He had always loved her, despite his unwillingness to admit it. No other woman would do for him.

Chris's first stop would be Amanda Dartmore's spacious home in Berkley Square. Even though she and Caldwell were no longer together, she might know where he could find the bounder. Chris retrieved his horse at the nearby livery and headed to Berkley Square. The butler opened the door to him. Chris knew him from his previous visits. His name was Warring.

"How may I help you, Captain?" Warring asked.

"Please announce me to Lady Dartmore."

"It's rather early, sir. Milady rarely leaves her bed before noon. Perhaps you can call later."

Chris pushed past him. "Tell her Captain Radcliff wishes to speak with her. It's important."

"Please wait here," Warring said as he started up the staircase. "I'll see if milady is receiving."

Chris didn't have long to wait. Amanda appeared at the top of the stairs, wearing a dressing gown that left little to the imagination.

"Chris!" she squealed. "I knew you would come to your senses. Come up, my love, I've been waiting forever for you."

His face grim, Chris mounted the stairs. When he reached the top, Amanda had already disappeared into her bedroom. Chris followed. He found her arrayed provocatively atop her bed, smiling coyly at him. She beckoned him forward.

"This isn't a social call, Amanda," Chris said.

"I don't care as long as you're here," Amanda purred.

"Where is Caldwell?"

Frowning, Amanda sat up, shrugging so that her gown slipped off her shoulders, baring her breasts. "He's gone. He meant nothing to me. He merely amused me for a time. Now that you're here, I need no other man."

"Can you give me the direction to Caldwell's lodgings?"

"What is this about, Chris? If you've come to berate me for taking up with Caldwell, I don't want to hear it."

"I'm not here for you, Amanda. I'm married. I love my wife."

"You love her?" Amanda choked out. "I don't believe you."

"Believe what you want. Did you know Caldwell has kidnapped Sophia?"

"Kidnapped her? Why ever for?"

"I was hoping you could tell me."

"I haven't seen him in days. His creditors are hounding him; he's probably left the country."

"With Sophia?"

She tapped her chin. "No, I don't think so. Why would he want her tagging along?"

"He took her for reasons I do not understand. Had he asked her for money, she might have given it to him. She had access to my bank account. Do you have any idea where he sought lodgings after you tossed him out?"

"Someplace cheap," Amanda guessed. "Why don't you ask his wife?"

"I intend to do just that. If you hear from him, please contact me at the Thorn and Thistle." He turned to leave.

"Chris, wait! Is this good-bye?"

"We said our good-byes a long time ago, Amanda. I'm going to find my wife and never let her out of my sight again."

Turning on his heel, he left her without another word.

Chris rode posthaste to the stately home of Lord and Lady Warpole, where Claire resided with her parents. He was told to wait in the parlor while the butler fetched Lady Caldwell. Claire, a plump, mousy woman, arrived a short time later.

"What can I do for you, Captain Radcliff?"

"Do you know where I can find your husband? It's vitally important that I locate him."

Claire grimaced, her disgust apparent. "Don't tell me he owes you money, too? If I never see that man again, it will be too soon."

"Have you seen him recently?" Chris asked, trying a different approach.

"He called here a few days ago. Papa sent him packing."

"Jeeters told me we had a visitor," Lord Warpole said as he strode into the room.

"Here's Papa now," Claire said. "Captain Radcliff is inquiring after Rayford."

Warpole acknowledged Chris with a nod. "That cur had the nerve to ask me for money. I sent him packing and told him never to darken my door again."

"Papa has friends in high places," Claire explained. "He has petitioned the court in my behalf for a divorce. When it's granted, I'll be rid of Rayford for good."

"Do you have any idea where I might find him?" Chris asked. "He kidnapped his stepsister."

Claire gasped. "Oh, poor Sophia!"

"Is he demanding ransom?" Warpole asked.

"Not that I know of, but I'm desperate to find him. Sophia and I were married in Jamaica some months ago."

"I didn't know that," Claire said. "I do wish I could help you, but Ray made no mention of Sophia during his brief visit."

"Caldwell's pockets are empty," Warpole said. "I took the liberty of having his finances looked into. He'll probably seek cheap lodgings."

"Thank you," Chris said. "I'll start with some of the dives along the waterfront. If you happen to hear from him, I can be reached at the Thorn and Thistle."

Chris took his leave and reined his horse toward the river. The sun was setting and all his leads had dried up. If he didn't find Caldwell soon, or find someone who knew where he had taken Sophia, he could lose her.

Chris spirits began to flag after visiting three waterfront inns without success. As he came out of the third, he ran into his brother.

"Justin, what are you doing here?"

"Dunning told me what happened. I knew you'd want to find Caldwell and decided to check on a few of the likely places he might be found. I guess we had the same idea."

"I don't know what I'll do if I don't find Sophia, Justin. I love her. I was going to tell her today."

Justin gripped Chris's shoulder. "Buck up, old boy. We'll find your wife. Shall we split up and meet back here in three hours?"

Chris nodded. "When I find Caldwell, I'm going to kill the bastard."

Three hours later, neither Chris nor Justin had found the missing Caldwell. But Justin had some good news to impart.

"I found where Caldwell has been staying," he informed Chris. "I suggest we wait and see if he turns up." Hope was a fragile emotion. Embracing it whole-heartedly, Chris followed Justin to the disreputable inn Caldwell called home.

Chapter Nineteen

A light flared in the cottage. Her heart pounding, Sophia faced her worst nightmare.

"We are finally alone," Sir Oscar Rigby drawled. "I've waited a long time for this."

Spinning on her heel, Sophia turned and ran. He caught her at the door.

"Oh, no, you don't. Not this time. You owe me, and it's long past time that you paid."

"If you don't release me immediately, you're the one who will pay. I would be very afraid of Chris if I were you."

"I think not," he sneered. "According to Caldwell, you and your husband are estranged. He says there is another woman waiting in the wings for Radcliff. Amanda Dartmore is a fetching piece."

"Then why don't you court her instead of coming after me?"

"You should know the answer to that. No one makes a fool of me and gets away with it. This time I have you right where I want you, and there is no one who cares enough about you to stop me."

Sophia prayed that wasn't true. Chris would care. He had to. She needed to believe he had been informed of her abduction and was searching for her. If she hadn't decided at the last minute to take Peg with her, no one would know she was missing until it was too late.

"You're wrong, many people care about me. I asked my maid Peg to accompany me. When I got into the carriage, Ray shoved her aside and took off with me in the carriage. Peg will tell Dunning what happened; he will inform the earl, and the earl will tell Chris. They will find Ray and force him to tell them where he has taken me. You're not as smart as you think, Sir Oscar."

Rigby cursed, raised his hand and slapped Sophia, knocking her head back. "Damn you and damn Caldwell! If you think to thwart me, you're mistaken. Caldwell knows better than to betray me. I paid a small fortune to get him out of debt."

"Why me when can have any woman you want?"

"I cannot forgive and forget. If you had submitted that night I came to your room, I would have taken my pleasure and forgotten you. But you thought yourself too good for me. You tricked me and broke a vase over my head. I almost had you in Jamaica, but then Radcliff foiled my plans."

"Let me go and I'll forget this ever happened," she pleaded.

"Do you think I'm stupid? I've booked passage on a ship sailing to Jamaica tomorrow. I'll release you in the morning and not before. I expect Caldwell to come for you long after I've left the cottage."

He grasped her arm and pulled her toward the bedroom. "Come along, I fancy you in a bed."

Sophia dug in her heels. "I'll fight you."

"I'm stronger than you are. I can hurt you if you refuse to accommodate me."

"If you hurt me, you'll hurt the innocent babe I'm carrying."

He stopped abruptly and stared at her middle. "I don't believe you."

"I'm not lying."

He shrugged. "It doesn't matter. Your stomach won't get in my way. It's up to you whether or not you get hurt, Sophia."

"Please," she begged, "don't do this."

"There's no escape," Rigby sneered. "I want you beneath me, just like Caldwell promised. Not just once, but many times. We have until daybreak."

He set down the lamp, grabbed her arm with both hands and dragged her into the bedroom. Sophia punched him with her free hand and aimed for his groin with her foot. To her surprise, she connected. Her success prompted her to kick him again. Rigby roared and clutched his privates with one hand while maintaining his grip on her with the other.

His face turned white with pain. "Wildcat! You've unmanned me. You'll pay dearly for that."

He shoved her to the floor and limped out of the room. Sophia fell hard, clutching her stomach to protect her babe. "Come at me again and I'll make sure you never assault another woman," she threatened with more bravado than she felt.

The door slammed in her face, leaving her in total darkness. She heard the key turn in the lock. "You can't escape—the windows are shuttered," Rigby called through the door. His voice sounded unnaturally high. "As soon as I've recovered, I'm coming in with a rope to bind you. Then we'll see how brave you are."

Sophia picked herself up from the floor and huddled in her cloak. It was cold in the bedroom; no fire had been lit in the fireplace. Had kicking Rigby bought her sufficient time for help to arrive? Her hopes rested on Chris's ability to find Rayford. Knowing Ray, he would cave in during questioning and reveal her location. But only if he could be found.

It was growing dark when Caldwell returned to his lodgings. Hiding in an alley way beside the building, Chris could tell that Ray had been drinking by the way he staggered through the door.

"There he is," Justin said quietly. "I was beginning to fear he wasn't going to show up."

"I was prepared to wait forever. Caldwell is the only lead we have. Let's follow him up to his room." Chris's lips curled in a grim smile. "Our business with him is best conducted in private."

Apparently, Caldwell didn't see them as they followed him up two flights of stairs. It took him several tries to find the keyhole, but when he finally unlocked the door, Chris pushed him inside while Justin entered behind them and closed the door. A chambermaid must have been in earlier to light a lamp, for dim light chased away the dark inside the tiny room.

"Wha—" Caldwell said, staring bleary-eyed at Chris. "Get out of my room."

"You call this a room? I'd call it a pigsty," Chris said, kicking debris out of his way. "You really have fallen low, haven't you? Where have you taken my wife?"

"I don't know what you're talking about."

Chris grabbed Caldwell by the collar and shoved him against the wall. "You're lying." A menacing growl rumbled low in his throat. "I want the truth, Caldwell. My servants saw you carry Sophia off in your carriage. Where did you take her?"

"Why do you care? You're not together. Did you think I wouldn't know? You never did care about her, did you?"

"You're wrong, Caldwell, dead wrong. As dead as you're going to be if you don't tell me where you took Sophia and why."

Caldwell gave him a mutinous glare. "He'll kill me if I betray him."

"Not if I kill you first."

Chris dragged Caldwell to the window and threw open the sash.

"Wha . . . what are you going to do?"

"Remember how we used to play pirates when we were young, Justin? We would make each other walk a plank and jump into the lake."

"I remember," Justin answered.

"I've a fancy to make Caldwell walk the plank. Since we don't have a plank, this window will have to do. And in lieu of a lake, the cobblestone courtyard below will have to suffice."

Caldwell's face contorted in fear. "You can't throw me out the window."

"Of course not," Chris replied. "You're going to jump."

"I won't do it."

Calmly Chris removed a wicked-looking blade from his boot and pressed it against Caldwell's throat. "Either you jump or I'll slice you up piece by piece, starting with your ears, which I'll toss to the dogs below."

Caldwell began to blubber. "I can't tell you. He'll kill me."

"I'll kill you if you don't."

"Get on with it, Chris," Justin said, stifling a yawn as if bored with the whole business. "We're wasting time."

Chris made a small nick behind Caldwell's ear but stopped short of removing it. "Tell you what, Caldwell. I'll make a deal with you. Tell me where to find Sophia and who paid you to abduct her, and I will see that you are escorted aboard a fast mail packet to France. Your marriage will be annulled soon, and you can find a rich Frenchwoman to wed."

Caldwell glanced down at the courtyard, two stories below. "Do you swear it?"

"Of course. I wouldn't say it if I didn't mean it. Talk, Caldwell, and it had better be the truth."

Caldwell sagged, apparently overcome with relief. "Rigby has her. He paid all my outstanding debts. In return, I was to bring Sophia to a cottage he rented in the country. I had no choice. My creditors were hounding me. I was one step away from debtor's prison."

"There is always a choice, Caldwell," Chris spat. "What is Rigby doing in London?"

"He's here on business, same as you. He left Jamaica shortly after you did."

Chris cursed violently. "Bastard! Tell me where to find Rigby."

Caldwell gave him directions to a cottage near a little village north of London. "It's a two-hour drive by carriage," Caldwell revealed.

"I can make it in one," Chris vowed. "Justin will remain here to guard you. If I return without Sophia, your life is forfeit. If I find Sophia unharmed, Justin will purchase passage for you to France and see you off."

"Good luck," Justin called as Chris hastened from the room.

"It may be too late," Caldwell muttered after Chris had left.

"You'd better start praying that Rigby hasn't harmed Sophia," Justin replied.

Chris left London and rode north at breakneck speed. If Caldwell had lied to him, he would cheerfully strangle the man. And if Rigby had hurt Sophia, he was as good as dead. Chris would make sure of it.

Chris blamed himself for Sophia's problems. Had he stayed with her instead of storming off and finding separate lodgings, he would have been able to stop Rigby's nefarious plan. But no, he had stubbornly refused to acknowledge his love for Sophia. Had he spoken the words she wanted to hear, none of this would have happened.

Chris would be eternally grateful for the full moon. It shed enough light for him to avoid the pitfalls in the rutted road. He passed through a small village, pushing his horse to its limit. Nevertheless, it took more than an hour for Chris to locate the narrow lane leading to the cottage Caldwell had described.

Sophia knew the moon had risen, for ribbons of light streamed through the slats of the shuttered window. She had heard nothing from Rigby in a long time and hoped she had done him permanent damage. Her hopes were dashed when she heard movement in the main part of the cottage.

Stumbling in the darkness, she had searched the room for a weapon. There was no pitcher, no bowl, nothing with which to inflict damage. She had only her wits to rely upon. She watched the door with growing apprehension. Rigby was a strong man. It wouldn't take much for him to subdue her.

Revealing her delicate condition hadn't deterred him, nor had it dampened his enthusiasm for assaulting her. Rigby was bent on revenge. Was there some way she could hurt him again? Unfortunately, he would be more alert to her tricks now and less likely to succumb.

Sophia heard the key turn in the lock and the doorknob rattle, and braced herself. Frantic, her gaze flew from one dark corner of the room to the other, searching for nonexistent help.

A sense of self-preservation told Sophia to flatten herself against the wall behind the door. The door opened. Muted light spilled through the opening. Rigby entered the room; he carried a coiled rope over his arm.

"Where are you?" Rigby bellowed, blinking in the darkness. He advanced into the room. "Don't think you can hide from me. This time I'm going to tie you to the bedposts and spend the remainder of the night taking my pleasure from you."

His back was turned to her. Sophia knew that if she hesitated she'd be lost. Holding her breath, she eased around the open door and out of the room. Her first thought was to flee into the night. But hard on the heels of that thought came another. Spinning around, she slammed the door and turned the key in the lock, imprisoning Rigby inside.

"No! Bitch! Stupid bitch," Rigby screamed. He began pounding on the door. Sophia backed away. Was he strong enough to batter the door down? Quite possibly he was. As Rigby cursed and kicked the door, Sophia fled. She had no idea where she was or in which direction to run, but she knew she had to get as far away from the cottage as possible.

Sophia ran down the lane, halting when she reached the road. She looked both ways, trying to decide which way to turn. Just then she heard hoofbeats pounding toward her and wondered if she should flee or wait for the horse and rider and plead for help. It wouldn't take long for a man Rigby's size and girth to kick down the door. He might already be free and closing in on her.

Her gut told her to wait for the rider and ask for help. Nothing could be worse than falling into Rigby's hands again.

Sophia hovered in the shadows at the side of the road as the horse and rider approached. The horse slowed as it approached the lane leading to the cottage. She stepped from the shadows and waved her arms.

Chris pulled on the reins. Frightened, Atlas reared. Chris brought him under control and leaped from the saddle.

"Sophia! Is that you? Thank God." He pulled her into his arms and hugged her so tightly, Sophia feared her ribs would crack. But she didn't complain. Her prayers had been answered. Chris cared for her enough to come to her rescue.

"Where is Rigby?" Chris asked. "How did you escape?"

"Please take me away from here. I'll explain later."

Chris lifted her onto Atlas's back and mounted behind her. Then he reined his mount back toward London. Sophia leaned against his solid, comforting form, too happy to break the silence. She was free of Rigby and in Chris's arms, exactly where she wanted to be. The tension of the past few hours caught up with her. She rested her head against Chris's chest and fell asleep.

Sophia didn't awaken until she felt herself being lifted from the saddle. She opened her eyes. "Where are we? We couldn't have reached London already."

"We're stopping at an inn. You can't go on, you're exhausted, and I need to find a constable. I'm not about to let Rigby get away with kidnapping you. Can you walk?"

"Of course, put me down."

He eased her onto her feet and, keeping his arm about her waist, conducted her into the inn. The innkeeper met them at the door.

"We'd like your best room," Chris said in a commanding voice, "and a bath for my wife and supper for two."

The innkeeper sized Chris up, came to a conclusion and grinned. "Immediately, sir, whatever you wish." He plucked a key from a drawer and picked up a candlestick. "Please follow me."

Chris's hold tightened on Sophia as they followed the innkeeper up the stairs. The innkeeper unlocked the door, entered ahead of them and set down the candlestick.

"This is our finest room," he said proudly. "I'll order the bath and send up a maid to start a fire in the grate to take the chill off the room. Meanwhile, I'll set my wife to cooking your supper. She's an excellent cook. I think you'll be pleased."

"Thank you. The room is better than I expected for such a small village."

Beaming, the innkeeper bowed himself out of the room.

Chris led Sophia to a chair and knelt before her. "I

want to know what that bastard did to you before I find the constable."

Sophia twisted her fingers in her lap. "He didn't touch me. When he tried, I kicked him."

A laugh gurgled in Chris's throat. "You kicked him? Where?"

Sophia sent him an answering grin. "Where it hurt him the most. Then he locked me in the bedroom and threatened to return with a rope."

"You kicked him in the balls?"

Her smile widened. "Twice. He was limping when he left the room and didn't return for a long time."

Chris sobered. "But he did return."

Sophia nodded. "He returned with a rope in his hands and vengeance in his heart."

"Dear God, how did you escape him?" He searched her face, saw the purple bruise on her cheek and cursed. "He hurt you!"

Her hand flew to her cheek. "Not too badly. He—"

A knock interrupted their conversation. Chris went to the door, admitting the maid who had been sent to build a fire in the hearth. When flames danced merrily in the grate, the maid bobbed a curtsy and left. Chris returned to Sophia's side and crouched before her.

"Tell me what Rigby did to you."

"He slapped me—nothing more."

Chris visibly relaxed. "How did you escape? You said he returned to the bedroom with a rope."

"It was quite simple, really. I hid behind the door. The room was dark and he didn't see me. When he charged deeper into the room, I slipped out the door and locked him inside. He couldn't get out without breaking the door down. I didn't wait around to find out if he succeeded. I turned and fled."

Chris gave her a hug. "You're amazing. I raced to your rescue only to find you'd rescued yourself. Your courage is one of the reasons I love you."

"What? What did you say?"

A very unwelcome knock forestalled Chris's reply. "Later," he said. "That will be your bath."

He opened the door to servants bearing a tub and buckets of hot and cold water. "Enjoy your bath, my love. I'm going to rouse the constable from his bed and explain the situation. With any luck, Rigby will rot in Newgate for what he's done this night."

Sophia watched the man she loved leave the room. This time, however, she knew he would return and they would be together forever. She smiled dreamily as the maid removed her cloak, helped her to undress and climb into the tub. She dismissed the girl, sank down into the water and closed her eyes.

Chris loved her. She had heard him say the words. She hadn't been dreaming. The words still rang in her ears. *I love you.* No words had ever sounded sweeter. Her ordeal with Rigby faded from her memory, replaced by Chris's tender gaze as he'd spoken the words she had waited forever to hear.

The door opened. Chris stepped into the room. "Still soaking in the tub?"

"Hand me the towel and I'll get out."

Chris found the towel on a bench near the blazing fire and held it out for Sophia to step into. She walked into his arms and felt the warm towel surround her. He dried her with loving hands, then carried her to the bed and placed her beneath the covers.

"I'll bathe while we wait for supper."

He undressed, eased into the tub and washed quickly. Sophia watched him, a half smile curving her lips. No man should be that good to look at. His firm, tanned flesh held her spellbound. An aura of power, sexuality, confidence and virility surrounded him.

His eyes smoldering, Chris said, "Keep looking at me like that and we'll never get to our supper."

Sophia was about to say she didn't care about supper when someone rapped on the door. "That must be our food," Chris said as he stepped out of the water, quickly dried himself and pulled on his trousers.

Sophia dragged the sheet up to her neck as Chris admitted the innkeeper.

"Just set the tray on the table," Chris instructed.

The innkeeper did as Chris directed and left. Wrapping herself in a sheet, Sophia sat down in the chair Chris held out for her. They both ate heartily of potato soup, delicate white fish, plump sausages and slices of freshly baked bread dripping with butter. They washed it all down with a decent red wine. For dessert, the innkeeper had provided juicy fruit tarts.

"Did you find the constable?" Sophia asked after she had eaten her fill.

"He wasn't too happy to be roused from his bed, but he promised to gather some men and take Rigby into custody."

Sophia merely nodded. Rigby was no longer her problem. He had done his worst and failed. Nothing mattered now but Chris, her unborn child and their future as a family. It was time to tell Chris he was going to be a father.

Chris's eyes darkened with desire, his voice husky as he asked, "Have you finished eating, love?" Sophia nodded. "I'll tuck you into bed. You've been through a lot today."

"Christian Radcliff!" Sophia scolded as she rose to

her feet and faced him squarely. "You finally tell me you love me and expect me to sleep? Oh, no, you don't. You're not getting off that easily."

Chris's eyes twinkled. "I thought you were tired."

"You thought wrong. Do you know how long I've loved you?"

"No, tell me."

"Practically forever. I fell in love with you the day we met at my debut."

"I've loved you almost as long," Chris admitted. "You broke my heart when you chose Desmond. I understand the reason now, but I didn't then. For years I refused to speak your name. I didn't even want to think about you, for when I did, overwhelming guilt over Desmond's death plunged me into the deepest hell."

Sophia sighed. "We need to bury the past if we are to survive as a family."

Chris pulled her into his arms. "I already have. I realize now that I can't live in the past forever. The future awaits us, my love. Shall we embrace it together?"

"Oh, yes. Kiss me, Chris."

His kiss was long, hard and hungry, and she reveled in his unspoken demands. He pulled the sheet away from her, baring her flesh to his sensual touch. His hands roamed freely, exploring the curves and valleys of her voluptuous body, eliciting sighs and moans of pleasure.

"I don't know what you've been doing, but I love your new curves," Chris whispered into her ear. He tweaked her nipple. "Your breasts are magnificent."

He swept her into his arms and placed her on the bed, following her down. He showed her just how much he loved her breasts by pressing sweet kisses upon them and laving her nipples with his tongue. A whimper escaped her when his hand searched lower, the pad of his thumb finding the sensitive nub nestled between her feminine folds.

Sophia cried out, arching up against him, her body aching for more. He played with her, lowering his head and using his tongue to lap her with languid strokes, then thrusting his fingers inside her. Shuddering violently, Sophia quickly approached the point of no return. He must have sensed her imminent surrender, for he rose up and planted frantic kisses on her mouth. She kissed him back, hungrily, drawing his tongue into her mouth, sliding hers along it.

With a deep groan of pleasure, he stroked a hand over her belly. Suddenly he paused and raised his head, his blue eyes staring intently into hers.

"Is there something you wish to tell me, Sophia?"

"Not now," Sophia panted. "Please, Chris, I want you. Don't make me wait."

Chris stared at her a moment longer, then nodded. "Very well, my sweet, but we *will* have this conversation."

His hands continued their journey down her stomach, making her skin quiver. He slid his hand between her thighs to her sweet center. His fingers came away wet.

"It's time, love."

"Way past time," Sophia whispered. "Come inside me. I don't want to wait any longer."

A low chuckle rumbled from his chest. "Do you wish to be on top?"

"Oh, yes!"

He slid his hands beneath her and lifted her astride him. "Take me, Sophia. Ride me. I am yours to do with as you please."

Instead of taking him inside her immediately, she slid down his legs, curled her hand around his thick

349

length and stroked up and down. He groaned a deep, raw sound and thrust himself upward into her hand. Again and again she stroked the thick length of his erection, awed by the silky, warm weight of him and the raw, unleashed power she held in her hand.

Then she bent her head and ran her tongue along his pulsing cock, up one side, over the throbbing head and down the other side. He lurched violently when she took him into her mouth. Paying him no heed, she tormented him mercilessly with her tongue and teeth, nipping and laving until he gave a roar and pulled her up and over him. Then abruptly he rolled, trapping her beneath him. He crouched over her, his eyes dark with untamed desire. Looking deep into her eyes, he lifted her legs over his shoulders and sheathed himself inside her.

Sophia raised her hips to take him deeper, tightening her sheath around his pulsing heat. He growled his approval and began the dance of love. He thrust and withdrew, again and again, pulling out, then pushing deep, faster, harder, sweetly caressing her body with each powerful stroke.

The ragged hum of his breathing resonated like sweet music in her ears. She felt her body begin to tremble, heard herself moaning. Chris buried himself deep with a guttural groan, and then Sophia soared, tasting Paradise. Shuddering, his name on her lips, she was tossed upon turbulent waves of shimmering pleasure.

Dimly she heard Chris shout, felt his body stiffen, and then she sank beneath the waves. Sophia was nearly asleep when she felt Chris slide away and settle down beside her. Then he curled himself around her and drew her into the curve of his body.

"Do you have any idea how much I love you?" he whispered against her neck.

"Not until tonight. Never stop loving me, Chris."

"I couldn't possibly." His hand closed over her breast and then slid down to her stomach. He splayed his fingers over the barely discernible bulge. "When were you going to tell me about our babe?"

Sophia sighed. "I never intended to tell you if you continued to punish yourself for Desmond's death. I needed to hear you admit that you loved me."

Astounded, Chris asked, "You would have let me return to Jamaica without telling me you were carrying my child?"

"If I had to. I couldn't live with you until you purged your heart of guilt and forgave yourself."

"Thank God I came to my senses in time. Will you return to Jamaica with me after the Christmas holidays? Justin and Grace have their hearts set on having the family together for the holidays. I can't wait to tell them we're having a child. I'll bet Casper is thrilled."

"I've told no one but Grace, but I wouldn't count on her keeping it a secret from her husband. We can tell Casper together. He's part of our family."

Chris caressed her creamy cheek. She was so dear to him. How could he have been so stupid? He should have realized that his determination to marry Sophia had been based on more than his desire to protect her. He had loved her even then. He rose up on his elbow to tell her, but subsided when he saw she had fallen asleep.

Chris had scarcely settled down to sleep when someone tapped lightly on the door. Cursing softly, he rolled out of bed, dragged on his trousers and cracked the door open. "I thought I told you I didn't want to be disturbed until morning."

The innkeeper scraped and bowed. "Forgive me, sir, but the constable is below. He asked me to fetch you."

"Tell him I'll be right down."

Chris closed the door and donned his boots and shirt. Then he left the room, closing the door softly behind him. When he returned a short time later, he found Sophia sitting up in bed.

"Did I awaken you?" Chris asked.

Sophia chewed on her bottom lip. "I sensed you weren't in bed beside me and woke up."

Chris quickly undressed and joined her. "Oh, my love, did you think I wasn't coming back?"

"I suppose I haven't fully accepted yet that you love me."

"Believe it, love."

"Where did you go?"

"The constable came to the inn to tell me that Rigby was gone when he arrived at the cottage. The bedroom door had been kicked in."

"Rigby said he was sailing for Jamaica in the morning," she said.

"Let him go," Chris said. "One day he'll pay for what he tried to do to you. Before we leave London, I'll obtain a warrant for his arrest and let the Jamaican authorities take care of him."

Sophia relaxed beside him. "There are still three weeks left until Christmas. What shall we do until then?"

"Why not just have fun doing all the things we can't do in Jamaica? We can go to the theater, attend plays, explore the city with Casper, visit Justin and his family, and shop. Would you like that?"

"As long as I'm with you, I don't care what we do.

I'm sure Casper would enjoy your company as well. Perhaps we can take his tutor to Jamaica with us, if he's agreeable."

"We'll ask him. Can you sleep now?"

She turned in his arms. "Not yet. I want to taste Paradise again."

"The baby—"

"He won't object."

"*He?*"

"Or she. Just shut up and love me."

He moved over her. "Nothing would give me greater pleasure."

Epilogue

Their time in London was everything Sophia could have hoped for. Because of the Earl of Standish's influence, Chris and Sophia were accepted into Society once again. Not that they cared. They attended plays and the opera, went to Vauxhall gardens, enjoyed leisurely strolls in the park when the weather permitted such activity, and took Casper on a variety of outings.

Christmas was spent quietly with Justin and his family. It was the first Christmas Sophia had celebrated since her mother's death many years ago. It was Chris's first Christmas with family in seven years and Casper's first family Christmas ever. But after celebrating the New Year at a ball, Sophia, Chris and Casper were anxious to return to their home in Jamaica. As it turned out, Mr. Dexter, Casper's tutor, happily agreed to accompany them.

On the fifth of January, a cool but rather pleasant winter day, the *Intrepid* slipped her moorings and set a course for Jamaica. A noticeably pregnant Sophia, along with Chris, Casper and Mr. Dexter, were joined by Lord Chester and his family.

Sophia rarely left the cabin the first two weeks of the voyage. The biting wind and intermittent snow kept the passengers from straying topside. But once the ship entered warm waters, the passengers spent their days strolling about the deck, enjoying the sun and tropical breezes. The heavier London clothes were packed away, replaced by lighter garments. Sophia renewed her friendship with Dirk Blaine and some of the sailors she had gotten to know during her previous voyage to Jamaica.

They arrived in Kingston at the end of January, three weeks and two days after they had departed London. The moment he stepped ashore, Chris became aware of a pall hanging over the city. There were no smiling black faces hawking their wares, no one, either white or black, strolling along the sun-drenched streets.

"Something is wrong," Chris said, voicing everyone's fears.

Chris and Lord Chester had planned to go directly to the livery, where they had left their carriages in anticipation of their return, but changed their minds. With wives and children in tow, they walked to the King's Arms.

Mr. Ludlow seemed surprised to see them. "This is a bad time to be returning to Jamaica," he said grimly.

"What happened?" Chris asked. "Did something unforeseen take place after we left the island?"

Ludlow's eyes looked haunted. "It was terrible. Too many people died. I suppose word hasn't reached England yet. 'Twas a catastrophe, right enough."

Lady Agatha herded the children into the common

room. "You can tell me about it later," she told her husband. "This is probably something the children shouldn't hear."

"Was it a slave rebellion?" Chris guessed. "I thought the danger had passed."

"After you left," Ludlow began, "stirrings of rebellion flared up again. "Daddy" Sam Sharp continued to preach passive resistance, and it looked like the slaves took his words to heart. But then things took a violent turn. Over Christmas and into the New Year, marauding slaves, some say up to twenty thousand, began burning plantations and murdering planters all over the island."

"Oh, no!" Sophia cried. "Is Sunset Hill gone?"

"Your plantation was left untouched. Your workers protected your property, and Sam Sharp and his people joined them in holding off rampaging slaves."

Chris let out a whoosh of breath. Sunset Hill had been spared. He couldn't believe it. Thank God he had freed his slaves.

"What happened at Orchid Manor?" Lord Chester asked.

"Gone," Ludlow said, shaking his head. "I'm sorry."

"We'll rebuild," Chester vowed.

"What about our neighbors?" Sophia asked.

"Some of your neighbors survived and others didn't. Wombly and Humbart escaped with their lives but lost their plantations. Sir Rigby died when his plantation was set afire. He arrived in Kingston aboard the *Mary Deare* a few days before the onset of the rebellion. He picked the wrong time to return."

"Rigby got just what he deserved," Chris muttered.

"How did the rebellion end?" Chester asked. "Everything seems quiet enough now."

"It was a dreadful time," Ludlow said sadly. "The slaves were tricked into laying down their arms with false promises of freedom. Over four hundred were hanged immediately, and hundreds more were whipped. Terrible, just terrible," he repeated. "Christmas of 1831 will long be remembered in the archives of Jamaican history as a bloodbath."

Sophia turned so pale that Chris reached for her, fearing she would faint. Mr. Dexter looked equally pale.

"I want to go home to Sunset Hill," Sophia whispered, "and you must invite Lord Chester and his family to stay with us until his new home is built."

"What about it, Chester? Will you accept our hospitality?"

"Thank you, that's very kind of you. Agatha insisted that Sophia should have a woman who knows about childbirth with her when she delivers," Chester said. "I should have listened to you, Radcliff. I should have freed my slaves. Had I done so, Orchid Manor might still be standing. I think we all learned a lesson from this. Human life is valuable, no matter what color a person's skin. I intend to free my slaves at once and pay them decent wages to work my land."

"Well said," Chris agreed. "It's settled, then. Let's fetch our carriages and take the women and children to Sunset Hill. We can pick up our luggage later."

"I'm coming with you," Casper said. "I'm not a child."

Chris clapped the lad on the shoulder. "Indeed you're not, my boy. And Mr. Dexter can come along, too, if he wishes."

During the ride to Sunset Hill, they encountered acres and acres of tobacco, sugar and coffee that had been torched and destroyed during the rebellion. But when they reached the outer limits of Chris's lands, the difference was glaringly apparent. Flowers still bloomed, birds still sang their sweet songs, and crops were flourishing. The house rose tall and majestic against a blue-bell sky.

"Home," Sophia whispered as Chris handed her down from the carriage. "I hope Jamaica never experiences another bloodbath. I can't wait to see Kateena and the others. London is nice to visit, but this is home. This is where our family will grow and prosper. Sunset Hill is our own personal Paradise."

"You are *my* personal Paradise," Chris said as they entered the house arm in arm. "Thank God we found our way back to one another."

Five months later.

Chris was holding Sophia's hand when their daughter was born. It was an easy birth, according to Lady Agatha and the midwife. They named her Angela, because Casper thought she looked like an angel. The following week, the Chesters moved into their new home and the island slowly returned to normal.

AUTHOR'S NOTE

I hope you enjoyed *A Taste of Paradise*. I have been to Jamaica several times and was impressed with the beauty of the island. Many disasters have plagued Jamaica over the years, including volcano eruptions and hurricanes. But no disaster was more horrific than the island's frequent slave rebellions, including the one that took place over Christmas of 1831.

After four hundred slaves were hanged and thousands of others whipped, a wave of revulsion swept England, prompting the British Parliament to abolish slavery on August 1, 1834. Although free, the slaves were still bound to slave owners' compensation schemes, which could be likened to apprenticeships, until 1838. The freed slaves still faced extreme hardship, marked by another rebellion in 1865. It was brutally repressed and the island subsequently became a Crown Colony.

My next book will be a Scottish themed Medieval romance. Look for it in the spring of 2007.

I enjoy hearing from readers. For a newsletter and bookmark, please send a business-sized self-addressed stamped envelope with your request to me at P.O. Box 3471, Holiday, FL 34692. For more information about my books, visit my Web site at www.conniemason.com or contact me by e-mail at conmason@aol.com.